CHAPTER THREE

Writer, Letterer
Robert Kirkman

Penciler, Inker
Cory Walker

Colorist
Bill Crabtree

DARKWING SEQUENCE
TERRY STEVENS
PENCILER & INKER

RED RUSH SEQUENCE
MATT ROBERTS
PENCILER
TONY MOORE
INKER

WAR WOMAN SEQUENCE
MARK ENGLERT
PENCILER
ERIK LARSEN
INKER

AQUARUS SEQUENCE
DAVE JOHNSON
PENCILER & INKER

GREEN GHOST & MARTIAN
MAN SEQUENCE
CLIFF RATHBURN
PENCILER & INKER

CHAPTER FOUR

Writer, Letterer
Robert Kirkman

Penciler, Inker
RYAN OTTLEY

Colorist
Bill Crabtree

INVINCIBLE INTRODUCTION
by Erik Larsen

Robert Kirkman has inextricably wormed his way into my life.

It started out innocently enough. Robert was a rabid Savage Dragon enthusiast and he'd arranged to interview me for some nitwit Internet outfit. I saw no reason to say no figuring that any publicity was good publicity and all the rest. The introduction having been made, Robert took his first step toward wiggling himself irreversibly into my life.

Robert was, at the time, working on a little independent book called Battle Pope in which he had taken a few of the themes I'd touched on in Savage Dragon and nudged them a few steps further in the direction of poor taste. Robert had the notion of sticking Savage Dragon into a yarn and managed to talk me into it. Another step.

Robert offered to haul my exhausted carcass to the airport after a convention in Chicago. It took him a week and a half to find the place but we arrived nevertheless, I miraculously made my flight and I was forever in his dept.

It was just where he wanted me.

I'm not sure what possessed young Cory Walker to dash off a splendid SuperPatriot pinup for inclusion in an issue of Savage Dragon but in all likelihood Robert put him up to it. Robert Kirkman and Cory Walker were all set to pitch a book called Science Dog to Image and Robert most likely thought it would be a dandy notion to get in the good graces with one of the founding fat-heads over at that half-assed organization.

The ploy worked. Both Jungle Jim Valentino and Erroneous Eric Stephenson were enthusiastic about said pulse-pounding pinup. They weren't quite as taken with the scintillating Science Dog pitch but thought it might be a good start for these fine fellows if I could convince them to perhaps do something with SuperPatriot while they brainstormed on a more Image-worthy effort.

Like I had to twist their arms...

I let the boys loose on SuperPatriot, giving them only the smallest suggestions to help guide them on their way. They batted out a spiffy miniseries in two shakes of a lamb's tail to the thunderous applause to everyone that happened across it.

It was solid entertainment for the funnybook dollar right out of the gate.

Robert's next step was pointing me in the direction of Mighty Mark Englert. Mark had taken it upon himself to begin illustrating an unused plot for an abandoned miniseries that I'd printed in the back pages of an issue of Savage Dragon. It was a way for him to scrape some samples together to try and break into this beastly biz. Mark would have, no doubt, shown me his energetic efforts himself at an upcoming comic book convention but Robert beat him to the punch and added yet another feather to his cap in the process. Offering to letter the story Mark had pencilled once I'd arranged to have it run in Savage Dragon only helped ingratiate himself to me.

By this point, Robert was practically family. I'd have invited him over to Thanksgiving dinner if I thought that it would balance the books but I suspected my wife wouldn't stand for his sorry sucking up related shenanigans. Besides, that kid looked like he could put away more than his fair share of turkey.

When it was decided that Image would launched a few new superhero books, Robert and Cory concocted a character called Invincible. As it turned out, their prodigious project needed no push from me. I could score no brownie pointclaiming to have horsewhipped those inbred idiots at Image into picking up their book—the fine folks at Image central had nothing but high praise for their peerless pitch. They made that perfectly clear and green-lit their marvelous mag in a heartbeat and a half.

But I owed Robert Kirkman. I knew it and he knew it.

And he wouldn't have it any other way.

Robert has often said to me, "I'm stealing all of your moves" but I'm so far in his debt how could I begin to get pissed? Invincible was, as they say, a critical hit. Critics adored it even though some retailers neglected to order it in suitable numbers. Still, it had a good buzz about it, sales were climbing and people seemed to genuinely love the gook. Stealing my moves or not, Robert was making all the right moves. In a short while Robert was adding other Image titles to his ever-growing Image workload.

Cory, on the other hand, seemed to have hit a wall. Pages came slower and slower. The pressures of a monthly book were something Cory was not prepared for.

The book began to fall behind schedule.

In short order Cory ground to a near halt and it became apparent that he wasn't going to continue. Robert, with Cory's blessing, called in a few favors. Enter: me, Mark Englert and a handful of other fellows looking to help out the poor guy in his time of need. I inked Mark's pristine pencils just as I was doing over on the Mighty Man backup story in Savage Dragon. Cory Walker concluded his run and managed to outshine us all on his way out the door. Knowing he could no longer keep up, Cory graciously stepped aside, for the good of the book.

So, what was Robert to do now—with his partner in crime and Invincible's co-creator, Cory Walker, no longer in tow? If it were anybody else I'd suggest to him that he call it a day and fold up his tent. What chance would a series have with the odds stacked so seriously against it? Here was a book, the sole semi-success story in a superhero launch that failed to catch fire, which was slipping swiftly off schedule and had lost a good chunk of its drawing power with the sudden departure of a rising talent that gave it visual vitality! What chance would it have in this maddeningly competitive market?

A damned good chance as it turned out.

Raucous Robert Kirkman struck gold—again! He managed to dig up yet another hungry, talented, fresh-faced illustrator eager to take the comic book world by storm! Enter: Ryan Ottley! His first effort, reprinted here, was a worthy accomplishment from a capable newcomer but in a matter of a few issues, produced at an amazing pace, Ryan Ottley not only managed to get the book back on schedule but grew into a terrific artist in his own right in the process of doing it! It's safe to say that not only is the book back on track but that its future has never looked brighter!

So, how does Robert do this? Is he that talented? Well, sure, there is a good deal of that, no question. But it's more than that. This is a guy who's a fan. A fan of comics, a fan of superheroes, and he's got an inexhaustible enthusiasm and drive that is not only amazing to behold but infectious as all hell. This guy wants to produce comics. He wants to produce good comics—and he'll do anything in his power to accomplish that goal.

And if he can ingratiate himself to an alleged big shot like me to the extent that I'm willing to stay up well past my bedtime writing a halfwit introduction to his second Invincible collection on a night when I desperately need some shuteye so that I can get those little nippers of mine off to school in the morning—all the better.

Robert Kirkman is a hell of a guy.

Invincible is one hell of a comic.

If you've never read an issue before, prepare yourself. You're gonna have a blast!

I sure did.

Erik Larsen
Creator/writer/artist of Savage Dragon

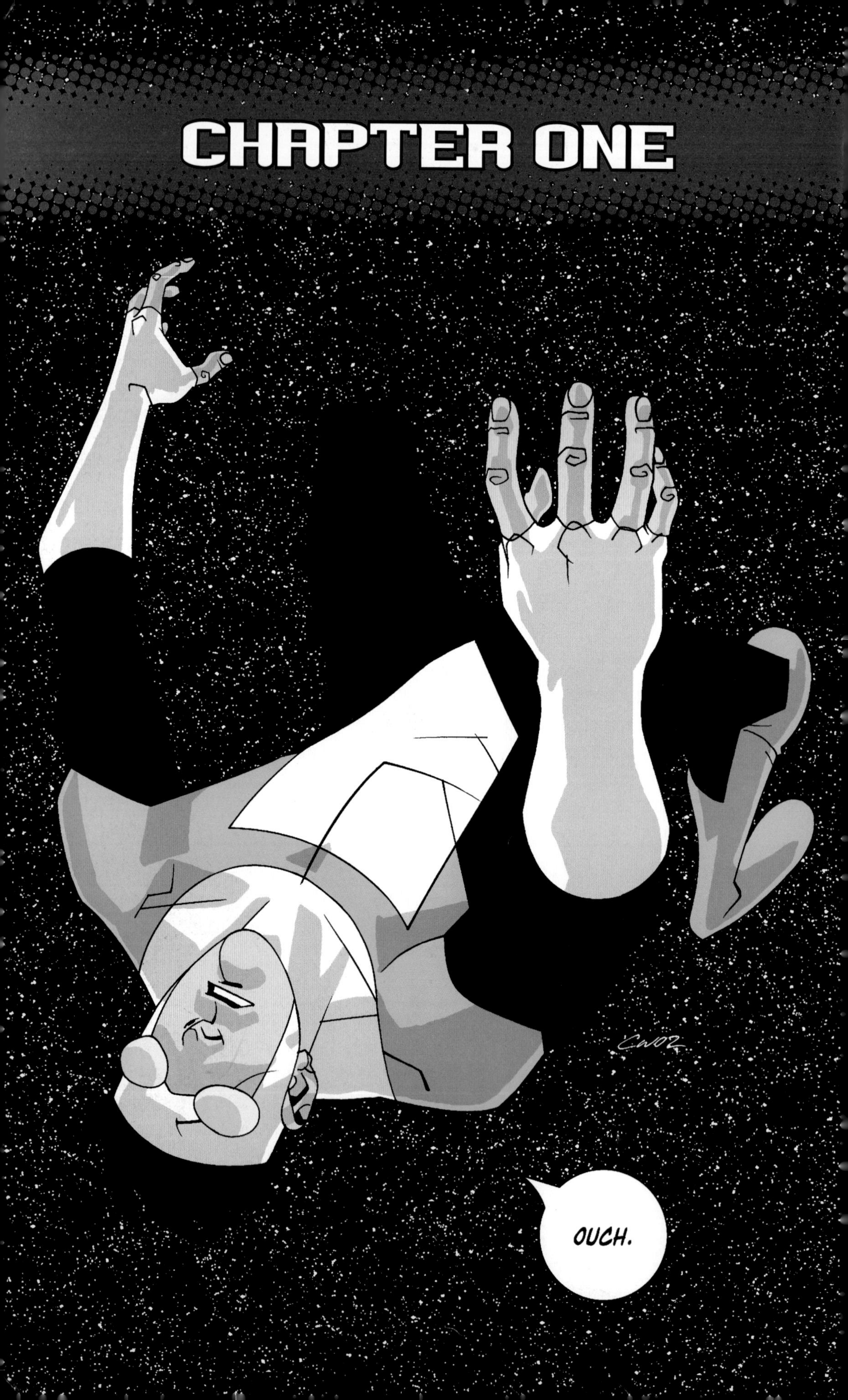
CHAPTER ONE
OUCH.

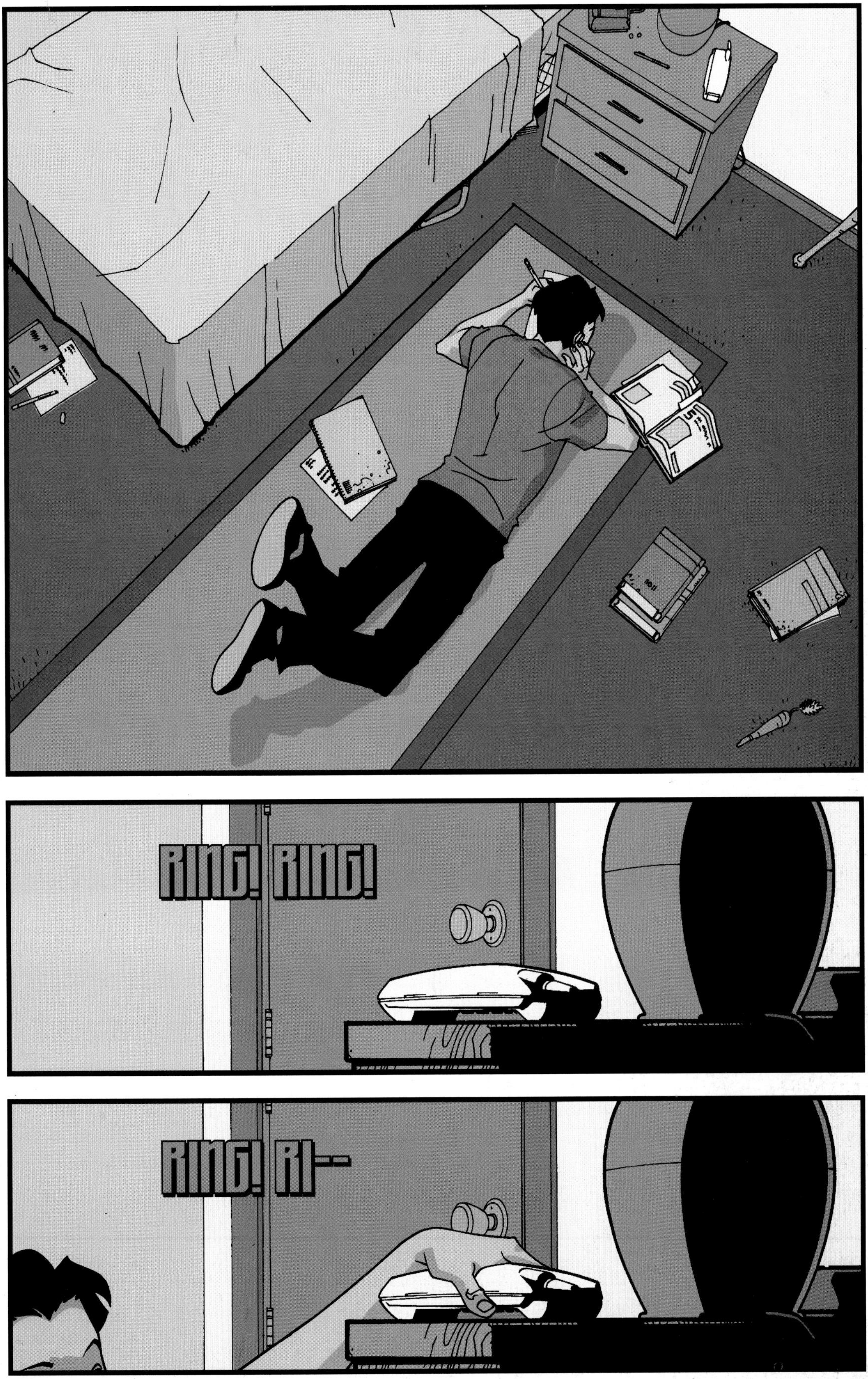
RING! RING!
RING! RI--

DEBBIE, I NEED TO SPEAK WITH MARK, *QUICK!* OKAY, HON... I'LL GO GET HIM.

I GOT IT, MOM. YOU CAN HANG UP.

WHAT'S GOING ON, DAD?

PAY ATTENTION, SON... I'M NOT GOING TO HAVE TIME TO *REPEAT* ANY OF THIS.

I NEED YOUR HELP.

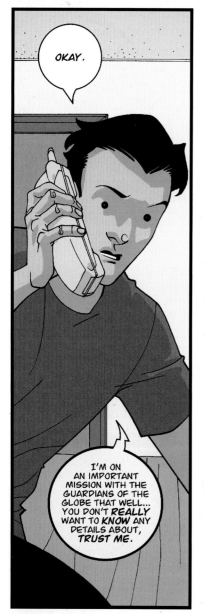

OKAY.

I'M ON AN IMPORTANT MISSION WITH THE GUARDIANS OF THE GLOBE THAT WELL... YOU DON'T *REALLY* WANT TO *KNOW* ANY DETAILS ABOUT, *TRUST ME.*

ANYWAY, I JUST GOT ALERTED TO A *MAJOR BADDIE* COMING INTO OUR SOLAR SYSTEM, HEADED STRAIGHT FOR *EARTH.*

I'VE FOUGHT THIS GUY *BEFORE*, HE'S NOT OUT OF YOUR *LEAGUE*, BUT HE'S GOING TO BE THE TOUGHEST GUY YOU'VE FACED *SO FAR.*

I'M NOT WORRIED. WHAT DO YOU WANT ME TO DO?

JUST BEAT THE GUY UP, KEEP HIM FROM ENTERING EARTH'S ATMOSPHERE AND RUNNING AMOK. IT'S NOT ROCKET SCIENCE.

YOU'VE GOT ABOUT *TWELVE* MINUTES TO GET INTO ORBIT.

OKAY, DAD. GOT IT.

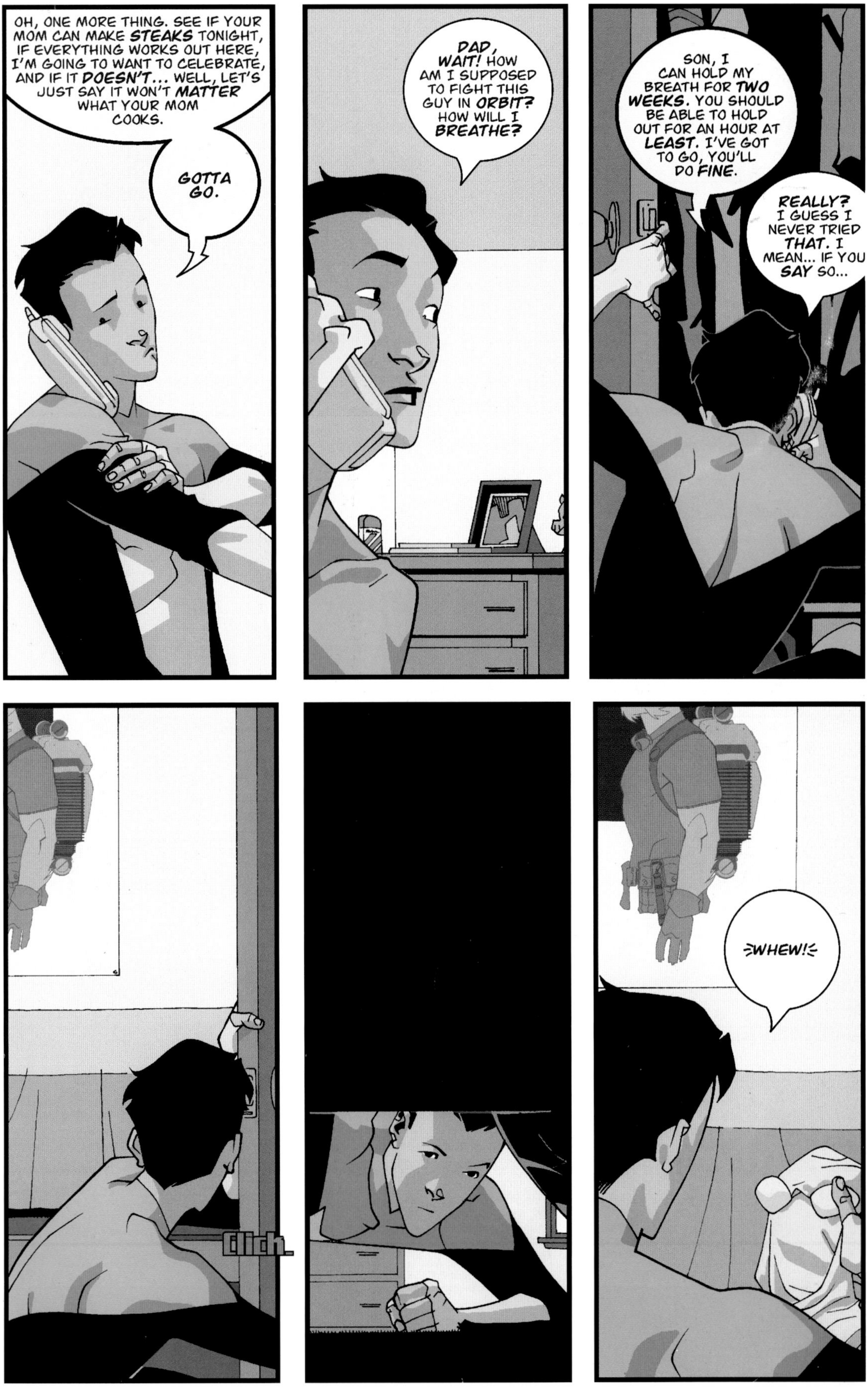

OH, ONE MORE THING. SEE IF YOUR MOM CAN MAKE STEAKS TONIGHT, IF EVERYTHING WORKS OUT HERE, I'M GOING TO WANT TO CELEBRATE, AND IF IT DOESN'T... WELL, LET'S JUST SAY IT WON'T MATTER WHAT YOUR MOM COOKS.
GOTTA GO.
DAD, WAIT! HOW AM I SUPPOSED TO FIGHT THIS GUY IN ORBIT? HOW WILL I BREATHE?
SON, I CAN HOLD MY BREATH FOR TWO WEEKS. YOU SHOULD BE ABLE TO HOLD OUT FOR AN HOUR AT LEAST. I'VE GOT TO GO, YOU'LL DO FINE.
REALLY? I GUESS I NEVER TRIED THAT. I MEAN... IF YOU SAY SO...
Click.
WHEW!

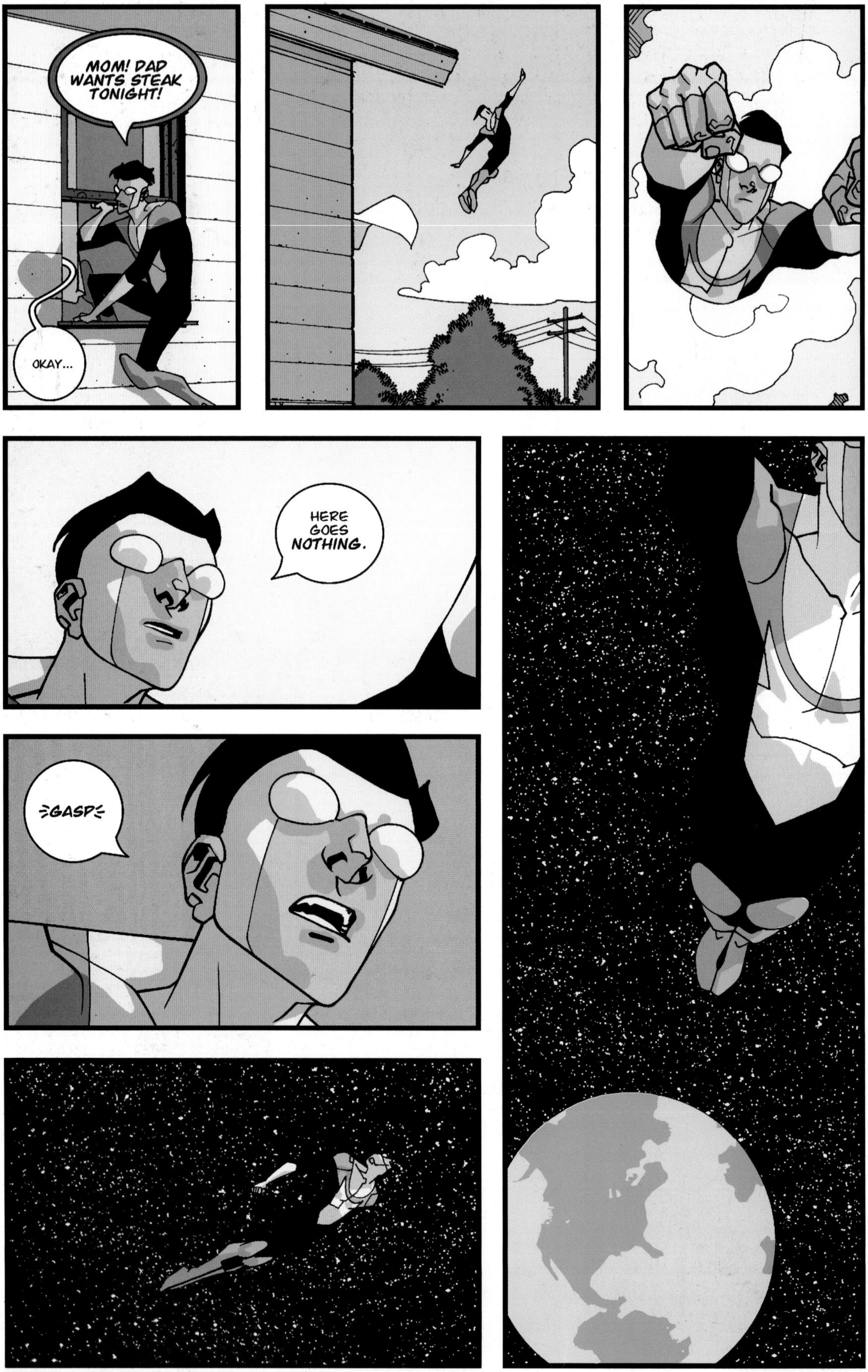
MOM! DAD WANTS STEAK TONIGHT!
OKAY...
HERE GOES NOTHING.
GASP

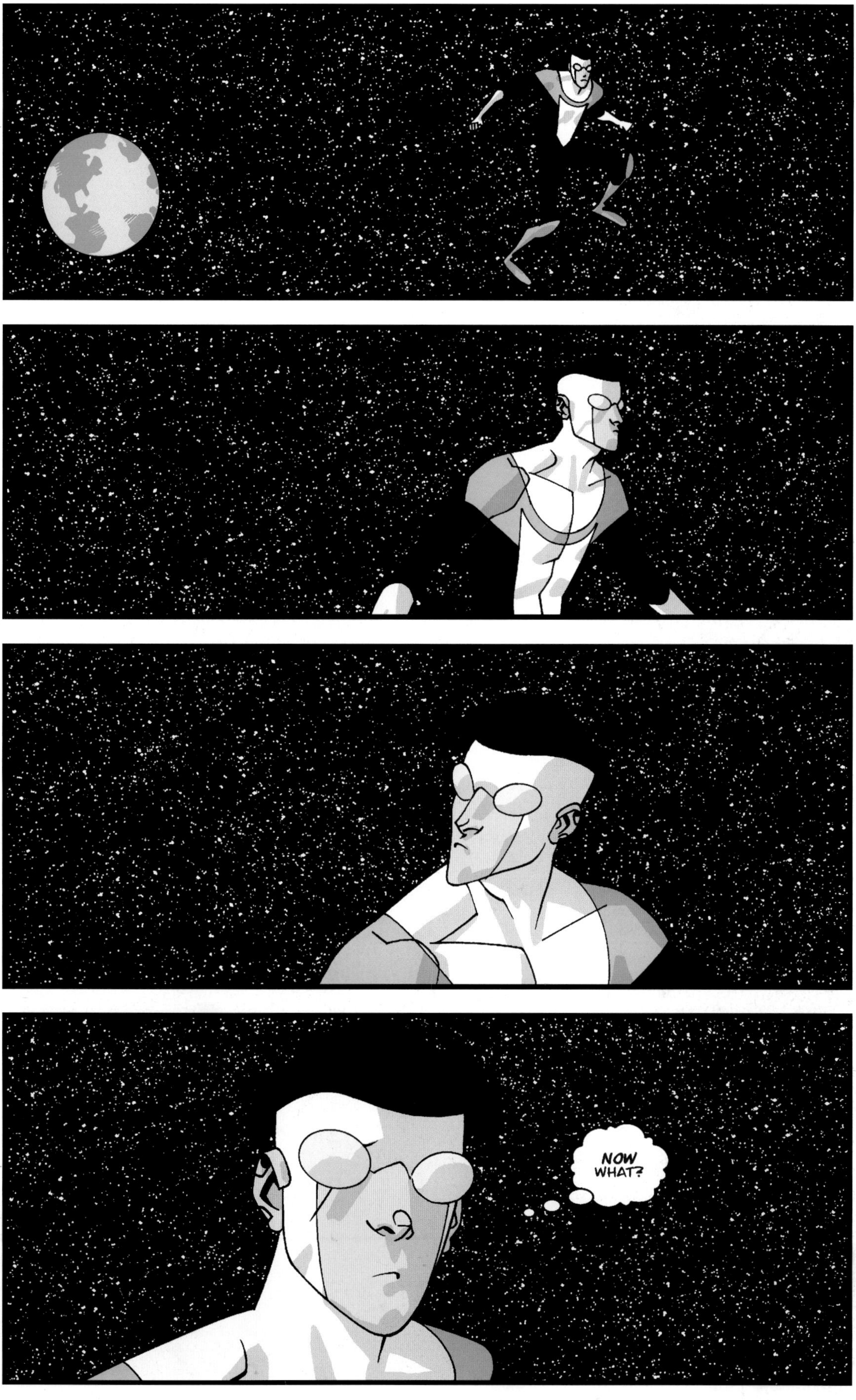
NOW WHAT?

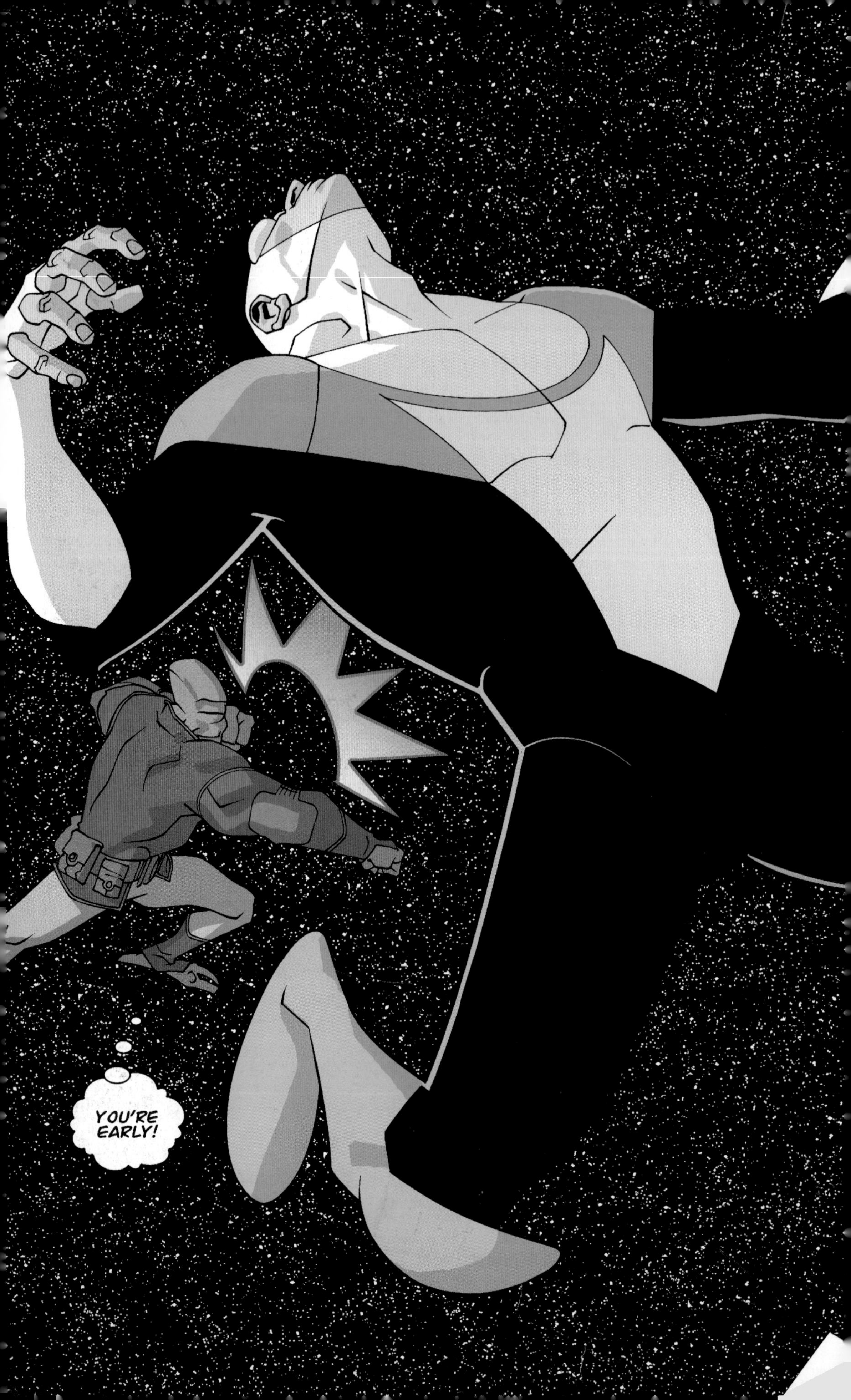
YOU'RE EARLY!

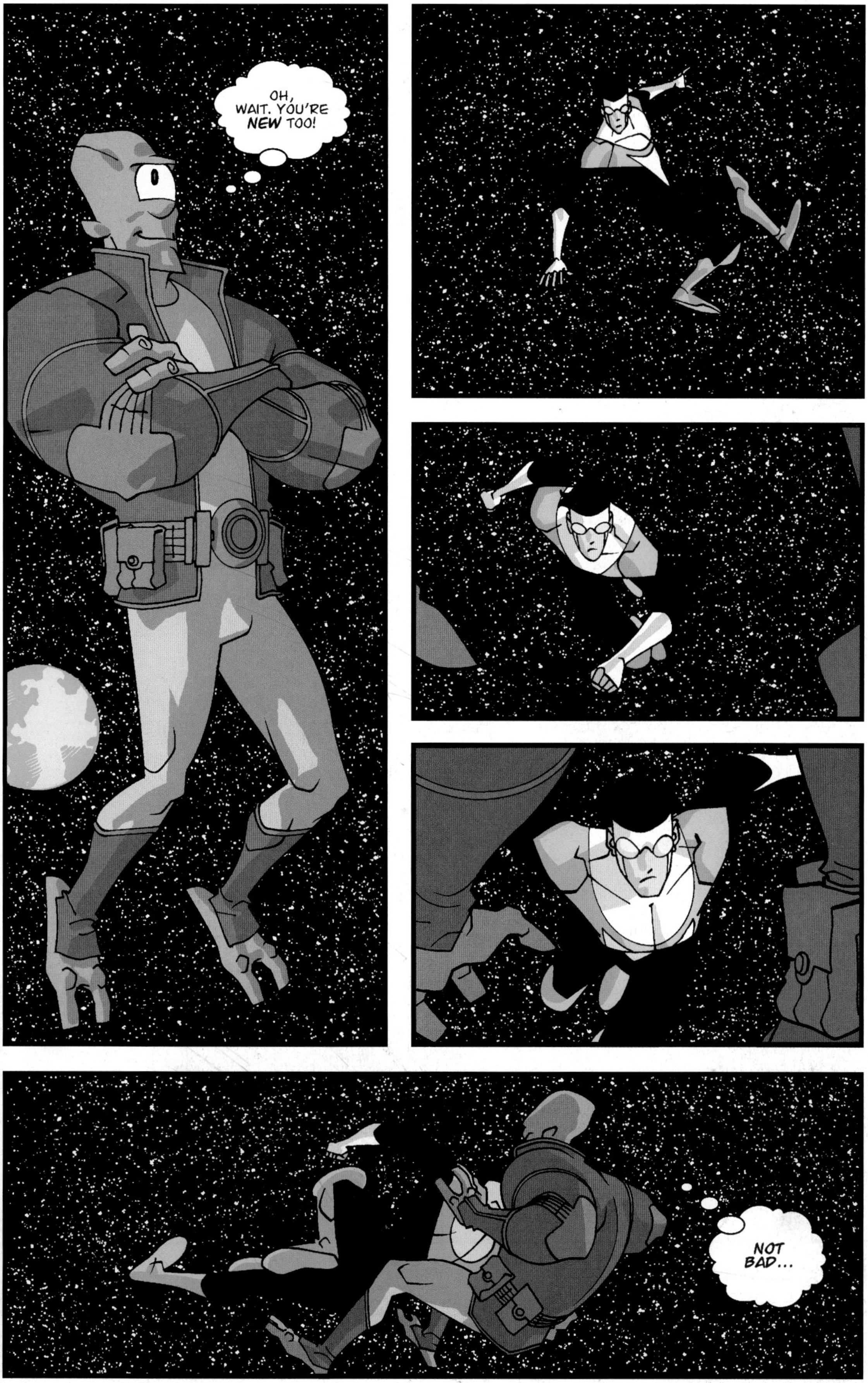
OH, WAIT. YOU'RE NEW TOO!
NOT BAD...

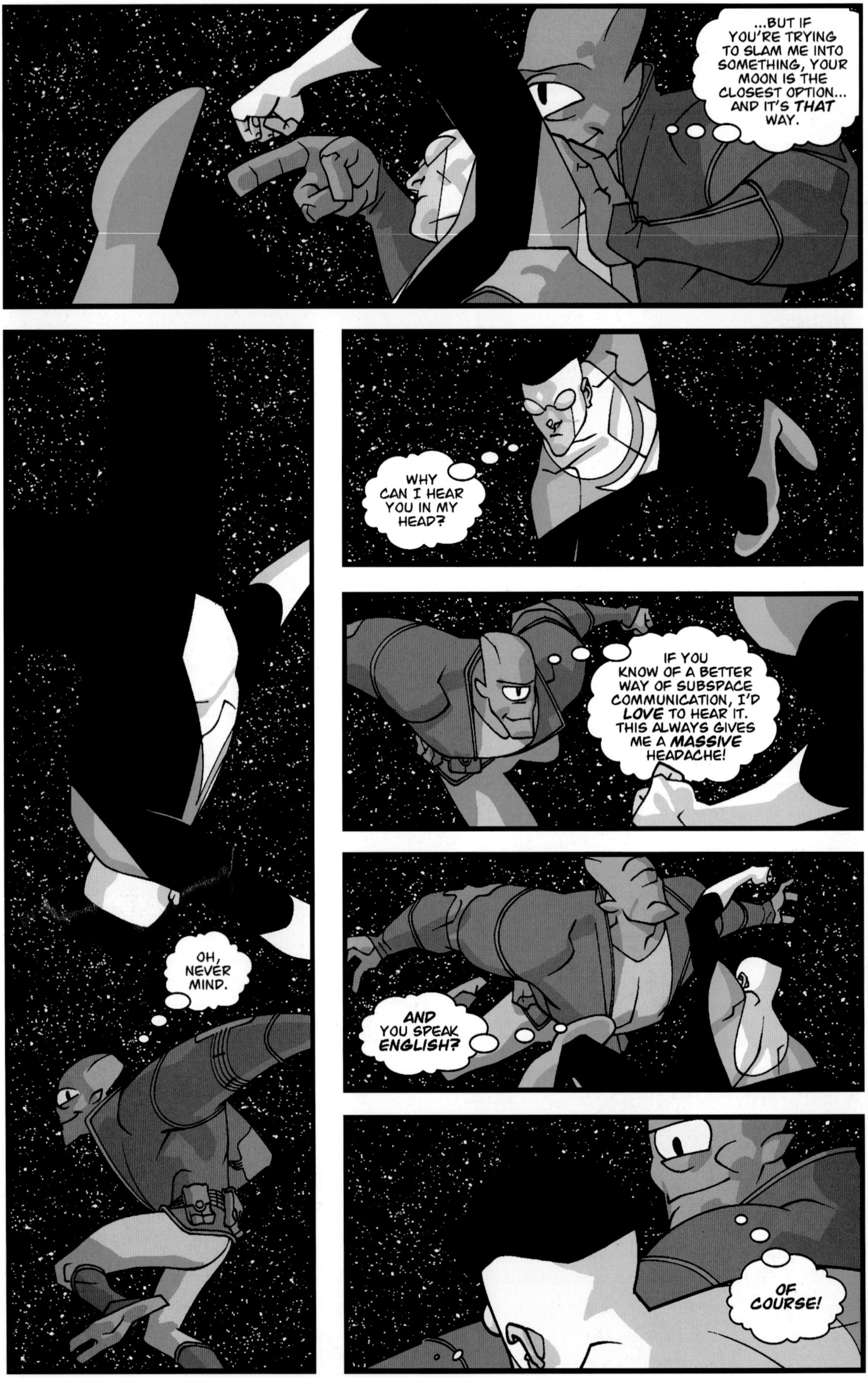
...BUT IF YOU'RE TRYING TO SLAM ME INTO SOMETHING, YOUR MOON IS THE CLOSEST OPTION... AND IT'S *THAT* WAY.
OH, NEVER MIND.
WHY CAN I HEAR YOU IN MY HEAD?
IF YOU KNOW OF A BETTER WAY OF SUBSPACE COMMUNICATION, I'D *LOVE* TO HEAR IT. THIS ALWAYS GIVES ME A *MASSIVE* HEADACHE!
AND YOU SPEAK ENGLISH?
OF COURSE!

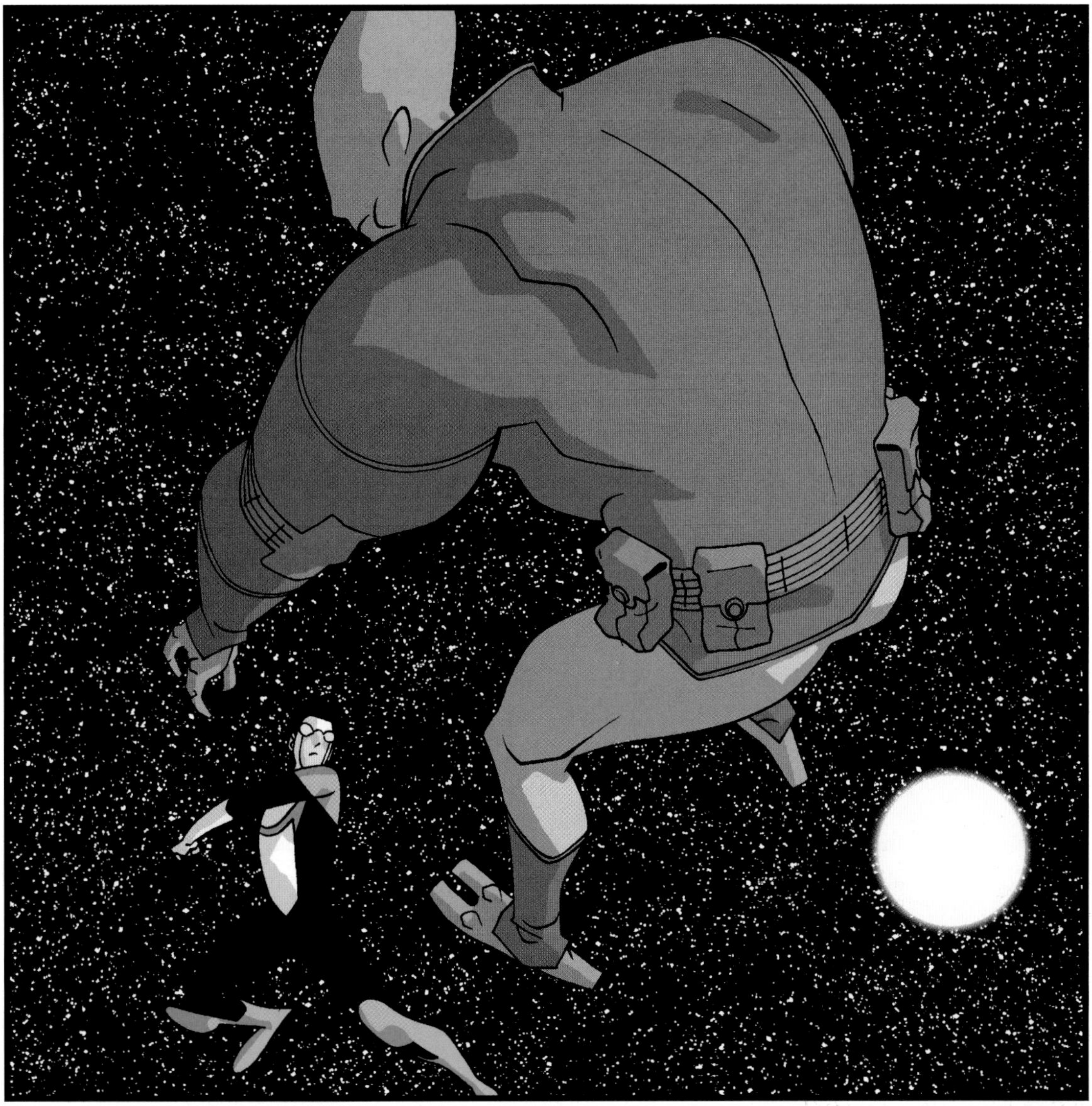

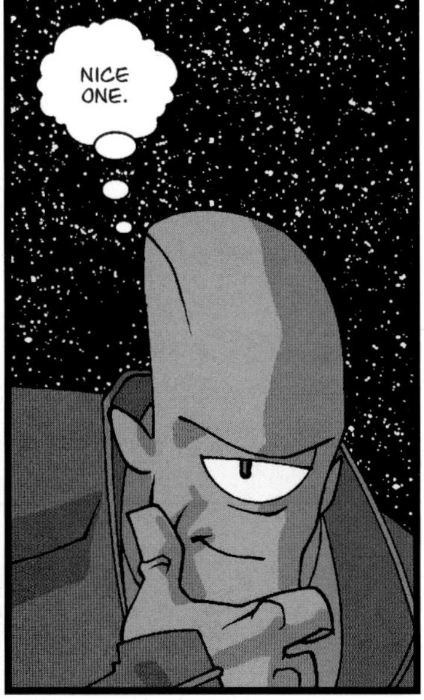
NICE ONE.

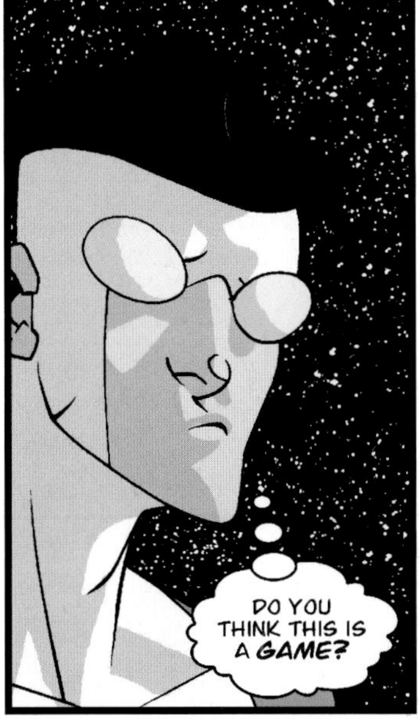
DO YOU THINK THIS IS A GAME?

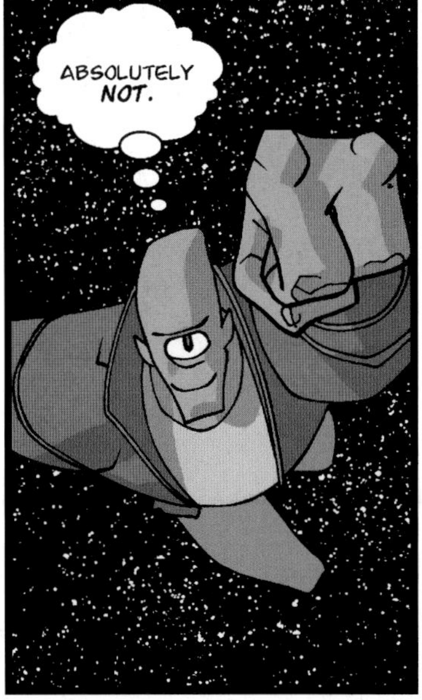
ABSOLUTELY NOT.

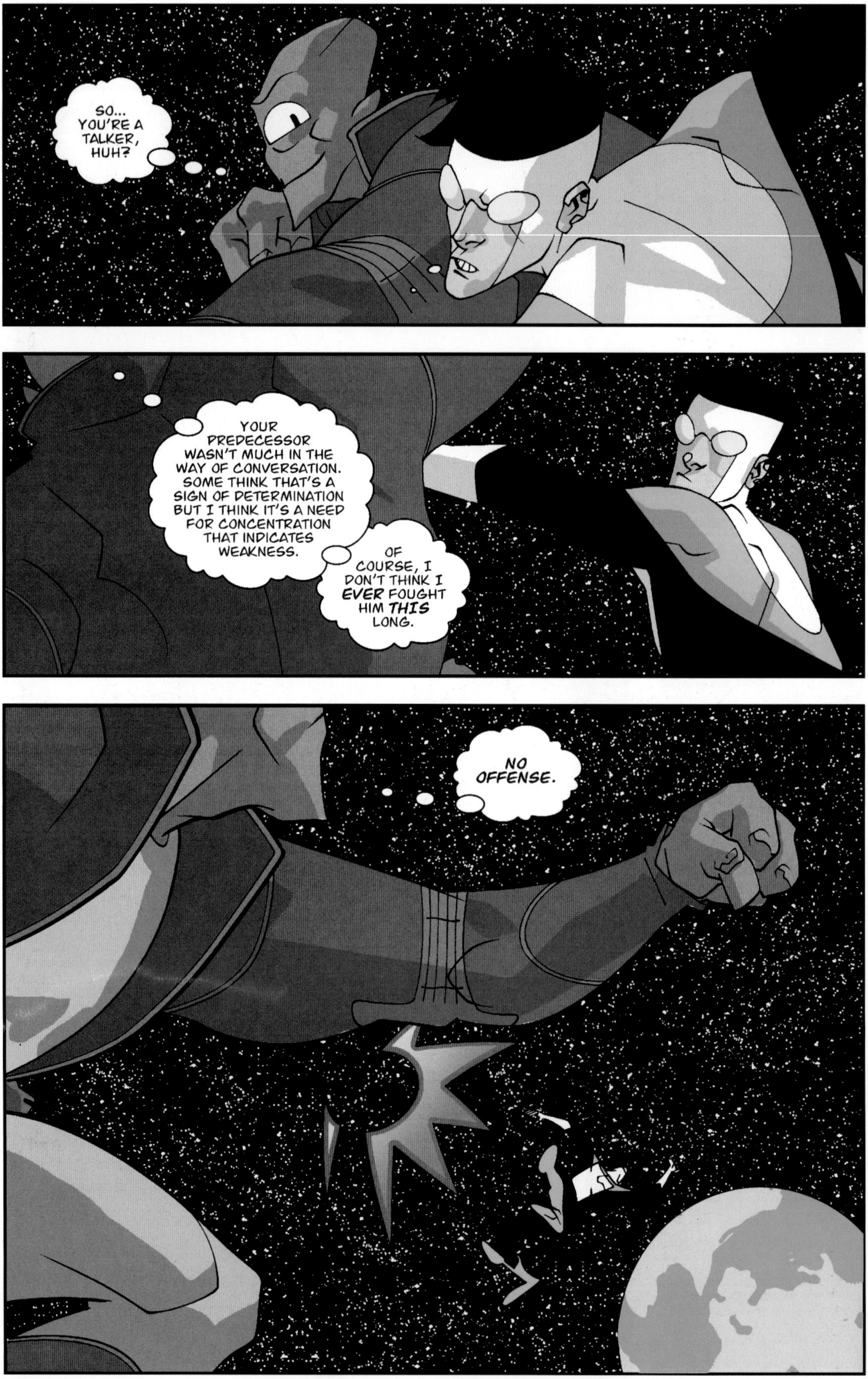
SO... YOU'RE A TALKER, HUH?
YOUR PREDECESSOR WASN'T MUCH IN THE WAY OF CONVERSATION. SOME THINK THAT'S A SIGN OF DETERMINATION BUT I THINK IT'S A NEED FOR CONCENTRATION THAT INDICATES WEAKNESS.
OF COURSE, I DON'T THINK I EVER FOUGHT HIM THIS LONG.
NO OFFENSE.

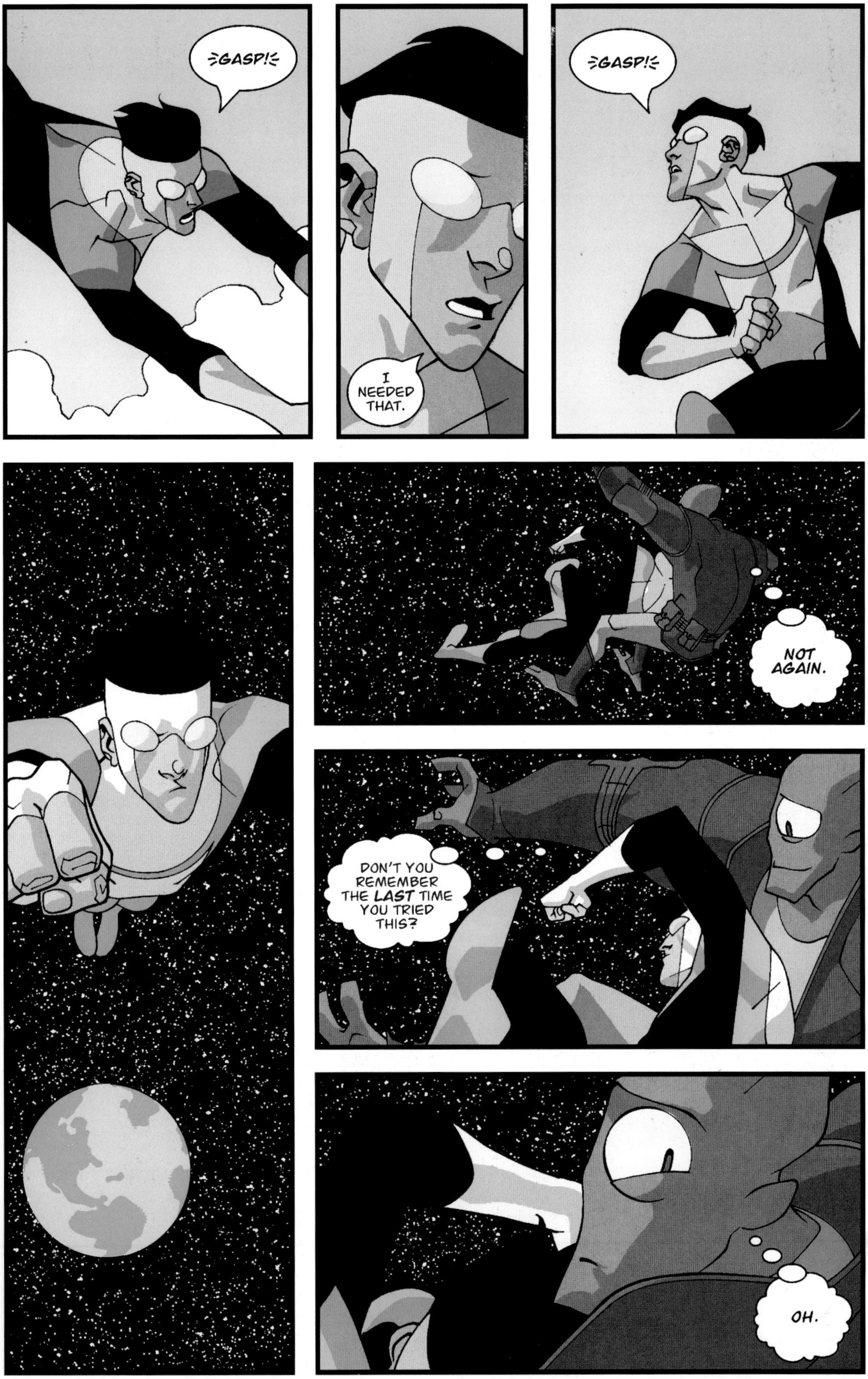
GASP!
I NEEDED THAT.
GASP!
NOT AGAIN.
DON'T YOU REMEMBER THE LAST TIME YOU TRIED THIS?
OH.

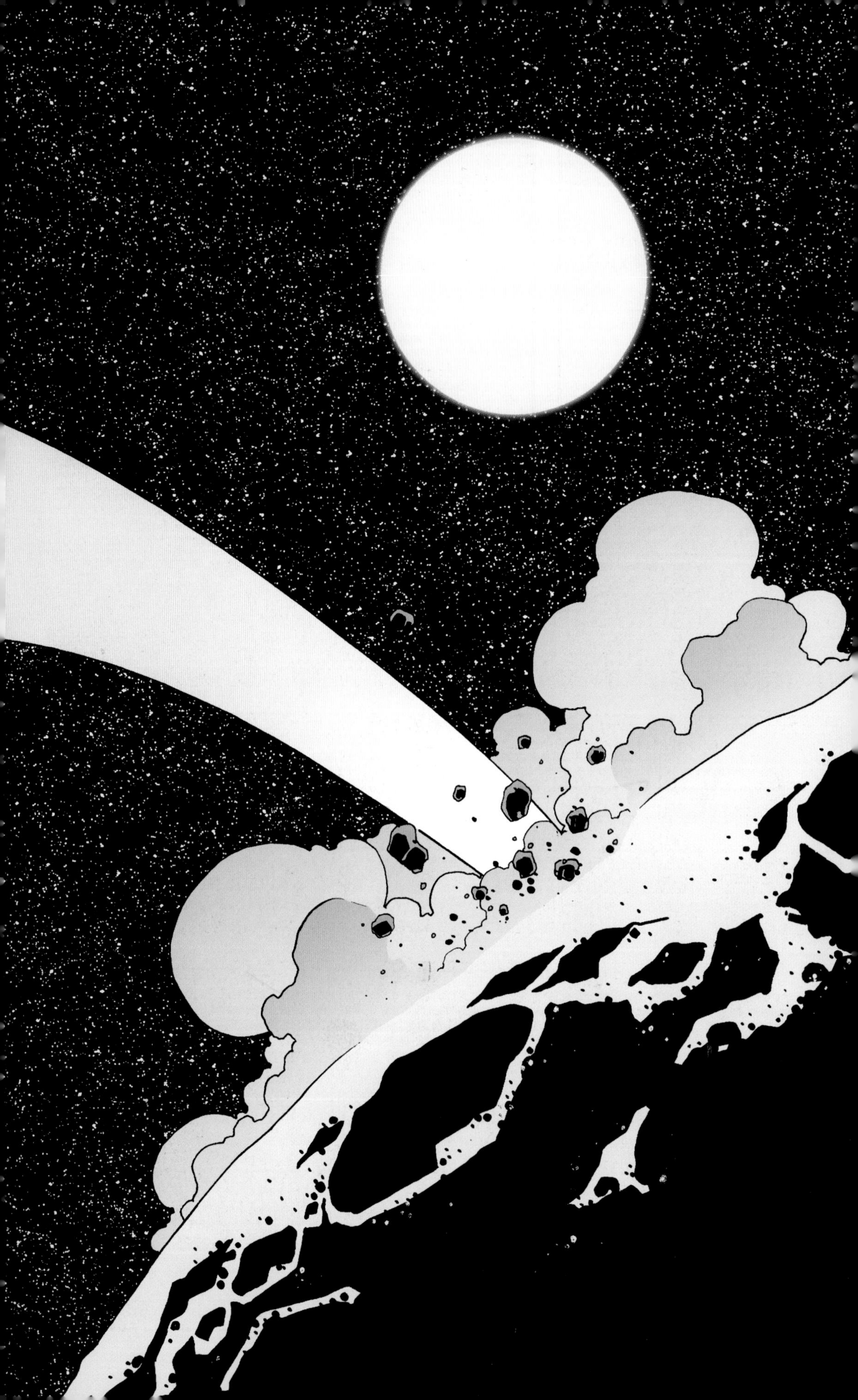

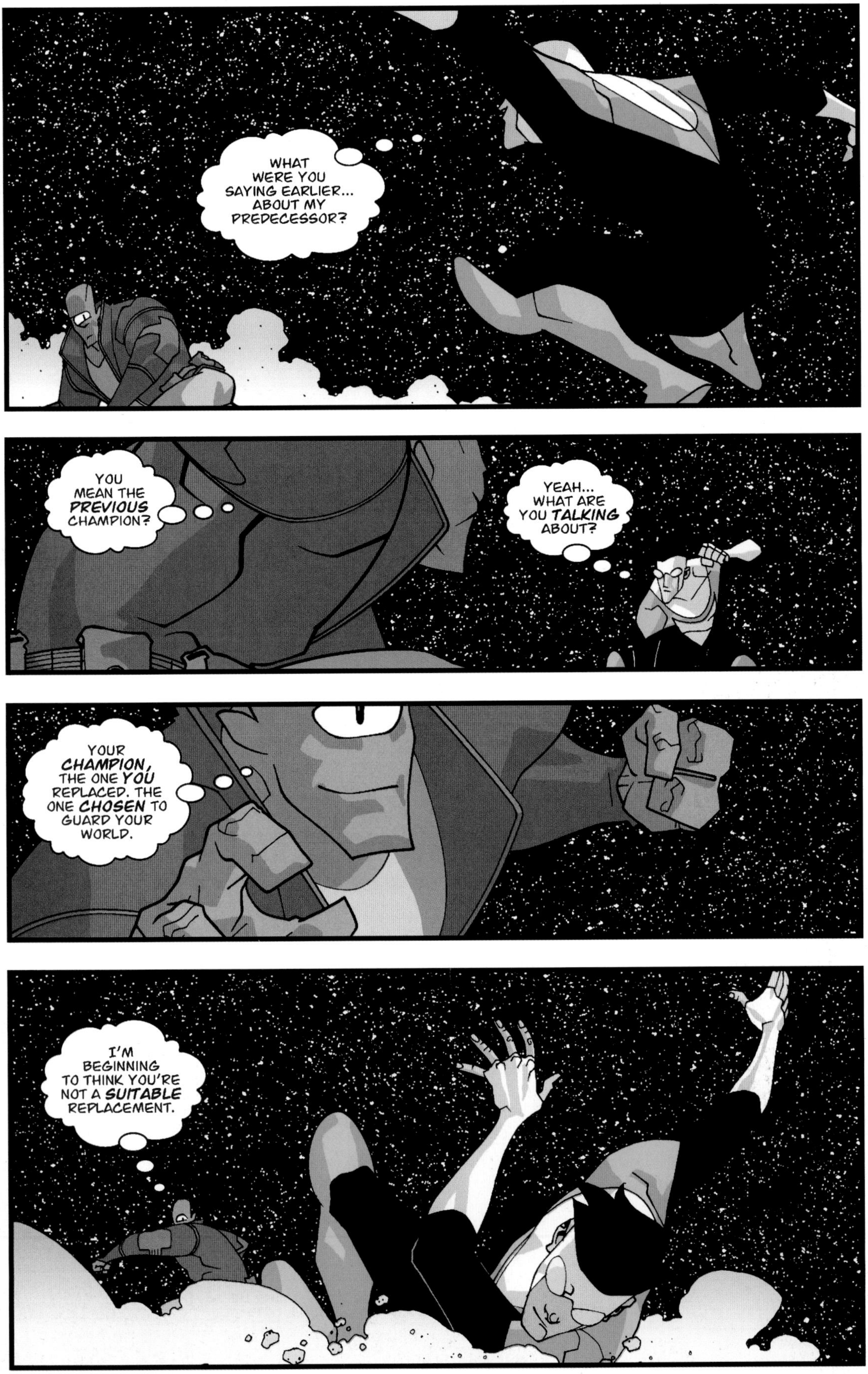
WHAT WERE YOU SAYING EARLIER... ABOUT MY PREDECESSOR?
YOU MEAN THE PREVIOUS CHAMPION?
YEAH... WHAT ARE YOU TALKING ABOUT?
YOUR CHAMPION, THE ONE YOU REPLACED. THE ONE CHOSEN TO GUARD YOUR WORLD.
I'M BEGINNING TO THINK YOU'RE NOT A SUITABLE REPLACEMENT.

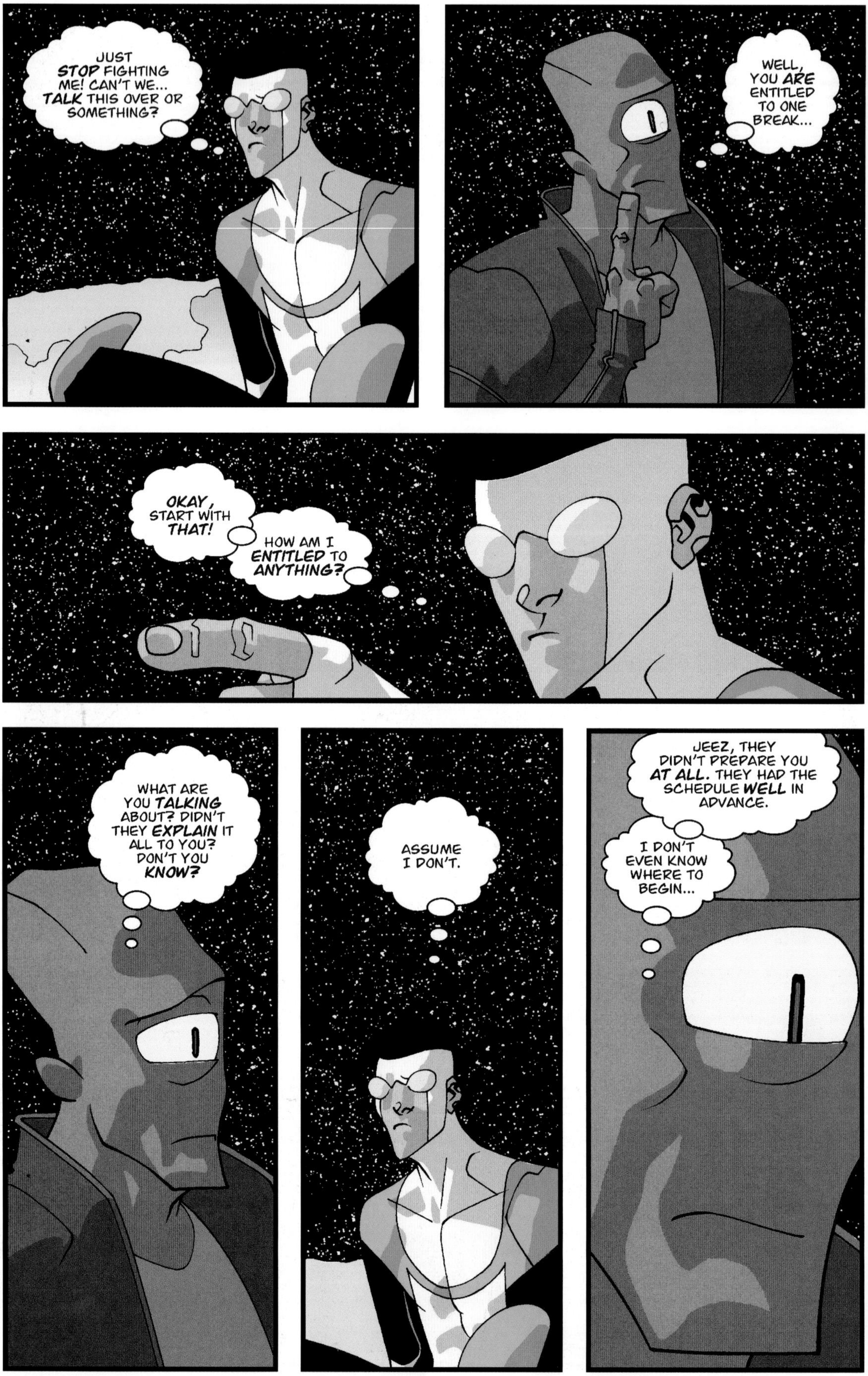
JUST STOP FIGHTING ME! CAN'T WE... TALK THIS OVER OR SOMETHING?
WELL, YOU ARE ENTITLED TO ONE BREAK...
OKAY, START WITH THAT!
HOW AM I ENTITLED TO ANYTHING?
WHAT ARE YOU TALKING ABOUT? DIDN'T THEY EXPLAIN IT ALL TO YOU? DON'T YOU KNOW?
ASSUME I DON'T.
JEEZ, THEY DIDN'T PREPARE YOU AT ALL. THEY HAD THE SCHEDULE WELL IN ADVANCE.
I DON'T EVEN KNOW WHERE TO BEGIN...

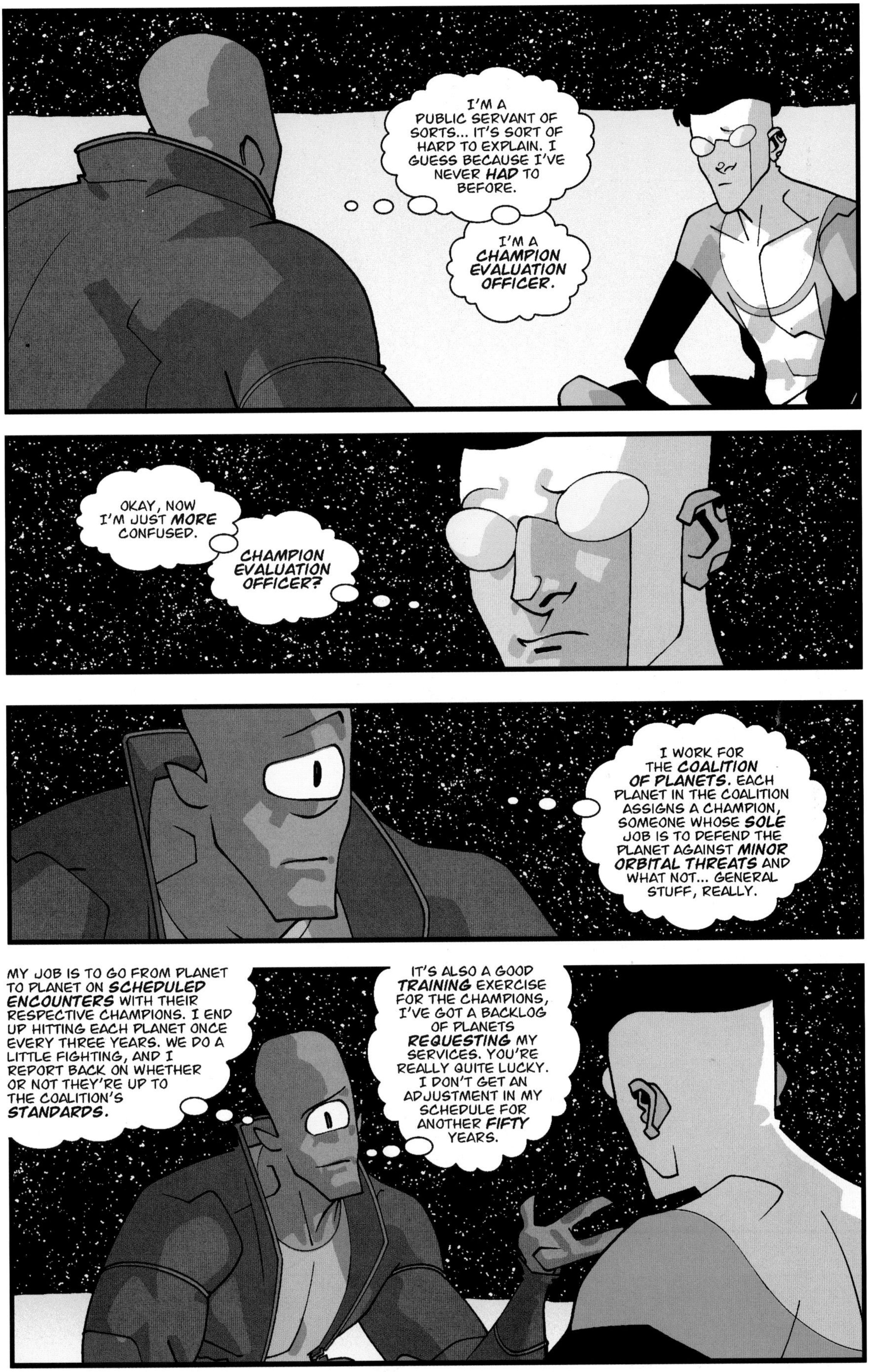

I'M A PUBLIC SERVANT OF SORTS... IT'S SORT OF HARD TO EXPLAIN. I GUESS BECAUSE I'VE NEVER HAD TO BEFORE.
I'M A CHAMPION EVALUATION OFFICER.
OKAY, NOW I'M JUST MORE CONFUSED.
CHAMPION EVALUATION OFFICER?
I WORK FOR THE COALITION OF PLANETS. EACH PLANET IN THE COALITION ASSIGNS A CHAMPION, SOMEONE WHOSE SOLE JOB IS TO DEFEND THE PLANET AGAINST MINOR ORBITAL THREATS AND WHAT NOT... GENERAL STUFF, REALLY.
MY JOB IS TO GO FROM PLANET TO PLANET ON SCHEDULED ENCOUNTERS WITH THEIR RESPECTIVE CHAMPIONS. I END UP HITTING EACH PLANET ONCE EVERY THREE YEARS. WE DO A LITTLE FIGHTING, AND I REPORT BACK ON WHETHER OR NOT THEY'RE UP TO THE COALITION'S STANDARDS.
IT'S ALSO A GOOD TRAINING EXERCISE FOR THE CHAMPIONS, I'VE GOT A BACKLOG OF PLANETS REQUESTING MY SERVICES. YOU'RE REALLY QUITE LUCKY. I DON'T GET AN ADJUSTMENT IN MY SCHEDULE FOR ANOTHER FIFTY YEARS.

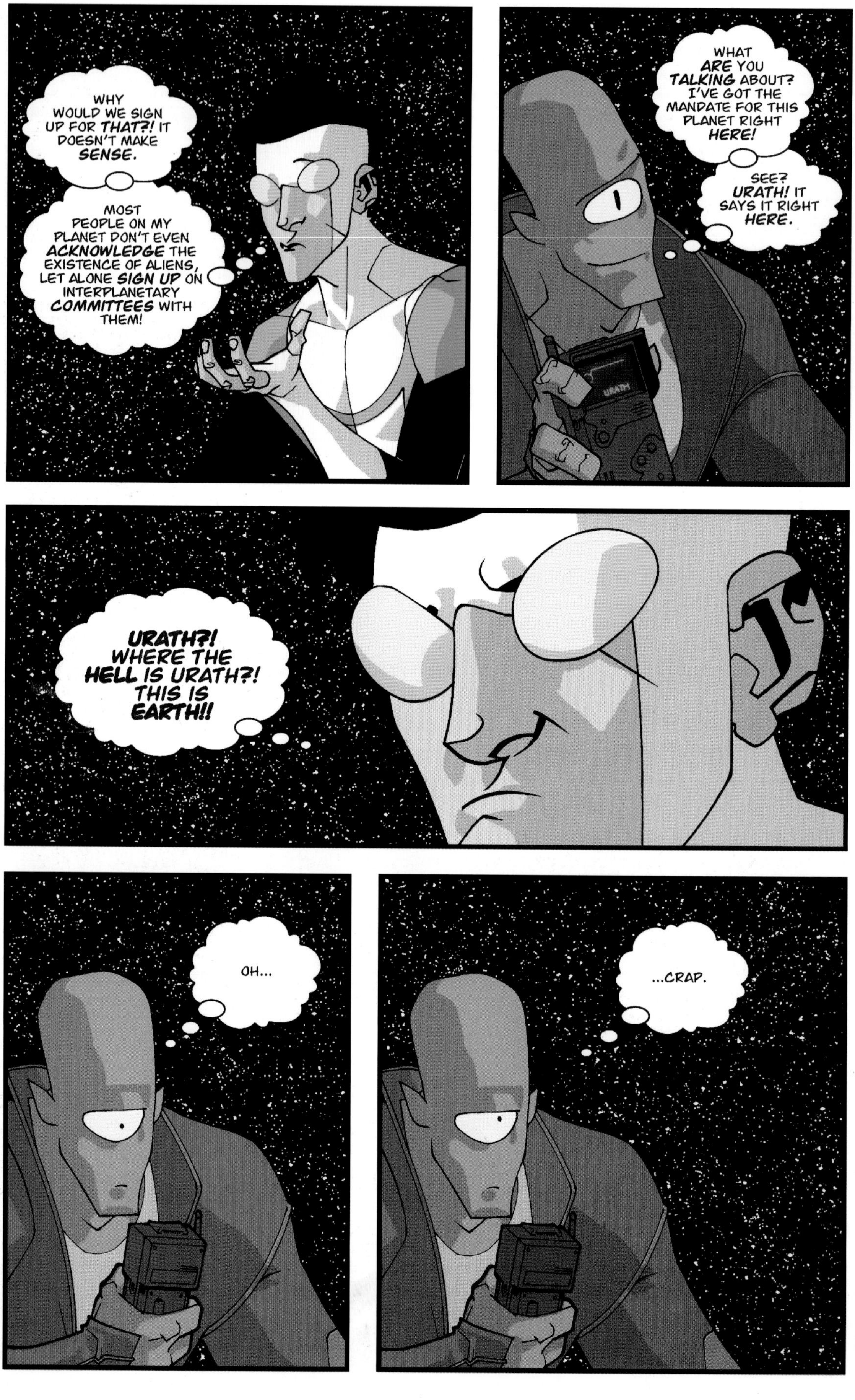
WHY WOULD WE SIGN UP FOR THAT?! IT DOESN'T MAKE SENSE.
MOST PEOPLE ON MY PLANET DON'T EVEN ACKNOWLEDGE THE EXISTENCE OF ALIENS, LET ALONE SIGN UP ON INTERPLANETARY COMMITTEES WITH THEM!
WHAT ARE YOU TALKING ABOUT? I'VE GOT THE MANDATE FOR THIS PLANET RIGHT HERE!
SEE? URATH! IT SAYS IT RIGHT HERE.
URATH
URATH?! WHERE THE HELL IS URATH?! THIS IS EARTH!!
OH...
...CRAP.

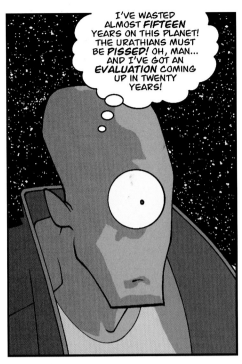

I'VE WASTED ALMOST **FIFTEEN** YEARS ON THIS PLANET! THE URATHIANS MUST BE **PISSED!** OH, MAN... AND I'VE GOT AN **EVALUATION** COMING UP IN TWENTY YEARS!

SORRY TO HAVE TO BREAK THE NEWS TO YOU, MAN.

DON'T WORRY ABOUT IT. IF IT WASN'T FOR YOU I MIGHT HAVE BEEN **FIRED** WHEN MY EVALUATION CAME UP... COME TO THINK OF IT, I MIGHT **STILL** BE...

...I GOTTA GO.

AGAIN, THANKS FOR ALL THE HELP. MY NAME'S **ALLEN**, I DIDN'T CATCH YOURS.

INVINCIBLE.

SEE YOU AROUND, INVINCIBLE.

WHOA...

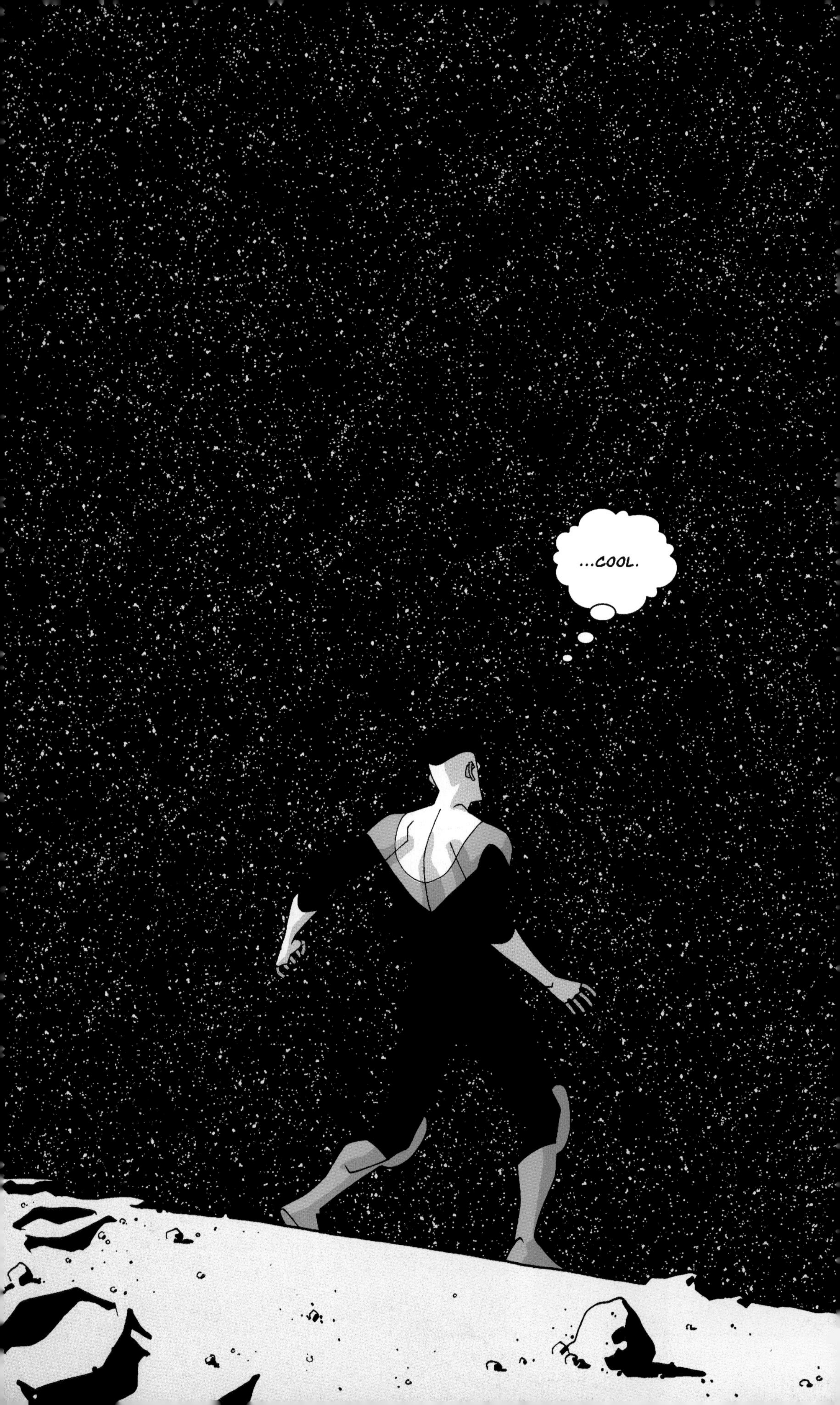
...COOL.

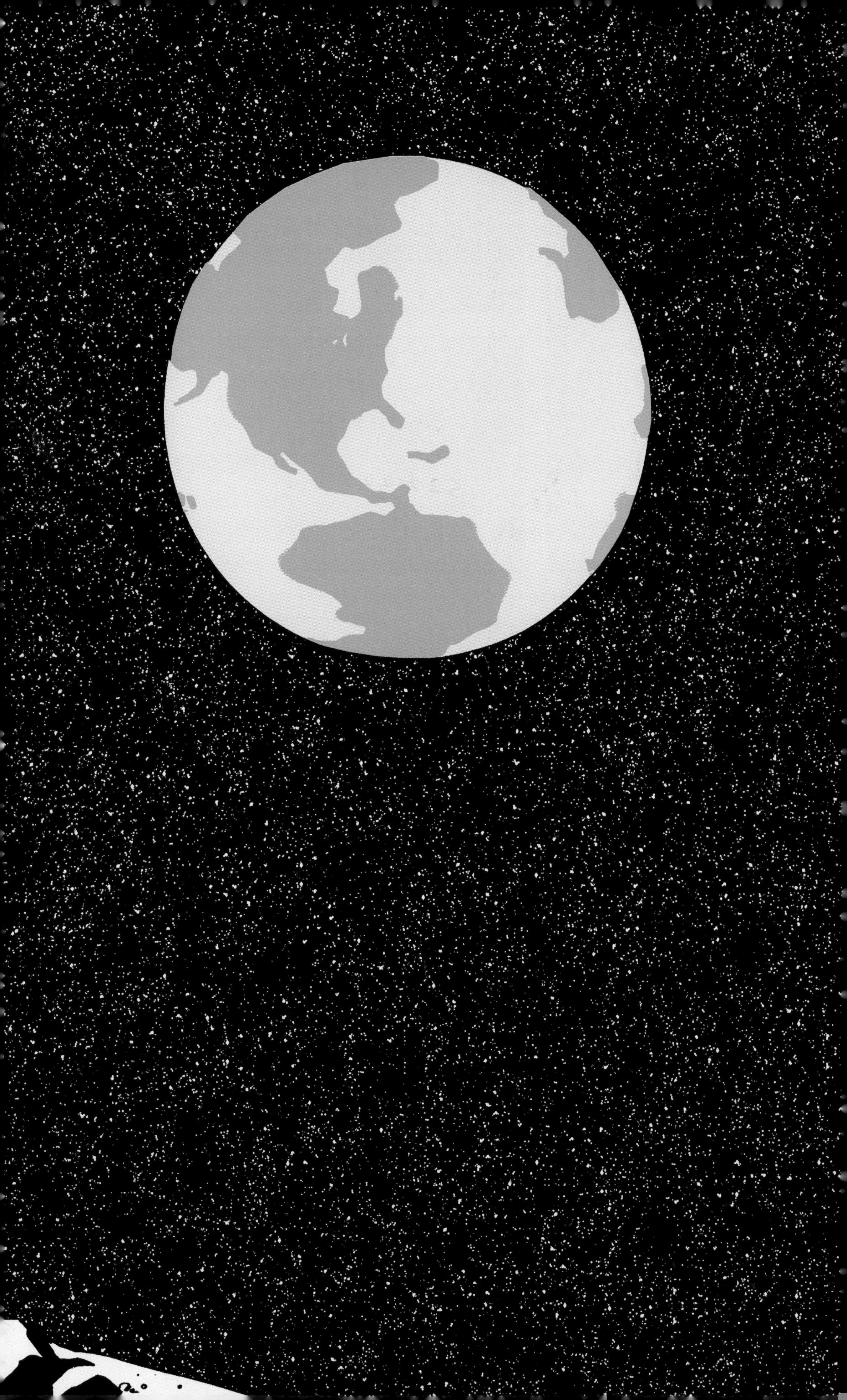

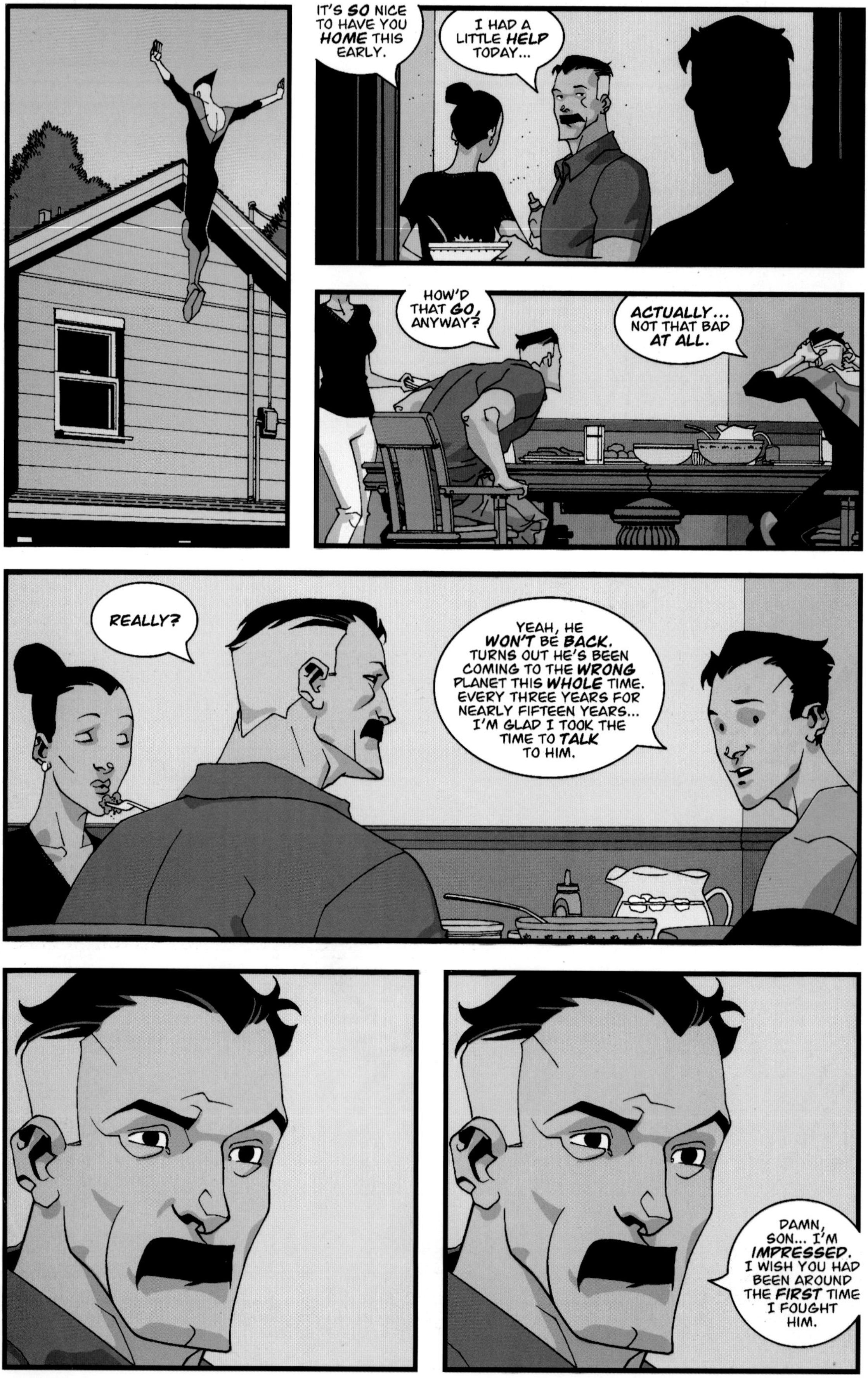
IT'S SO NICE TO HAVE YOU HOME THIS EARLY.
I HAD A LITTLE HELP TODAY...
HOW'D THAT GO, ANYWAY?
ACTUALLY... NOT THAT BAD AT ALL.
REALLY?
YEAH, HE WON'T BE BACK. TURNS OUT HE'S BEEN COMING TO THE WRONG PLANET THIS WHOLE TIME. EVERY THREE YEARS FOR NEARLY FIFTEEN YEARS... I'M GLAD I TOOK THE TIME TO TALK TO HIM.
DAMN, SON... I'M IMPRESSED. I WISH YOU HAD BEEN AROUND THE FIRST TIME I FOUGHT HIM.

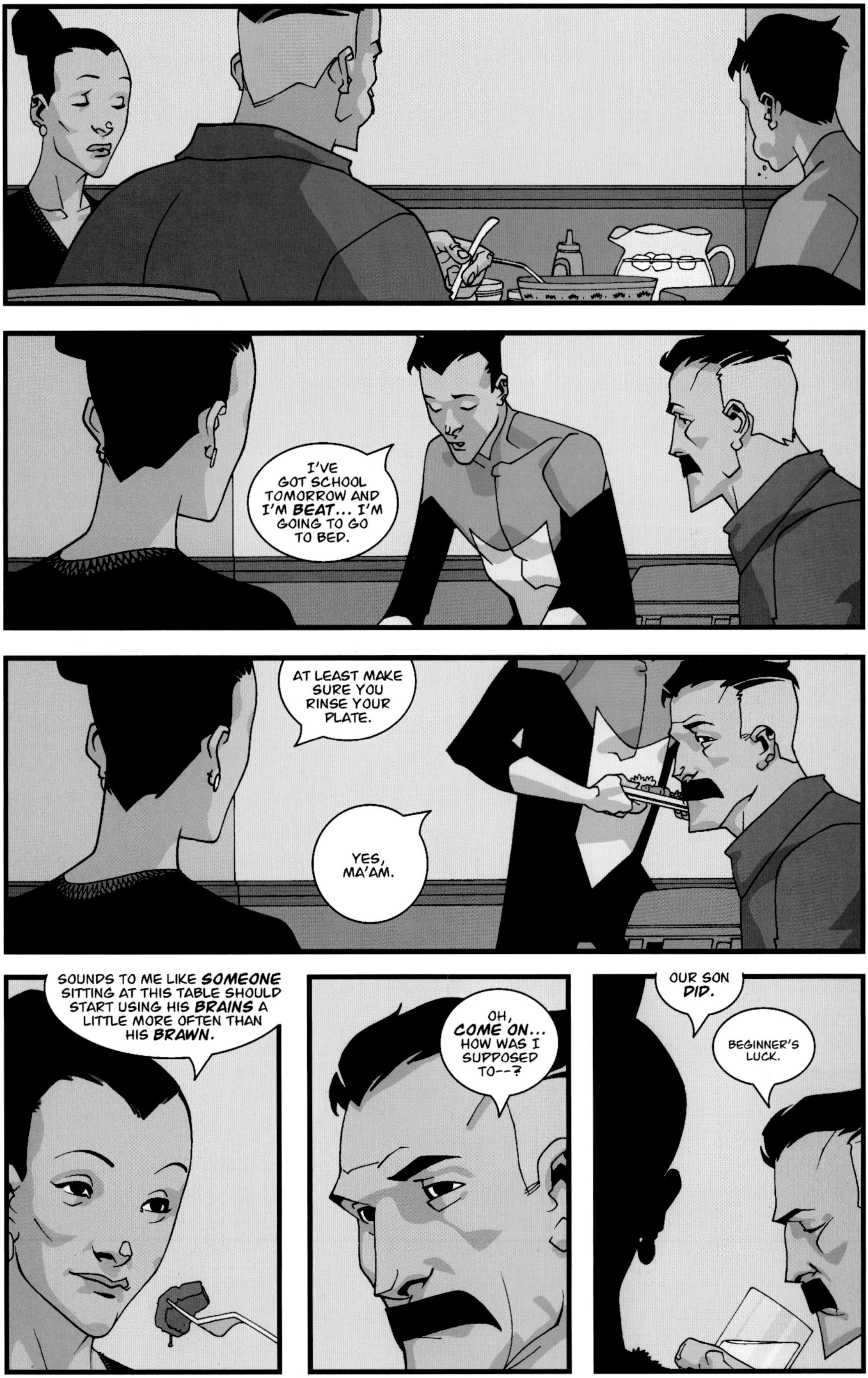
I'VE GOT SCHOOL TOMORROW AND I'M BEAT... I'M GOING TO GO TO BED.
AT LEAST MAKE SURE YOU RINSE YOUR PLATE.
YES, MA'AM.
SOUNDS TO ME LIKE SOMEONE SITTING AT THIS TABLE SHOULD START USING HIS BRAINS A LITTLE MORE OFTEN THAN HIS BRAWN.
OH, COME ON... HOW WAS I SUPPOSED TO--?
OUR SON DID.
BEGINNER'S LUCK.

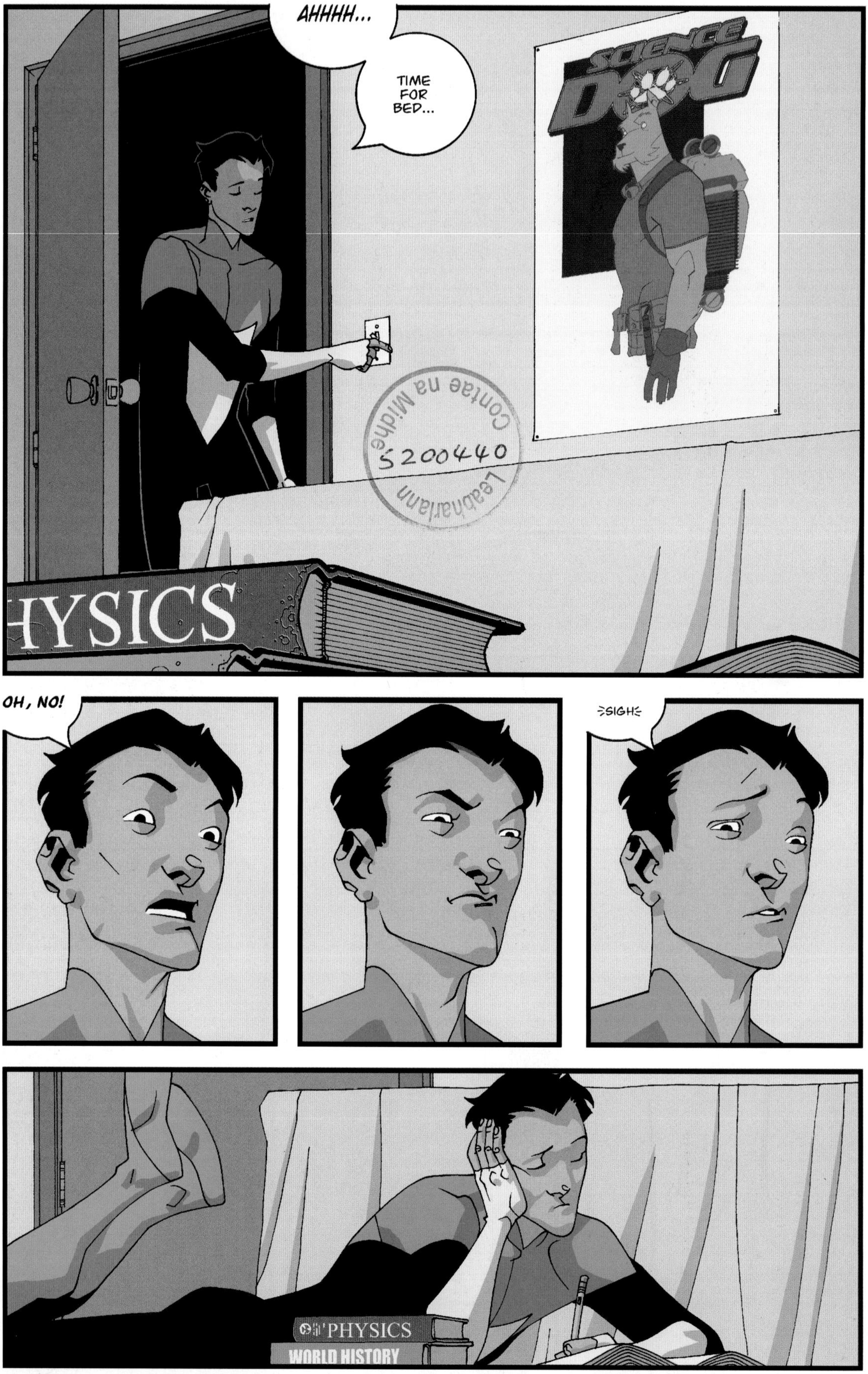
AHHHH...
TIME FOR BED...
SCIENCE DOG
HYSICS
OH, NO!
SIGH
PHYSICS
WORLD HISTORY

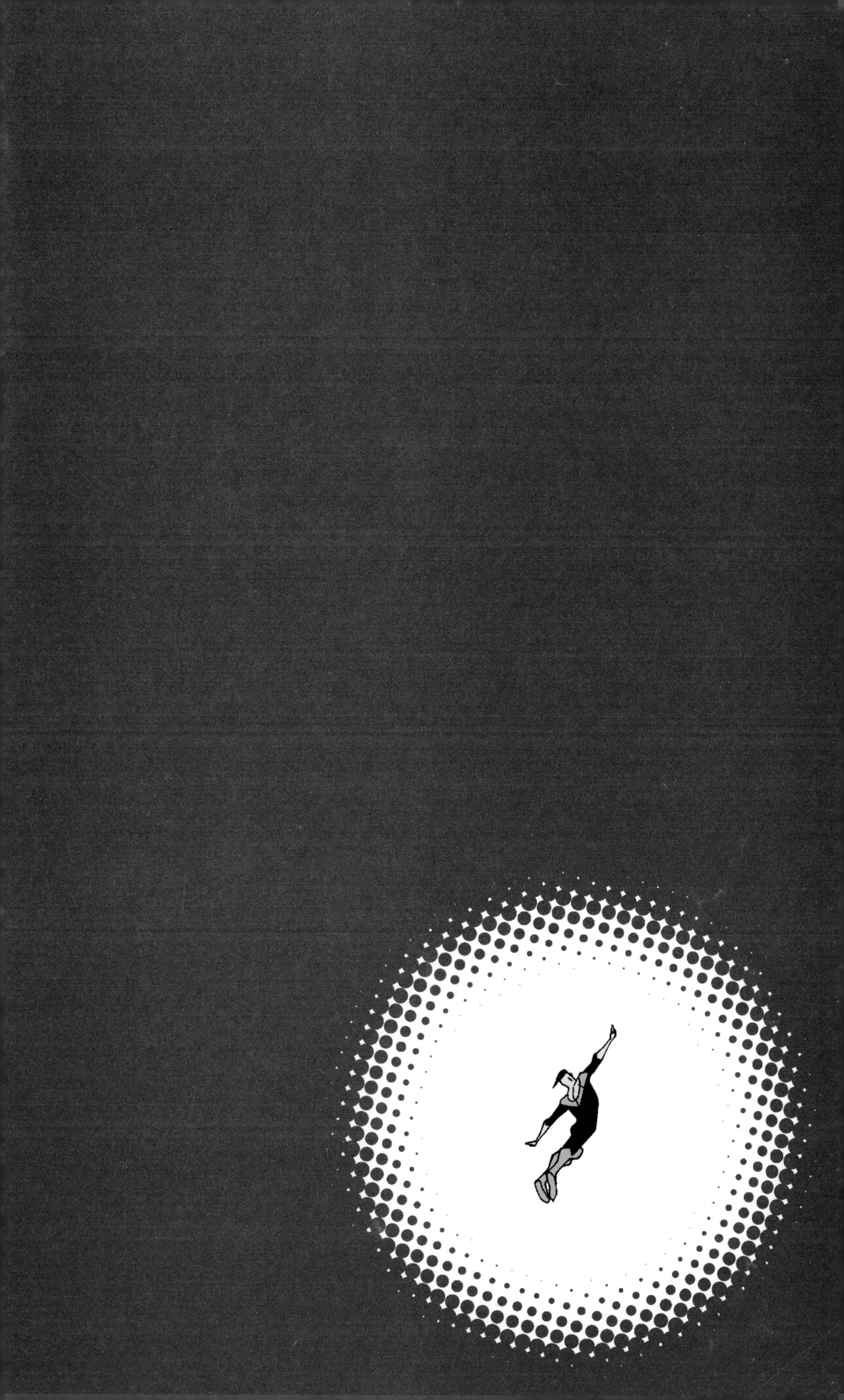

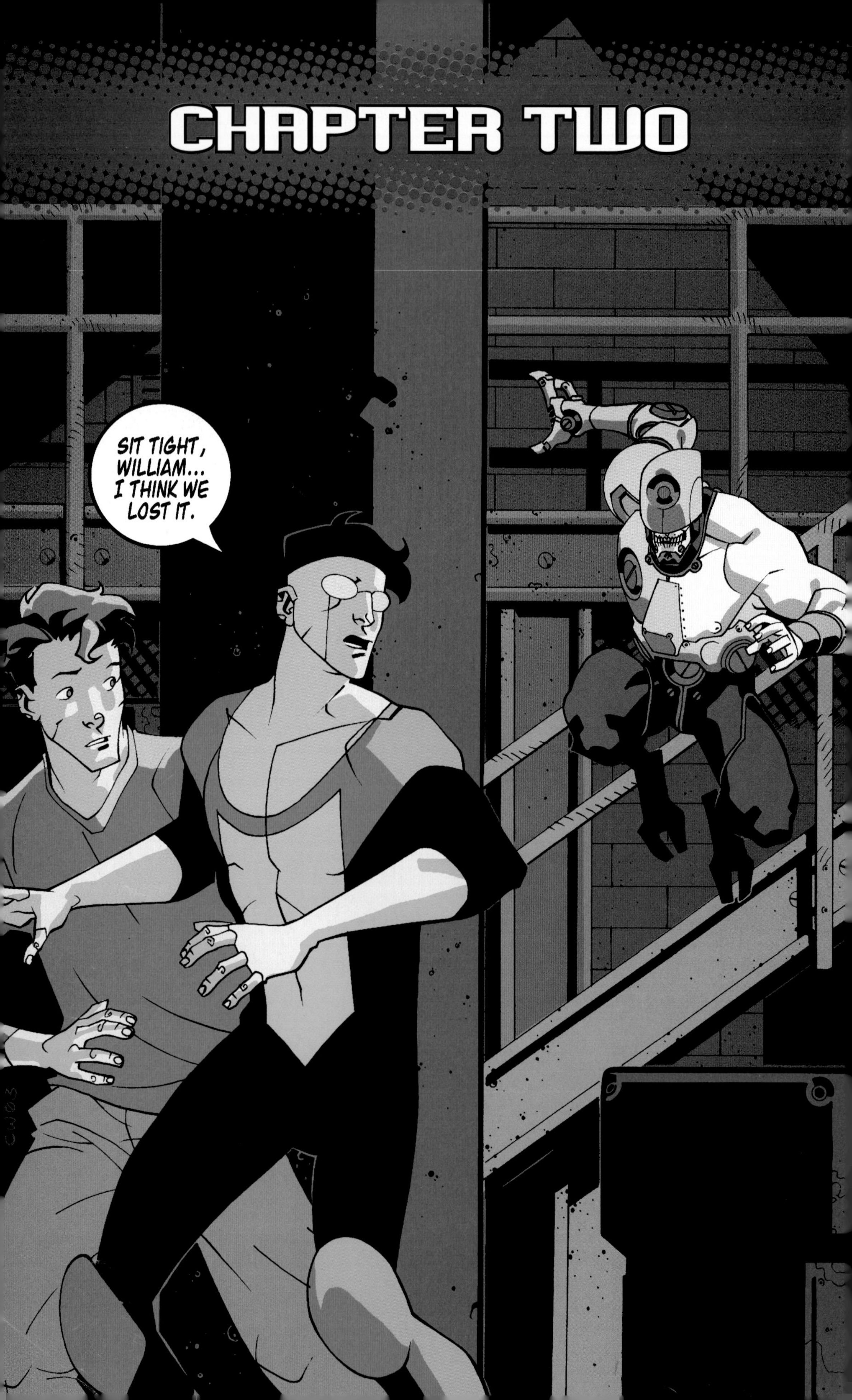
CHAPTER TWO
SIT TIGHT, WILLIAM... I THINK WE LOST IT.

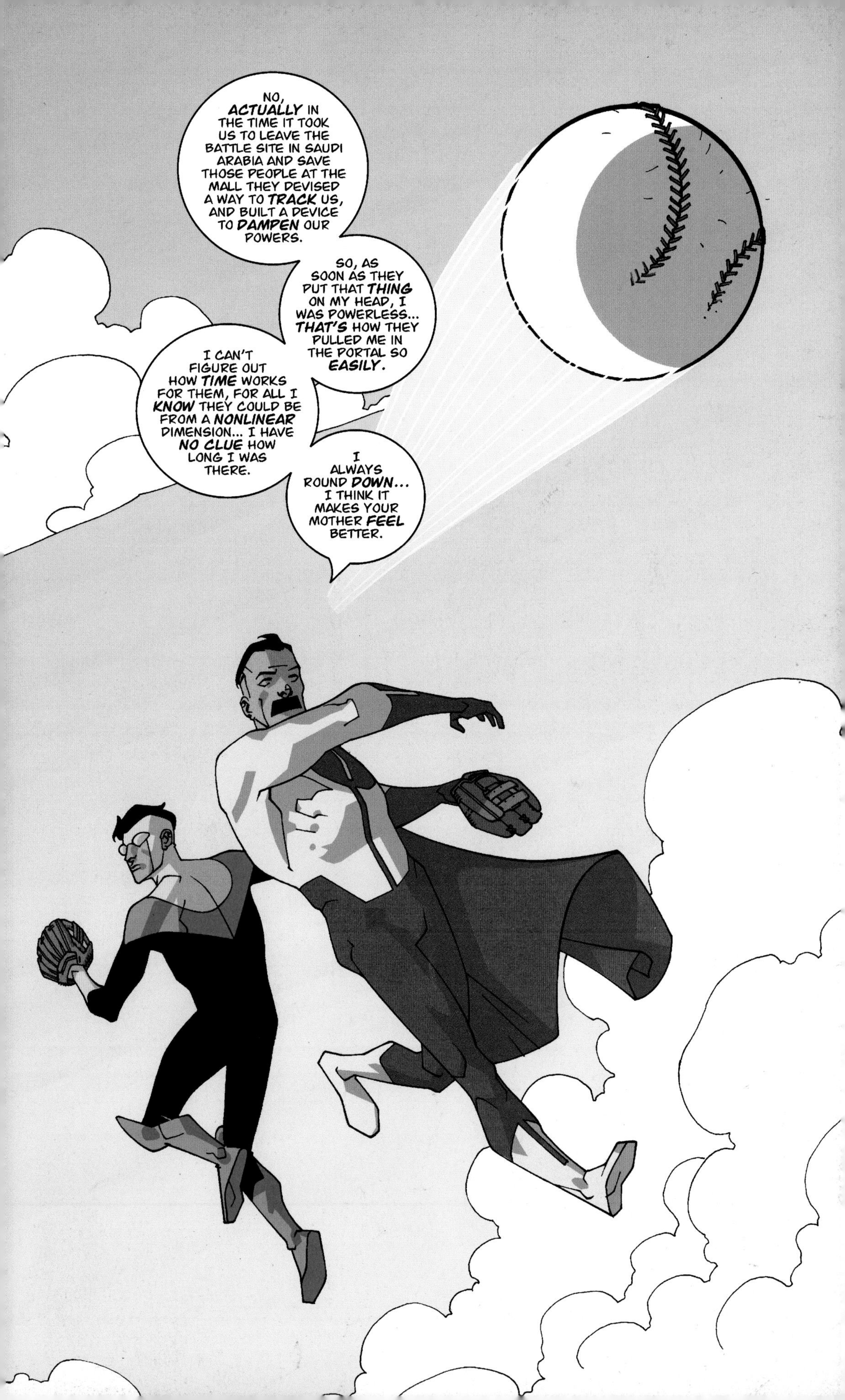
NO, ACTUALLY IN THE TIME IT TOOK US TO LEAVE THE BATTLE SITE IN SAUDI ARABIA AND SAVE THOSE PEOPLE AT THE MALL THEY DEVISED A WAY TO TRACK US, AND BUILT A DEVICE TO DAMPEN OUR POWERS.
SO, AS SOON AS THEY PUT THAT THING ON MY HEAD, I WAS POWERLESS... THAT'S HOW THEY PULLED ME IN THE PORTAL SO EASILY.
I CAN'T FIGURE OUT HOW TIME WORKS FOR THEM, FOR ALL I KNOW THEY COULD BE FROM A NONLINEAR DIMENSION... I HAVE NO CLUE HOW LONG I WAS THERE.
I ALWAYS ROUND DOWN... I THINK IT MAKES YOUR MOTHER FEEL BETTER.

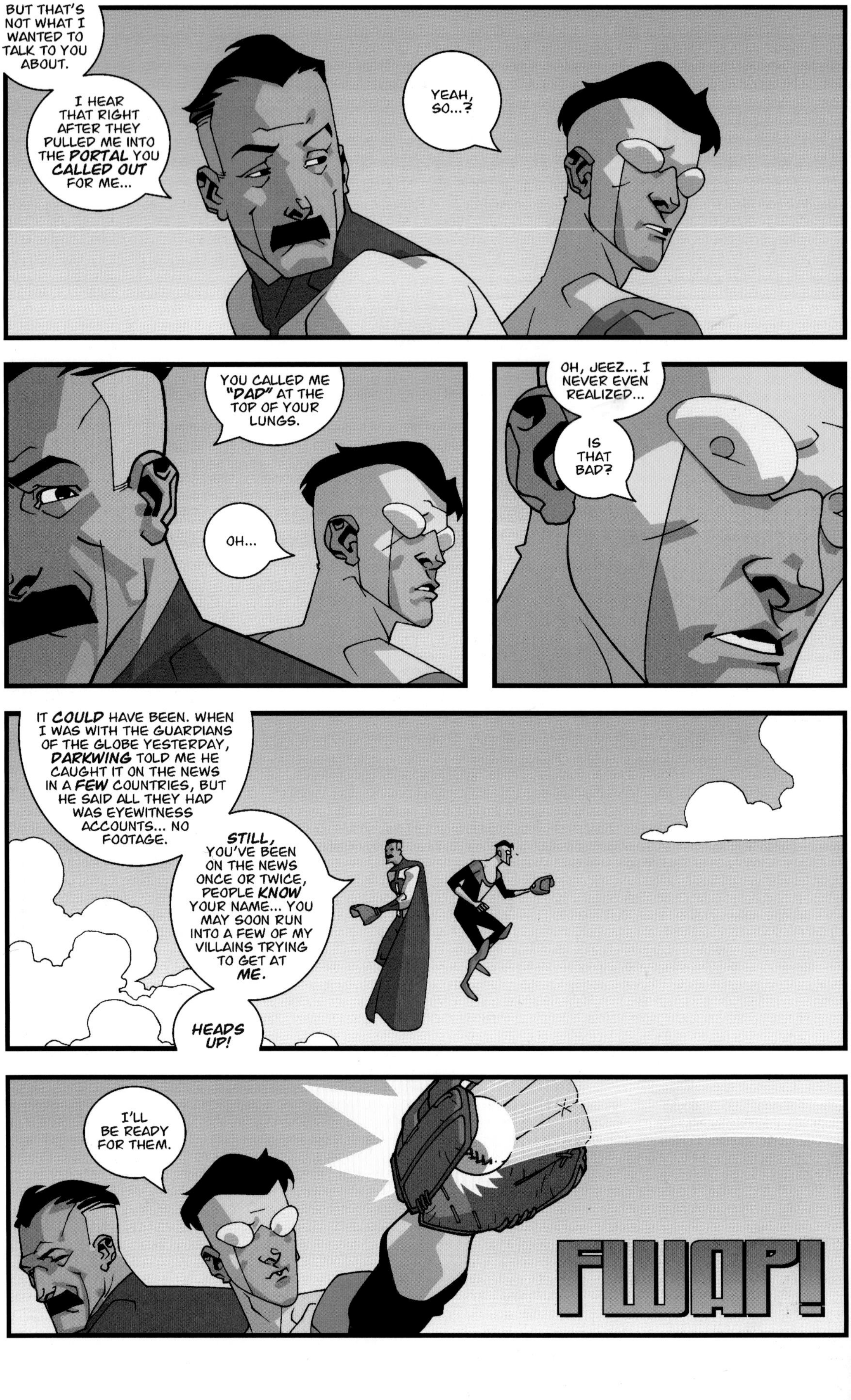
BUT THAT'S NOT WHAT I WANTED TO TALK TO YOU ABOUT.
I HEAR THAT RIGHT AFTER THEY PULLED ME INTO THE PORTAL YOU CALLED OUT FOR ME...
YEAH, SO...?
YOU CALLED ME "DAD" AT THE TOP OF YOUR LUNGS.
OH...
OH, JEEZ... I NEVER EVEN REALIZED...
IS THAT BAD?
IT COULD HAVE BEEN. WHEN I WAS WITH THE GUARDIANS OF THE GLOBE YESTERDAY, DARKWING TOLD ME HE CAUGHT IT ON THE NEWS IN A FEW COUNTRIES, BUT HE SAID ALL THEY HAD WAS EYEWITNESS ACCOUNTS... NO FOOTAGE.
STILL, YOU'VE BEEN ON THE NEWS ONCE OR TWICE, PEOPLE KNOW YOUR NAME... YOU MAY SOON RUN INTO A FEW OF MY VILLAINS TRYING TO GET AT ME.
HEADS UP!
I'LL BE READY FOR THEM.
FWAP!

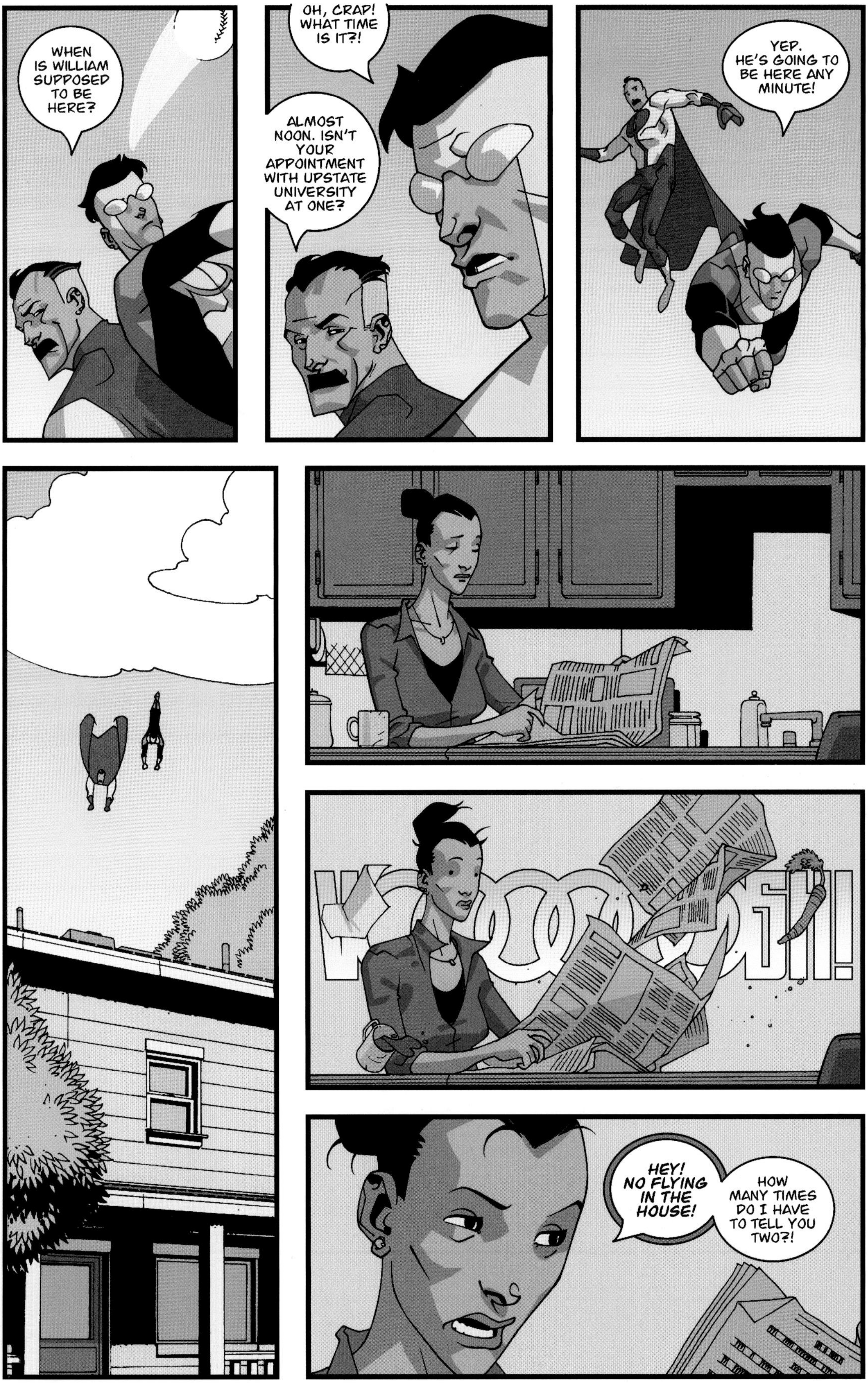
WHEN IS WILLIAM SUPPOSED TO BE HERE?
OH, CRAP! WHAT TIME IS IT?!
ALMOST NOON. ISN'T YOUR APPOINTMENT WITH UPSTATE UNIVERSITY AT ONE?
YEP. HE'S GOING TO BE HERE ANY MINUTE!
HEY! NO FLYING IN THE HOUSE!
HOW MANY TIMES DO I HAVE TO TELL YOU TWO?!

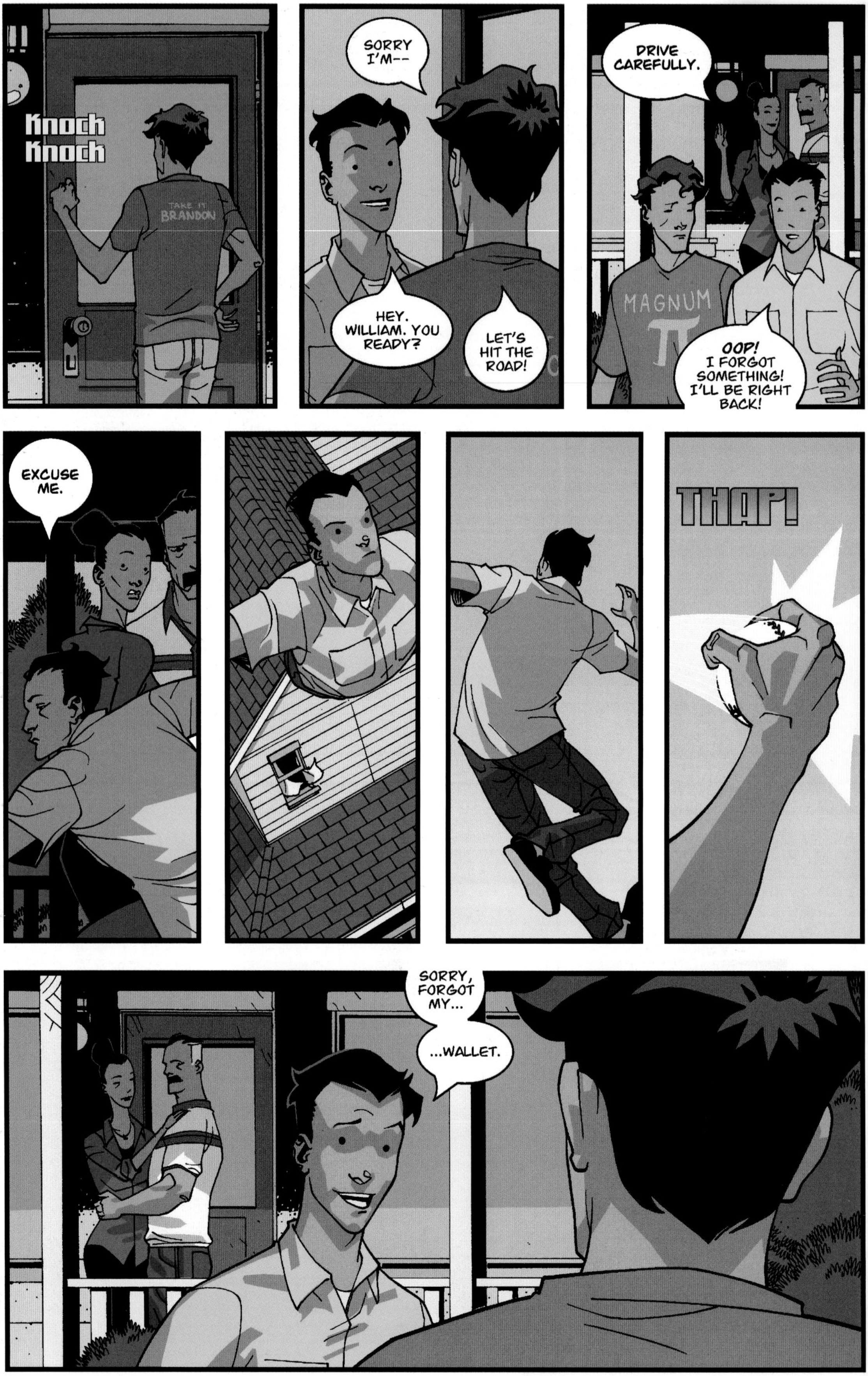
KNOCK KNOCK
TAKE IT BRANDON
SORRY I'M--
HEY. WILLIAM. YOU READY?
LET'S HIT THE ROAD!
DRIVE CAREFULLY.
MAGNUM
OOP! I FORGOT SOMETHING! I'LL BE RIGHT BACK!
EXCUSE ME.
THAP!
SORRY, FORGOT MY...
...WALLET.

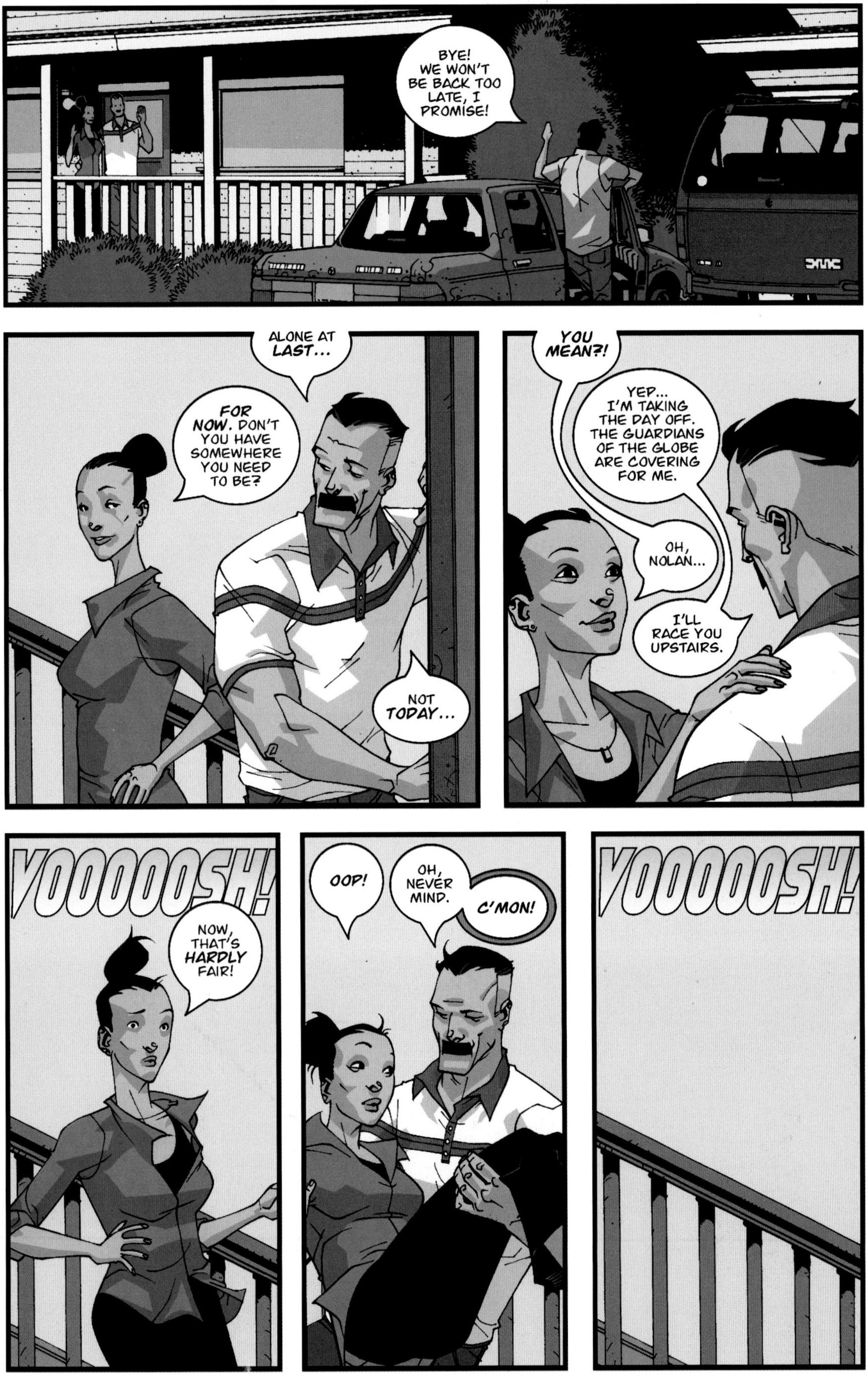
BYE! WE WON'T BE BACK TOO LATE, I PROMISE!
ALONE AT LAST...
FOR NOW. DON'T YOU HAVE SOMEWHERE YOU NEED TO BE?
NOT TODAY...
YOU MEAN?!
YEP... I'M TAKING THE DAY OFF. THE GUARDIANS OF THE GLOBE ARE COVERING FOR ME.
OH, NOLAN...
I'LL RACE YOU UPSTAIRS.
VOOOOOOSH!
NOW, THAT'S HARDLY FAIR!
OOP!
OH, NEVER MIND.
C'MON!
VOOOOOOSH!

I SUPPOSE YOU'RE ALL WONDERING **WHY** I CALLED YOU HERE.

IF THERE IS **ONE** THING I HAVE LEARNED IN MY LIFE THUS FAR IT'S THAT **THINGS CHANGE.** I REMEMBER ALMOST FOUR YEARS AGO WHEN WE STARTED TO WORK TOGETHER HOW **NEW** AND **EXCITING** THINGS WERE... HOW **DIFFERENT** WE ALL WERE BACK THEN.

WE WERE YOUNG, AND RECKLESS... WE WEREN'T QUITE AS **EFFECTIVE** AS WE ARE NOW. THINGS **CHANGED...** AND NOW IT LOOKS LIKE WE'RE IN FOR **ANOTHER** ONE.

I HAVE BEEN INVITED TO TRY OUT FOR THE GUARDIANS OF THE GLOBE.

OH, **ROBOT-- THAT'S GREAT!**

YEAH, MAN... WELL DONE! I'M SURE YOU'LL **REALLY** TURN SOME HEADS.

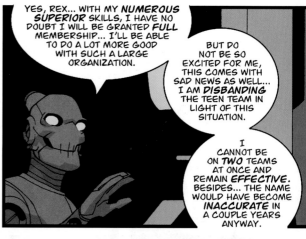

YES, REX... WITH MY **NUMEROUS SUPERIOR** SKILLS, I HAVE NO DOUBT I WILL BE GRANTED **FULL** MEMBERSHIP... I'LL BE ABLE TO DO A LOT MORE GOOD WITH SUCH A LARGE ORGANIZATION.

BUT DO NOT BE SO EXCITED FOR ME, THIS COMES WITH SAD NEWS AS WELL... I AM **DISBANDING** THE TEEN TEAM IN LIGHT OF THIS SITUATION.

I CANNOT BE ON **TWO** TEAMS AT ONCE AND REMAIN **EFFECTIVE.** BESIDES... THE NAME WOULD HAVE BECOME **INACCURATE** IN A COUPLE YEARS ANYWAY.

OF COURSE, THIS FACILITY WILL ALWAYS BE OPEN FOR YOUR **PRIVATE** USE AND I WILL **ALWAYS** ASSIST YOU IF I CAN.

THIS IS NOT THE **END,** IT IS A BEGINNING.

WE **TOTALLY** UNDERSTAND, MAN. C'MERE, YA BUCKET OF BOLTS. I'M PROUD OF YOU.

CONGRATULATIONS, ROBOT.

WE WILL MISS YOU.

I WILL MISS YOU ALL, AS WELL.

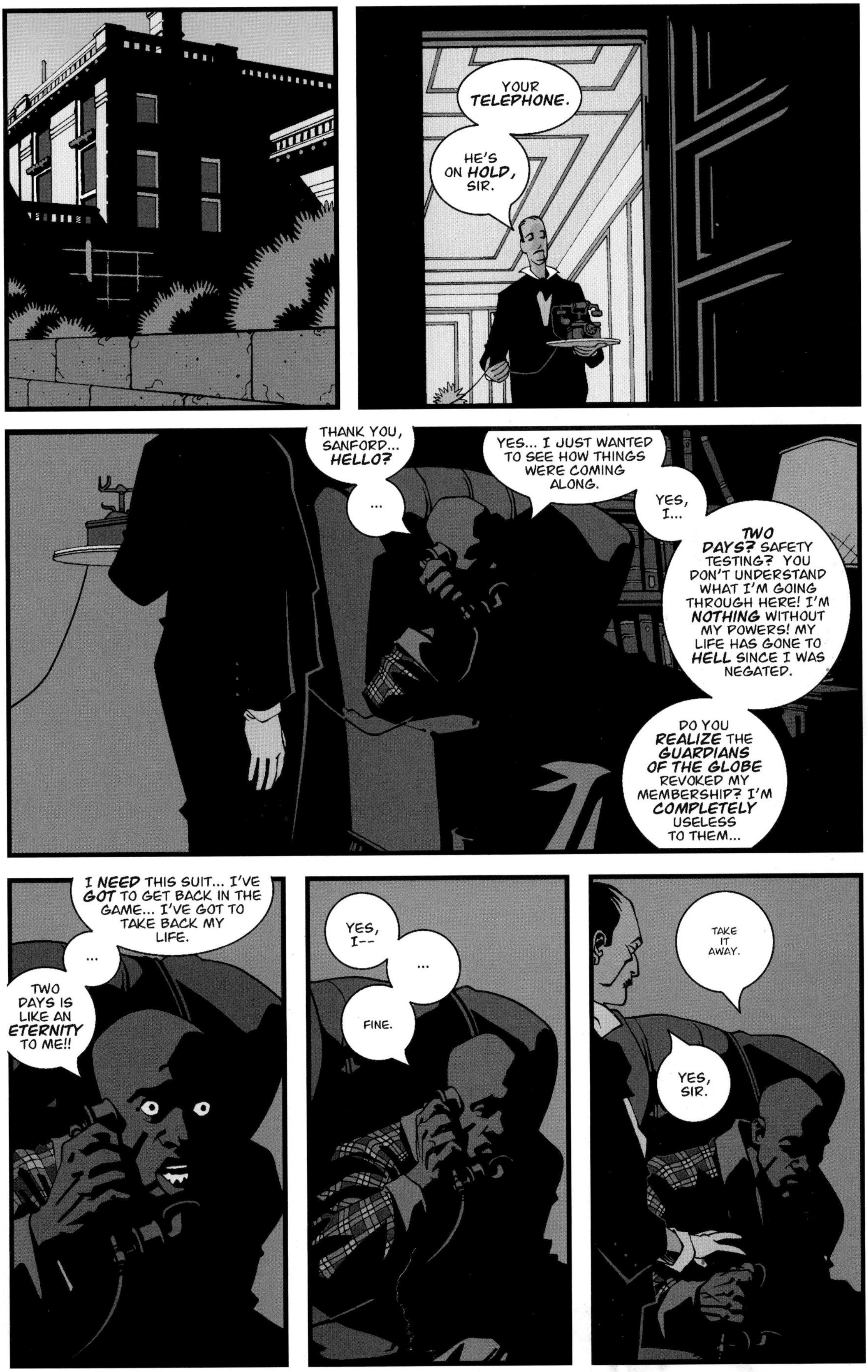
YOUR TELEPHONE.
HE'S ON HOLD, SIR.
THANK YOU, SANFORD... HELLO?
...
YES... I JUST WANTED TO SEE HOW THINGS WERE COMING ALONG.
YES, I...
TWO DAYS? SAFETY TESTING? YOU DON'T UNDERSTAND WHAT I'M GOING THROUGH HERE! I'M NOTHING WITHOUT MY POWERS! MY LIFE HAS GONE TO HELL SINCE I WAS NEGATED.
DO YOU REALIZE THE GUARDIANS OF THE GLOBE REVOKED MY MEMBERSHIP? I'M COMPLETELY USELESS TO THEM...
I NEED THIS SUIT... I'VE GOT TO GET BACK IN THE GAME... I'VE GOT TO TAKE BACK MY LIFE.
...
TWO DAYS IS LIKE AN ETERNITY TO ME!!
YES, I--
...
FINE.
TAKE IT AWAY.
YES, SIR.

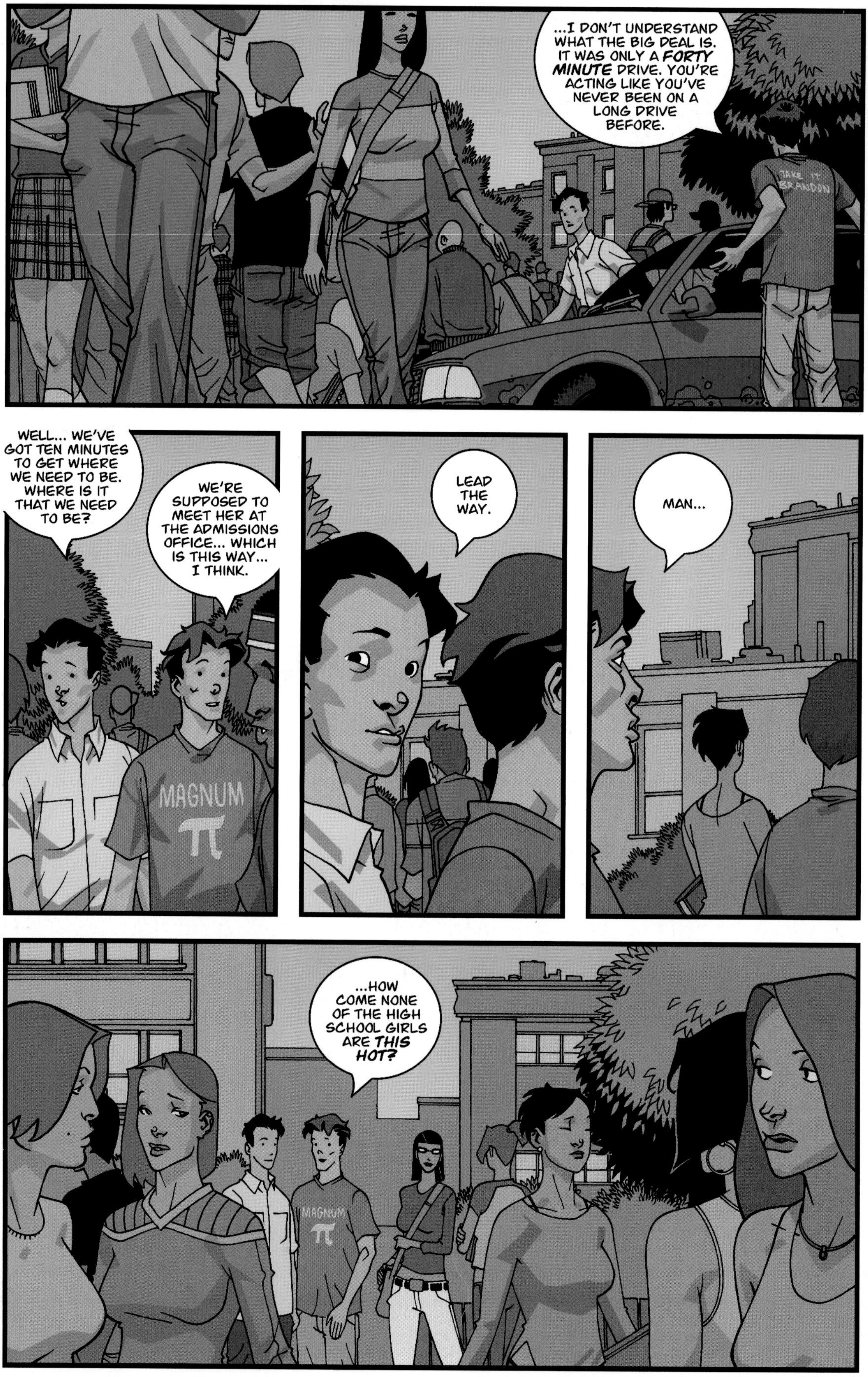
...I DON'T UNDERSTAND WHAT THE BIG DEAL IS. IT WAS ONLY A FORTY MINUTE DRIVE. YOU'RE ACTING LIKE YOU'VE NEVER BEEN ON A LONG DRIVE BEFORE.
TAKE IT BRANDON
WELL... WE'VE GOT TEN MINUTES TO GET WHERE WE NEED TO BE. WHERE IS IT THAT WE NEED TO BE?
WE'RE SUPPOSED TO MEET HER AT THE ADMISSIONS OFFICE... WHICH IS THIS WAY... I THINK.
MAGNUM π
LEAD THE WAY.
MAN...
...HOW COME NONE OF THE HIGH SCHOOL GIRLS ARE THIS HOT?
MAGNUM π

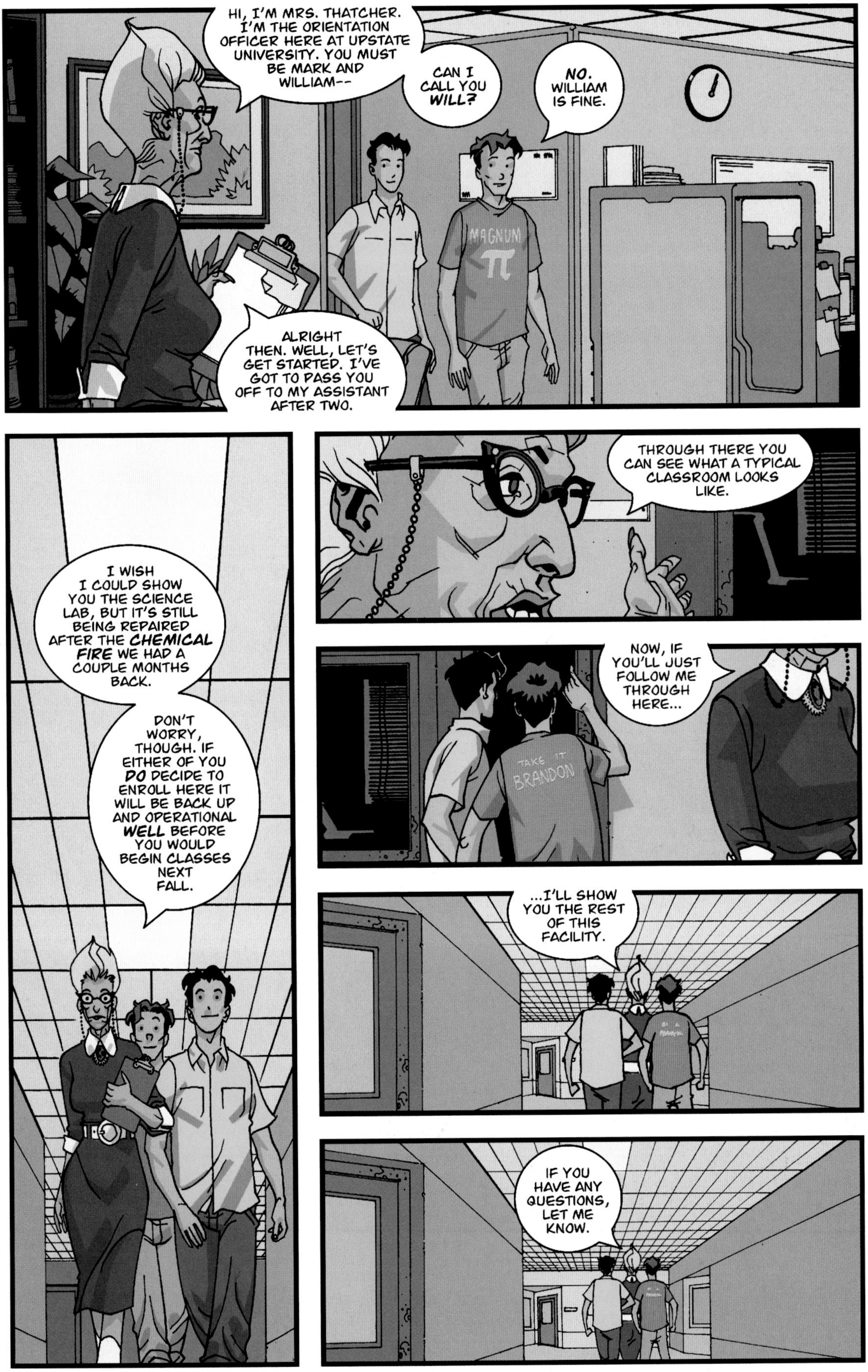
HI, I'M MRS. THATCHER. I'M THE ORIENTATION OFFICER HERE AT UPSTATE UNIVERSITY. YOU MUST BE MARK AND WILLIAM--
CAN I CALL YOU WILL?
NO. WILLIAM IS FINE.
MAGNUM π
ALRIGHT THEN. WELL, LET'S GET STARTED. I'VE GOT TO PASS YOU OFF TO MY ASSISTANT AFTER TWO.
I WISH I COULD SHOW YOU THE SCIENCE LAB, BUT IT'S STILL BEING REPAIRED AFTER THE CHEMICAL FIRE WE HAD A COUPLE MONTHS BACK.
DON'T WORRY, THOUGH. IF EITHER OF YOU DO DECIDE TO ENROLL HERE IT WILL BE BACK UP AND OPERATIONAL WELL BEFORE YOU WOULD BEGIN CLASSES NEXT FALL.
THROUGH THERE YOU CAN SEE WHAT A TYPICAL CLASSROOM LOOKS LIKE.
NOW, IF YOU'LL JUST FOLLOW ME THROUGH HERE...
TAKE IT BRANDON
...I'LL SHOW YOU THE REST OF THIS FACILITY.
IF YOU HAVE ANY QUESTIONS, LET ME KNOW.

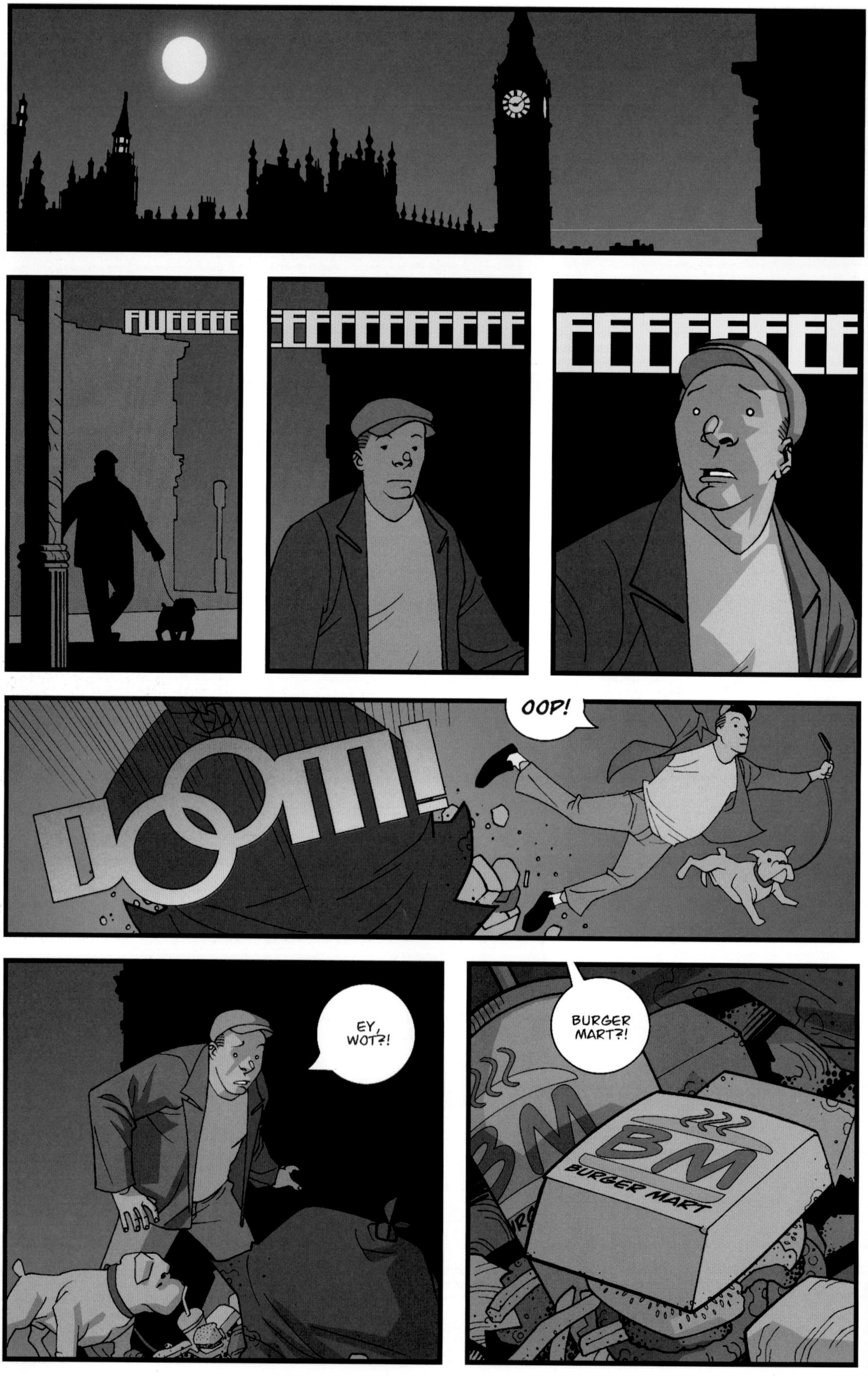
AWEEEEE
EEEEEEEEEEE
EEEEEEEE
DOOM!
OOP!
EY, WOT?!
BURGER MART?!
BM
BURGER MART

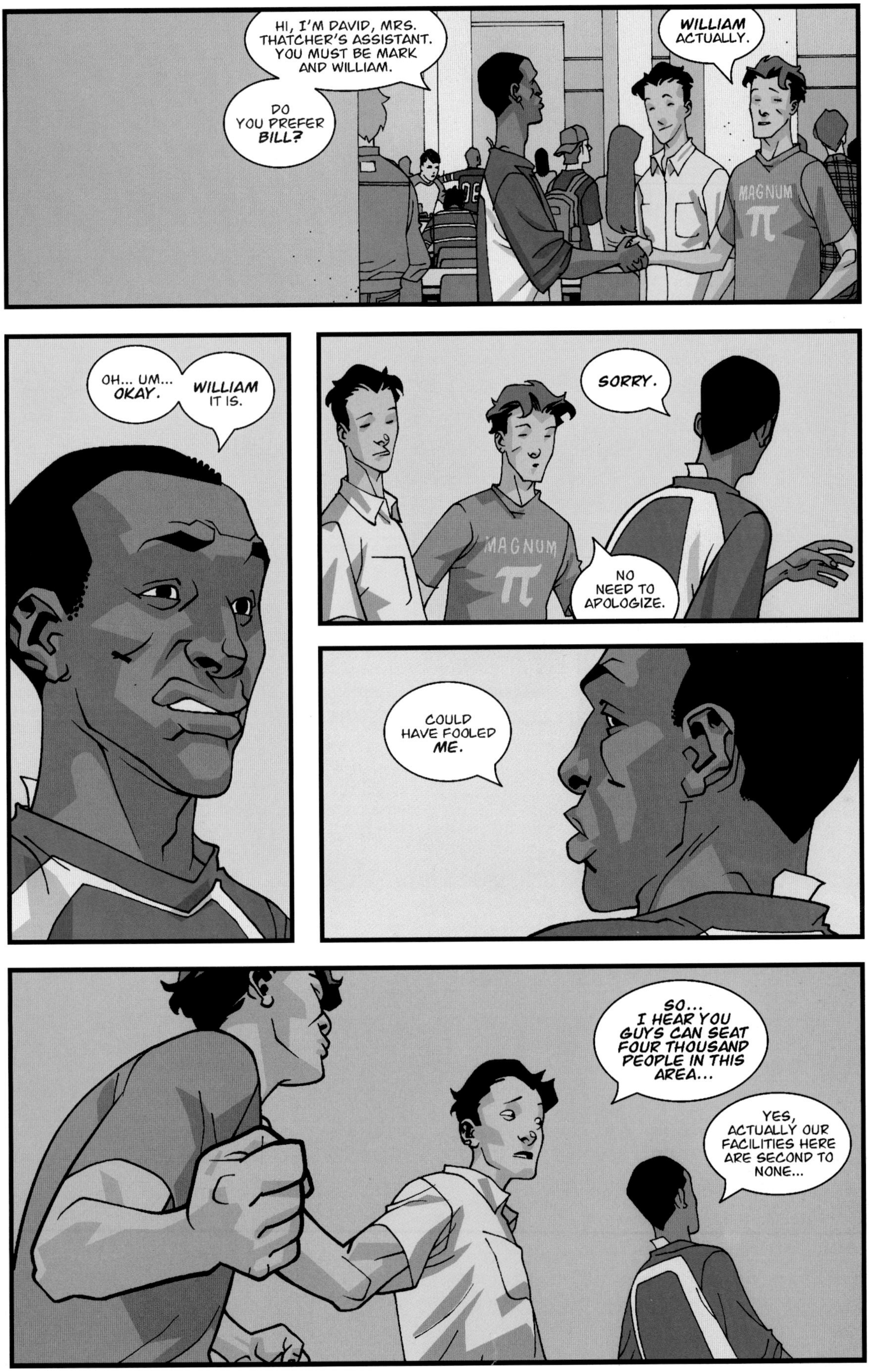
HI, I'M DAVID, MRS. THATCHER'S ASSISTANT. YOU MUST BE MARK AND WILLIAM.
DO YOU PREFER BILL?
WILLIAM ACTUALLY.
MAGNUM π
OH... UM... OKAY.
WILLIAM IT IS.
SORRY.
MAGNUM π
NO NEED TO APOLOGIZE.
COULD HAVE FOOLED ME.
SO... I HEAR YOU GUYS CAN SEAT FOUR THOUSAND PEOPLE IN THIS AREA...
YES, ACTUALLY OUR FACILITIES HERE ARE SECOND TO NONE...

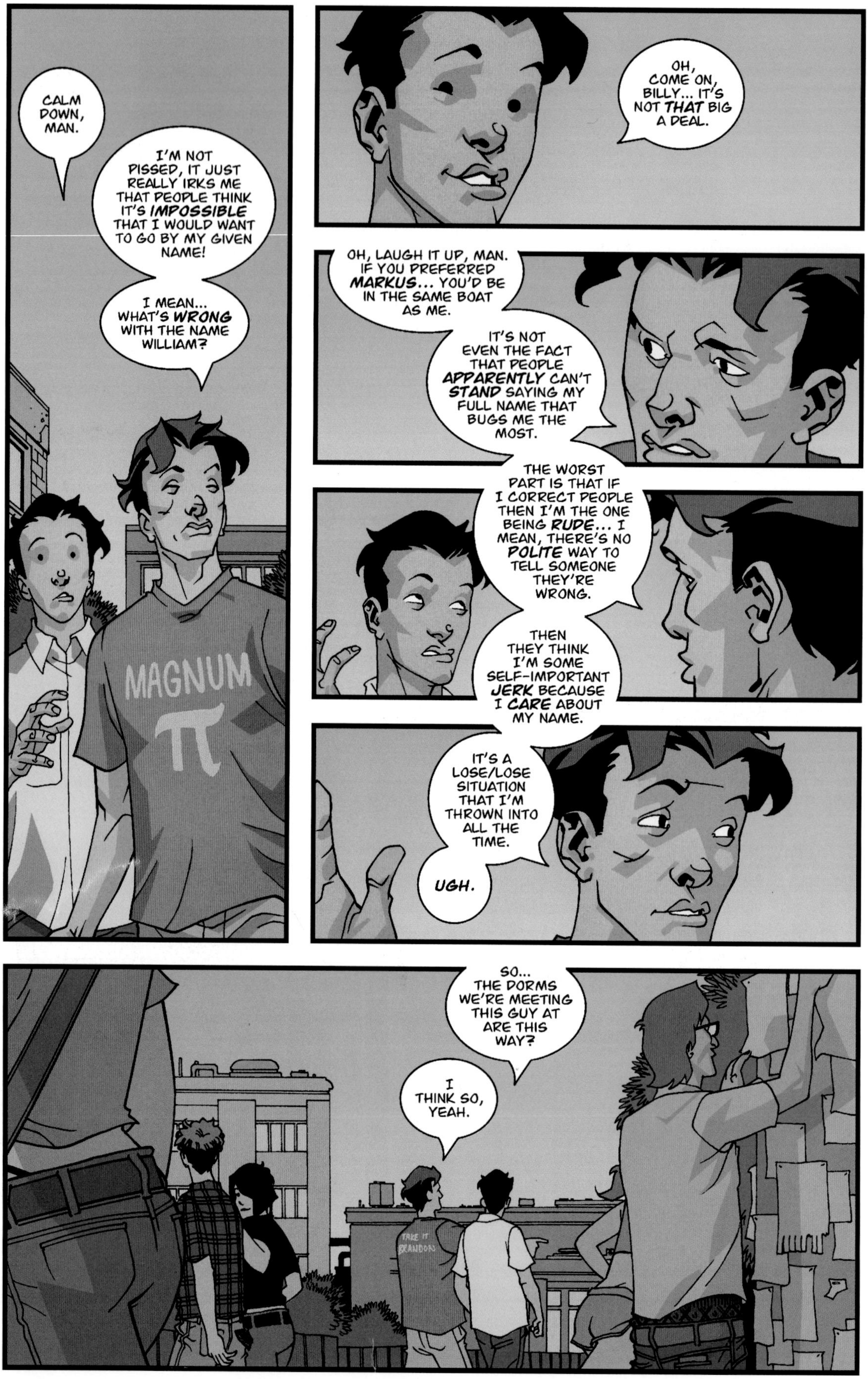

CALM DOWN, MAN.
I'M NOT PISSED, IT JUST REALLY IRKS ME THAT PEOPLE THINK IT'S IMPOSSIBLE THAT I WOULD WANT TO GO BY MY GIVEN NAME!
I MEAN... WHAT'S WRONG WITH THE NAME WILLIAM?
MAGNUM π
OH, COME ON, BILLY... IT'S NOT THAT BIG A DEAL.
OH, LAUGH IT UP, MAN. IF YOU PREFERRED MARKUS... YOU'D BE IN THE SAME BOAT AS ME.
IT'S NOT EVEN THE FACT THAT PEOPLE APPARENTLY CAN'T STAND SAYING MY FULL NAME THAT BUGS ME THE MOST.
THE WORST PART IS THAT IF I CORRECT PEOPLE THEN I'M THE ONE BEING RUDE... I MEAN, THERE'S NO POLITE WAY TO TELL SOMEONE THEY'RE WRONG.
THEN THEY THINK I'M SOME SELF-IMPORTANT JERK BECAUSE I CARE ABOUT MY NAME.
IT'S A LOSE/LOSE SITUATION THAT I'M THROWN INTO ALL THE TIME.
UGH.
SO... THE DORMS WE'RE MEETING THIS GUY AT ARE THIS WAY?
I THINK SO, YEAH.

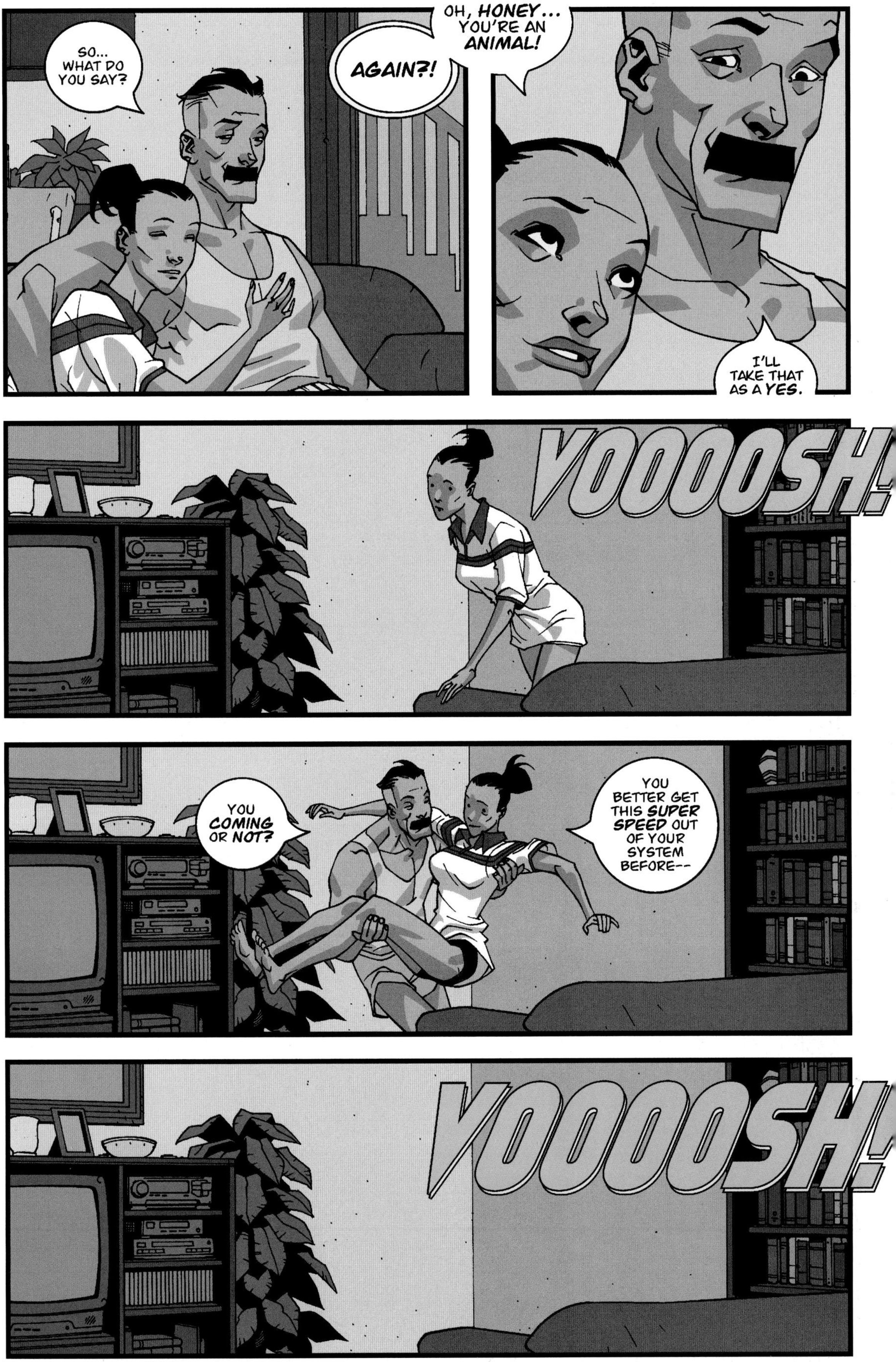
SO... WHAT DO YOU SAY?
AGAIN?!
OH, HONEY... YOU'RE AN ANIMAL!
I'LL TAKE THAT AS A YES.
VOOOOSH!
YOU COMING OR NOT?
YOU BETTER GET THIS SUPER SPEED OUT OF YOUR SYSTEM BEFORE--
VOOOOSH!

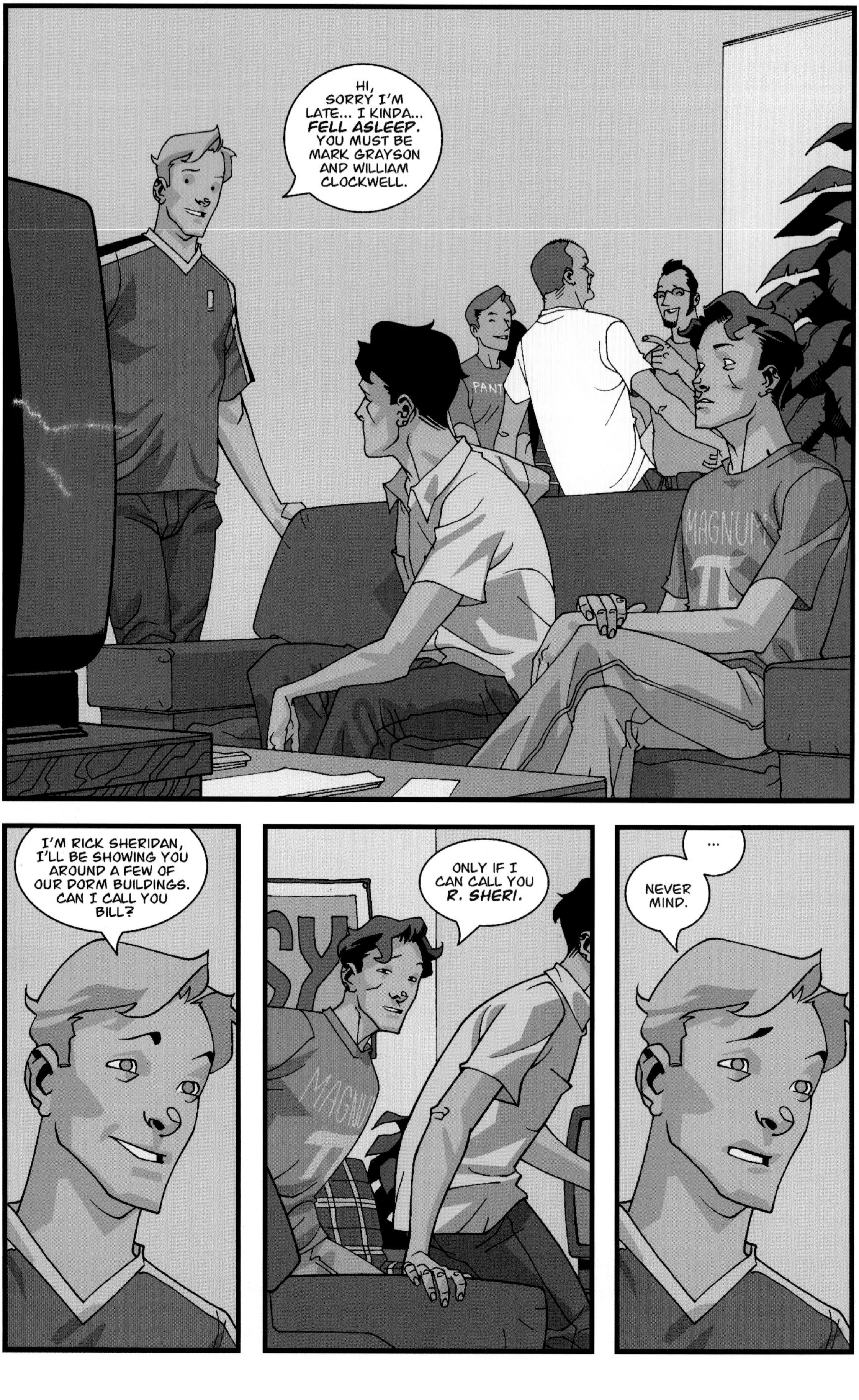
HI, SORRY I'M LATE... I KINDA... **FELL ASLEEP.** YOU MUST BE MARK GRAYSON AND WILLIAM CLOCKWELL.
MAGNUM
I'M RICK SHERIDAN, I'LL BE SHOWING YOU AROUND A FEW OF OUR DORM BUILDINGS. CAN I CALL YOU BILL?
ONLY IF I CAN CALL YOU **R. SHERI.**
...
NEVER MIND.

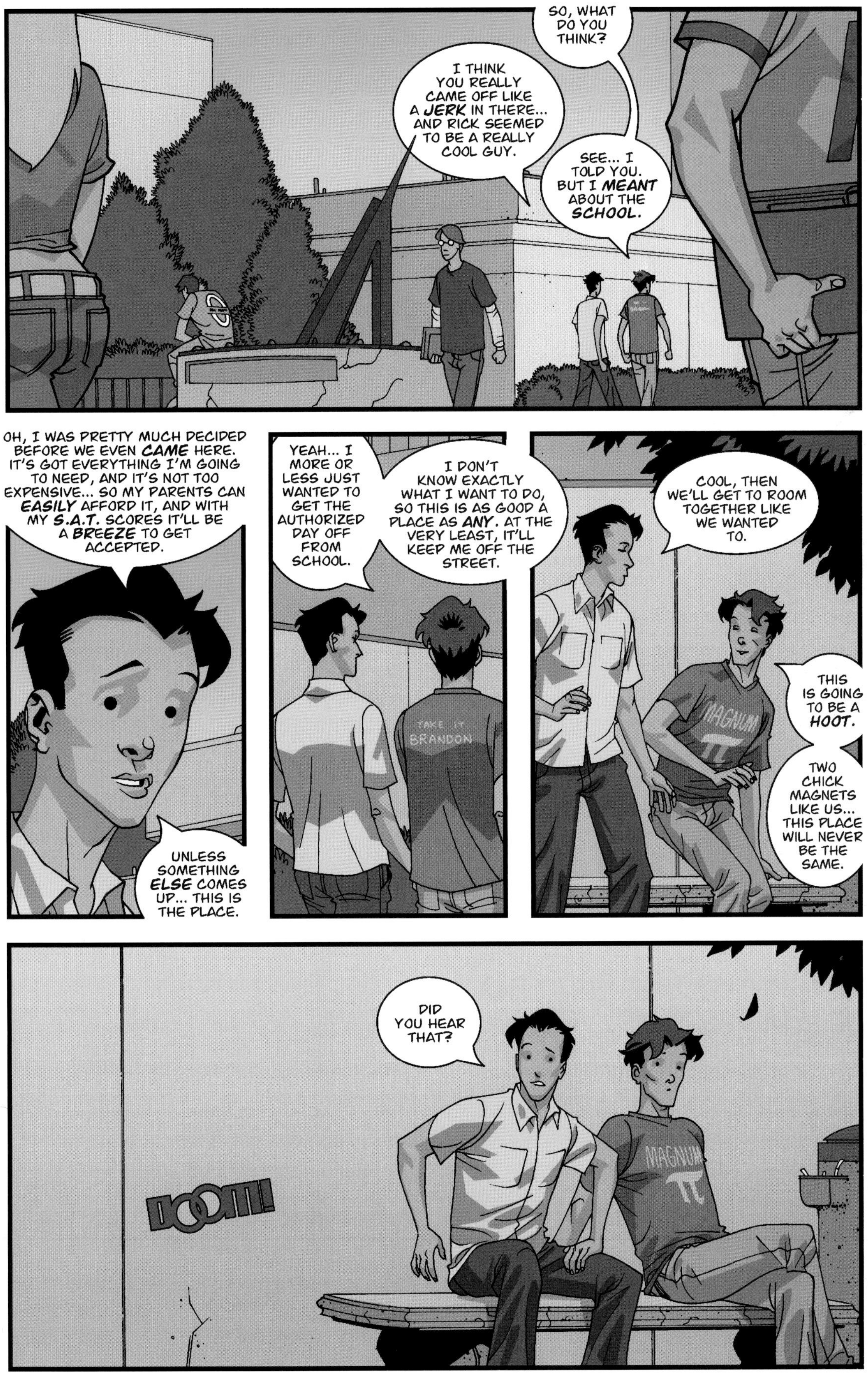
SO, WHAT DO YOU THINK?
I THINK YOU REALLY CAME OFF LIKE A JERK IN THERE... AND RICK SEEMED TO BE A REALLY COOL GUY.
SEE... I TOLD YOU. BUT I MEANT ABOUT THE SCHOOL.
OH, I WAS PRETTY MUCH DECIDED BEFORE WE EVEN CAME HERE. IT'S GOT EVERYTHING I'M GOING TO NEED, AND IT'S NOT TOO EXPENSIVE... SO MY PARENTS CAN EASILY AFFORD IT, AND WITH MY S.A.T. SCORES IT'LL BE A BREEZE TO GET ACCEPTED.
UNLESS SOMETHING ELSE COMES UP... THIS IS THE PLACE.
YEAH... I MORE OR LESS JUST WANTED TO GET THE AUTHORIZED DAY OFF FROM SCHOOL.
I DON'T KNOW EXACTLY WHAT I WANT TO DO, SO THIS IS AS GOOD A PLACE AS ANY. AT THE VERY LEAST, IT'LL KEEP ME OFF THE STREET.
TAKE IT BRANDON
COOL, THEN WE'LL GET TO ROOM TOGETHER LIKE WE WANTED TO.
MAGNUM
THIS IS GOING TO BE A HOOT.
TWO CHICK MAGNETS LIKE US... THIS PLACE WILL NEVER BE THE SAME.
DID YOU HEAR THAT?
DOOM!
MAGNUM

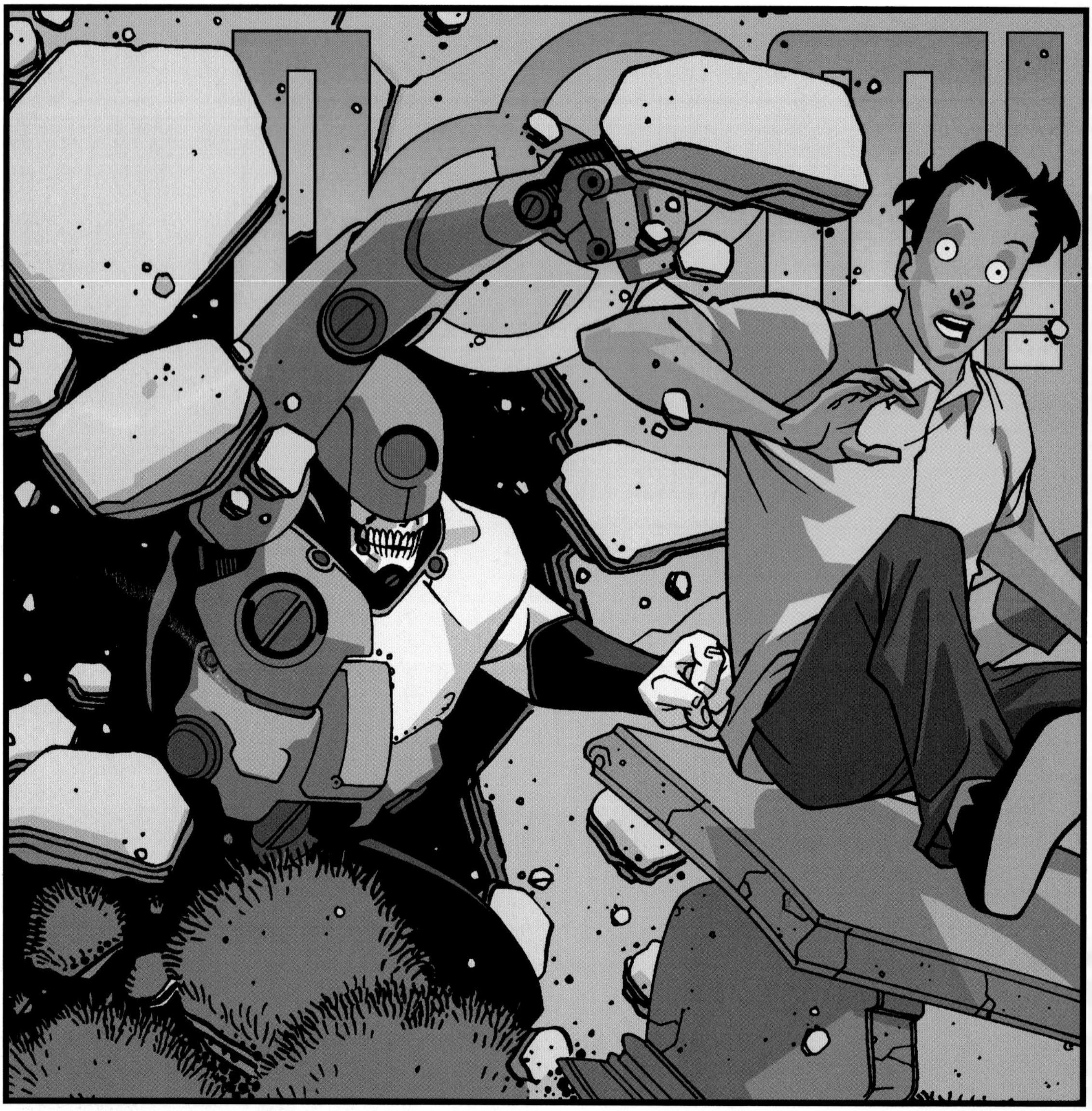

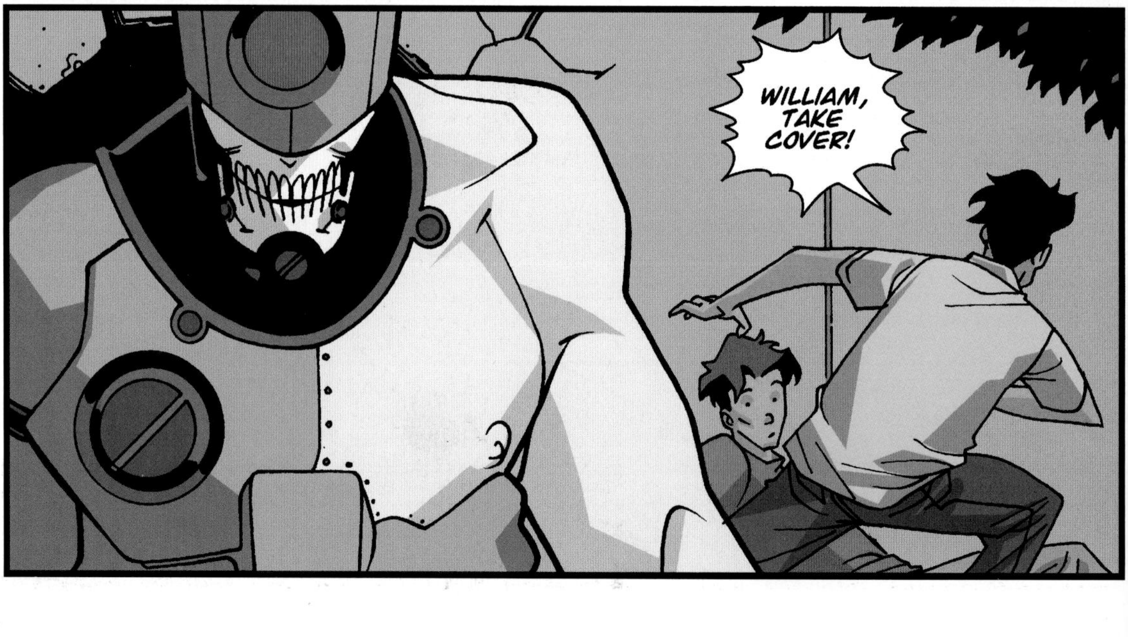
WILLIAM, TAKE COVER!

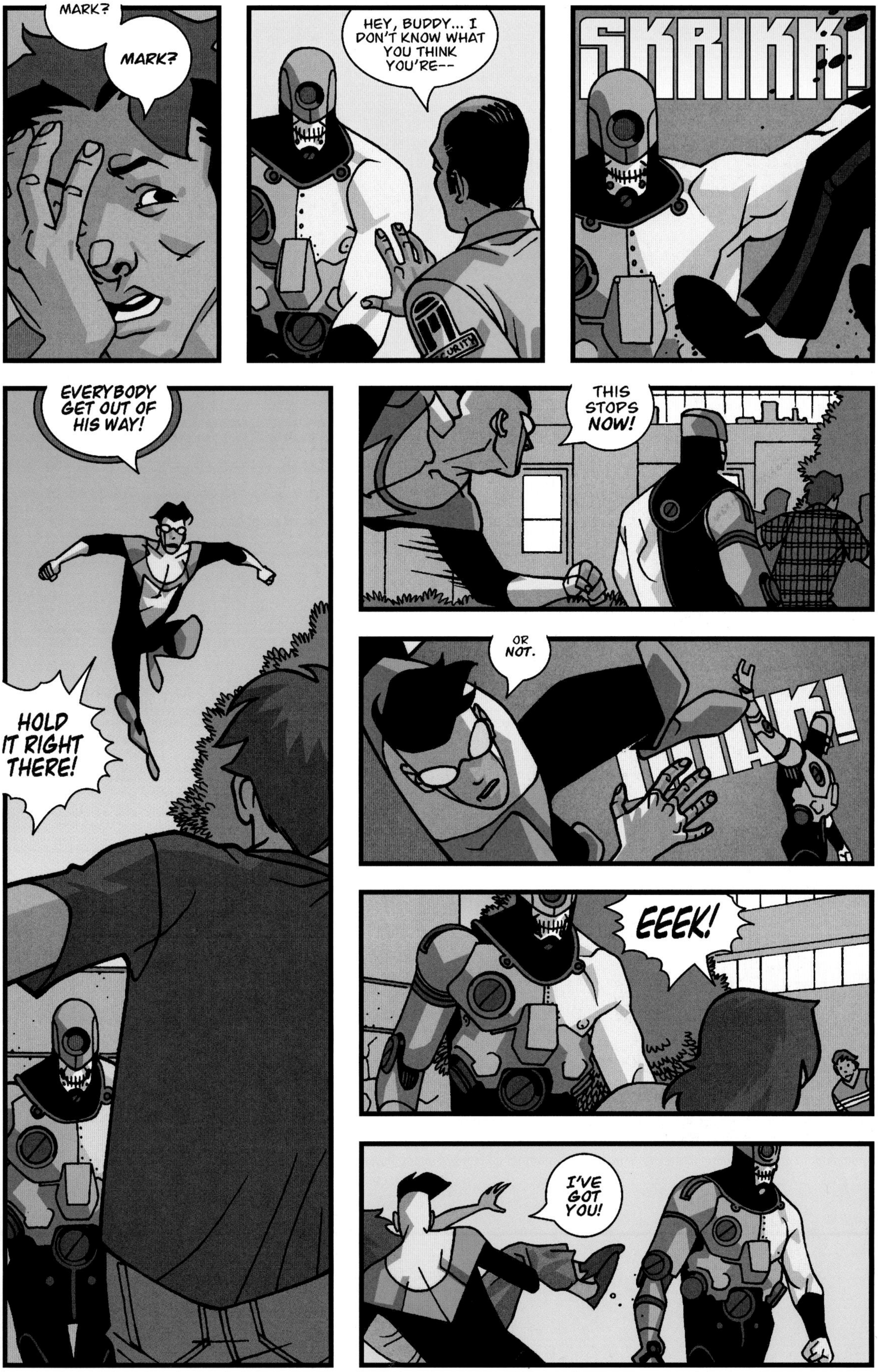
MARK?
MARK?
HEY, BUDDY... I DON'T KNOW WHAT YOU THINK YOU'RE--
SECURITY
SKRIKK!
EVERYBODY GET OUT OF HIS WAY!
HOLD IT RIGHT THERE!
THIS STOPS NOW!
OR NOT.
EEEK!
I'VE GOT YOU!

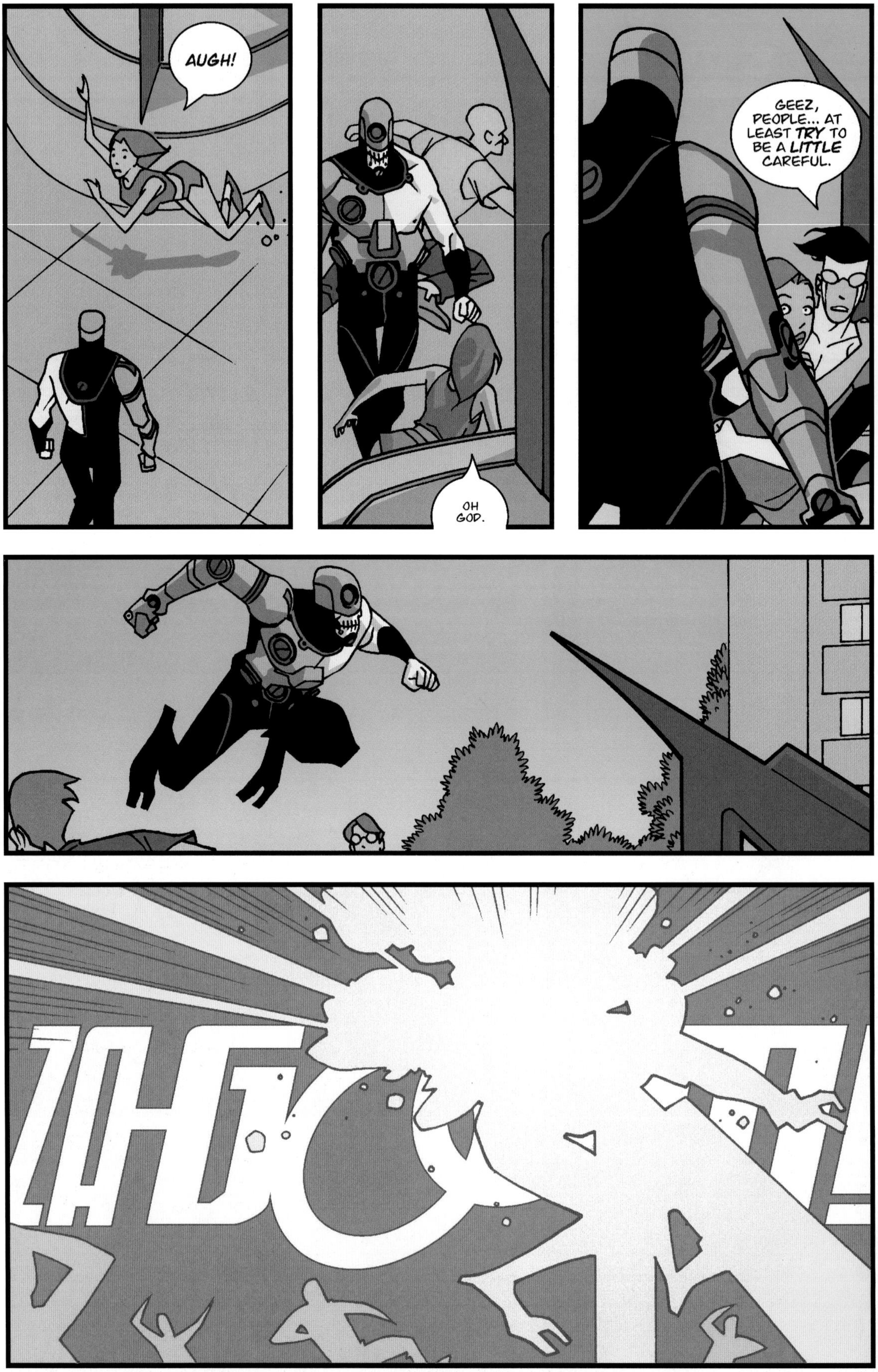
AUGH!
OH GOD.
GEEZ, PEOPLE... AT LEAST TRY TO BE A LITTLE CAREFUL.

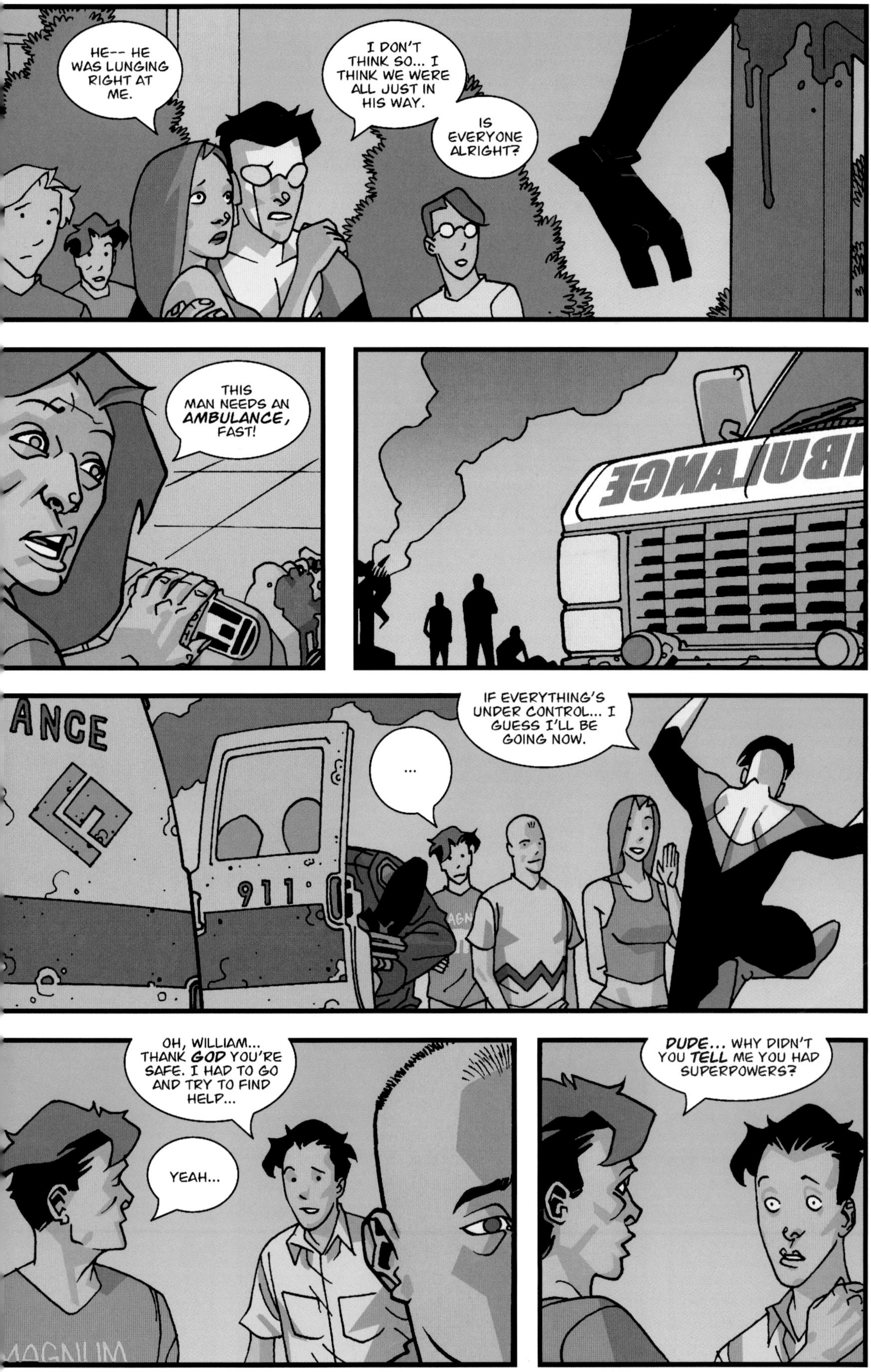
HE-- HE WAS LUNGING RIGHT AT ME.
I DON'T THINK SO... I THINK WE WERE ALL JUST IN HIS WAY.
IS EVERYONE ALRIGHT?
THIS MAN NEEDS AN AMBULANCE, FAST!
AMBULANCE
ANCE
911
...
IF EVERYTHING'S UNDER CONTROL... I GUESS I'LL BE GOING NOW.
OH, WILLIAM... THANK GOD YOU'RE SAFE. I HAD TO GO AND TRY TO FIND HELP...
YEAH...
MAGNUM
DUDE... WHY DIDN'T YOU TELL ME YOU HAD SUPERPOWERS?

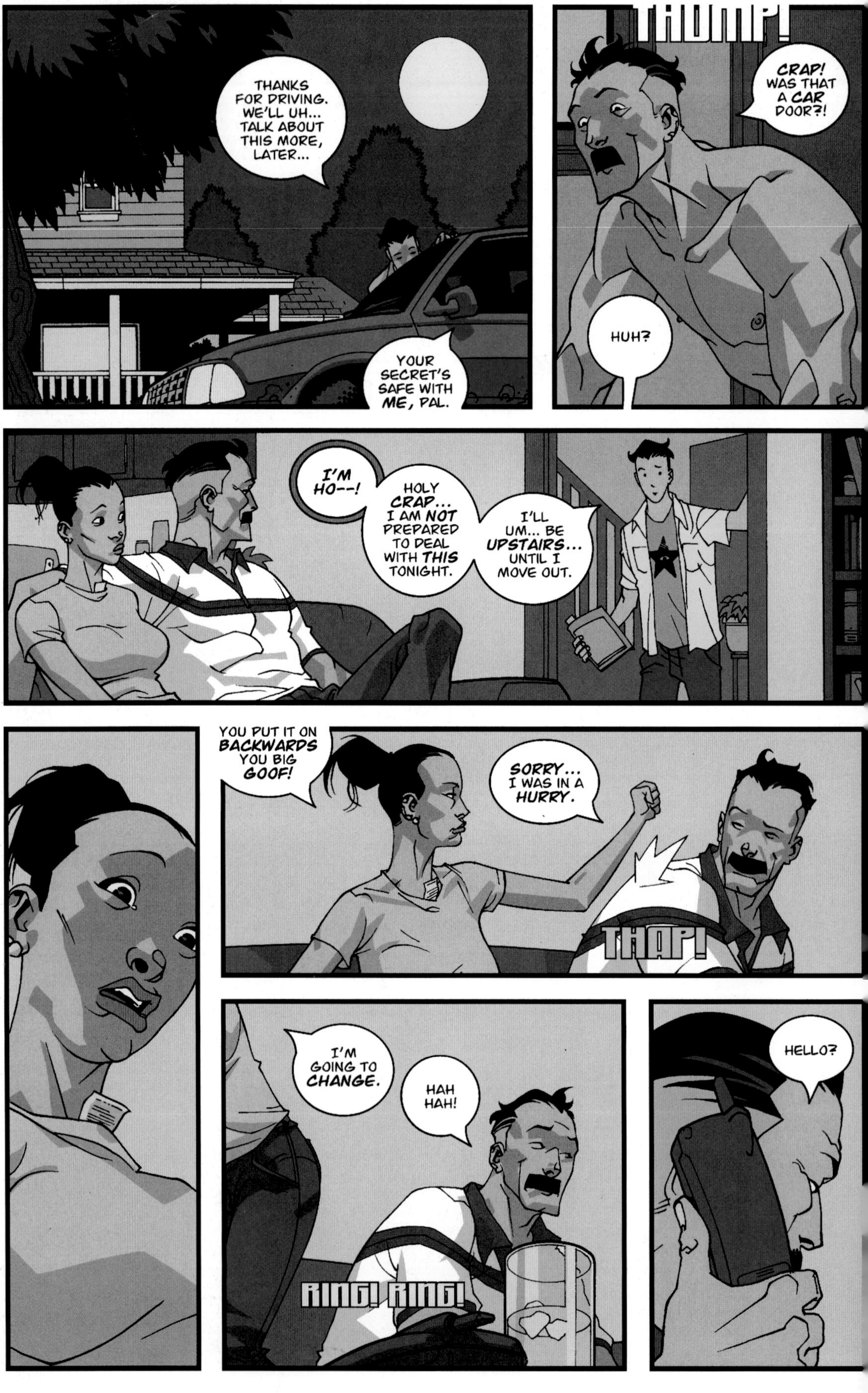
THANKS FOR DRIVING. WE'LL UH... TALK ABOUT THIS MORE, LATER...
YOUR SECRET'S SAFE WITH ME, PAL.
CRAP! WAS THAT A CAR DOOR?!
HUH?
I'M HO--!
HOLY CRAP... I AM NOT PREPARED TO DEAL WITH THIS TONIGHT.
I'LL UM... BE UPSTAIRS... UNTIL I MOVE OUT.
YOU PUT IT ON BACKWARDS YOU BIG GOOF!
SORRY... I WAS IN A HURRY.
THAP!
I'M GOING TO CHANGE.
HAH HAH!
RING! RING!
HELLO?

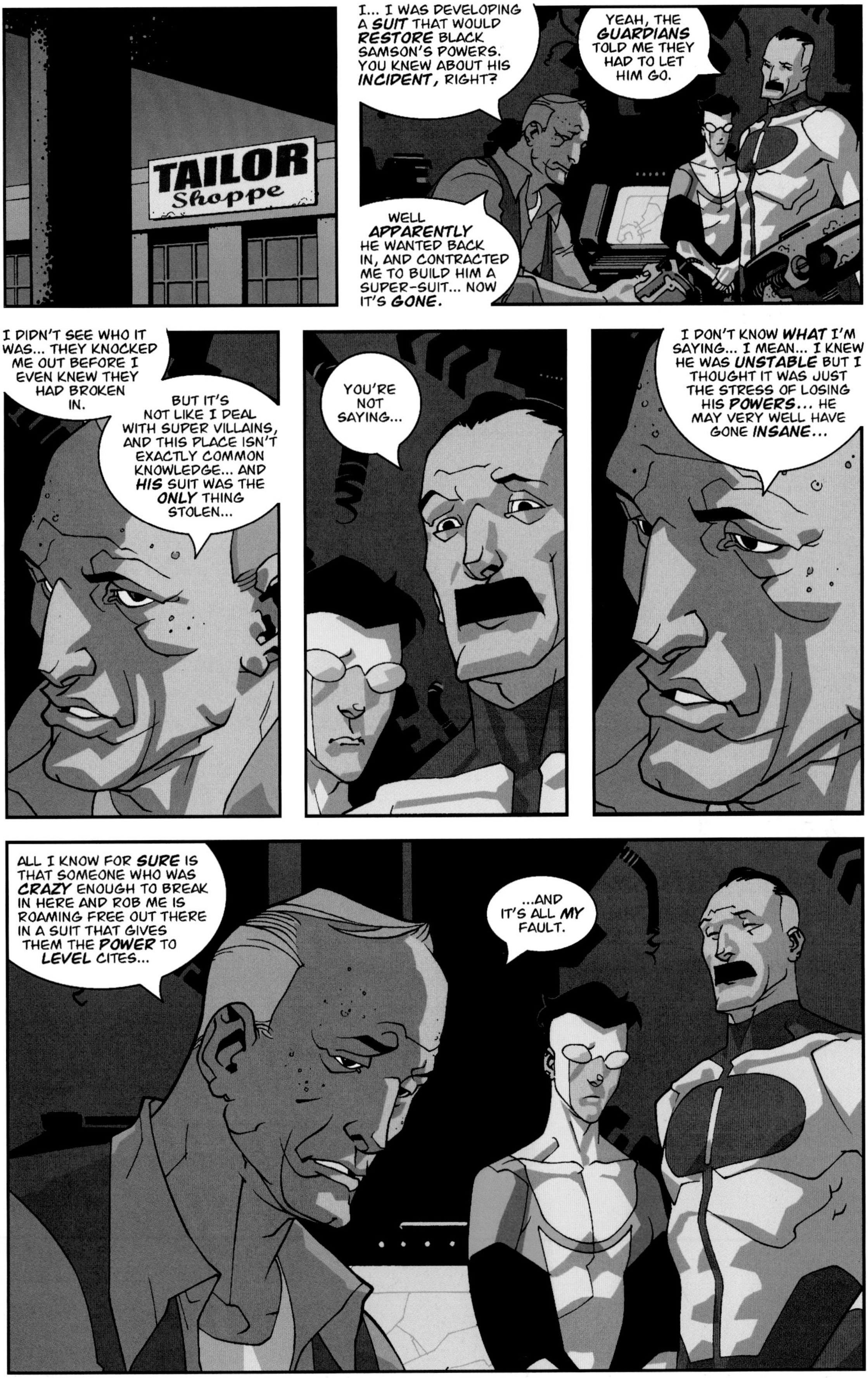
TAILOR Shoppe
I... I WAS DEVELOPING A SUIT THAT WOULD RESTORE BLACK SAMSON'S POWERS. YOU KNEW ABOUT HIS INCIDENT, RIGHT?
YEAH, THE GUARDIANS TOLD ME THEY HAD TO LET HIM GO.
WELL APPARENTLY HE WANTED BACK IN, AND CONTRACTED ME TO BUILD HIM A SUPER-SUIT... NOW IT'S GONE.
I DIDN'T SEE WHO IT WAS... THEY KNOCKED ME OUT BEFORE I EVEN KNEW THEY HAD BROKEN IN.
BUT IT'S NOT LIKE I DEAL WITH SUPER VILLAINS, AND THIS PLACE ISN'T EXACTLY COMMON KNOWLEDGE... AND HIS SUIT WAS THE ONLY THING STOLEN...
YOU'RE NOT SAYING...
I DON'T KNOW WHAT I'M SAYING... I MEAN... I KNEW HE WAS UNSTABLE BUT I THOUGHT IT WAS JUST THE STRESS OF LOSING HIS POWERS... HE MAY VERY WELL HAVE GONE INSANE...
ALL I KNOW FOR SURE IS THAT SOMEONE WHO WAS CRAZY ENOUGH TO BREAK IN HERE AND ROB ME IS ROAMING FREE OUT THERE IN A SUIT THAT GIVES THEM THE POWER TO LEVEL CITES...
...AND IT'S ALL MY FAULT.

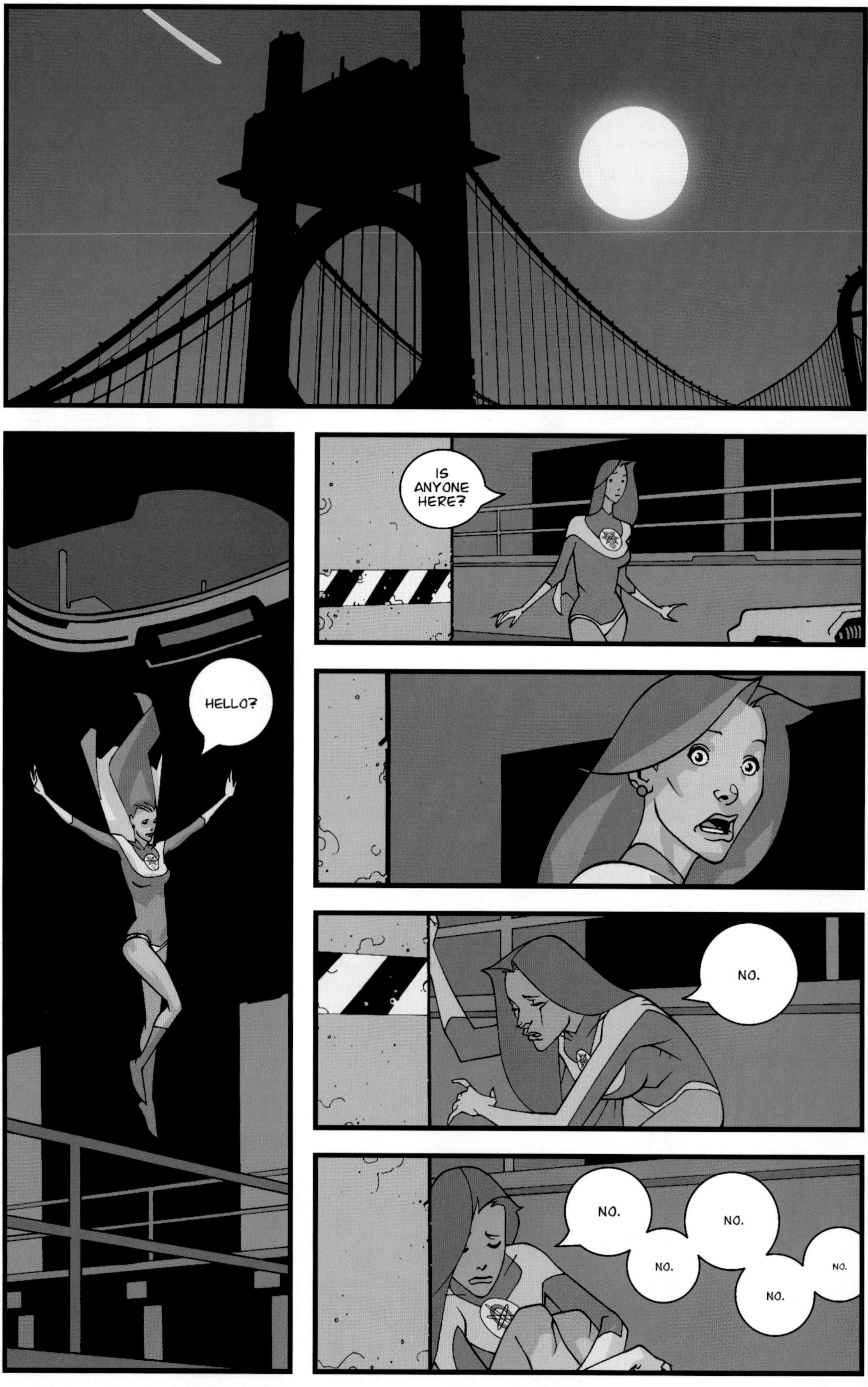
HELLO?
IS ANYONE HERE?
NO.
NO.
NO.
NO.
NO.
NO.

CHAPTER THREE

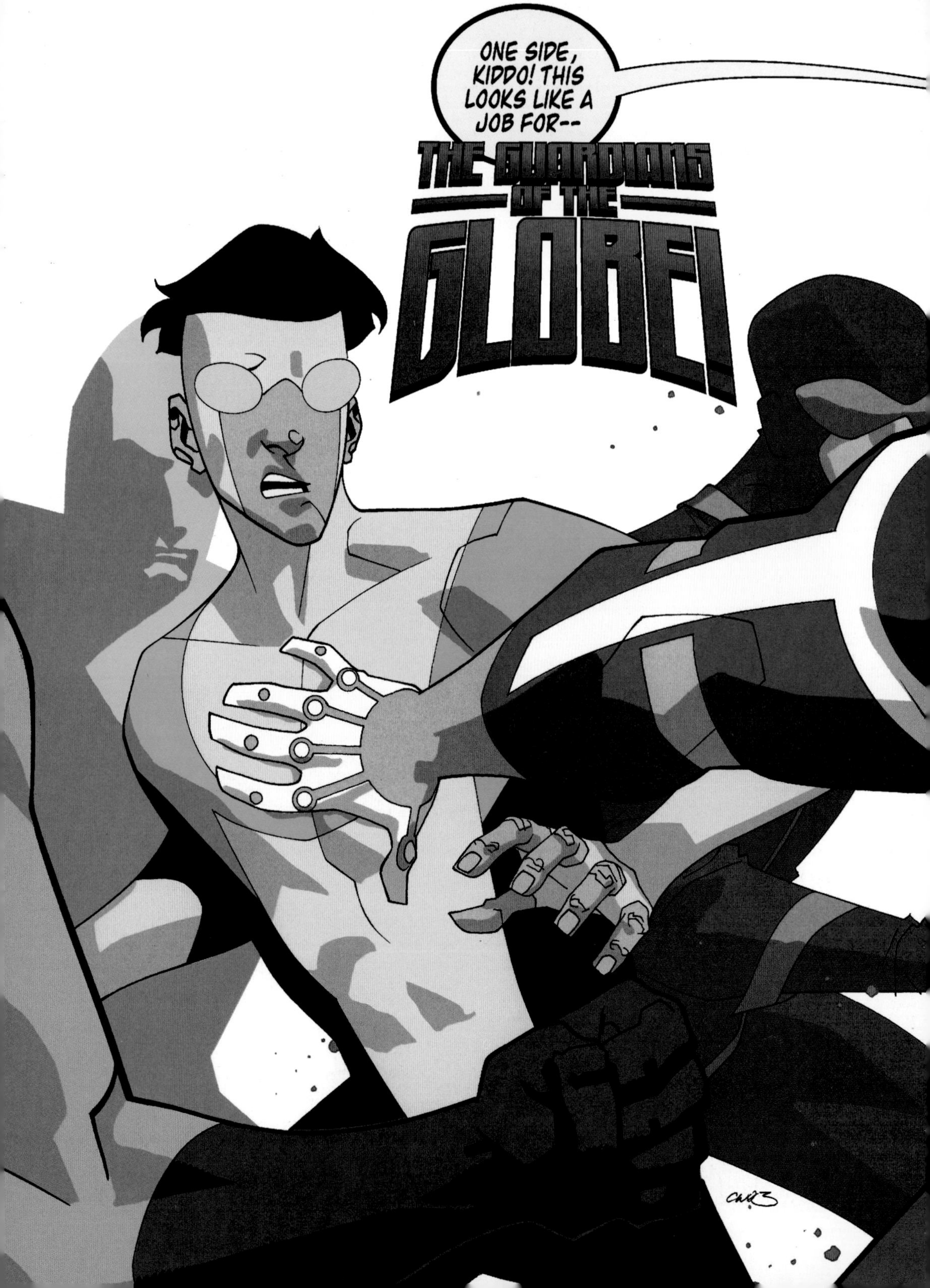
ONE SIDE, KIDDO! THIS LOOKS LIKE A JOB FOR--
THE GUARDIANS OF THE GLOBE!

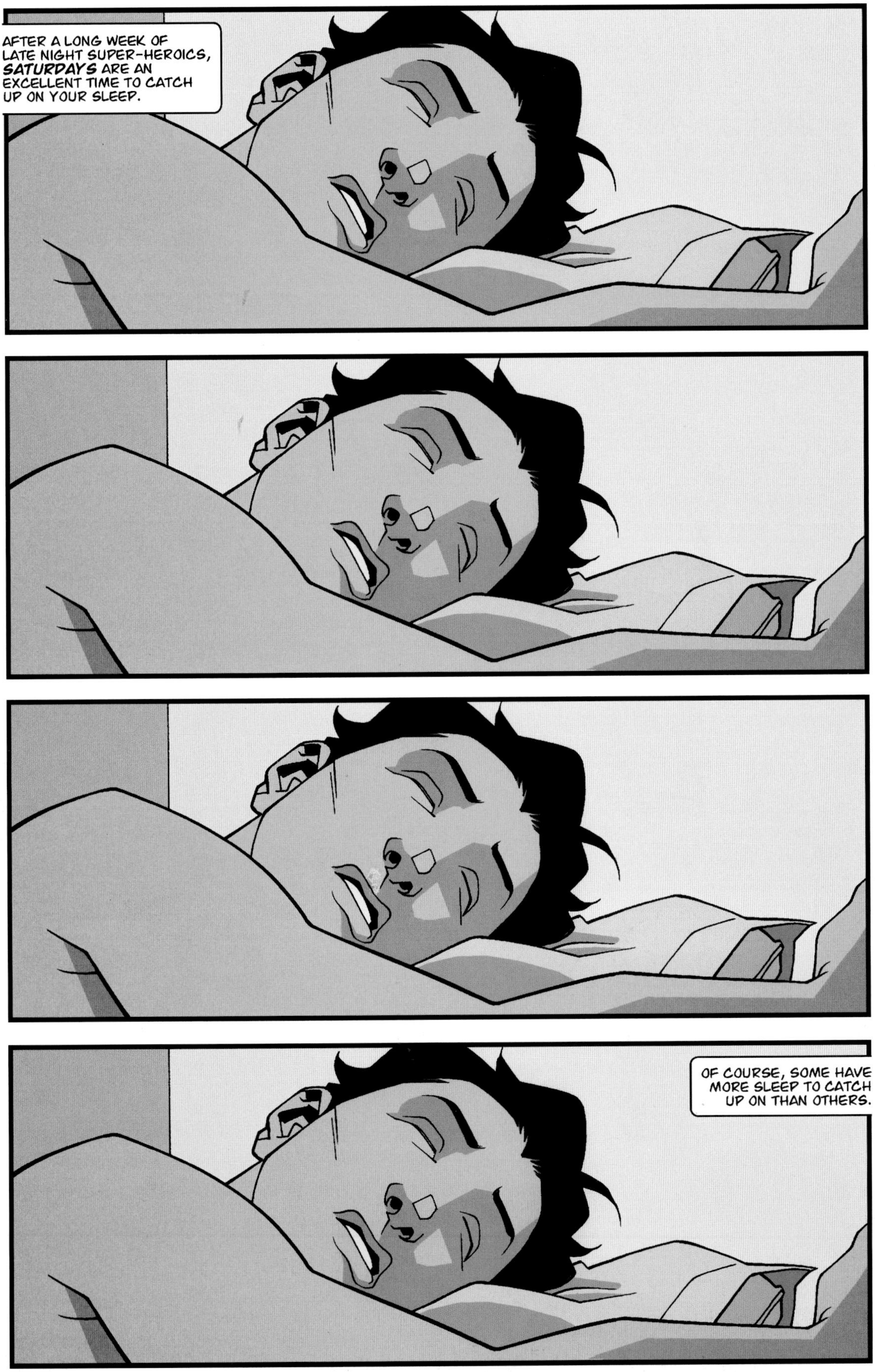
AFTER A LONG WEEK OF LATE NIGHT SUPER-HEROICS, **SATURDAYS** ARE AN EXCELLENT TIME TO CATCH UP ON YOUR SLEEP.
OF COURSE, SOME HAVE MORE SLEEP TO CATCH UP ON THAN OTHERS.

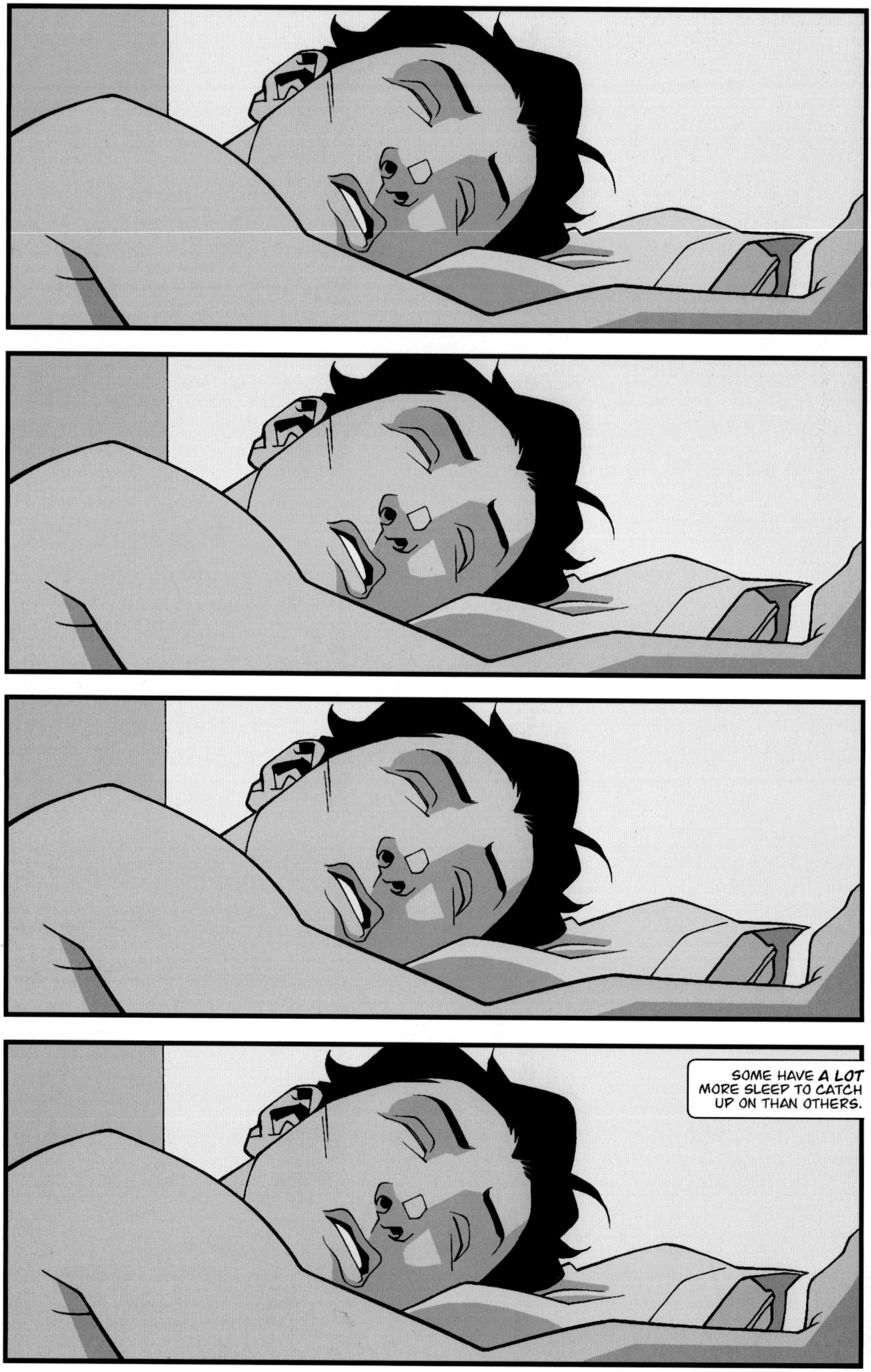
SOME HAVE A LOT MORE SLEEP TO CATCH UP ON THAN OTHERS.

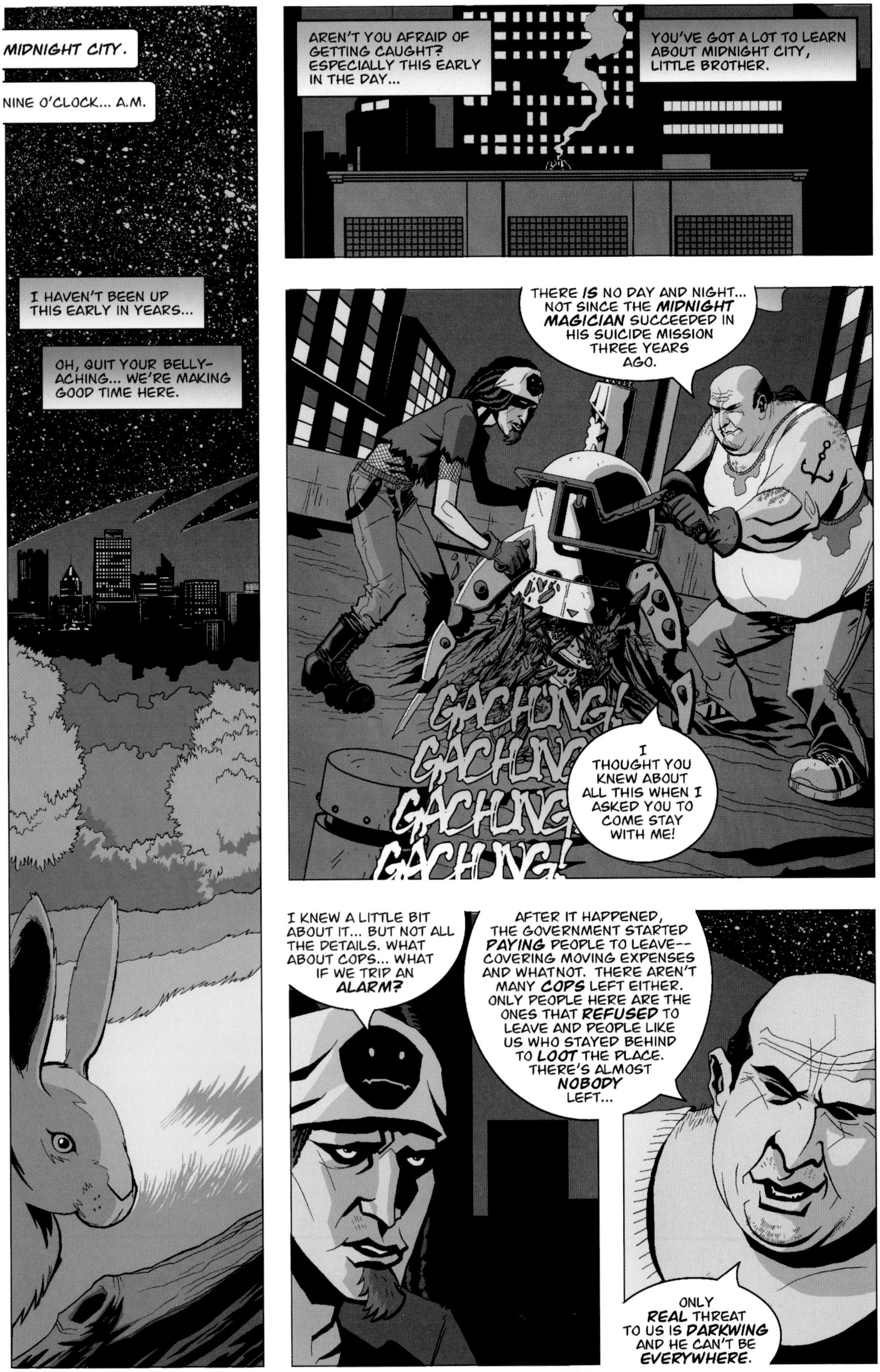
MIDNIGHT CITY.
NINE O'CLOCK... A.M.
I HAVEN'T BEEN UP THIS EARLY IN YEARS...
OH, QUIT YOUR BELLY-ACHING... WE'RE MAKING GOOD TIME HERE.
AREN'T YOU AFRAID OF GETTING CAUGHT? ESPECIALLY THIS EARLY IN THE DAY...
YOU'VE GOT A LOT TO LEARN ABOUT MIDNIGHT CITY, LITTLE BROTHER.
THERE IS NO DAY AND NIGHT... NOT SINCE THE MIDNIGHT MAGICIAN SUCCEEDED IN HIS SUICIDE MISSION THREE YEARS AGO.
GACHUNG! GACHUNG! GACHUNG! GACHUNG!
I THOUGHT YOU KNEW ABOUT ALL THIS WHEN I ASKED YOU TO COME STAY WITH ME!
I KNEW A LITTLE BIT ABOUT IT... BUT NOT ALL THE DETAILS. WHAT ABOUT COPS... WHAT IF WE TRIP AN ALARM?
AFTER IT HAPPENED, THE GOVERNMENT STARTED PAYING PEOPLE TO LEAVE-- COVERING MOVING EXPENSES AND WHATNOT. THERE AREN'T MANY COPS LEFT EITHER. ONLY PEOPLE HERE ARE THE ONES THAT REFUSED TO LEAVE AND PEOPLE LIKE US WHO STAYED BEHIND TO LOOT THE PLACE. THERE'S ALMOST NOBODY LEFT...
ONLY REAL THREAT TO US IS DARKWING AND HE CAN'T BE EVERYWHERE.

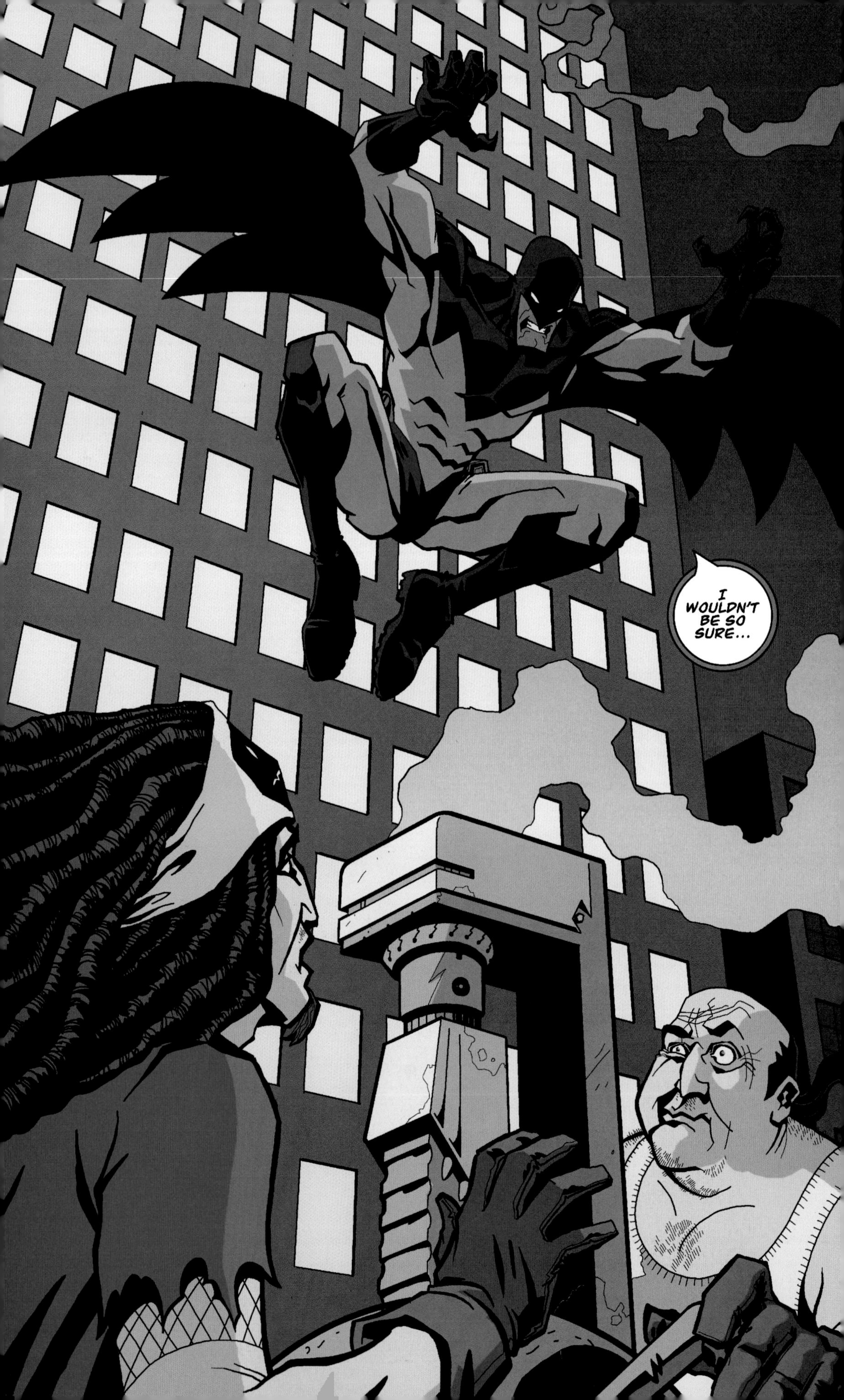
I WOULDN'T BE SO SURE...

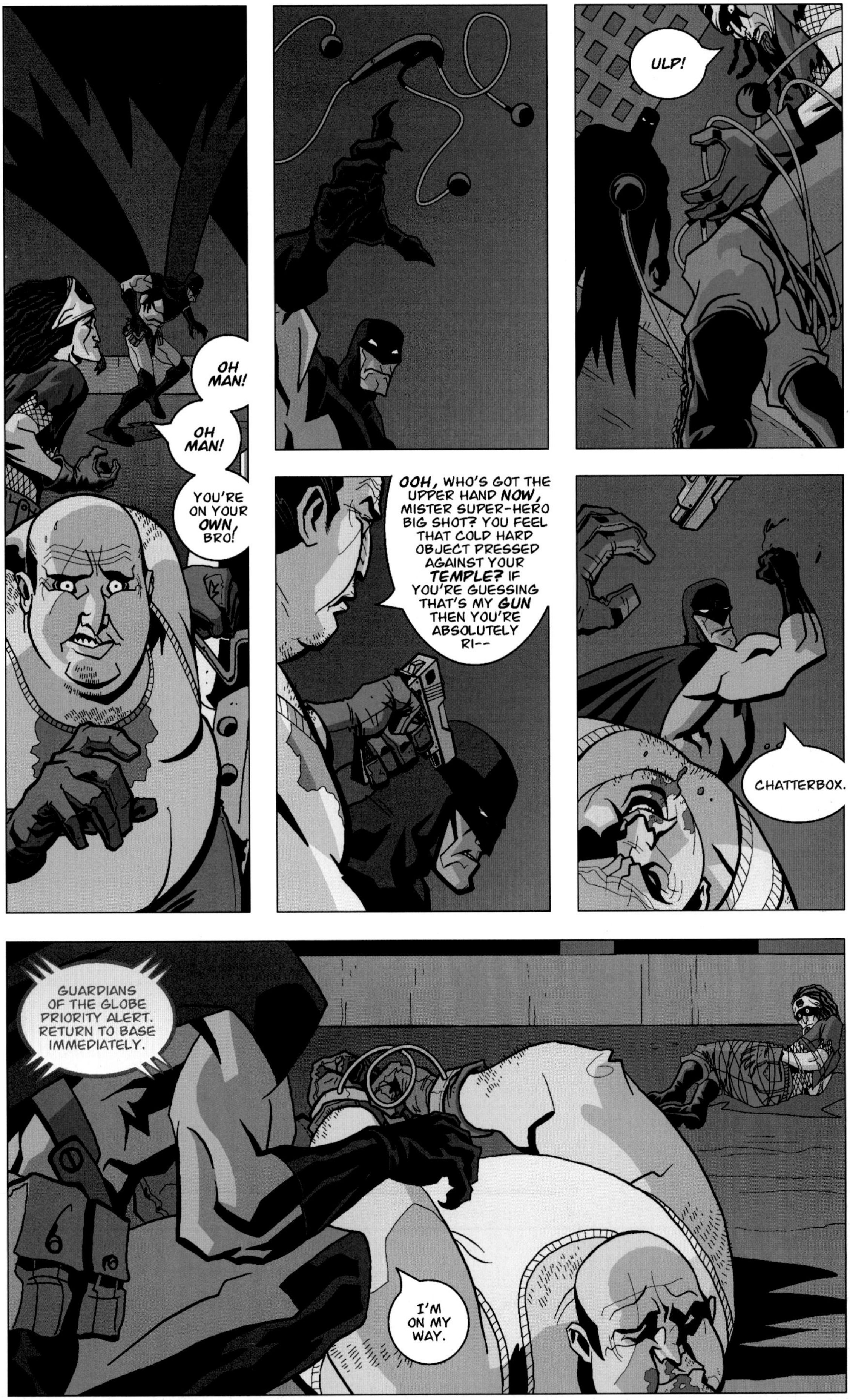
OH MAN!
OH MAN!
YOU'RE ON YOUR OWN, BRO!
ULP!
OOH, WHO'S GOT THE UPPER HAND NOW, MISTER SUPER-HERO BIG SHOT? YOU FEEL THAT COLD HARD OBJECT PRESSED AGAINST YOUR TEMPLE? IF YOU'RE GUESSING THAT'S MY GUN THEN YOU'RE ABSOLUTELY RI--
CHATTERBOX.
GUARDIANS OF THE GLOBE PRIORITY ALERT. RETURN TO BASE IMMEDIATELY.
I'M ON MY WAY.

WING
JET.

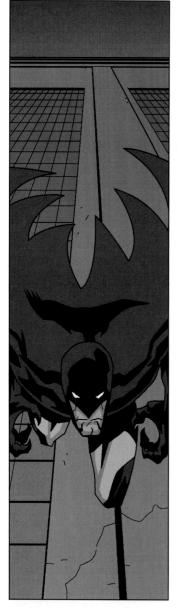

VOOSH!!!

BELVEDERE,
CONTACT THE
AUTHORITIES. I
LEFT A COUPLE
PERPS ON THE
BURNS TOWER.
I'VE BEEN
CALLED
AWAY.

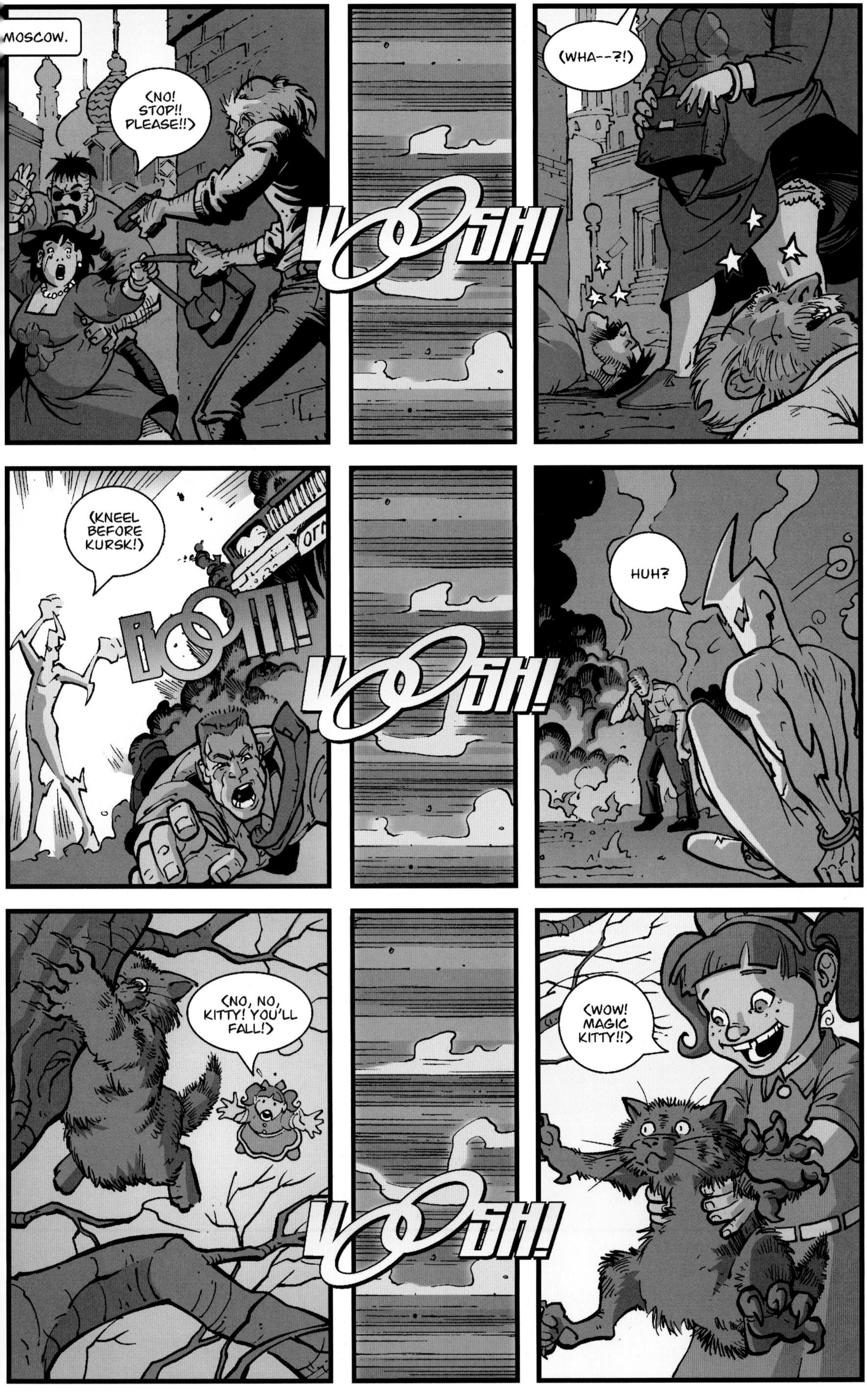
MOSCOW.
<NO! STOP!! PLEASE!!>
WOOSH!
(WHA--?!)
(KNEEL BEFORE KURSK!)
BOOM!
WOOSH!
HUH?
<NO, NO, KITTY! YOU'LL FALL!>
WOOSH!
<WOW! MAGIC KITTY!!>

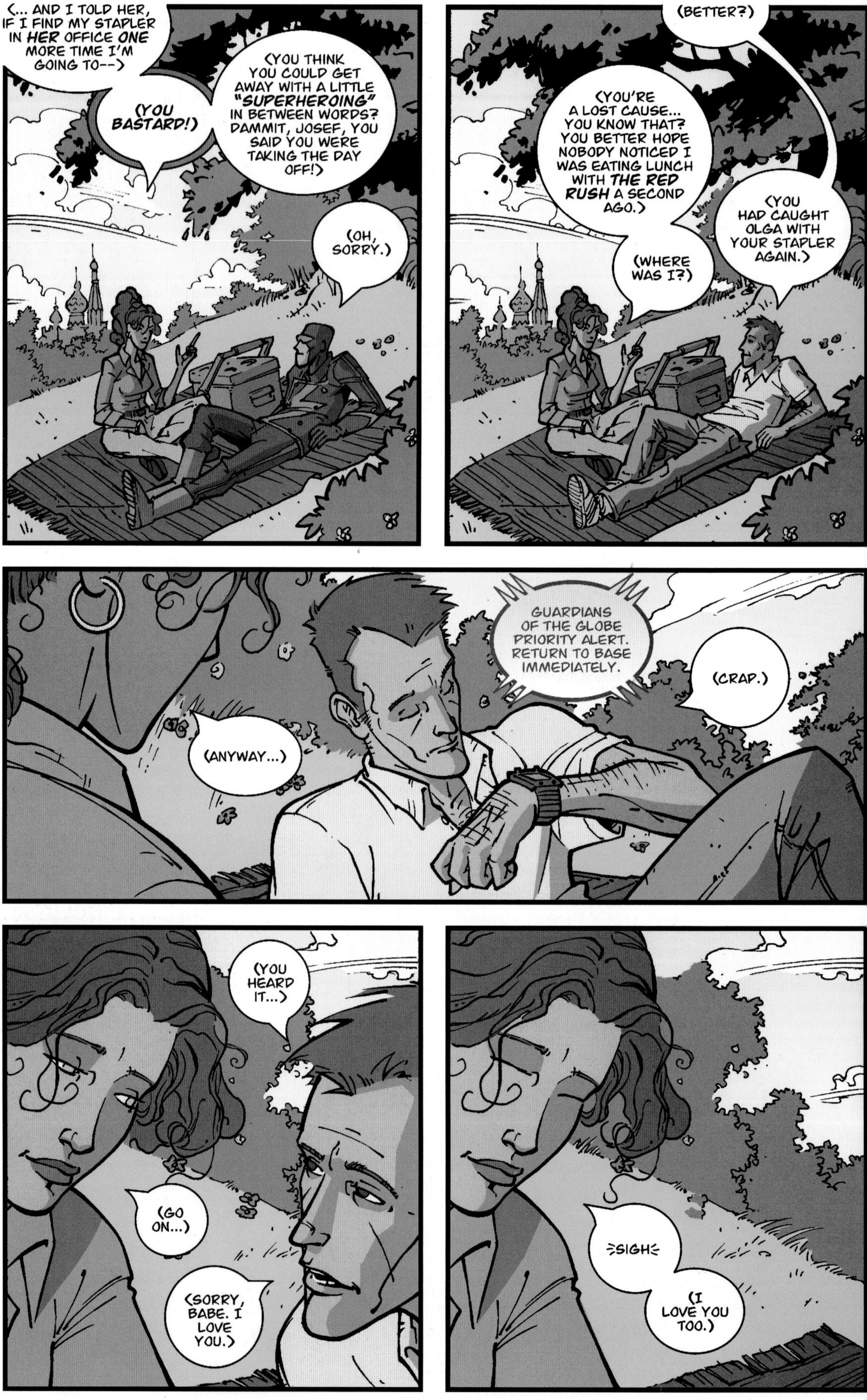
‹... AND I TOLD HER, IF I FIND MY STAPLER IN HER OFFICE ONE MORE TIME I'M GOING TO--›
(YOU BASTARD!)
‹YOU THINK YOU COULD GET AWAY WITH A LITTLE "SUPERHEROING" IN BETWEEN WORDS? DAMMIT, JOSEF, YOU SAID YOU WERE TAKING THE DAY OFF!›
(OH, SORRY.)
(BETTER?)
‹YOU'RE A LOST CAUSE... YOU KNOW THAT? YOU BETTER HOPE NOBODY NOTICED I WAS EATING LUNCH WITH THE RED RUSH A SECOND AGO.›
(WHERE WAS I?)
‹YOU HAD CAUGHT OLGA WITH YOUR STAPLER AGAIN.›
GUARDIANS OF THE GLOBE PRIORITY ALERT. RETURN TO BASE IMMEDIATELY.
(CRAP.)
‹ANYWAY...›
‹YOU HEARD IT...›
‹GO ON...›
‹SORRY, BABE. I LOVE YOU.›
≈SIGH≈
‹I LOVE YOU TOO.›

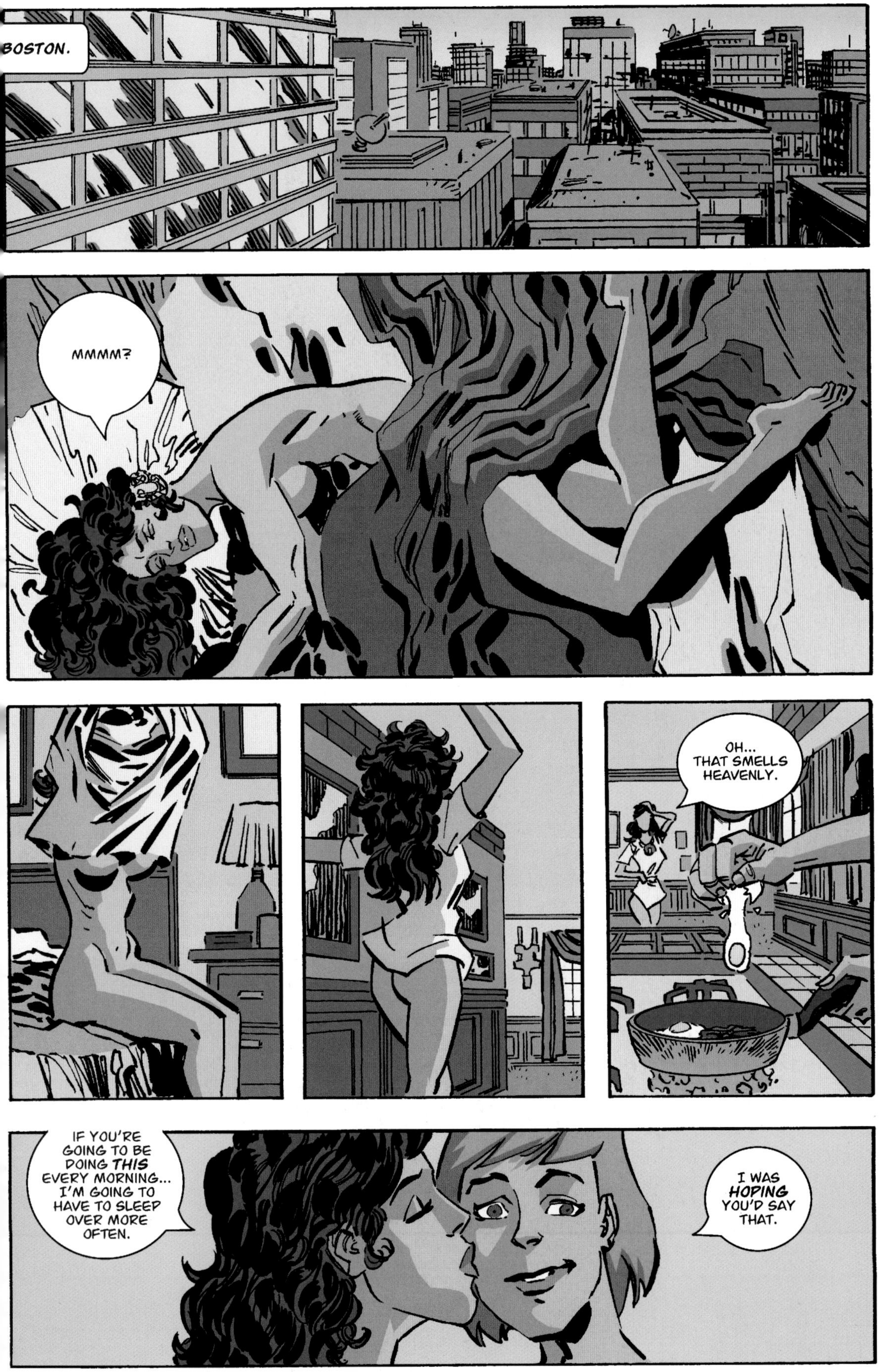
BOSTON.
MMMM?
OH... THAT SMELLS HEAVENLY.
IF YOU'RE GOING TO BE DOING THIS EVERY MORNING... I'M GOING TO HAVE TO SLEEP OVER MORE OFTEN.
I WAS HOPING YOU'D SAY THAT.

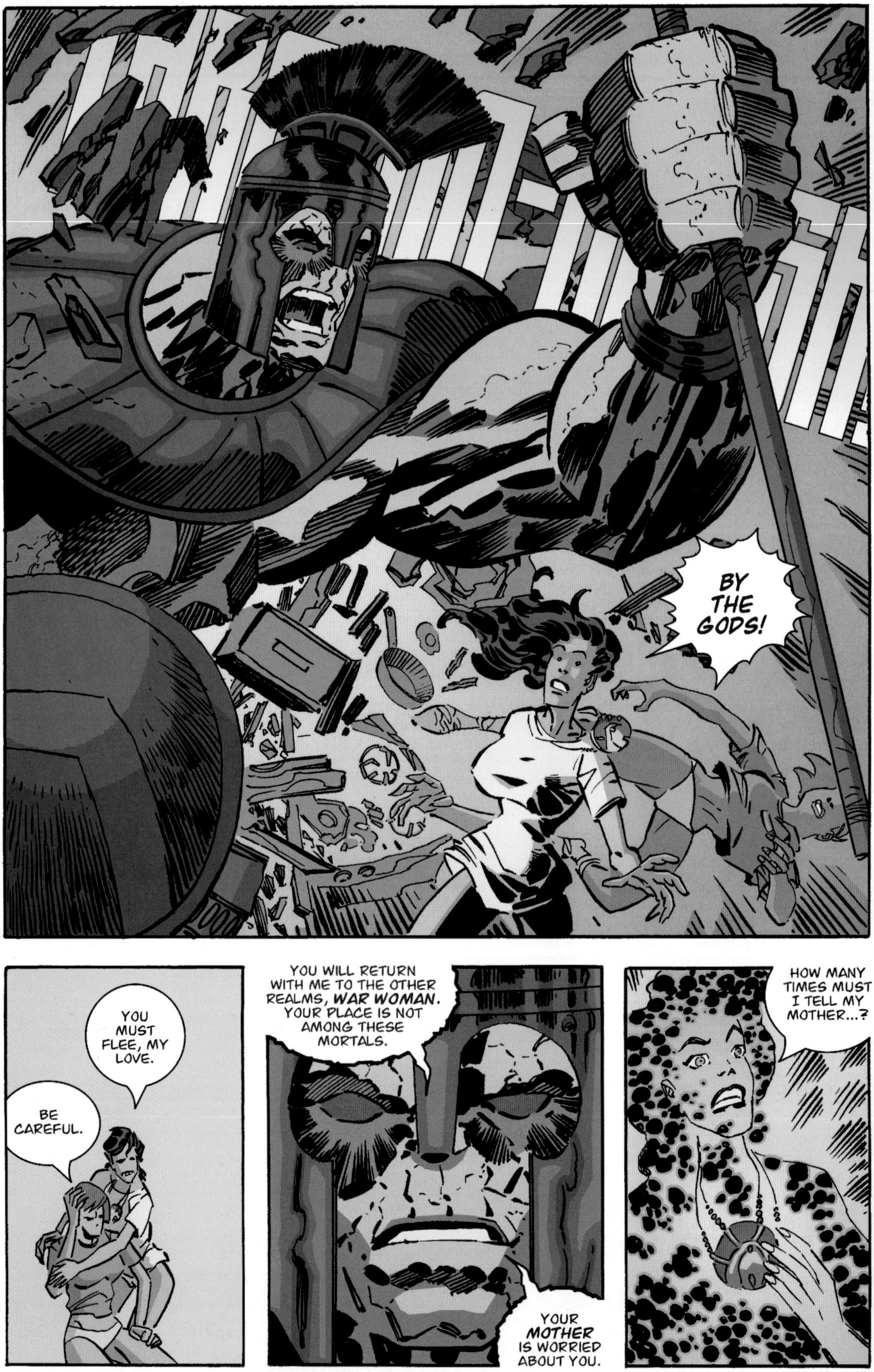
BY THE GODS!
YOU MUST FLEE, MY LOVE.
BE CAREFUL.
YOU WILL RETURN WITH ME TO THE OTHER REALMS, *WAR WOMAN*. YOUR PLACE IS NOT AMONG THESE MORTALS.
YOUR *MOTHER* IS WORRIED ABOUT YOU.
HOW MANY TIMES MUST I TELL MY MOTHER...?

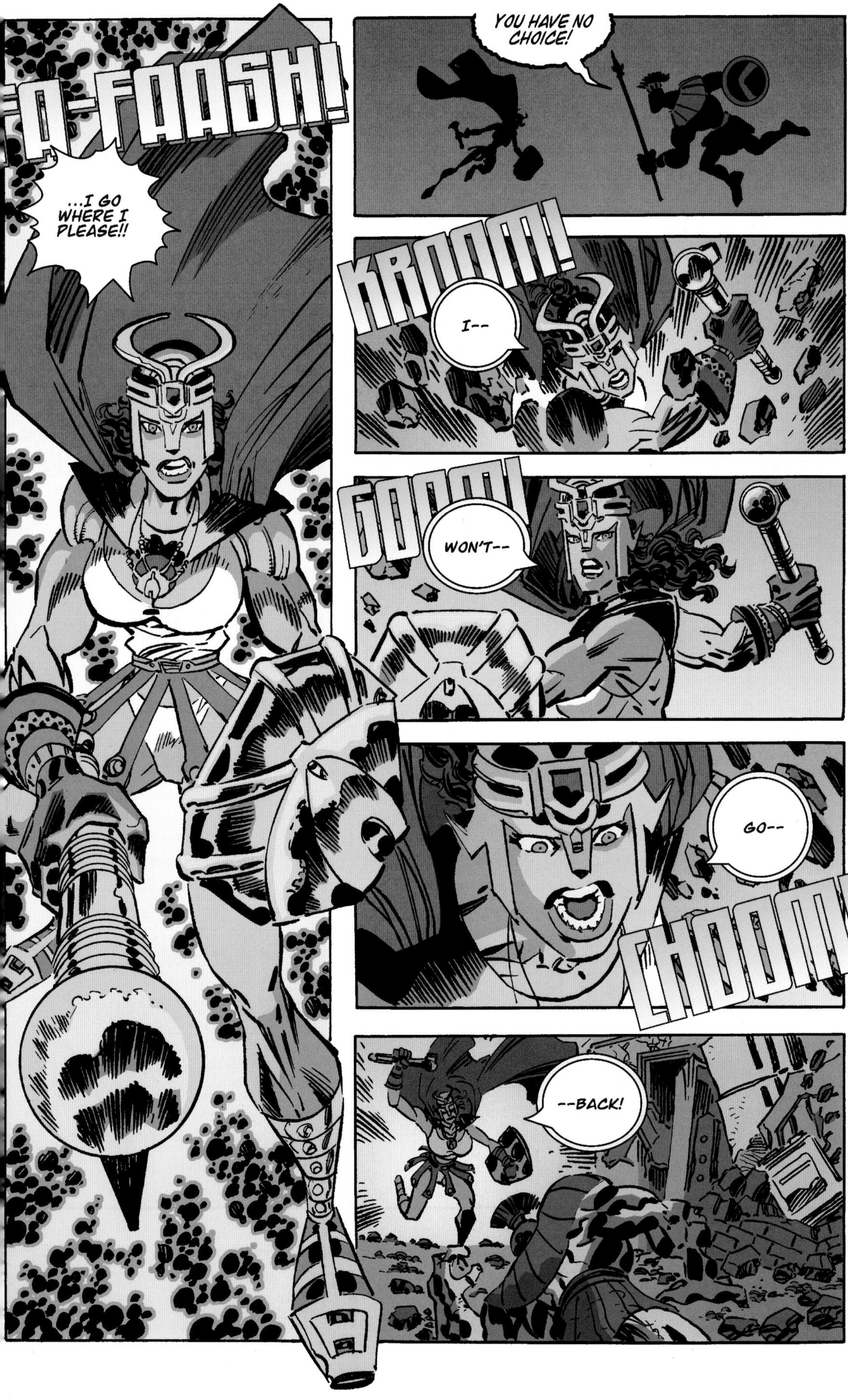
A-FAASH!
...I GO WHERE I PLEASE!!
YOU HAVE NO CHOICE!
KROOM!
I--
GOOM!
WON'T--
GO--
CHOOM!
--BACK!

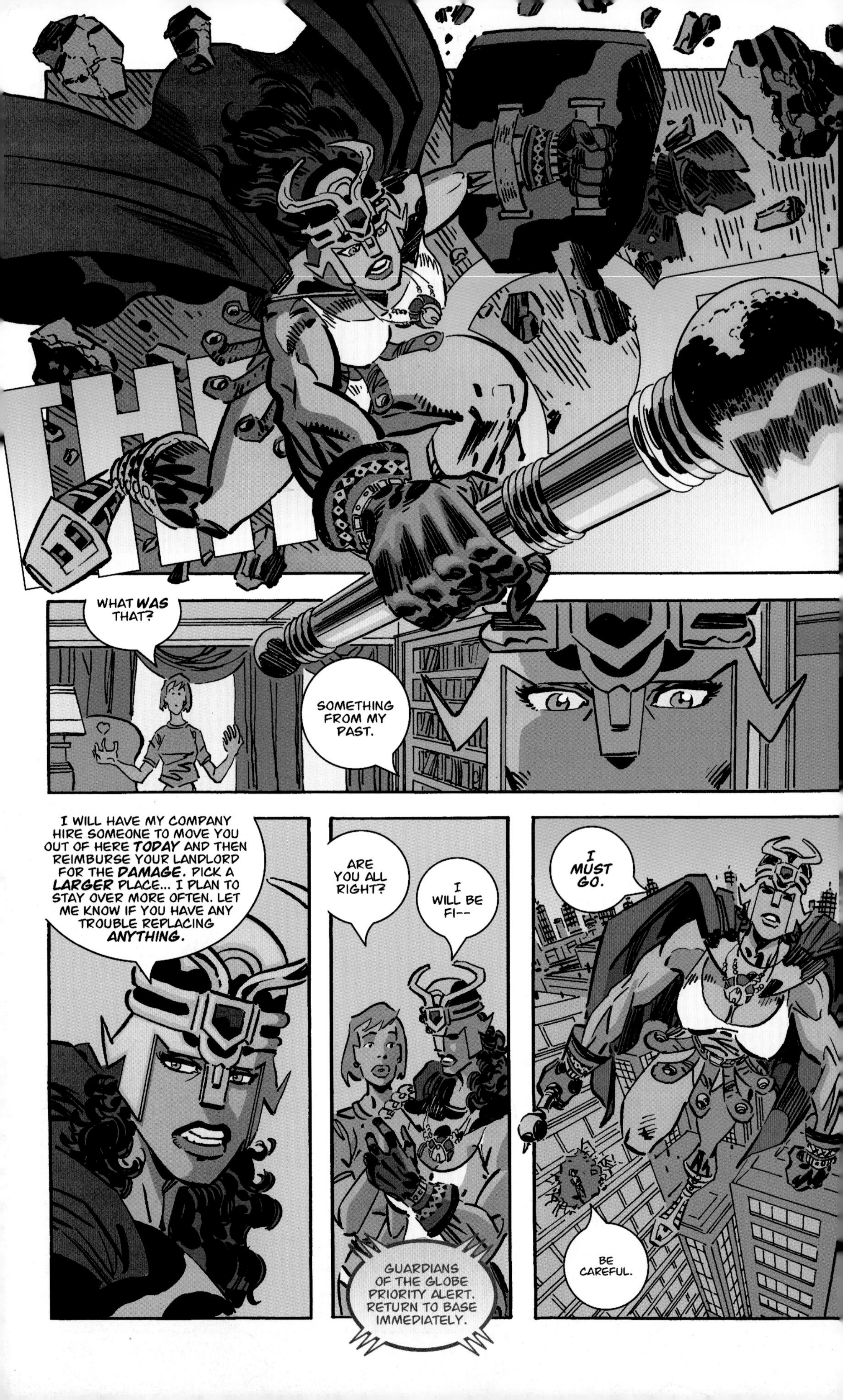
TH
WHAT WAS THAT?
SOMETHING FROM MY PAST.
I WILL HAVE MY COMPANY HIRE SOMEONE TO MOVE YOU OUT OF HERE TODAY AND THEN REIMBURSE YOUR LANDLORD FOR THE DAMAGE. PICK A LARGER PLACE... I PLAN TO STAY OVER MORE OFTEN. LET ME KNOW IF YOU HAVE ANY TROUBLE REPLACING ANYTHING.
ARE YOU ALL RIGHT?
I WILL BE FI--
GUARDIANS OF THE GLOBE PRIORITY ALERT. RETURN TO BASE IMMEDIATELY.
I MUST GO.
BE CAREFUL.

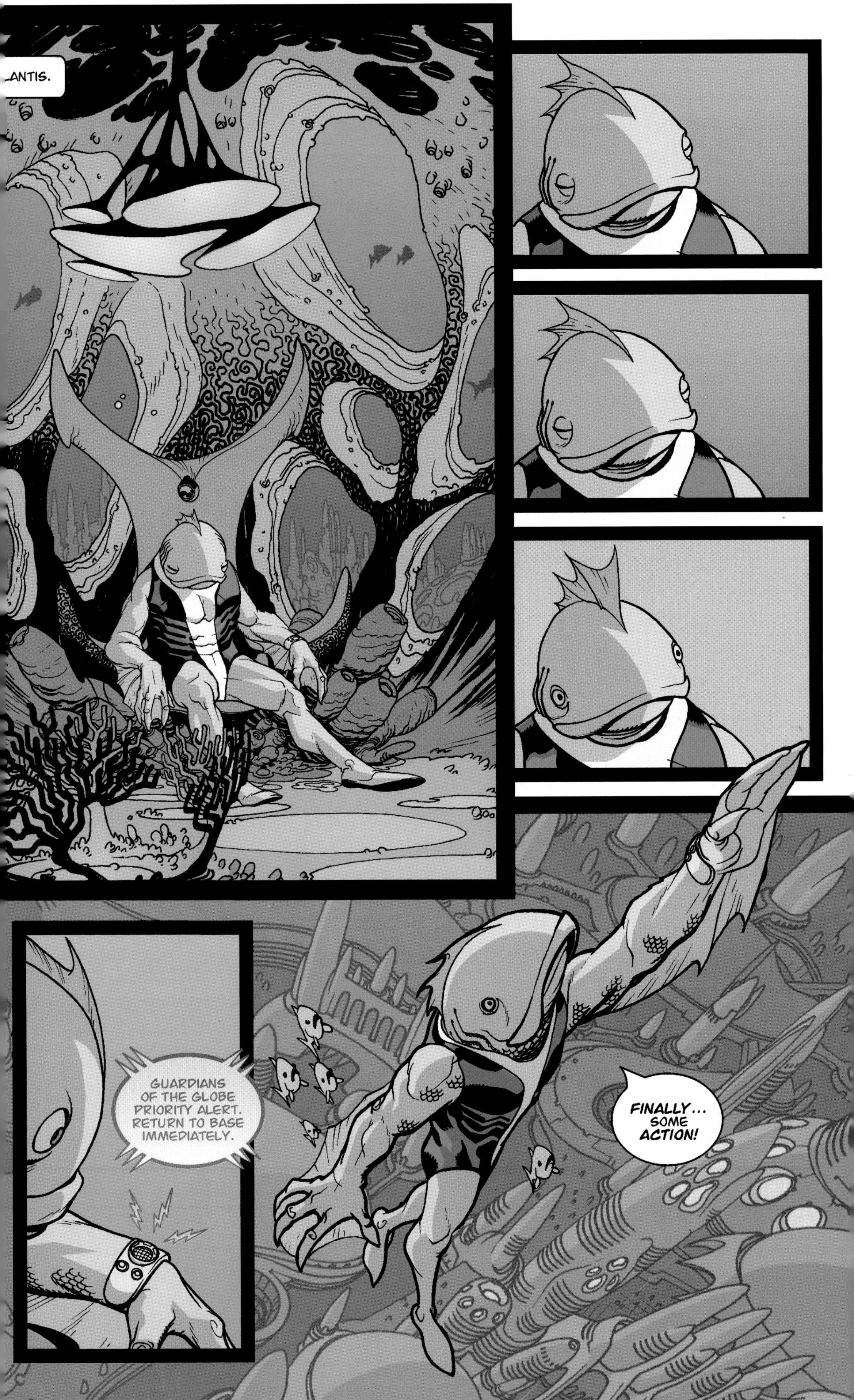

...ANTIS.
GUARDIANS OF THE GLOBE PRIORITY ALERT. RETURN TO BASE IMMEDIATELY.
FINALLY... SOME ACTION!

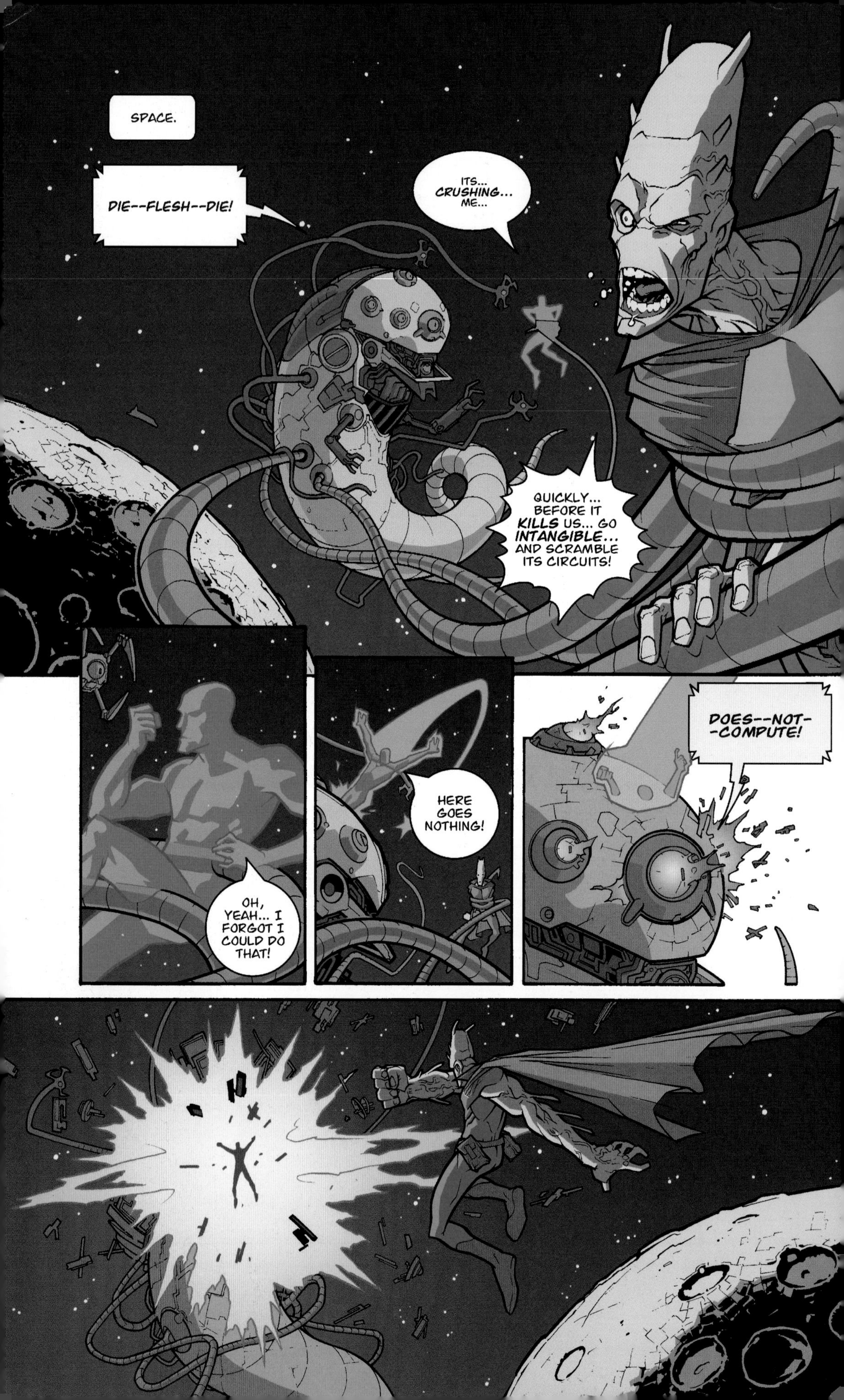
SPACE.
DIE--FLESH--DIE!
ITS... CRUSHING... ME...
QUICKLY... BEFORE IT KILLS US... GO INTANGIBLE... AND SCRAMBLE ITS CIRCUITS!
OH, YEAH... I FORGOT I COULD DO THAT!
HERE GOES NOTHING!
DOES--NOT--COMPUTE!

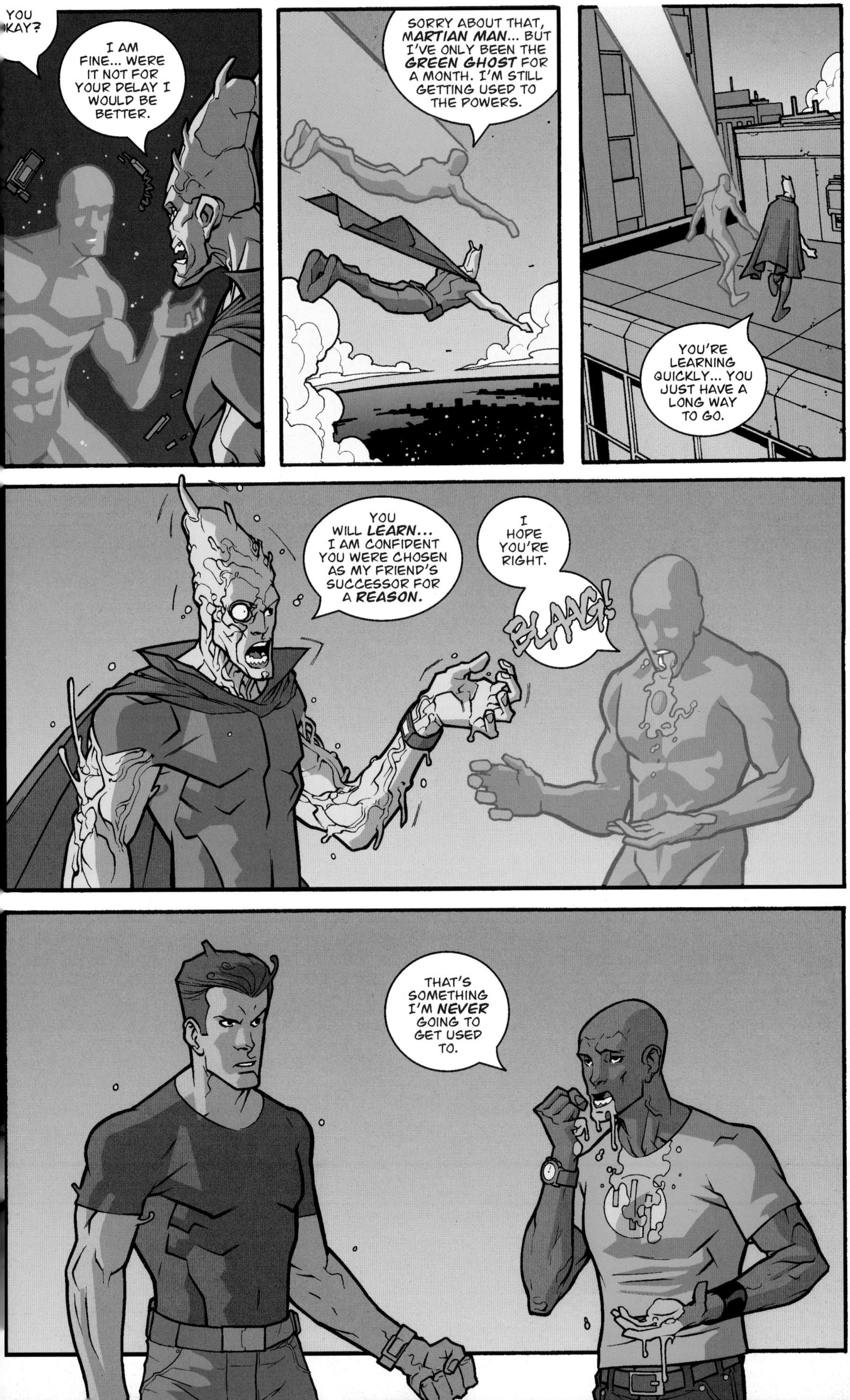
YOU
KAY?
I AM FINE... WERE IT NOT FOR YOUR DELAY I WOULD BE BETTER.
SORRY ABOUT THAT, MARTIAN MAN... BUT I'VE ONLY BEEN THE GREEN GHOST FOR A MONTH. I'M STILL GETTING USED TO THE POWERS.
YOU'RE LEARNING QUICKLY... YOU JUST HAVE A LONG WAY TO GO.
YOU WILL LEARN... I AM CONFIDENT YOU WERE CHOSEN AS MY FRIEND'S SUCCESSOR FOR A REASON.
I HOPE YOU'RE RIGHT.
BLAAG!
THAT'S SOMETHING I'M NEVER GOING TO GET USED TO.

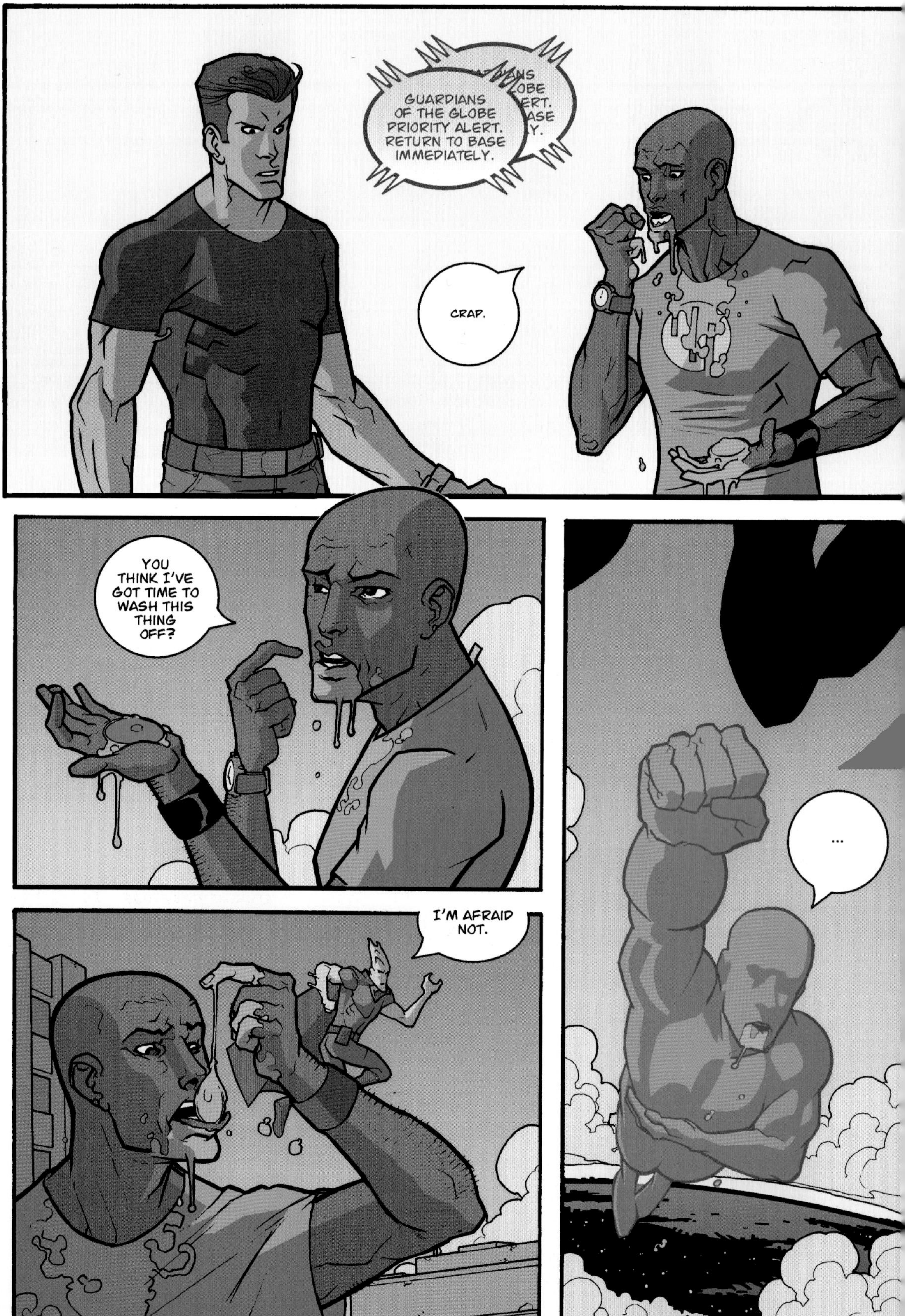
GUARDIANS OF THE GLOBE PRIORITY ALERT. RETURN TO BASE IMMEDIATELY.
CRAP.
YOU THINK I'VE GOT TIME TO WASH THIS THING OFF?
I'M AFRAID NOT.
...

HIGH ABOVE DENVER.

I THOUGHT I WAS **RID** OF ALL YOU RIDICULOUS VILLAINS!

YOU MAY THINK OF BI-PLANE AS A SILLY VILLAIN **NOW**, IMMORTAL... BUT SOON YOU'LL SEE THE DAMAGE I CAN DO.

PLEASE, CHILD... THE SUSPENSE IS **KILLING** ME.

THIS IS IT FOR ME... MY LAST HURRAH! I'VE GOT THE **CANCER**... IN MY LYMPH NODES... I'M A **GONER**. DOC SAYS I'VE GOT LESS THAN A **MONTH**.

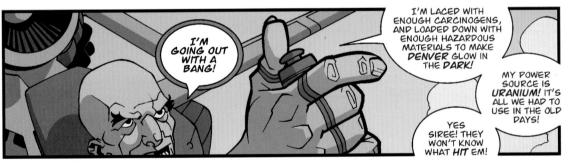

I'M GOING OUT WITH A BANG!

I'M LACED WITH ENOUGH CARCINOGENS, AND LOADED DOWN WITH ENOUGH HAZARDOUS MATERIALS TO MAKE **DENVER** GLOW IN THE **DARK**!

MY POWER SOURCE IS **URANIUM!** IT'S ALL WE HAD TO USE IN THE OLD DAYS!

YES SIREE! THEY WON'T KNOW WHAT **HIT** EM!

WAIT! WHAT'RE YOU--

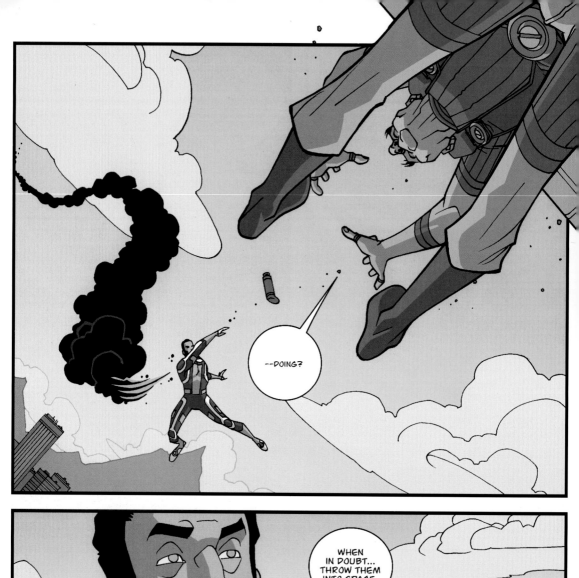

--DOING?

WHEN IN DOUBT... THROW THEM INTO SPACE.

GUARDIANS OF THE GLOBE PRIORITY ALERT. RETURN TO BASE IMMEDIATELY.

I'M ON THE WAY.

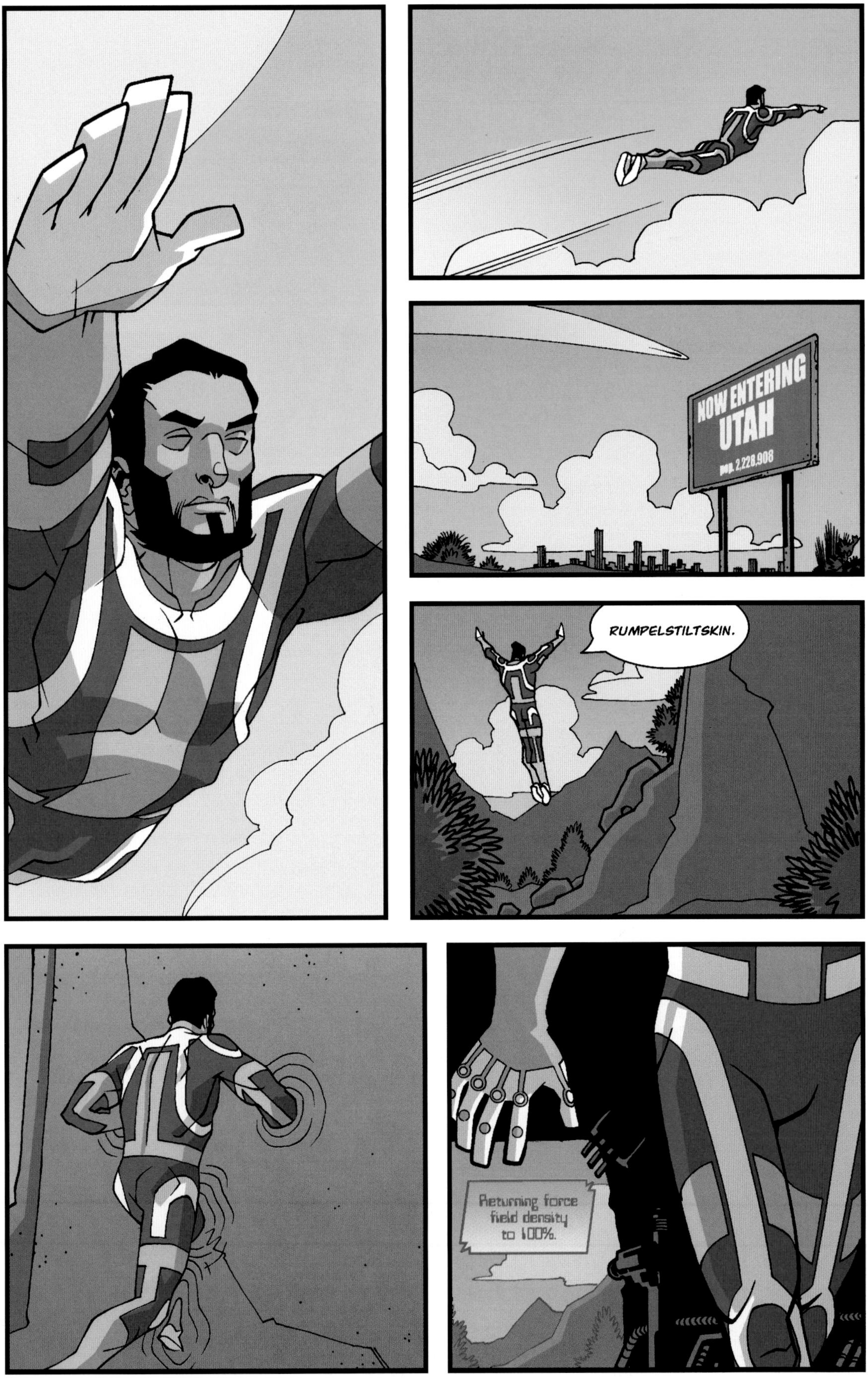
NOW ENTERING
UTAH
pop. 2,228,908
RUMPELSTILTSKIN.
Returning force field density to 100%.

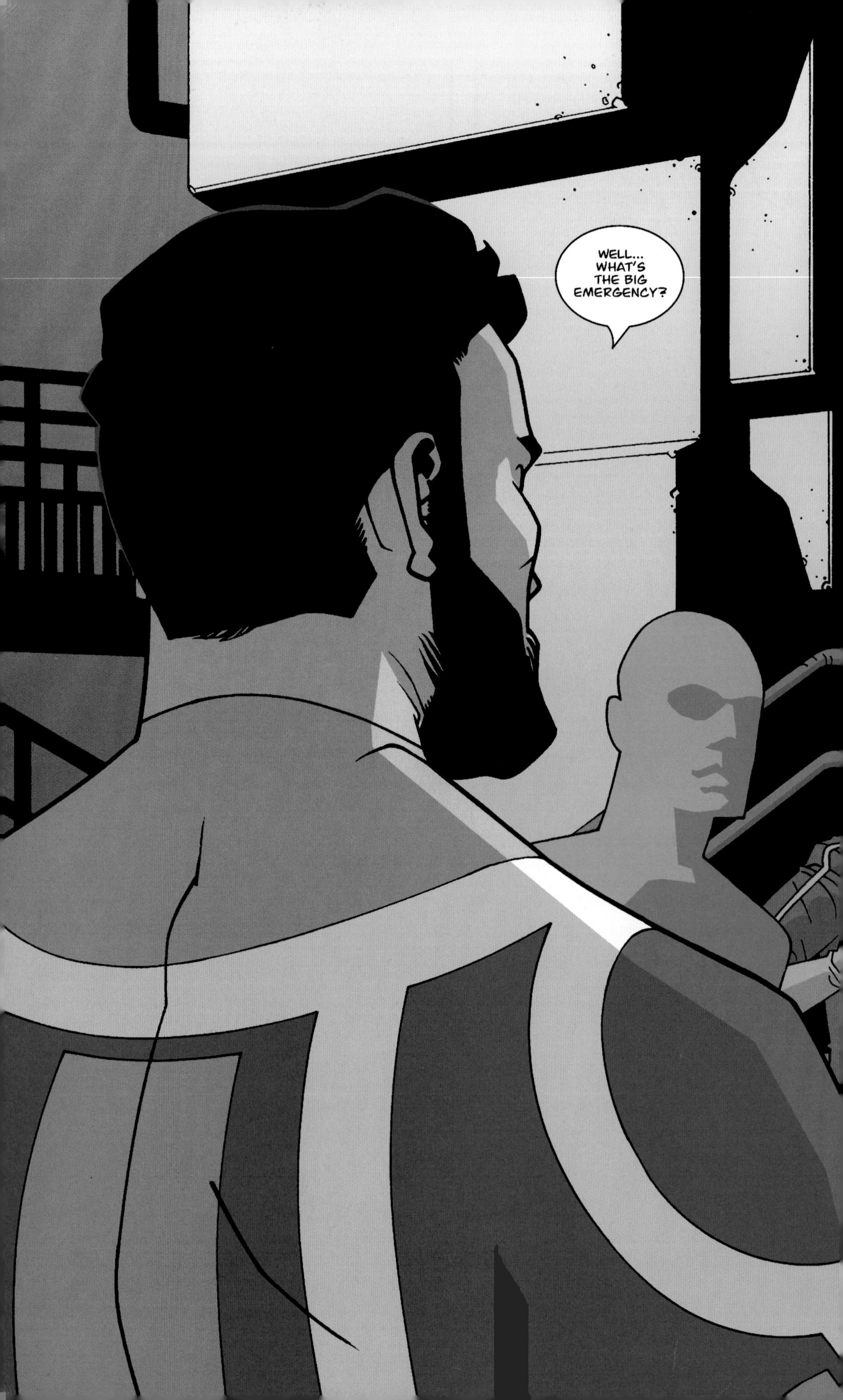
WELL... WHAT'S THE BIG EMERGENCY?

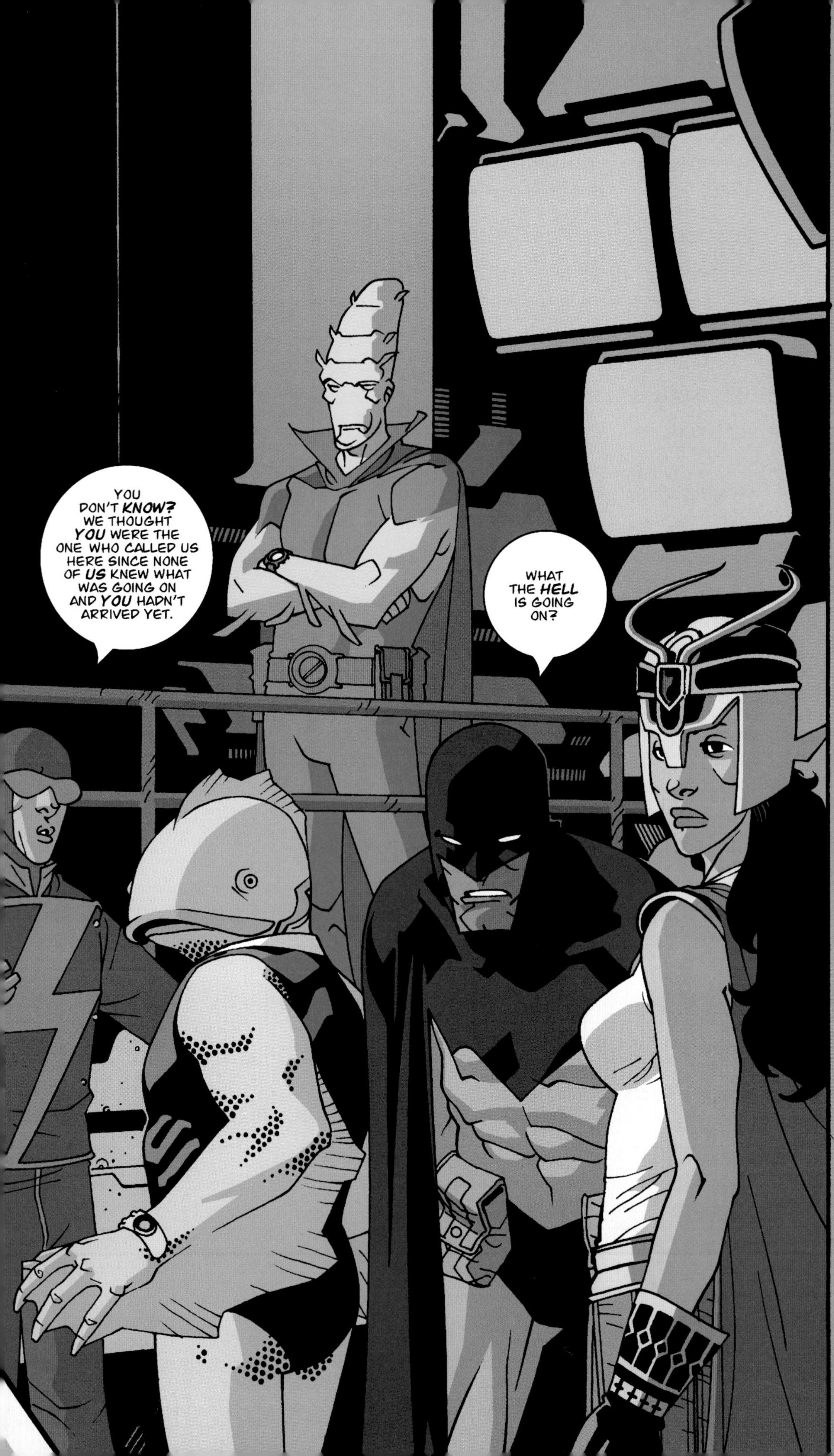
YOU DON'T KNOW? WE THOUGHT YOU WERE THE ONE WHO CALLED US HERE SINCE NONE OF US KNEW WHAT WAS GOING ON AND YOU HADN'T ARRIVED YET.
WHAT THE HELL IS GOING ON?

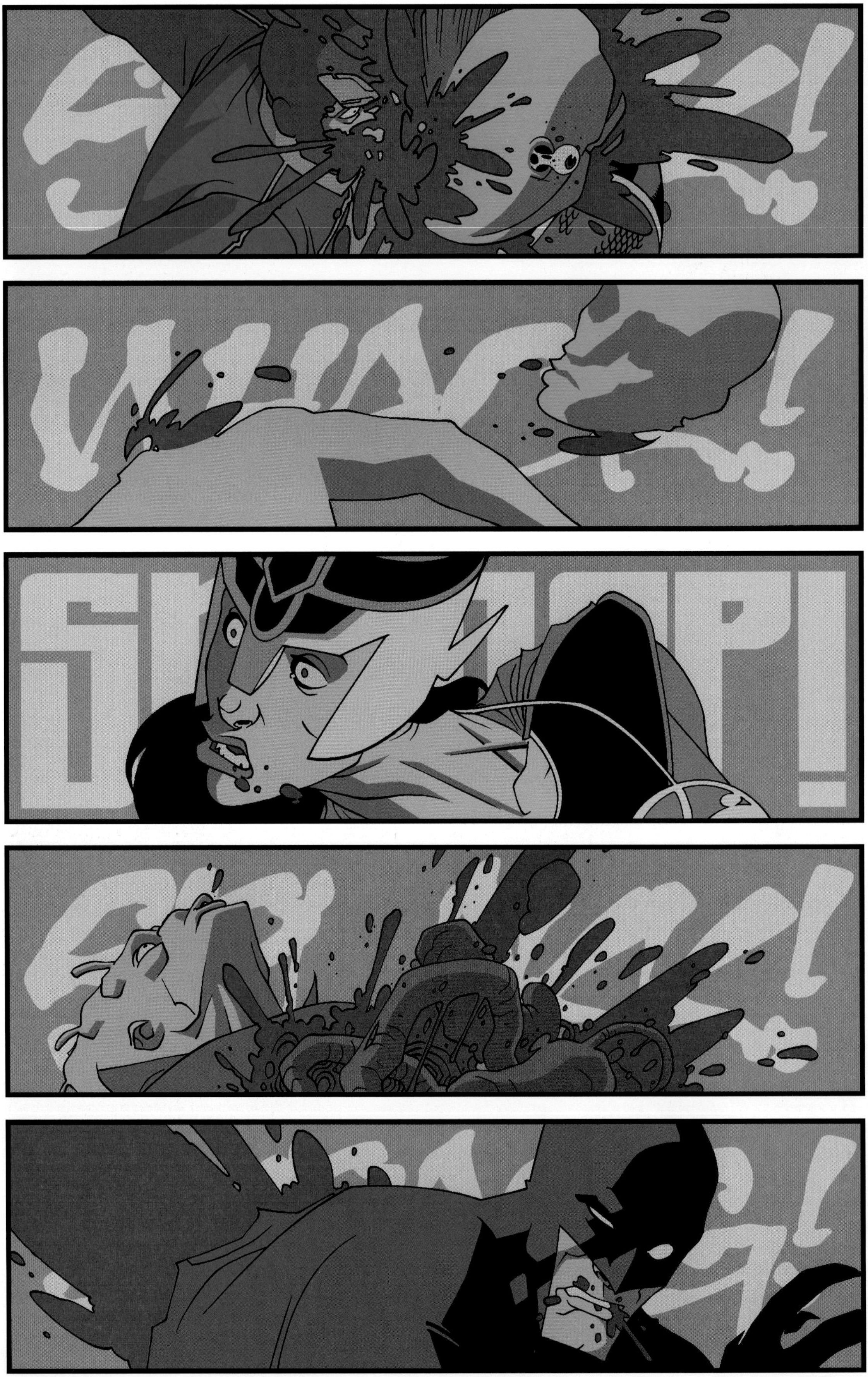

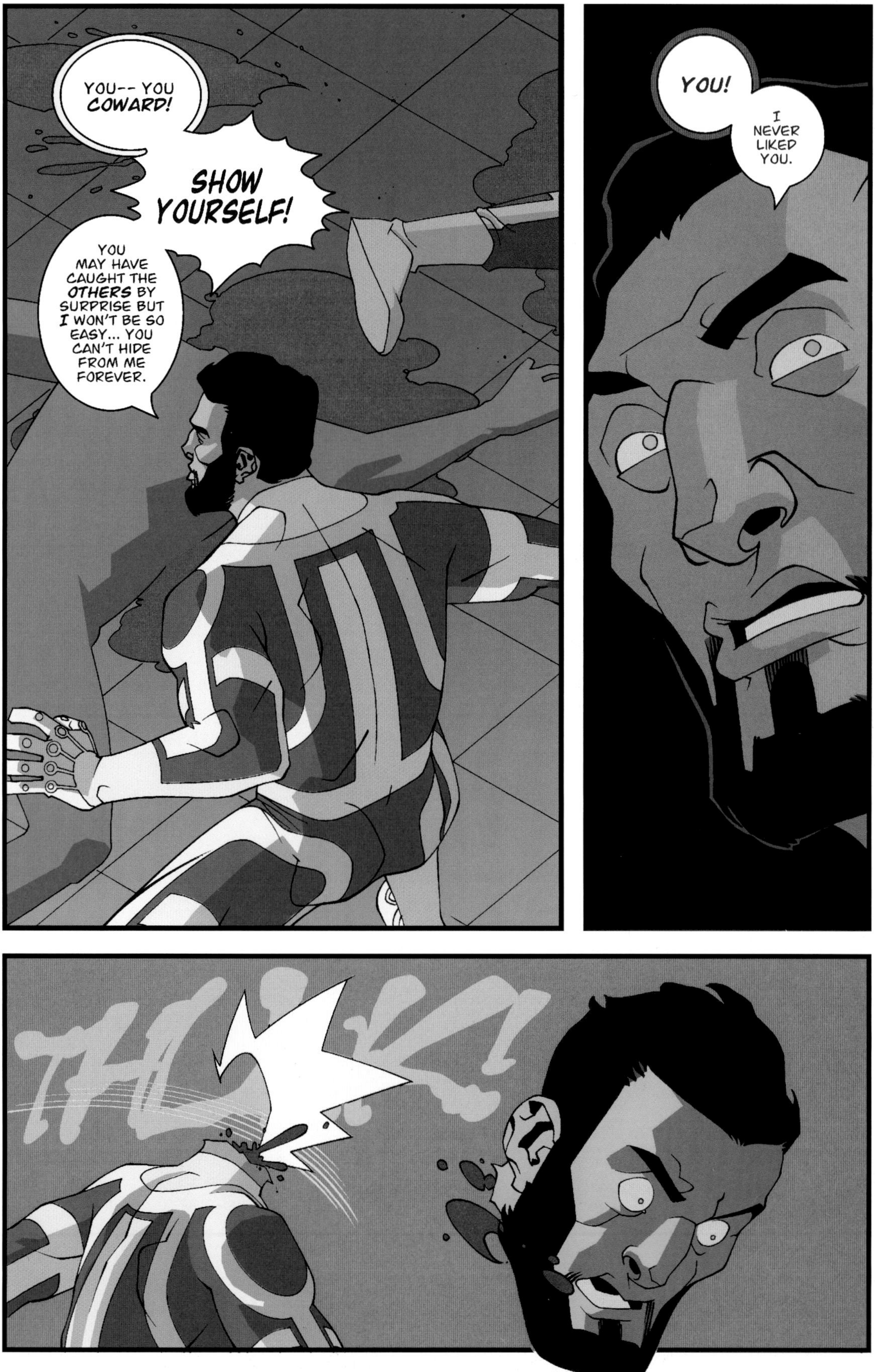
YOU-- YOU COWARD!
SHOW YOURSELF!
YOU MAY HAVE CAUGHT THE OTHERS BY SURPRISE BUT I WON'T BE SO EASY... YOU CAN'T HIDE FROM ME FOREVER.
YOU!
I NEVER LIKED YOU.

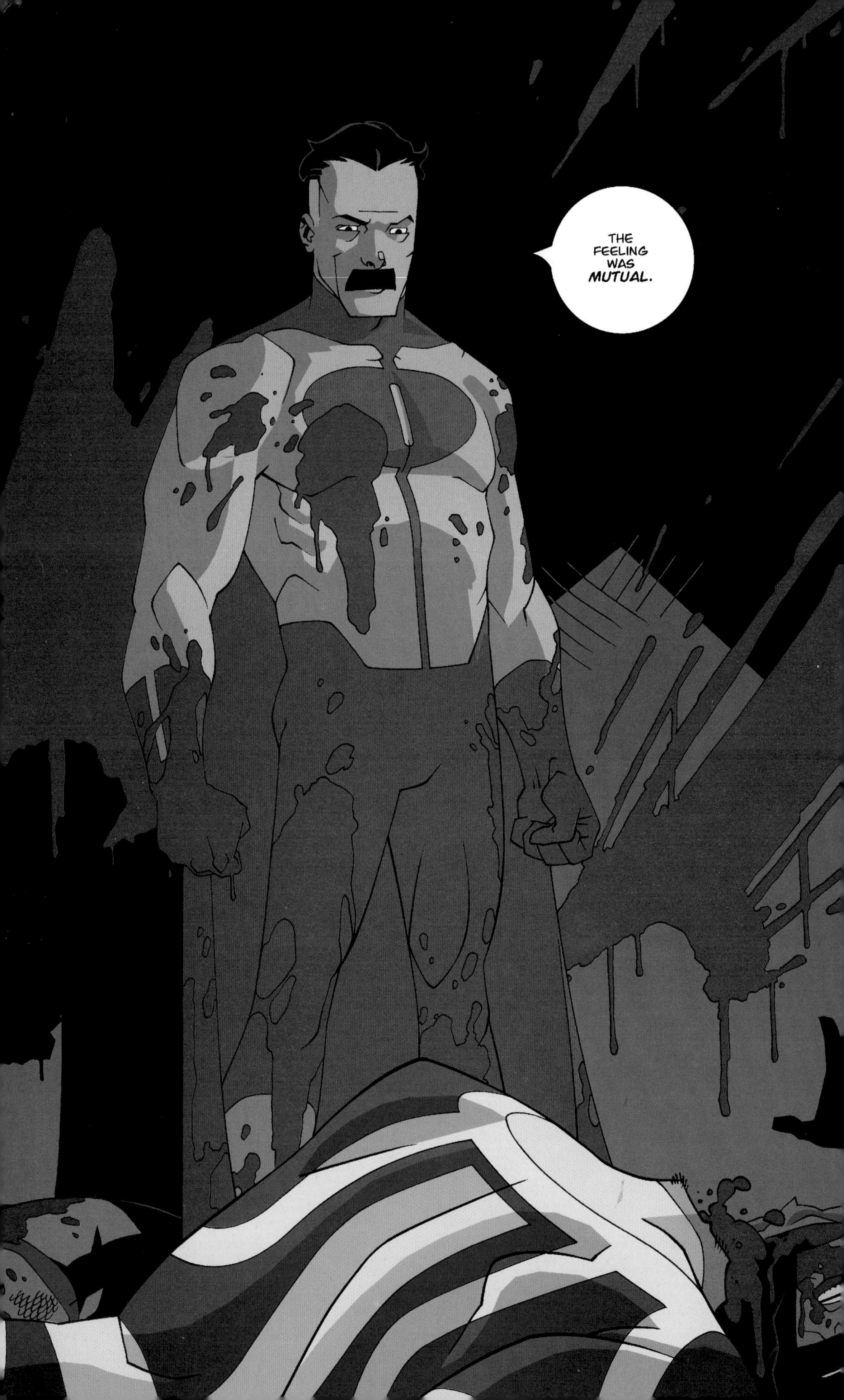
THE FEELING WAS *MUTUAL.*

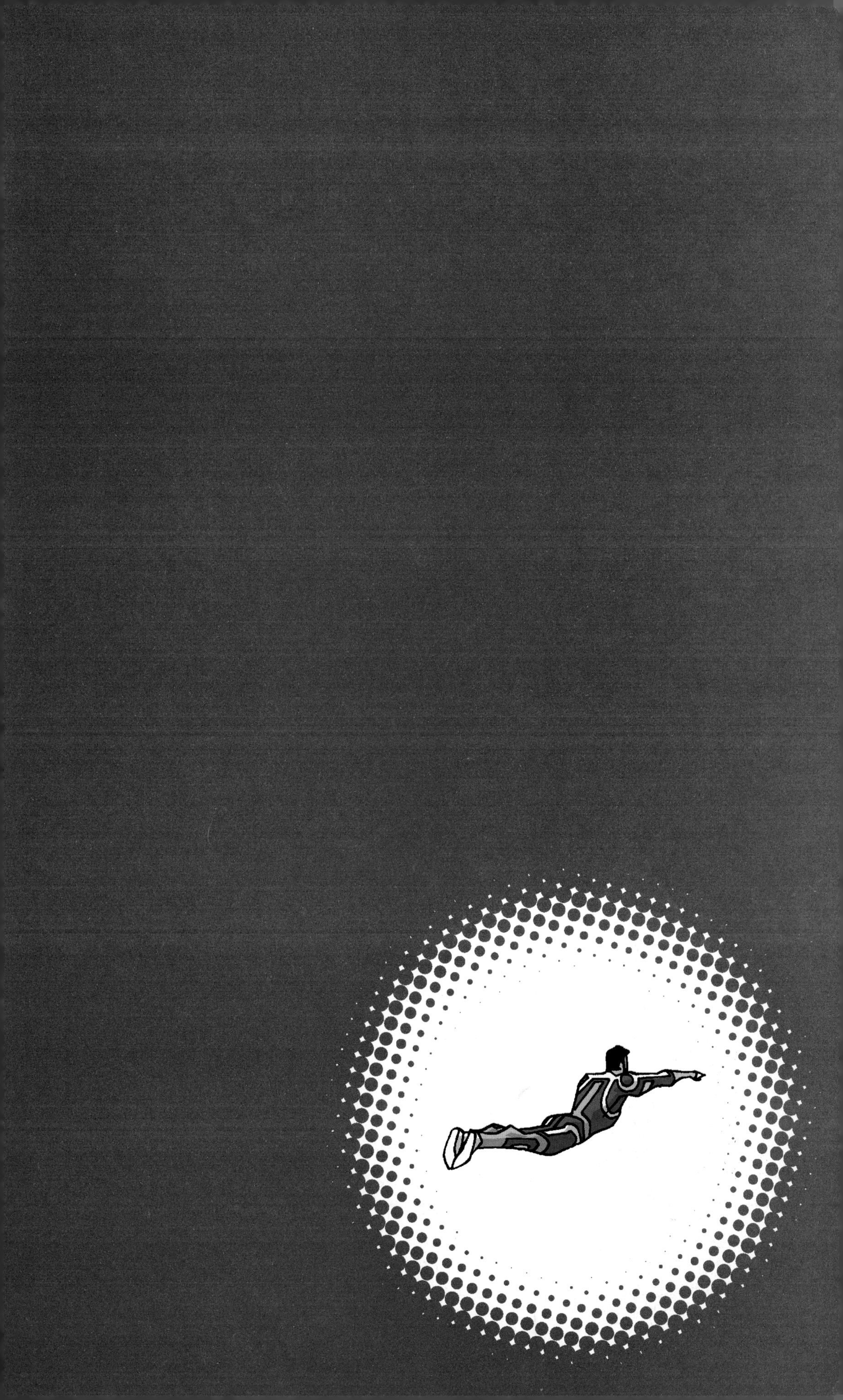

CHAPTER FOUR

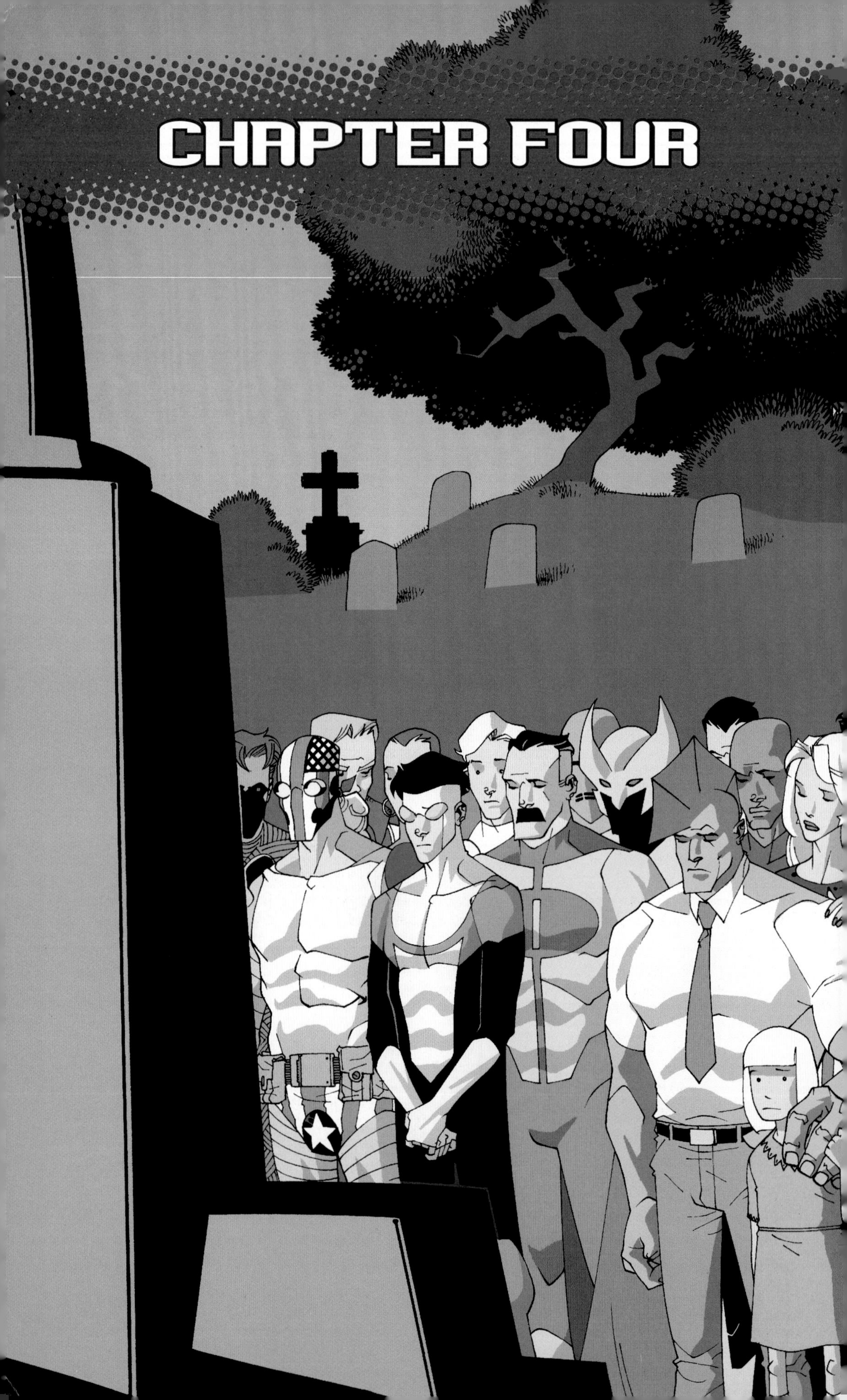

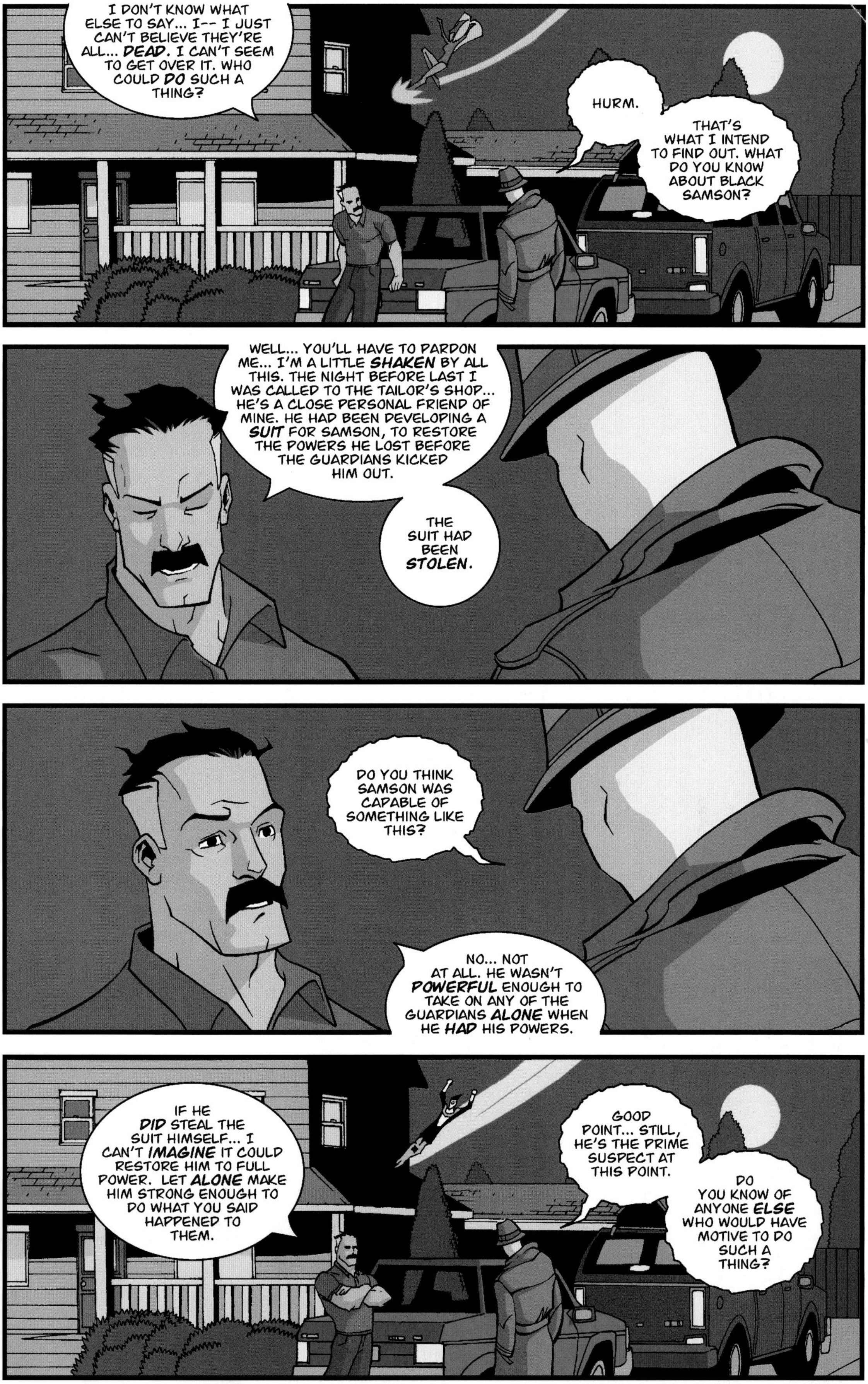

I DON'T KNOW WHAT ELSE TO SAY... I-- I JUST CAN'T BELIEVE THEY'RE ALL... DEAD. I CAN'T SEEM TO GET OVER IT. WHO COULD DO SUCH A THING?
HURM.
THAT'S WHAT I INTEND TO FIND OUT. WHAT DO YOU KNOW ABOUT BLACK SAMSON?
WELL... YOU'LL HAVE TO PARDON ME... I'M A LITTLE SHAKEN BY ALL THIS. THE NIGHT BEFORE LAST I WAS CALLED TO THE TAILOR'S SHOP... HE'S A CLOSE PERSONAL FRIEND OF MINE. HE HAD BEEN DEVELOPING A SUIT FOR SAMSON, TO RESTORE THE POWERS HE LOST BEFORE THE GUARDIANS KICKED HIM OUT.
THE SUIT HAD BEEN STOLEN.
DO YOU THINK SAMSON WAS CAPABLE OF SOMETHING LIKE THIS?
NO... NOT AT ALL. HE WASN'T POWERFUL ENOUGH TO TAKE ON ANY OF THE GUARDIANS ALONE WHEN HE HAD HIS POWERS.
IF HE DID STEAL THE SUIT HIMSELF... I CAN'T IMAGINE IT COULD RESTORE HIM TO FULL POWER. LET ALONE MAKE HIM STRONG ENOUGH TO DO WHAT YOU SAID HAPPENED TO THEM.
GOOD POINT... STILL, HE'S THE PRIME SUSPECT AT THIS POINT.
DO YOU KNOW OF ANYONE ELSE WHO WOULD HAVE MOTIVE TO DO SUCH A THING?

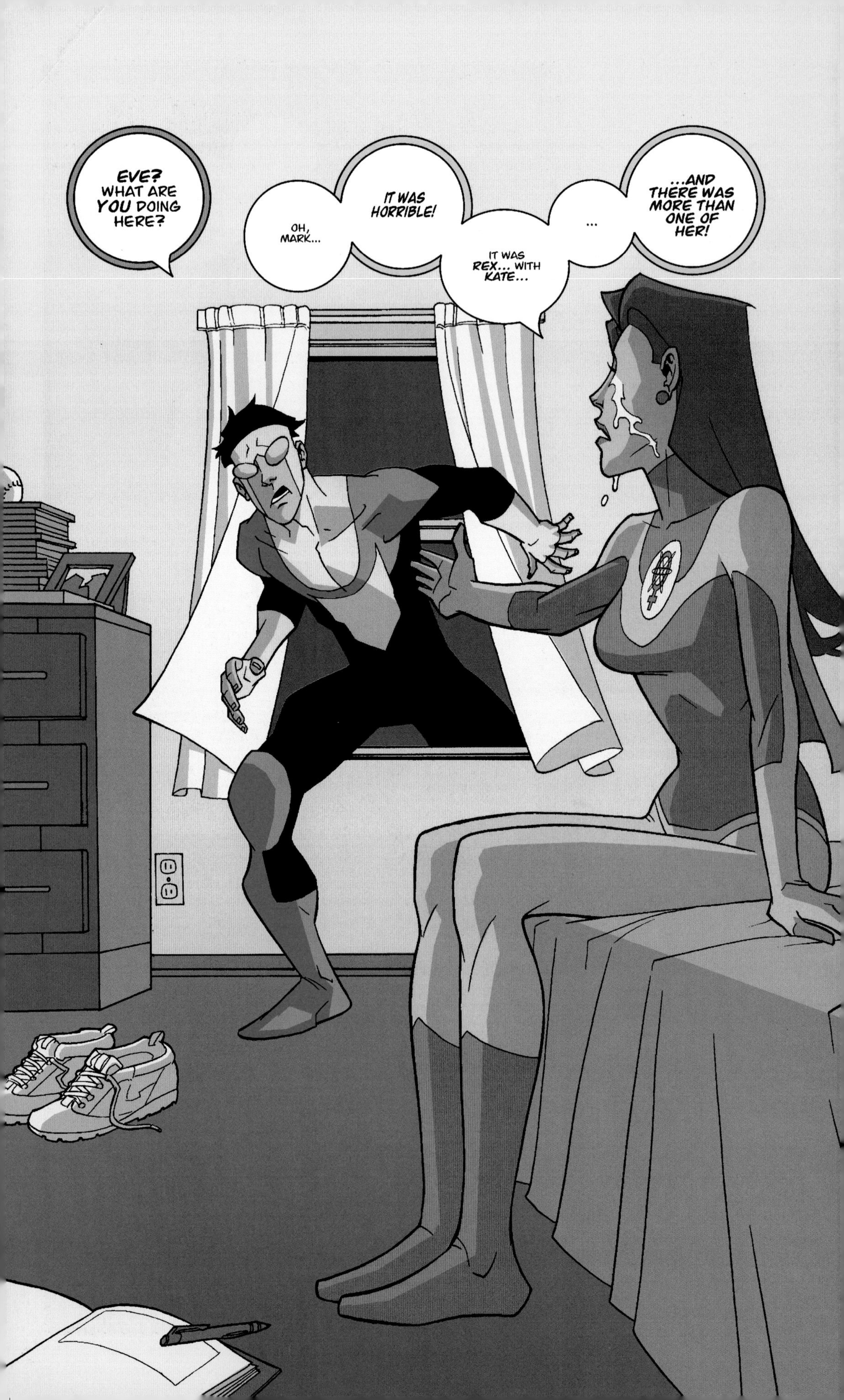
EVE? WHAT ARE YOU DOING HERE?
OH, MARK...
IT WAS HORRIBLE!
IT WAS REX... WITH KATE...
...
...AND THERE WAS MORE THAN ONE OF HER!

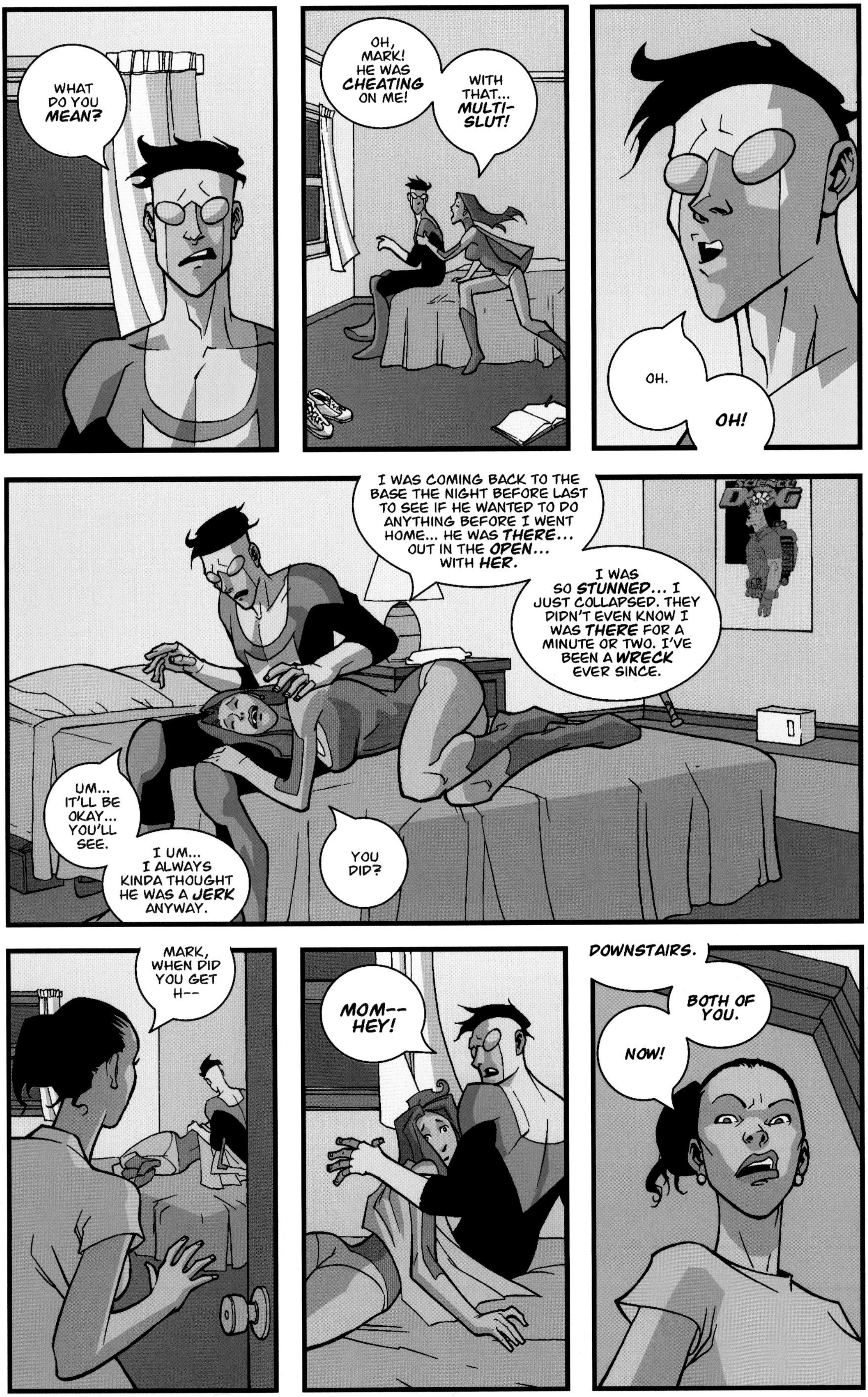
WHAT DO YOU MEAN?
OH, MARK! HE WAS CHEATING ON ME!
WITH THAT... MULTI-SLUT!
OH.
OH!
I WAS COMING BACK TO THE BASE THE NIGHT BEFORE LAST TO SEE IF HE WANTED TO DO ANYTHING BEFORE I WENT HOME... HE WAS THERE... OUT IN THE OPEN... WITH HER.
I WAS SO STUNNED... I JUST COLLAPSED. THEY DIDN'T EVEN KNOW I WAS THERE FOR A MINUTE OR TWO. I'VE BEEN A WRECK EVER SINCE.
UM... IT'LL BE OKAY... YOU'LL SEE.
I UM... I ALWAYS KINDA THOUGHT HE WAS A JERK ANYWAY.
YOU DID?
MARK, WHEN DID YOU GET H--
MOM-- HEY!
DOWNSTAIRS.
BOTH OF YOU.
NOW!

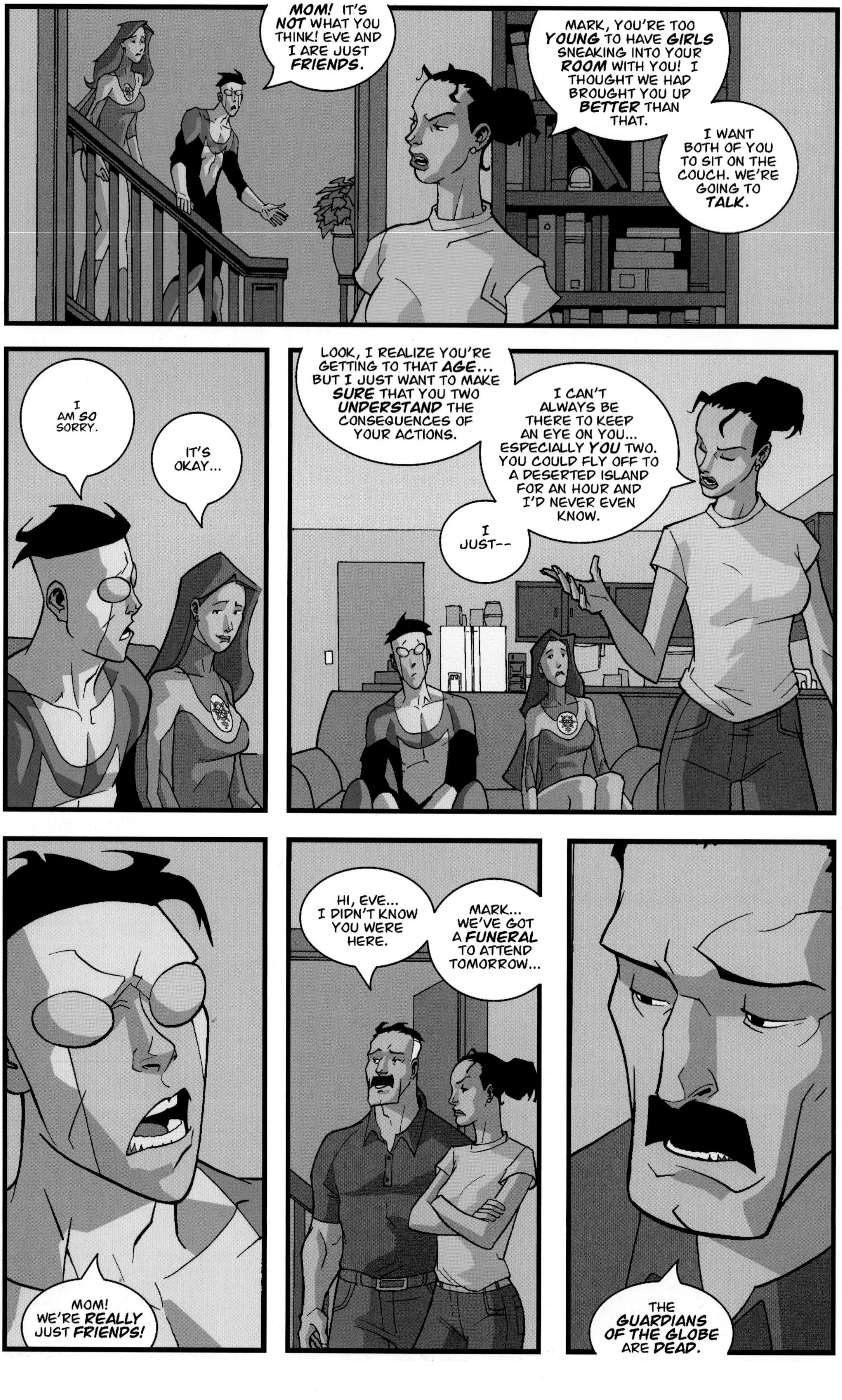
MOM! IT'S NOT WHAT YOU THINK! EVE AND I ARE JUST FRIENDS.
MARK, YOU'RE TOO YOUNG TO HAVE GIRLS SNEAKING INTO YOUR ROOM WITH YOU! I THOUGHT WE HAD BROUGHT YOU UP BETTER THAN THAT.
I WANT BOTH OF YOU TO SIT ON THE COUCH. WE'RE GOING TO TALK.
I AM SO SORRY.
IT'S OKAY...
LOOK, I REALIZE YOU'RE GETTING TO THAT AGE... BUT I JUST WANT TO MAKE SURE THAT YOU TWO UNDERSTAND THE CONSEQUENCES OF YOUR ACTIONS.
I CAN'T ALWAYS BE THERE TO KEEP AN EYE ON YOU... ESPECIALLY YOU TWO. YOU COULD FLY OFF TO A DESERTED ISLAND FOR AN HOUR AND I'D NEVER EVEN KNOW.
I JUST--
MOM! WE'RE REALLY JUST FRIENDS!
HI, EVE... I DIDN'T KNOW YOU WERE HERE.
MARK... WE'VE GOT A FUNERAL TO ATTEND TOMORROW...
THE GUARDIANS OF THE GLOBE ARE DEAD.

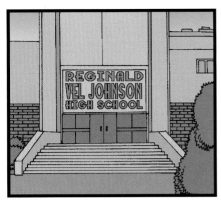

REGINALD VEL JOHNSON HIGH SCHOOL

HEY, MAN... WHAT'S GOING ON?

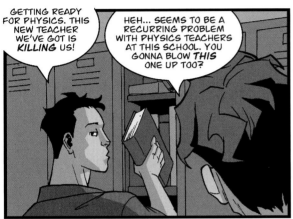

GETTING READY FOR PHYSICS. THIS NEW TEACHER WE'VE GOT IS *KILLING* US!

HEH... SEEMS TO BE A RECURRING PROBLEM WITH PHYSICS TEACHERS AT THIS SCHOOL. YOU GONNA BLOW *THIS* ONE UP TOO?

JEEZ, THAT'S NOT WHAT I MEANT... AND I DIDN'T BLOW UP MISTER HILES, HE BLEW HIMSELF UP-- AND KEEP IT *DOWN*. YOU WANT TO GIVE AWAY MY *SECRET IDENTITY?*

SORRY.

HERE.

...

OPEN IT LATER WHEN YOU GET HOME.

DID THAT JUST HAPPEN?

YEAH.. *WOW*.

HOLD THE PHONE...

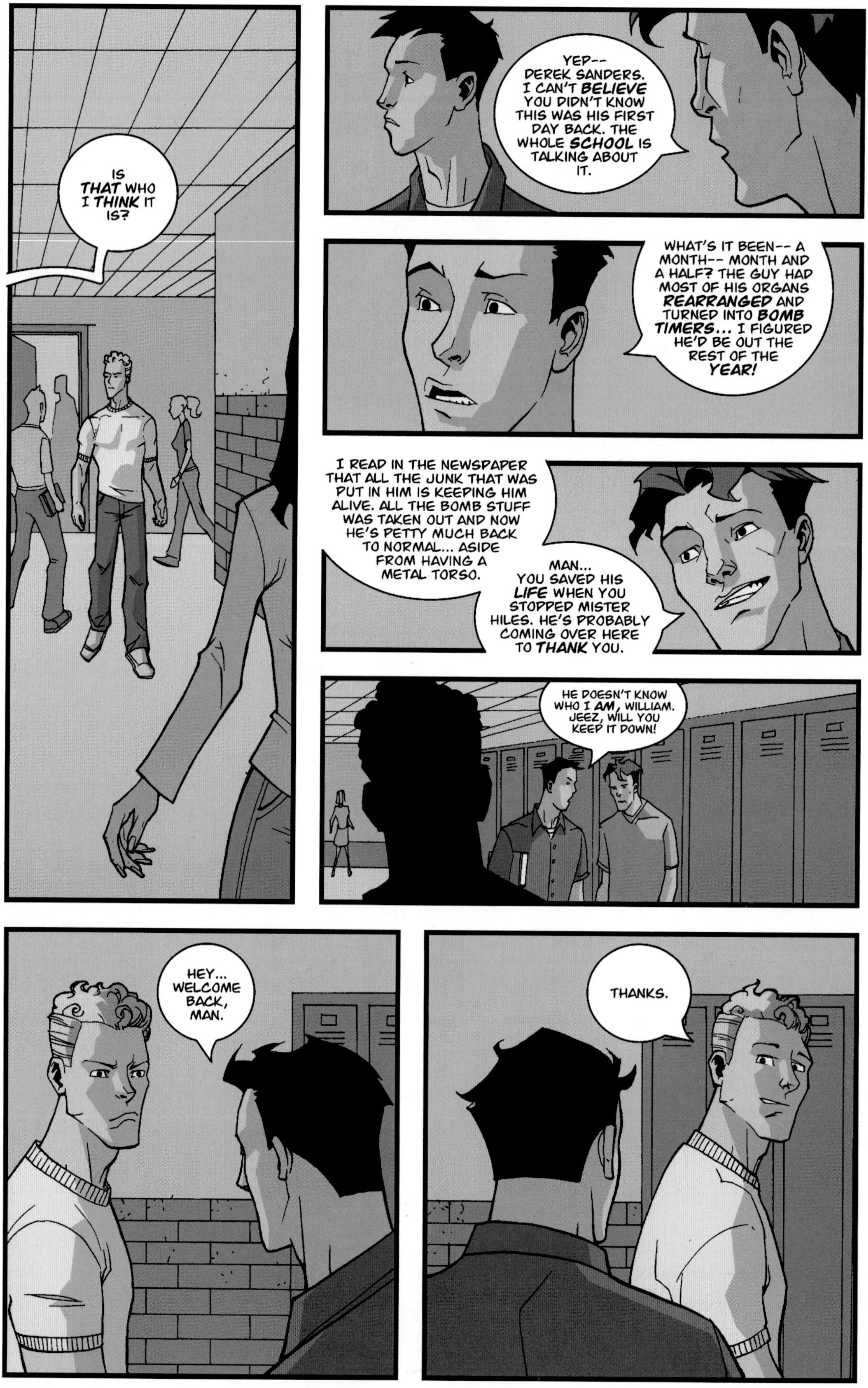
IS THAT WHO I THINK IT IS?
YEP-- DEREK SANDERS. I CAN'T BELIEVE YOU DIDN'T KNOW THIS WAS HIS FIRST DAY BACK. THE WHOLE SCHOOL IS TALKING ABOUT IT.
WHAT'S IT BEEN-- A MONTH-- MONTH AND A HALF? THE GUY HAD MOST OF HIS ORGANS REARRANGED AND TURNED INTO BOMB TIMERS... I FIGURED HE'D BE OUT THE REST OF THE YEAR!
I READ IN THE NEWSPAPER THAT ALL THE JUNK THAT WAS PUT IN HIM IS KEEPING HIM ALIVE. ALL THE BOMB STUFF WAS TAKEN OUT AND NOW HE'S PETTY MUCH BACK TO NORMAL... ASIDE FROM HAVING A METAL TORSO.
MAN... YOU SAVED HIS LIFE WHEN YOU STOPPED MISTER HILES. HE'S PROBABLY COMING OVER HERE TO THANK YOU.
HE DOESN'T KNOW WHO I AM, WILLIAM. JEEZ, WILL YOU KEEP IT DOWN!
HEY... WELCOME BACK, MAN.
THANKS.

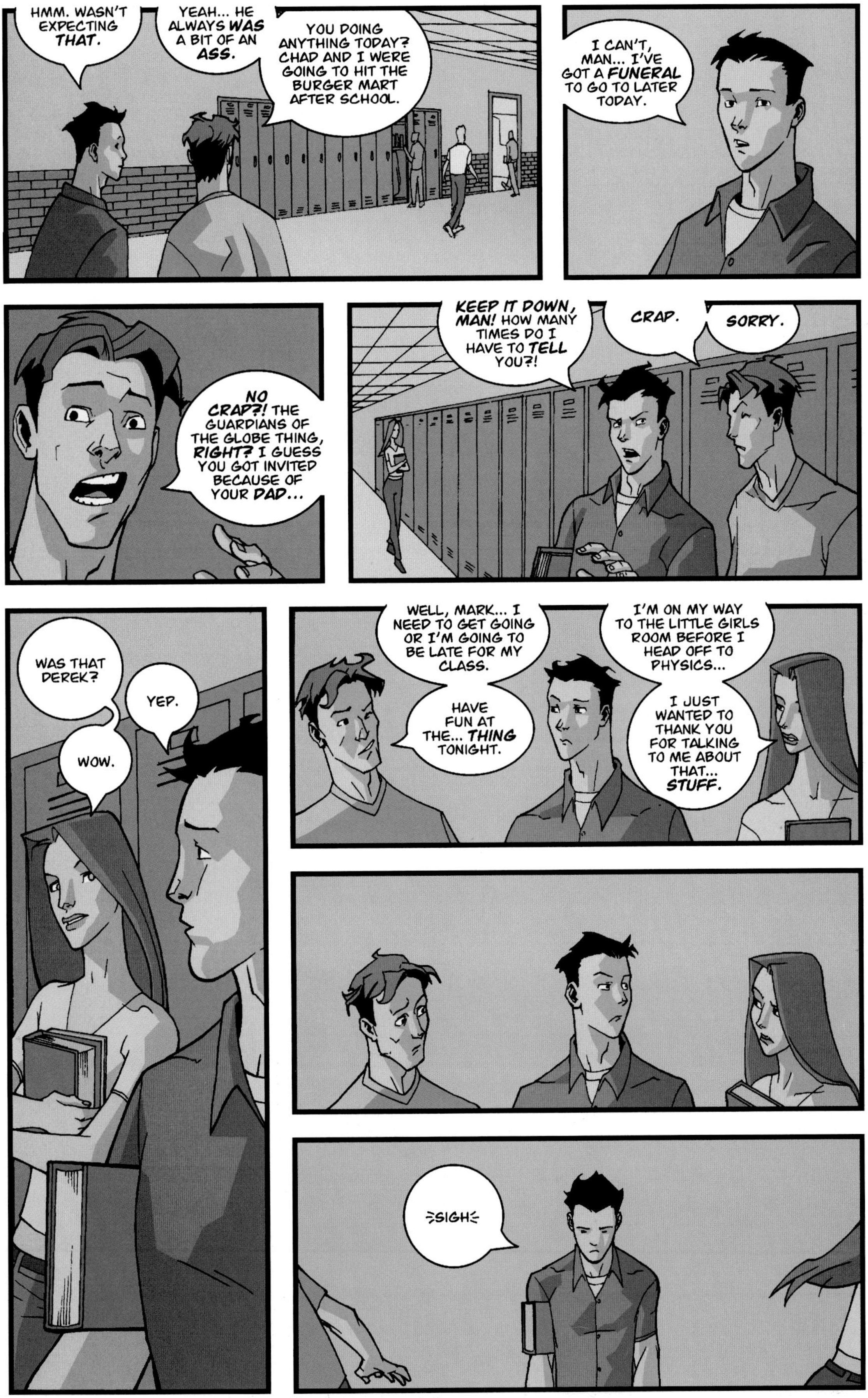
HMM. WASN'T EXPECTING THAT.
YEAH... HE ALWAYS WAS A BIT OF AN ASS.
YOU DOING ANYTHING TODAY? CHAD AND I WERE GOING TO HIT THE BURGER MART AFTER SCHOOL.
I CAN'T, MAN... I'VE GOT A FUNERAL TO GO TO LATER TODAY.
NO CRAP?! THE GUARDIANS OF THE GLOBE THING, RIGHT? I GUESS YOU GOT INVITED BECAUSE OF YOUR DAD...
KEEP IT DOWN, MAN! HOW MANY TIMES DO I HAVE TO TELL YOU?!
CRAP.
SORRY.
WAS THAT DEREK?
YEP.
WOW.
WELL, MARK... I NEED TO GET GOING OR I'M GOING TO BE LATE FOR MY CLASS.
HAVE FUN AT THE... THING TONIGHT.
I'M ON MY WAY TO THE LITTLE GIRLS ROOM BEFORE I HEAD OFF TO PHYSICS...
I JUST WANTED TO THANK YOU FOR TALKING TO ME ABOUT THAT... STUFF.
≈SIGH≈

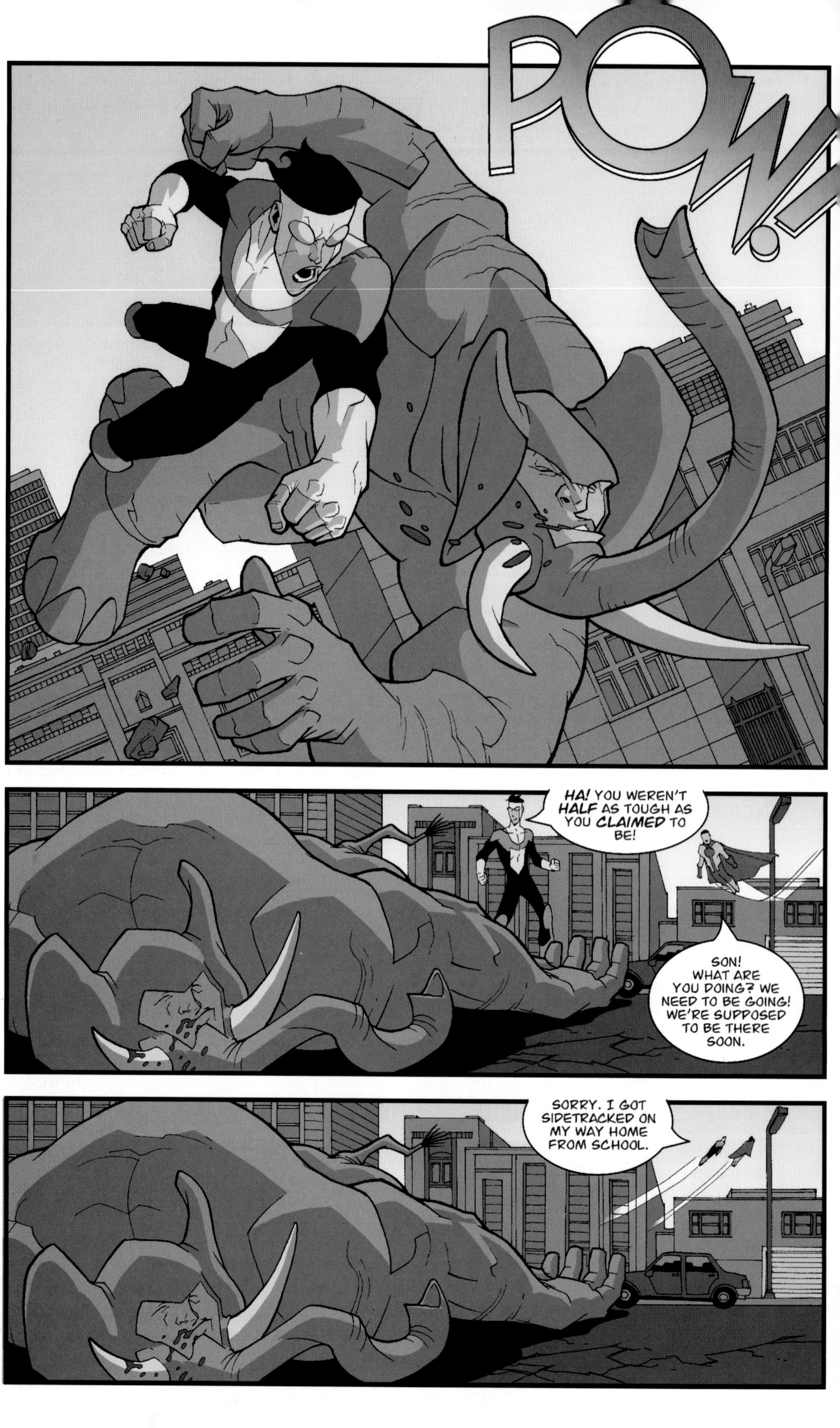
POW!
HA! YOU WEREN'T HALF AS TOUGH AS YOU CLAIMED TO BE!
SON! WHAT ARE YOU DOING? WE NEED TO BE GOING! WE'RE SUPPOSED TO BE THERE SOON.
SORRY. I GOT SIDETRACKED ON MY WAY HOME FROM SCHOOL.

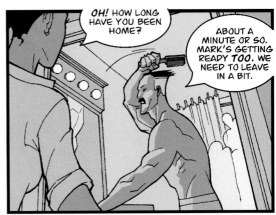

OH! HOW LONG HAVE YOU BEEN HOME?

ABOUT A MINUTE OR SO. MARK'S GETTING READY *TOO*. WE NEED TO LEAVE IN A BIT.

THE FUNERAL IS *TODAY?*

YEAH...

HEY... HAVE YOU THOUGHT ABOUT WHAT WE'RE GOING TO DO FOR MARK'S *BIRTHDAY* THIS YEAR?

MARK'S BIRTHDAY?

YEAH... YOU KNOW MARK... OUR *SON*. HIS BIRTHDAY IS *NEXT WEEK*. DON'T *TELL* ME YOU FORGOT!

I GUESS SO... WITH ALL THAT'S GOING ON...

OH, JEEZ, HON'. I'M SO *SORRY*... I DIDN'T REALIZE THIS WAS HITTING YOU SO *HARD*.

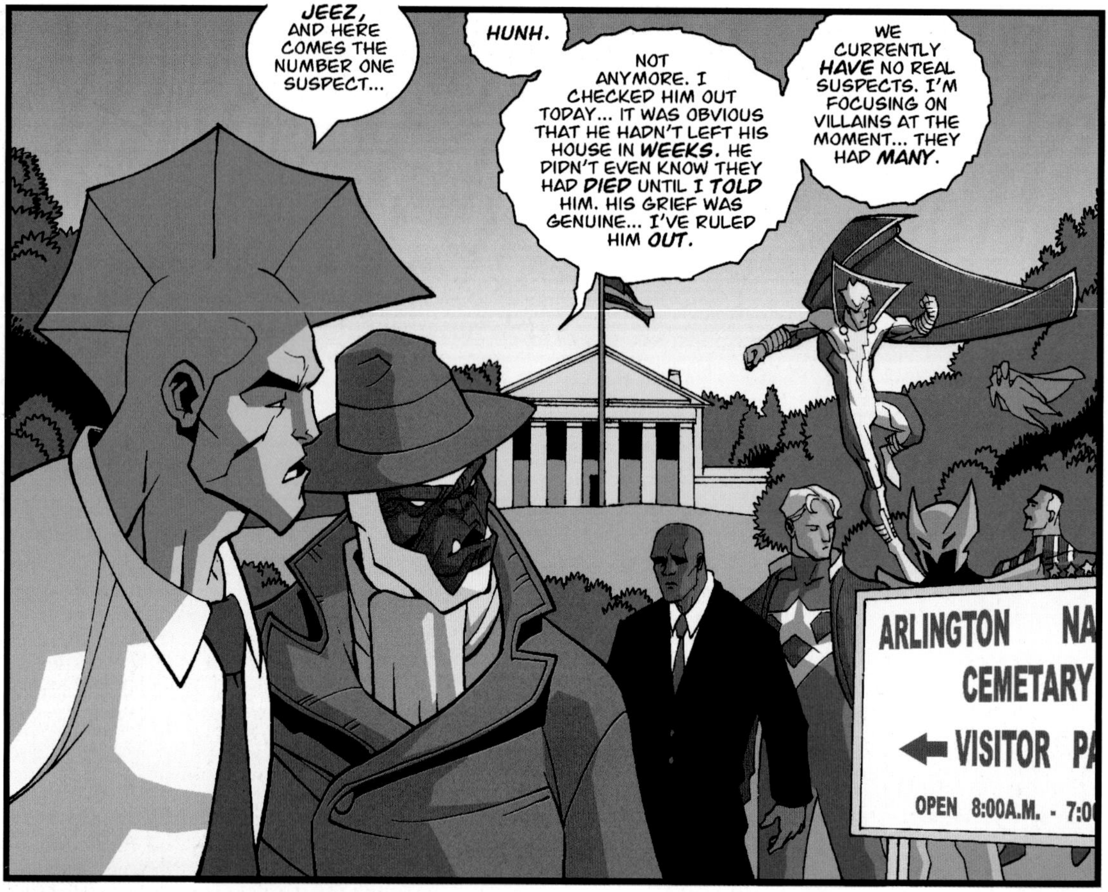
JEEZ, AND HERE COMES THE NUMBER ONE SUSPECT...
HUNH.
NOT ANYMORE. I CHECKED HIM OUT TODAY... IT WAS OBVIOUS THAT HE HADN'T LEFT HIS HOUSE IN WEEKS. HE DIDN'T EVEN KNOW THEY HAD DIED UNTIL I TOLD HIM. HIS GRIEF WAS GENUINE... I'VE RULED HIM OUT.
WE CURRENTLY HAVE NO REAL SUSPECTS. I'M FOCUSING ON VILLAINS AT THE MOMENT... THEY HAD MANY.
ARLINGTON NA
CEMETARY
VISITOR PA
OPEN 8:00A.M. - 7:0

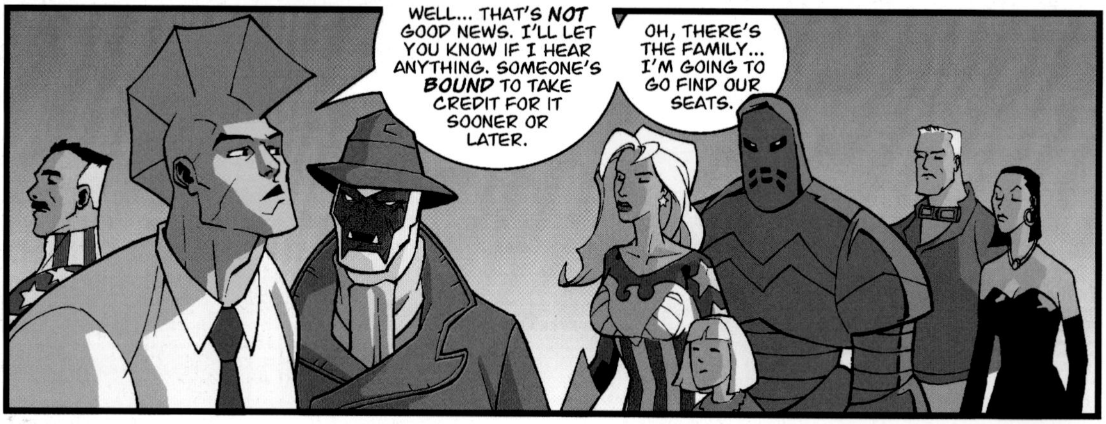
WELL... THAT'S NOT GOOD NEWS. I'LL LET YOU KNOW IF I HEAR ANYTHING. SOMEONE'S BOUND TO TAKE CREDIT FOR IT SOONER OR LATER.
OH, THERE'S THE FAMILY... I'M GOING TO GO FIND OUR SEATS.

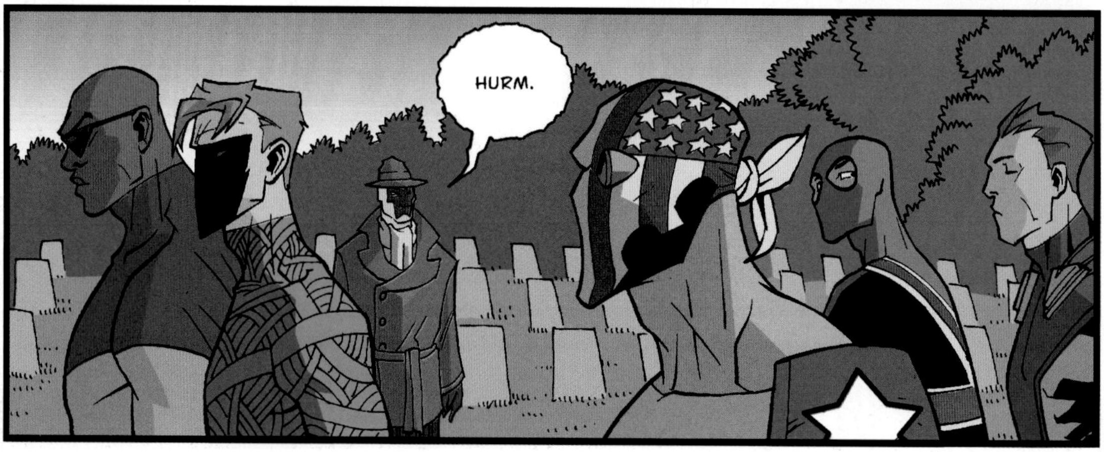
HURM.

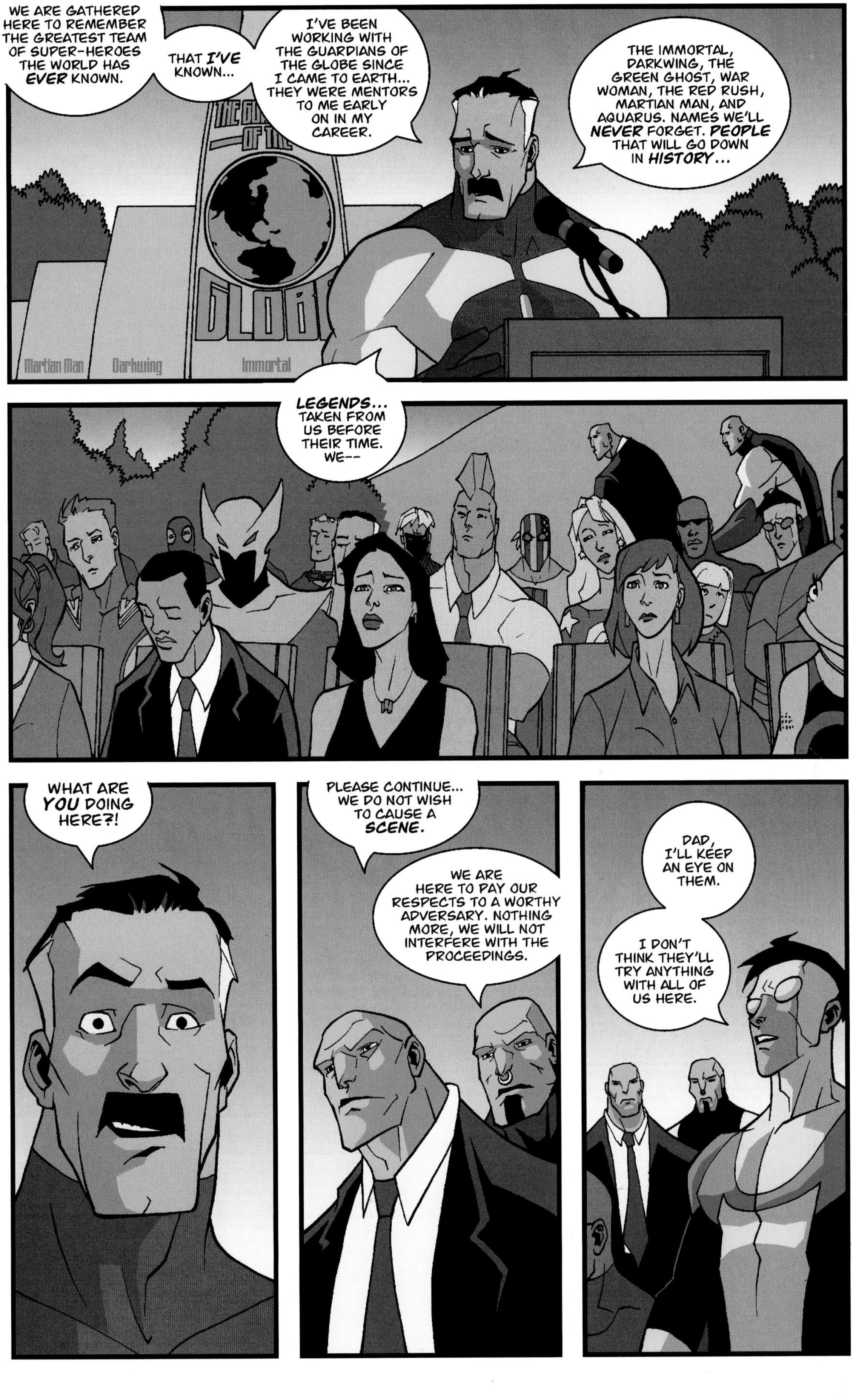
WE ARE GATHERED HERE TO REMEMBER THE GREATEST TEAM OF SUPER-HEROES THE WORLD HAS EVER KNOWN.
THAT I'VE KNOWN...
I'VE BEEN WORKING WITH THE GUARDIANS OF THE GLOBE SINCE I CAME TO EARTH... THEY WERE MENTORS TO ME EARLY ON IN MY CAREER.
THE IMMORTAL, DARKWING, THE GREEN GHOST, WAR WOMAN, THE RED RUSH, MARTIAN MAN, AND AQUARUS. NAMES WE'LL NEVER FORGET. PEOPLE THAT WILL GO DOWN IN HISTORY...
Martian Man
Darkwing
Immortal
LEGENDS... TAKEN FROM US BEFORE THEIR TIME. WE--
WHAT ARE YOU DOING HERE?!
PLEASE CONTINUE... WE DO NOT WISH TO CAUSE A SCENE.
WE ARE HERE TO PAY OUR RESPECTS TO A WORTHY ADVERSARY. NOTHING MORE, WE WILL NOT INTERFERE WITH THE PROCEEDINGS.
DAD, I'LL KEEP AN EYE ON THEM.
I DON'T THINK THEY'LL TRY ANYTHING WITH ALL OF US HERE.

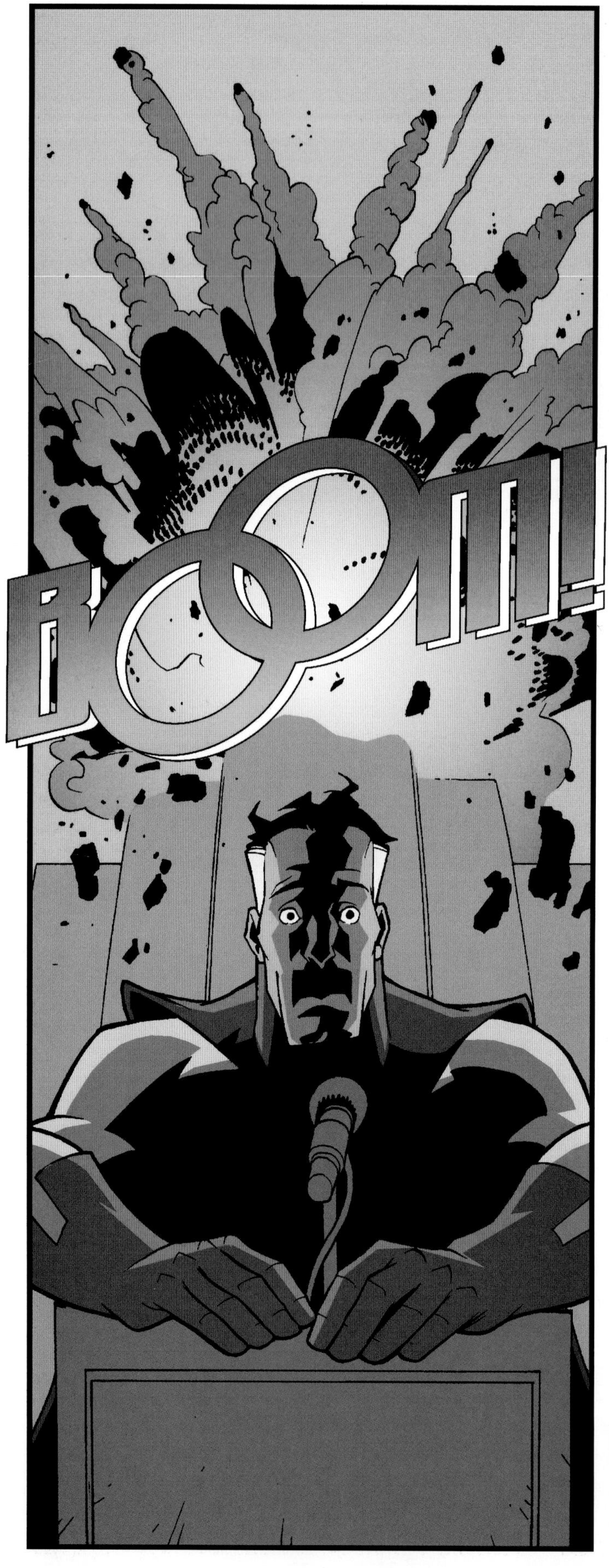
BOOM!!

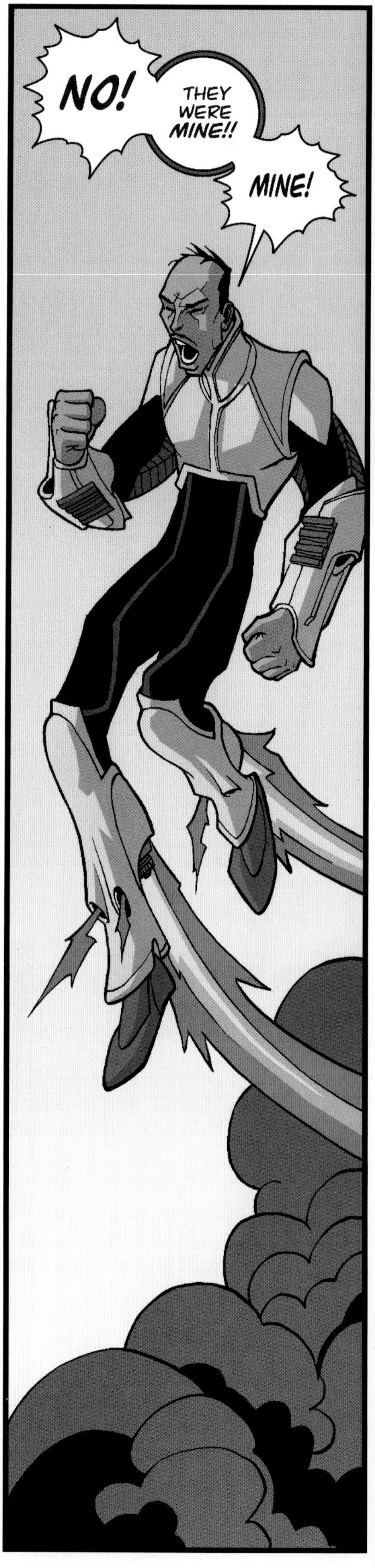
NO!
THEY WERE MINE!!
MINE!

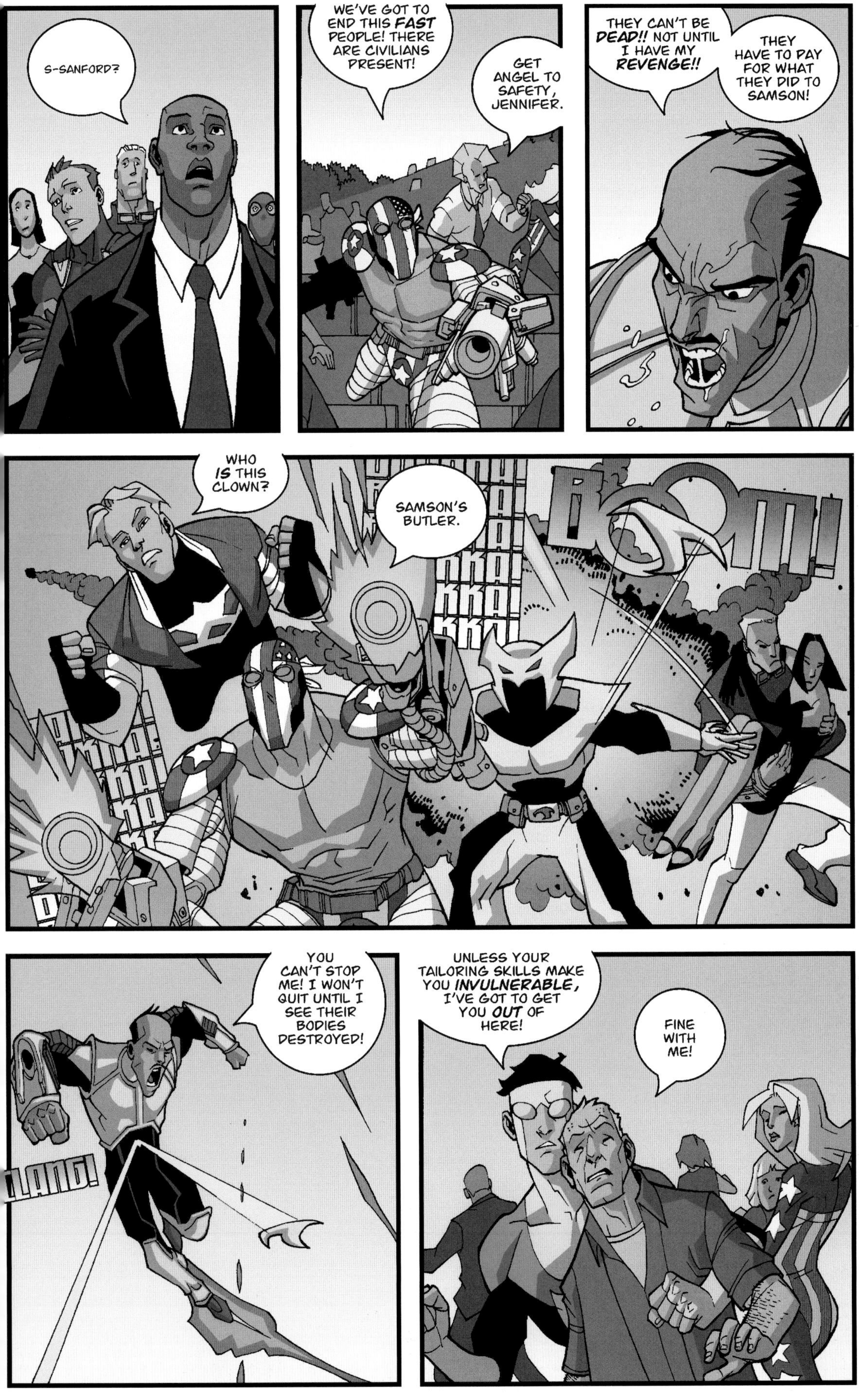
S-SANFORD?
WE'VE GOT TO END THIS FAST PEOPLE! THERE ARE CIVILIANS PRESENT!
GET ANGEL TO SAFETY, JENNIFER.
THEY CAN'T BE DEAD!! NOT UNTIL I HAVE MY REVENGE!!
THEY HAVE TO PAY FOR WHAT THEY DID TO SAMSON!
WHO IS THIS CLOWN?
SAMSON'S BUTLER.
BOOM!
YOU CAN'T STOP ME! I WON'T QUIT UNTIL I SEE THEIR BODIES DESTROYED!
UNLESS YOUR TAILORING SKILLS MAKE YOU INVULNERABLE, I'VE GOT TO GET YOU OUT OF HERE!
FINE WITH ME!

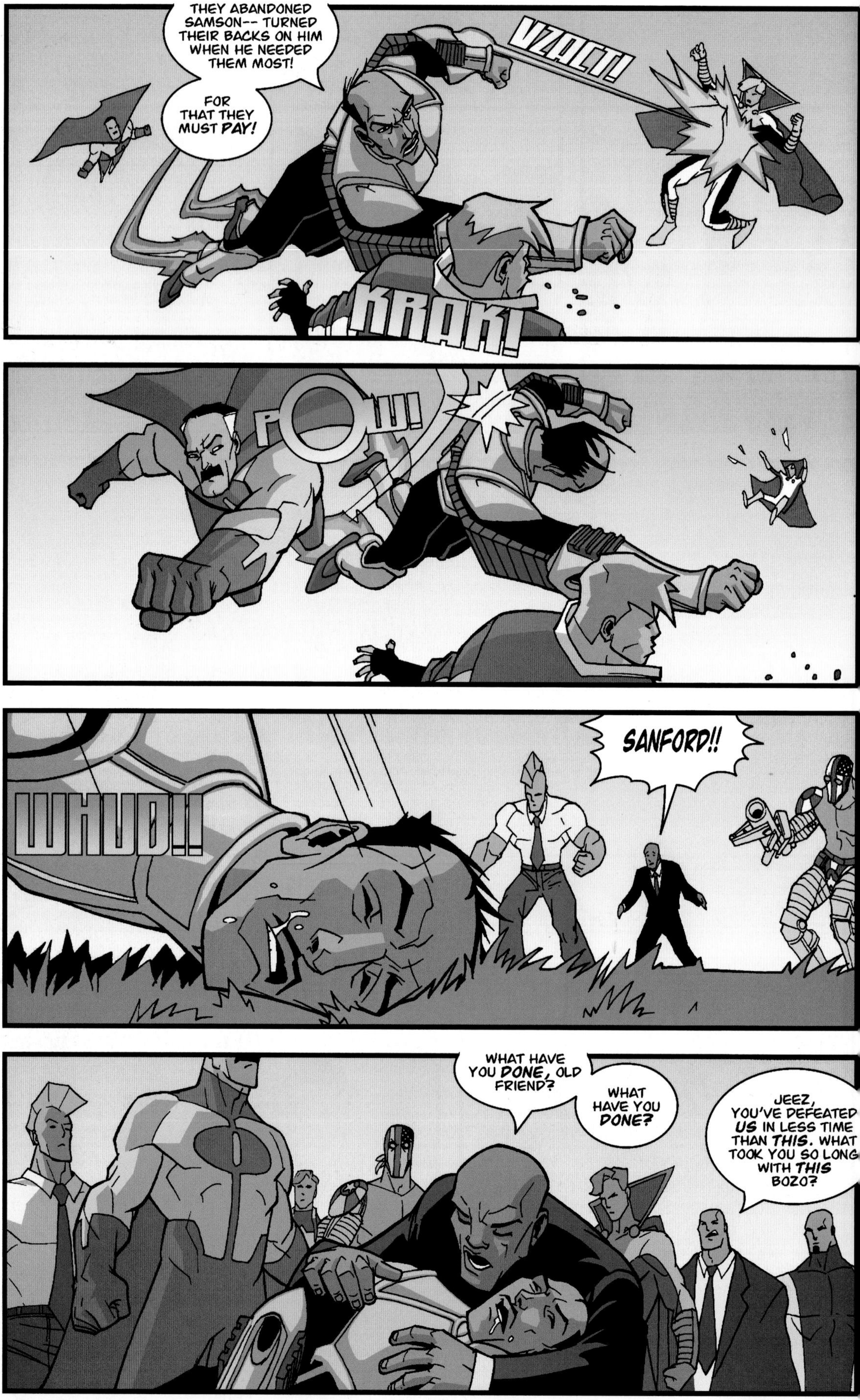
THEY ABANDONED SAMSON-- TURNED THEIR BACKS ON HIM WHEN HE NEEDED THEM MOST!
FOR THAT THEY MUST PAY!
VZACT!
KRAK!
POW!
WHUD!!
SANFORD!!
WHAT HAVE YOU DONE, OLD FRIEND?
WHAT HAVE YOU DONE?
JEEZ, YOU'VE DEFEATED US IN LESS TIME THAN THIS. WHAT TOOK YOU SO LONG WITH THIS BOZO?

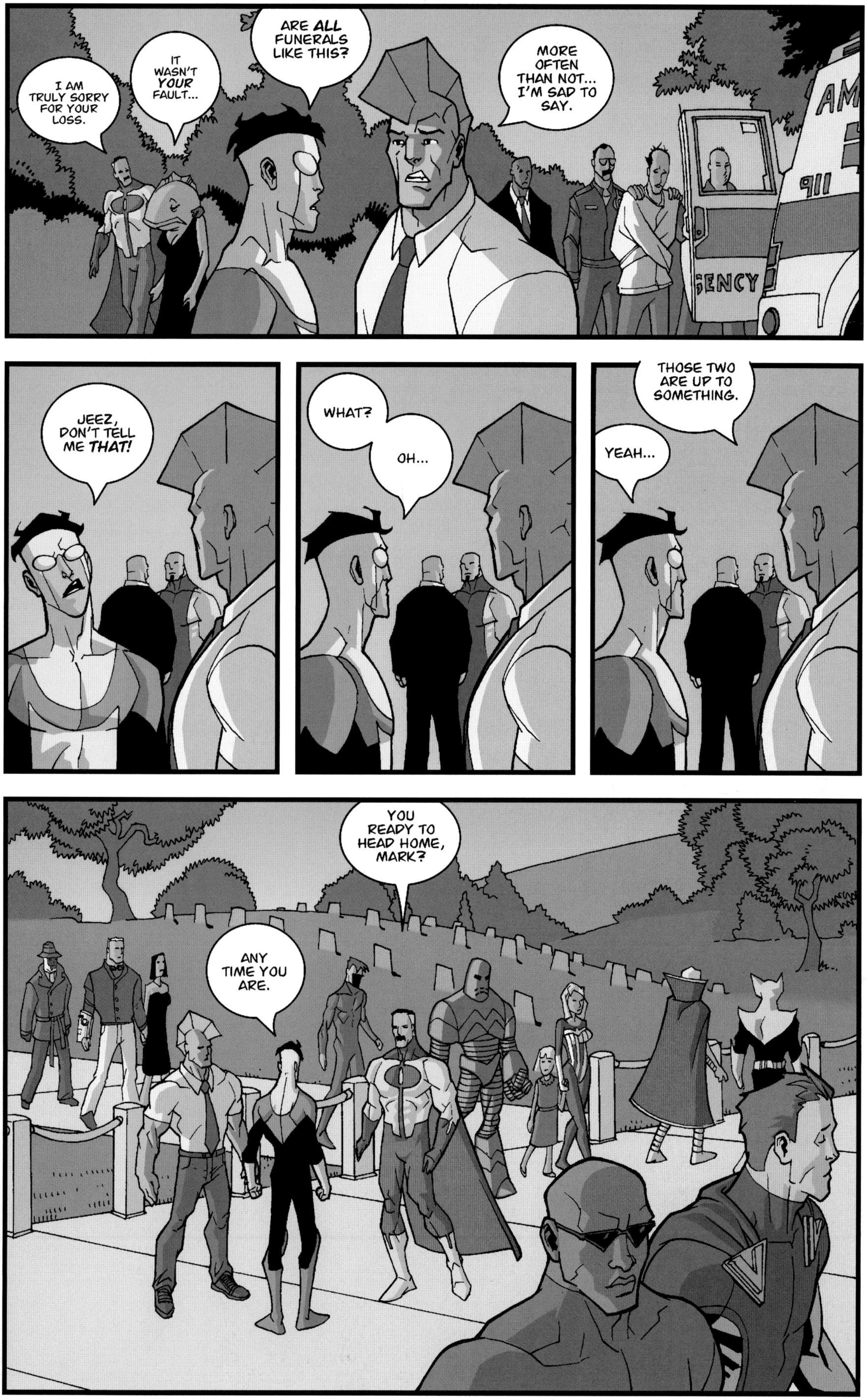
I AM TRULY SORRY FOR YOUR LOSS.
IT WASN'T YOUR FAULT...
ARE ALL FUNERALS LIKE THIS?
MORE OFTEN THAN NOT... I'M SAD TO SAY.
AM
911
GENCY
JEEZ, DON'T TELL ME THAT!
WHAT?
OH...
THOSE TWO ARE UP TO SOMETHING.
YEAH...
YOU READY TO HEAD HOME, MARK?
ANY TIME YOU ARE.

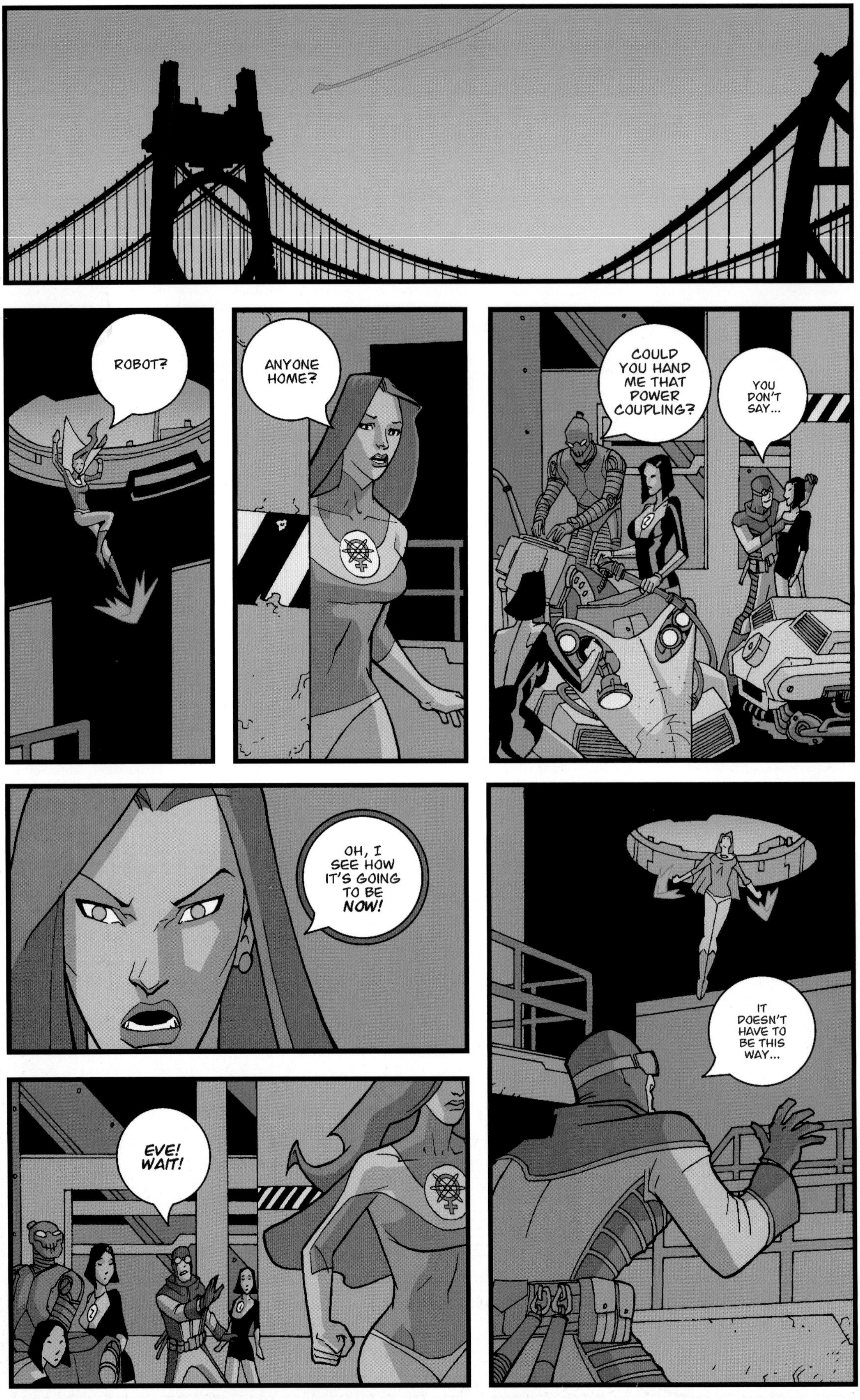
ROBOT?
ANYONE HOME?
COULD YOU HAND ME THAT POWER COUPLING?
YOU DON'T SAY...
OH, I SEE HOW IT'S GOING TO BE NOW!
IT DOESN'T HAVE TO BE THIS WAY...
EVE! WAIT!

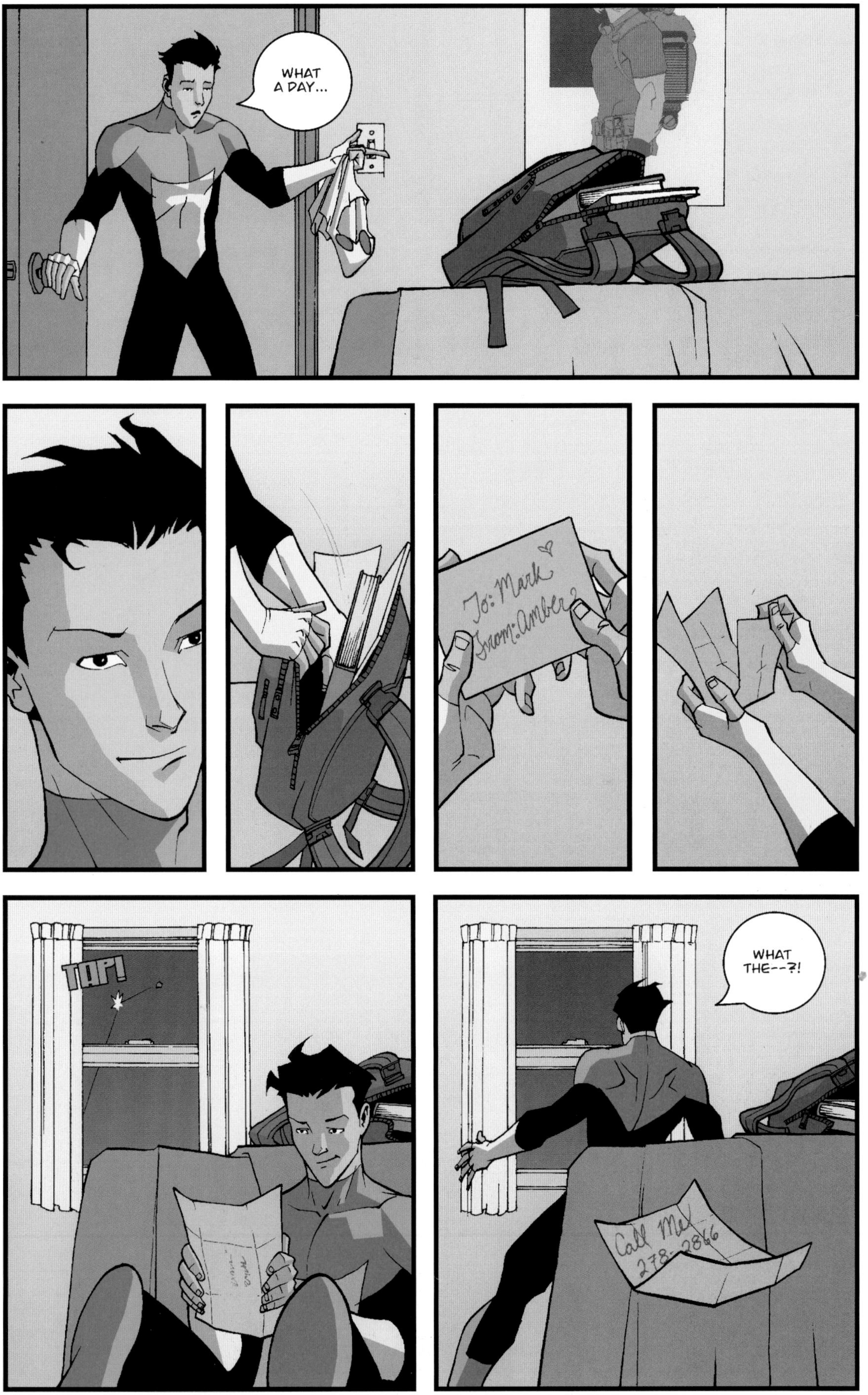
WHAT A DAY...
To: Mark
From: Amber
TAP!
WHAT THE--?!
Call Me!
278-2866

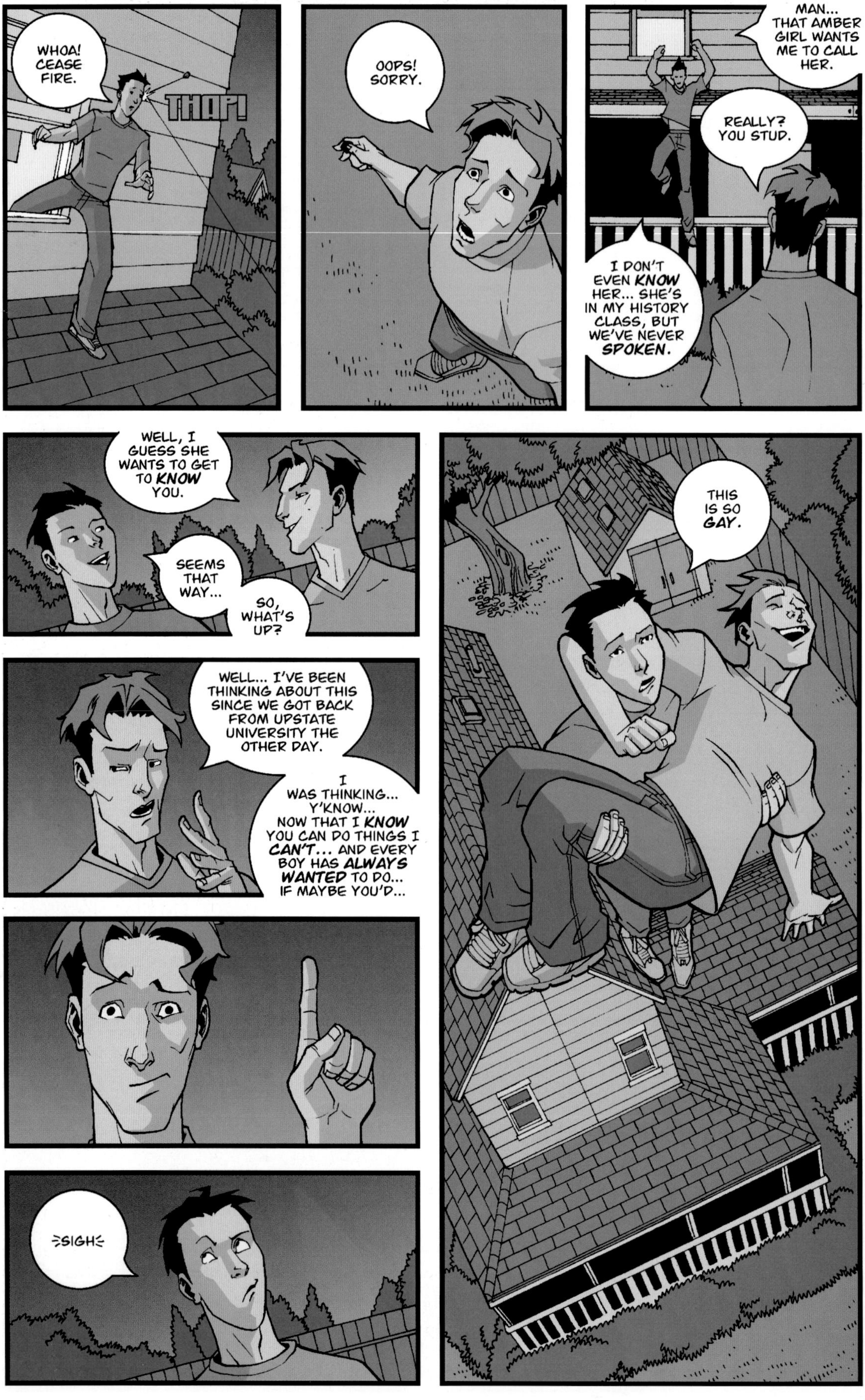
WHOA! CEASE FIRE.
THAP!
OOPS! SORRY.
MAN... THAT AMBER GIRL WANTS ME TO CALL HER.
REALLY? YOU STUD.
I DON'T EVEN KNOW HER... SHE'S IN MY HISTORY CLASS, BUT WE'VE NEVER SPOKEN.
WELL, I GUESS SHE WANTS TO GET TO KNOW YOU.
SEEMS THAT WAY...
SO, WHAT'S UP?
WELL... I'VE BEEN THINKING ABOUT THIS SINCE WE GOT BACK FROM UPSTATE UNIVERSITY THE OTHER DAY.
I WAS THINKING... Y'KNOW... NOW THAT I KNOW YOU CAN DO THINGS I CAN'T... AND EVERY BOY HAS ALWAYS WANTED TO DO... IF MAYBE YOU'D...
SIGH
THIS IS SO GAY.

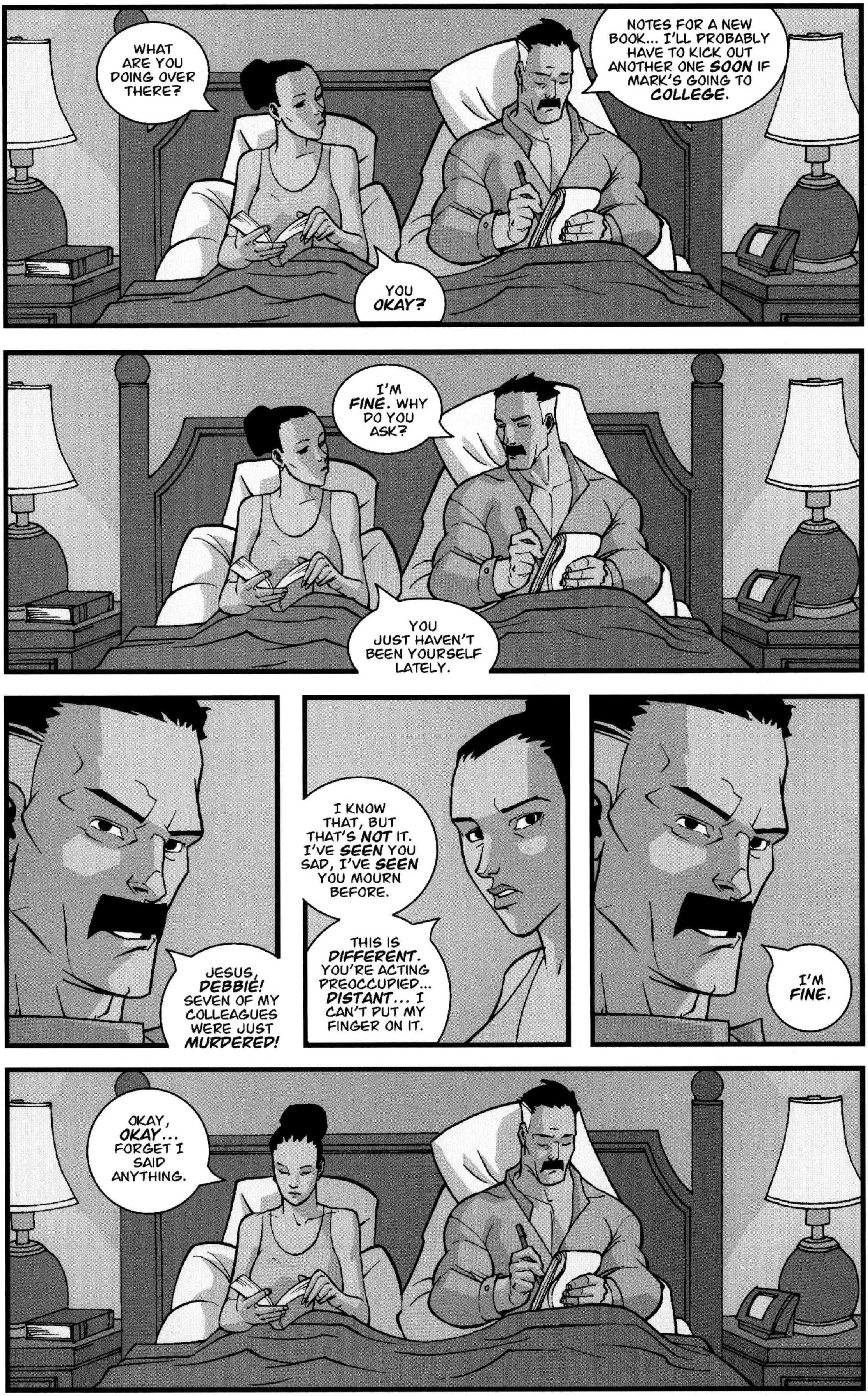

WHAT ARE YOU DOING OVER THERE?
NOTES FOR A NEW BOOK... I'LL PROBABLY HAVE TO KICK OUT ANOTHER ONE SOON IF MARK'S GOING TO COLLEGE.
YOU OKAY?
I'M FINE. WHY DO YOU ASK?
YOU JUST HAVEN'T BEEN YOURSELF LATELY.
JESUS, DEBBIE! SEVEN OF MY COLLEAGUES WERE JUST MURDERED!
I KNOW THAT, BUT THAT'S NOT IT. I'VE SEEN YOU SAD, I'VE SEEN YOU MOURN BEFORE.
THIS IS DIFFERENT. YOU'RE ACTING PREOCCUPIED... DISTANT... I CAN'T PUT MY FINGER ON IT.
I'M FINE.
OKAY, OKAY... FORGET I SAID ANYTHING.

ARLINGTON NAT...
CEMETARY
VISITOR PAR...

YOU SON OF A BITCH.

IT'S *NOT* A SHORT DRIVE OUT HERE Y'KNOW...

David Hiles
1944-2003

Forgive him, he lost his way.

I CAN'T *BELIEVE* THEY EVEN ALLOWED YOU TO BE BURIED *HERE*.

I GUESS YOUR EX-WIFE FELT *SORRY* FOR YOU-- PULLED SOME *STRINGS* SO YOU COULD BE BURIED WITH YOUR FELLOW *VETERANS*...

YOU WERE *WHAT*... A CLERK?

WELL, I DON'T FEEL SORRY FOR YOU... I DON'T CARE *WHAT* HAPPENED TO YOUR SON TO MAKE YOU DO WHAT YOU DID...

BUT Y'KNOW...

...I *DID* BRING YOU A GIFT.

ZIIIP!

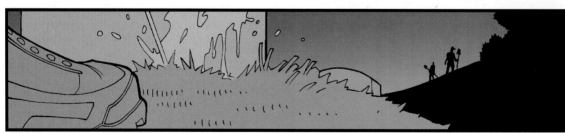

C'MON, *HURRY!* YOU WANNA GET CAUGHT?!

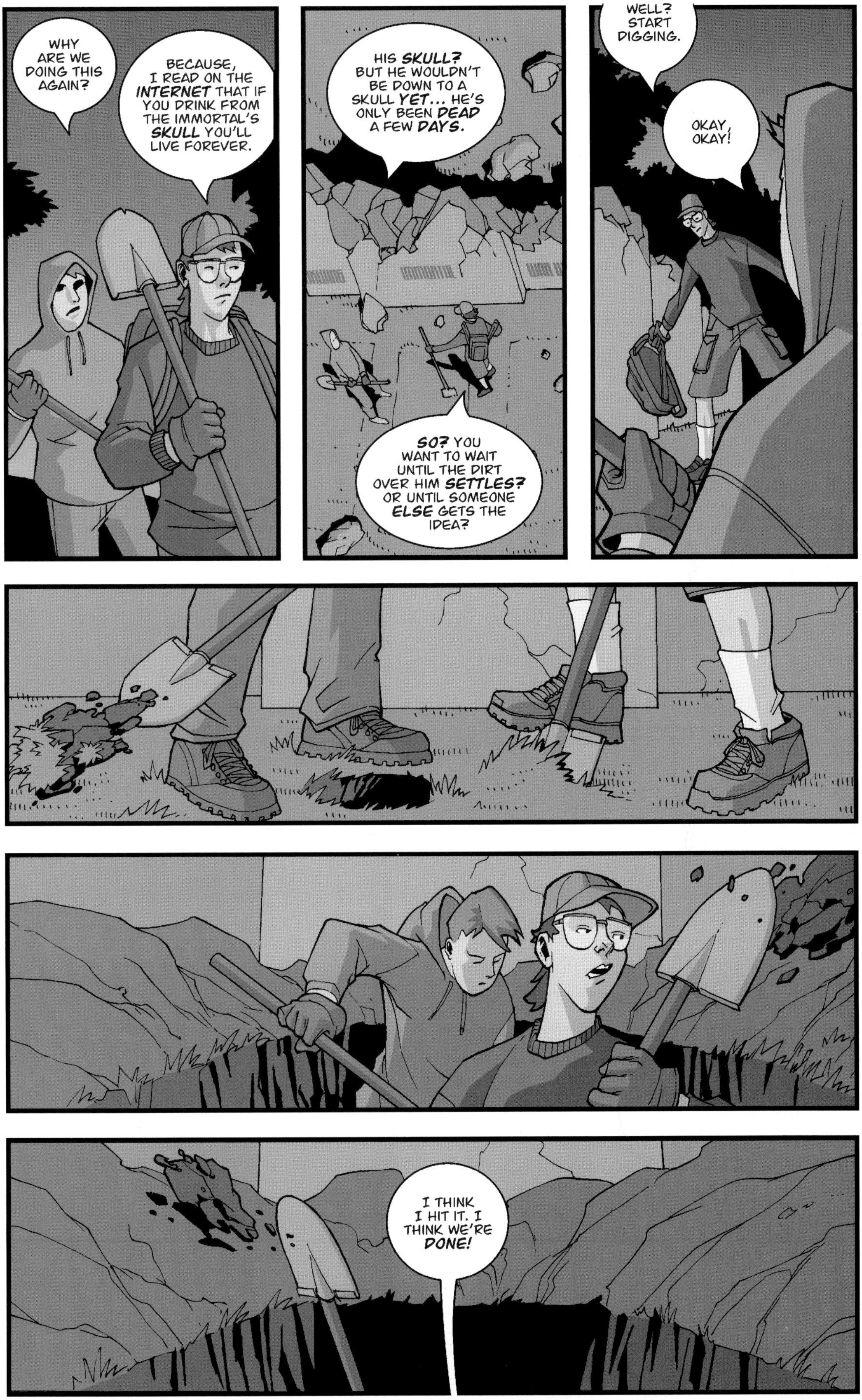
WHY ARE WE DOING THIS AGAIN?
BECAUSE, I READ ON THE INTERNET THAT IF YOU DRINK FROM THE IMMORTAL'S SKULL YOU'LL LIVE FOREVER.
HIS SKULL? BUT HE WOULDN'T BE DOWN TO A SKULL YET... HE'S ONLY BEEN DEAD A FEW DAYS.
IMMORTAL
SO? YOU WANT TO WAIT UNTIL THE DIRT OVER HIM SETTLES? OR UNTIL SOMEONE ELSE GETS THE IDEA?
WELL? START DIGGING.
OKAY, OKAY!
I THINK I HIT IT. I THINK WE'RE DONE!

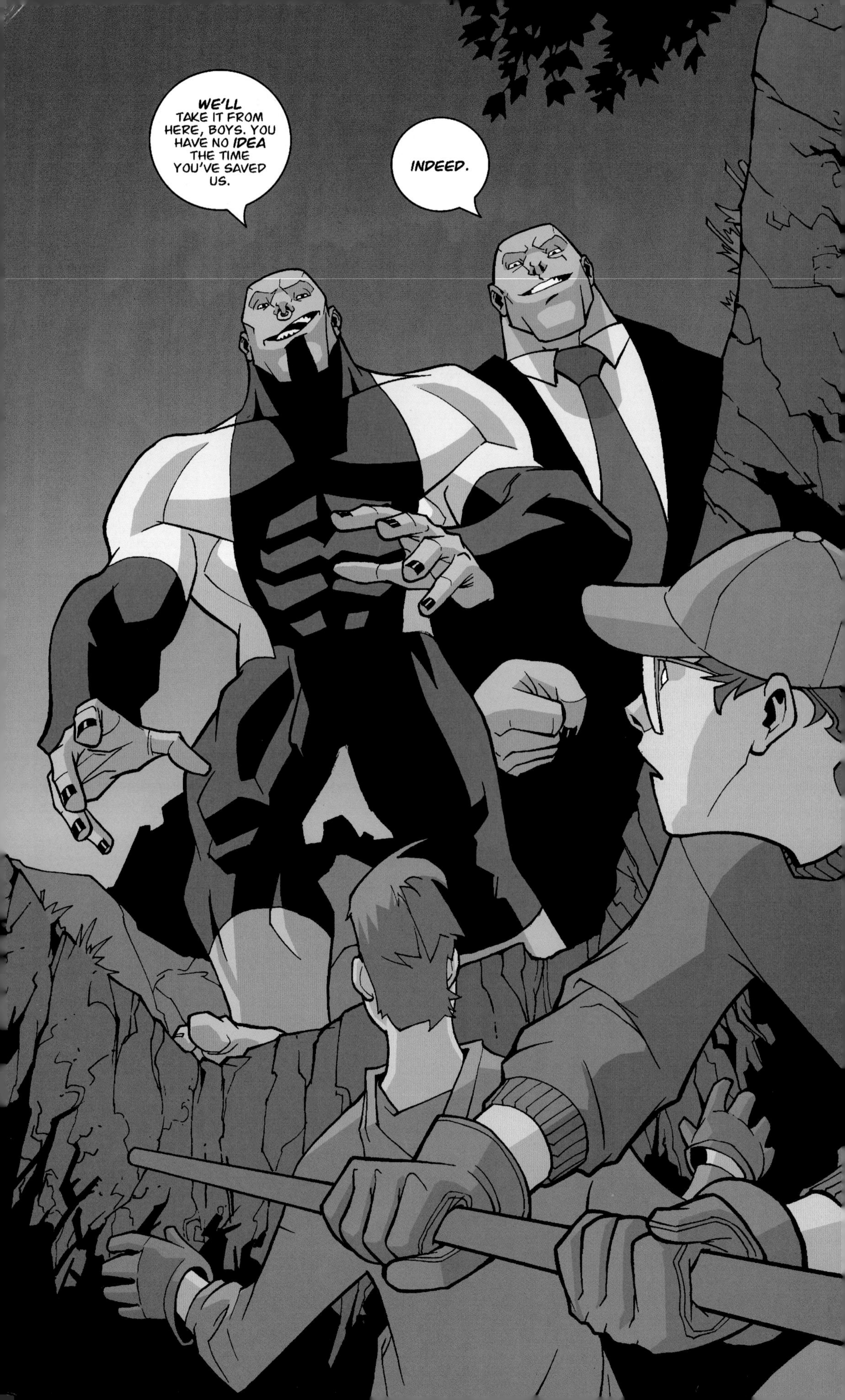
WE'LL TAKE IT FROM HERE, BOYS. YOU HAVE NO IDEA THE TIME YOU'VE SAVED US.
INDEED.

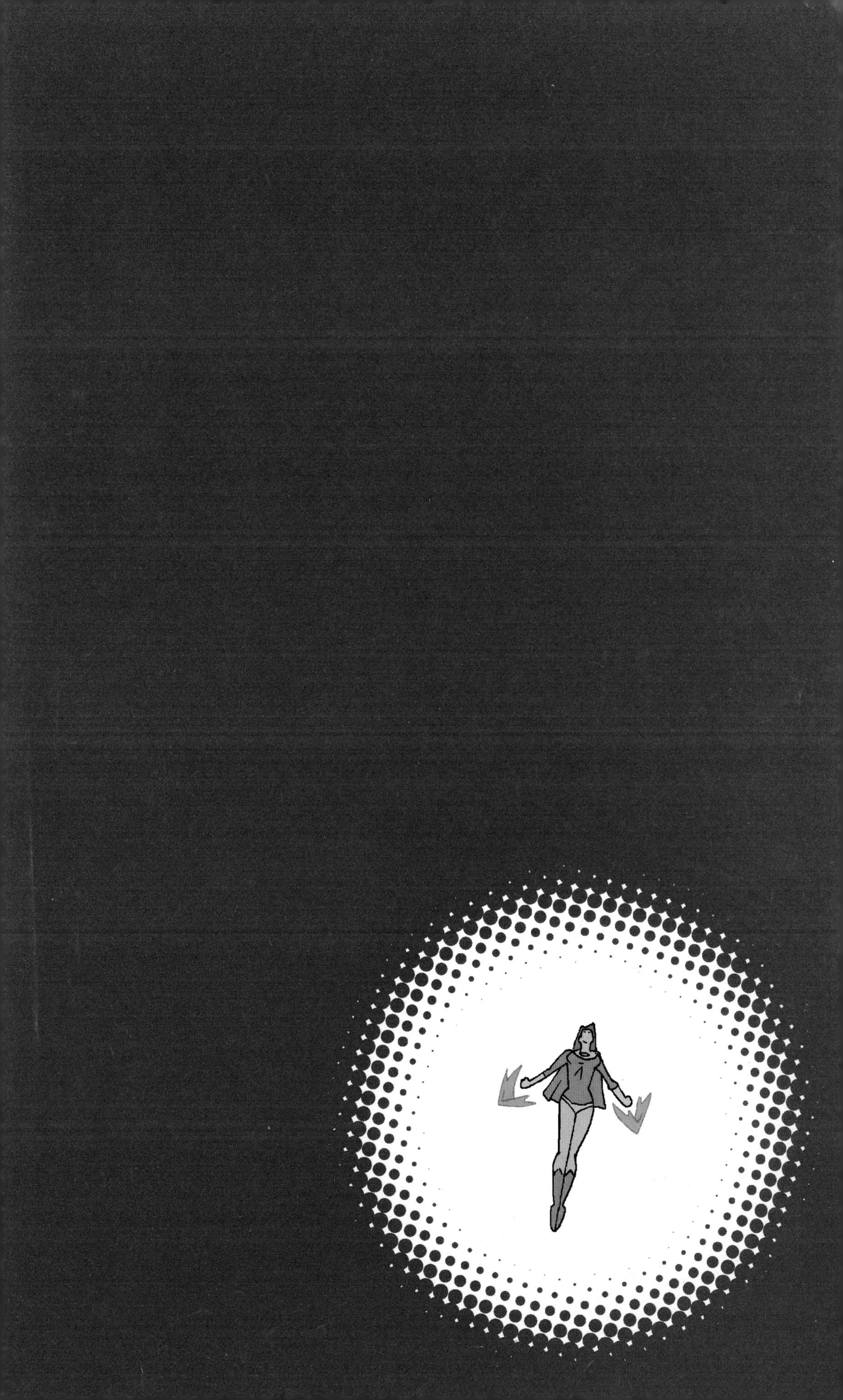

COVERS

SKETCHBOOK

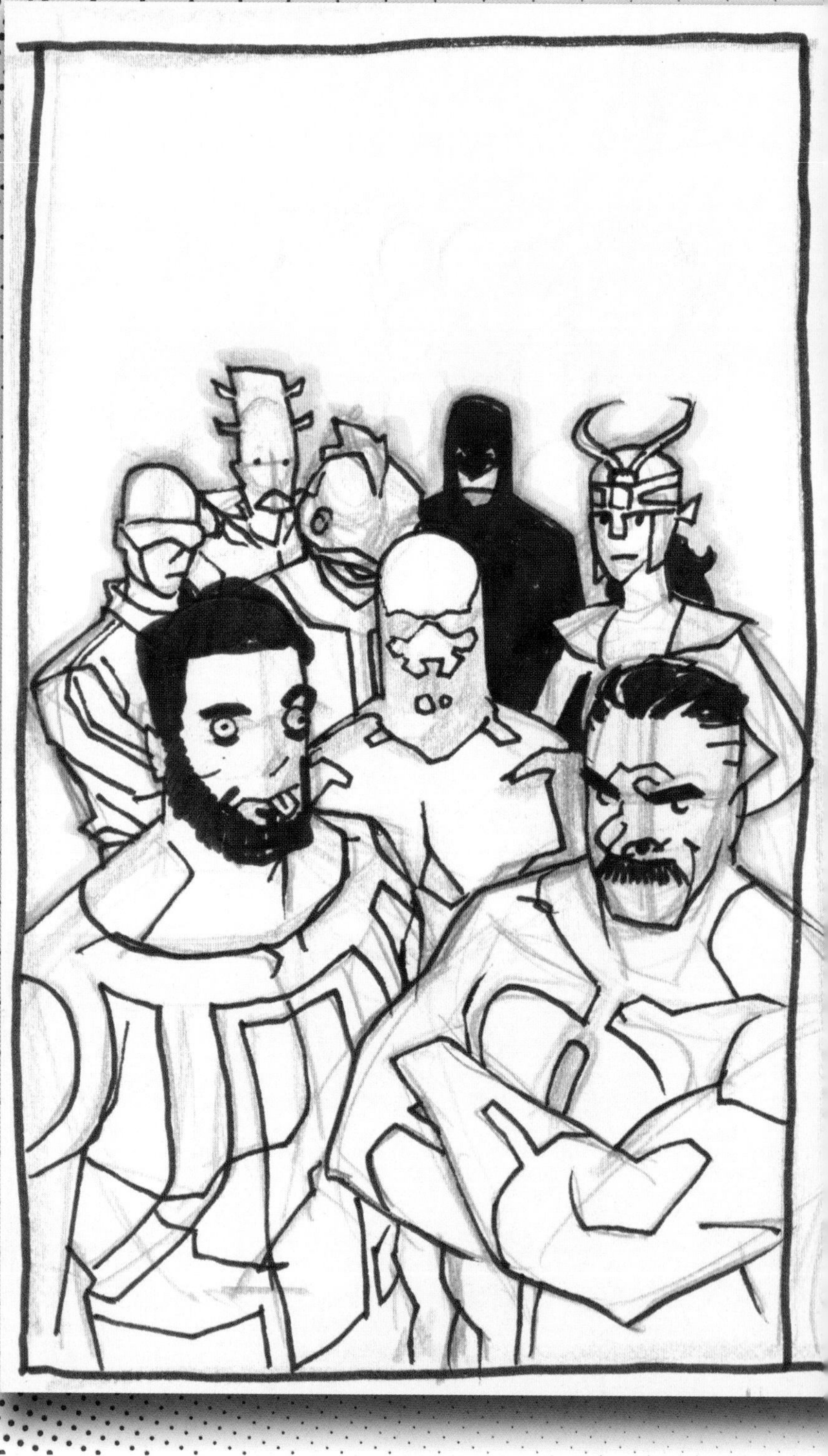

When it came time to do this collection... I'll be honest. I had no idea what to call this book, or what would be on the cover. The first arc was easy, I had that title planned early on, and Kurt Busiek was kind enough to suggest the cover image. This arc was different... it was almost all set up for things that are coming up. Of course, the big Omni-Man event in issue 7 is the most important thing in the book, but I didn't want to spoil that. Then I came up with "Eight is Enough," based on the fact that there's seven guardians of the globe, and with Omni-Man, that's eight. It worked. But then those fine folks at Image laid down more wisdom and said it probably wasn't a good idea to do a TPB without the title character on the cover. You'd think this is something we wouldn't need to be told... sigh. Anyway, changes were made but now you can see the first version of this trade in all it's glory as well as the design sketch Cory sent in before he drew it. Enjoy!

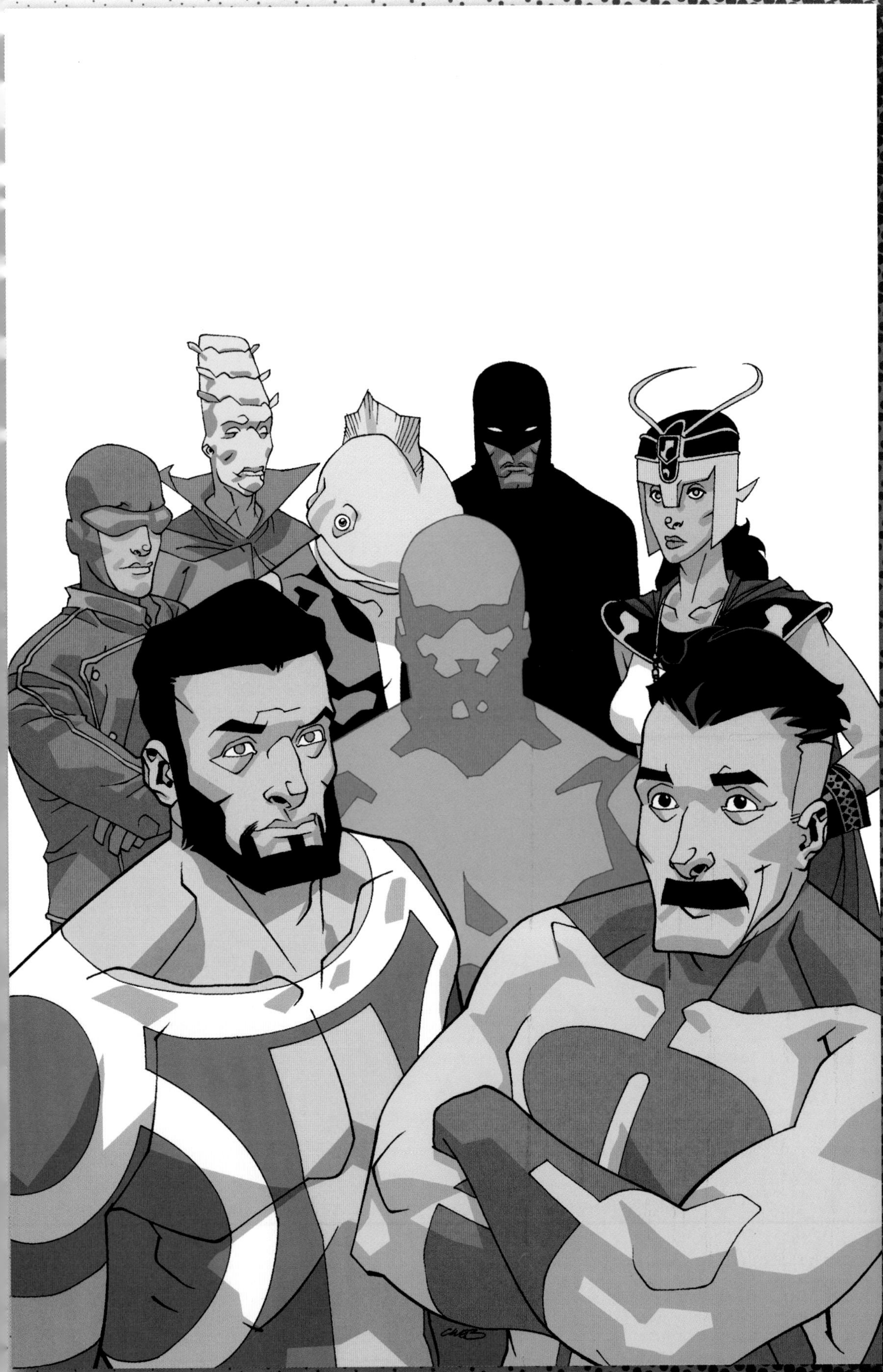

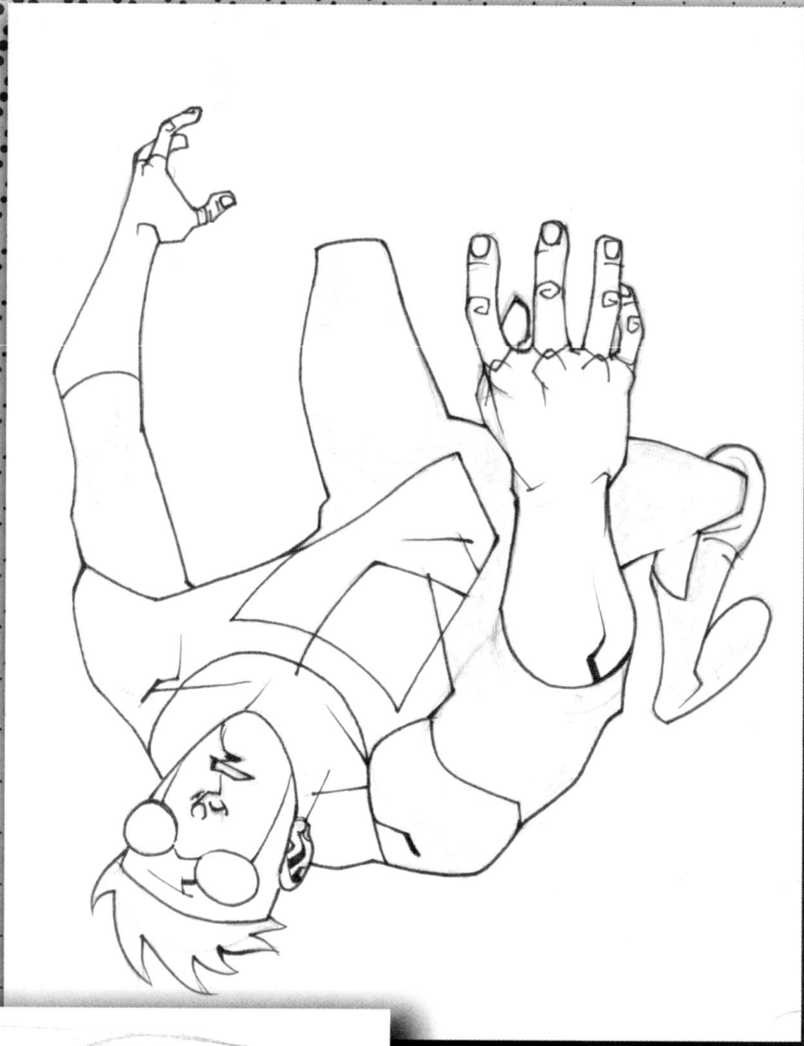

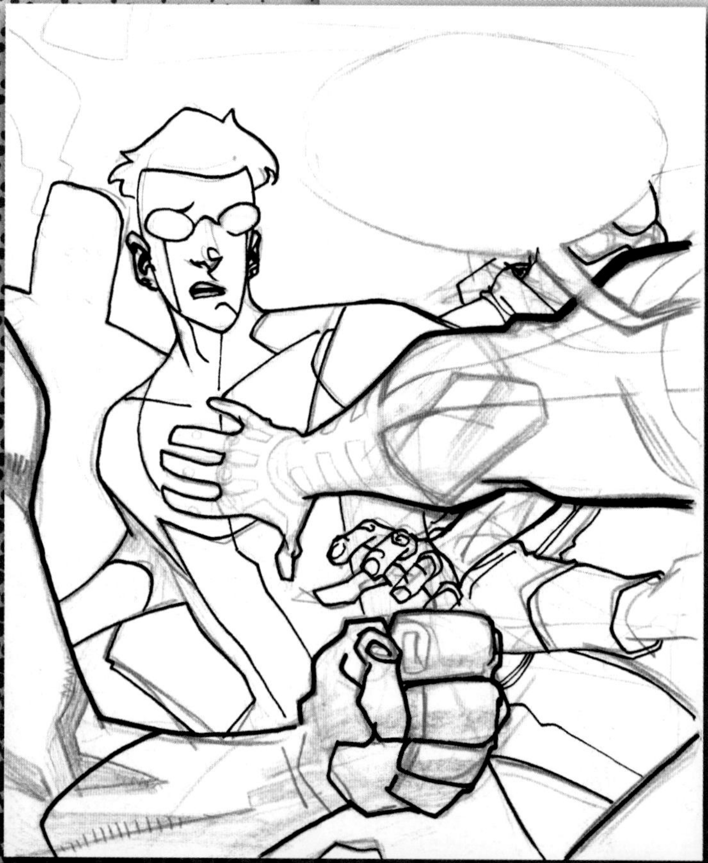

Here are Cory's layouts to the cover to issues 5 and 7. He pretty much nailed these on the first pass. In fact, I think Cory had the idea for the cover to issue 5 before we had decided what was going to be in issue 5. Meaning... he wanted to do Mark floating in space on a cover but had no idea what issue, if any, we could do it on. Accommodating fella that I am... I said: "That's cool, let's use it for the next issue."

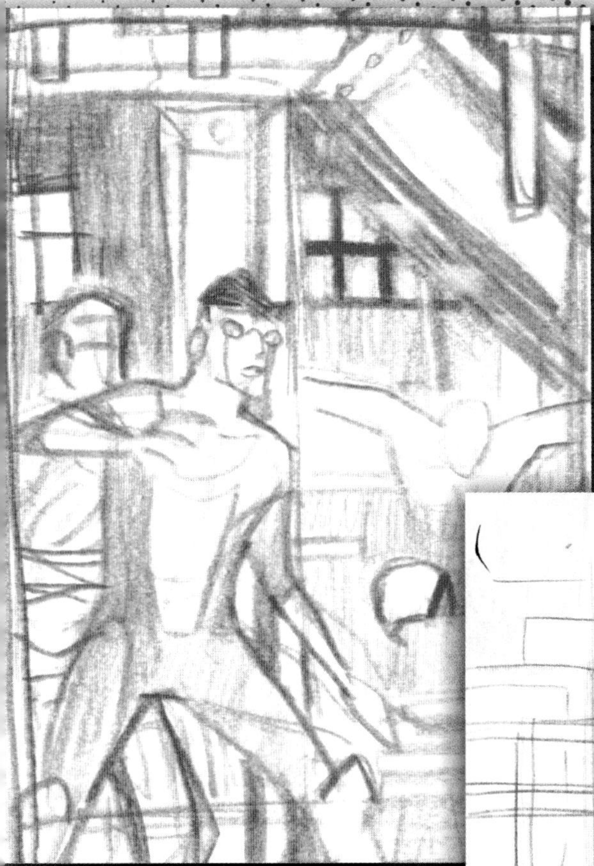

The cover to issue 6 didn't come on the first try but it came pretty easily. For this one I told Cory: "They visit the college in this issue, and they should fight something there... go crazy and I'll work it into the story." That to me is pretty fun, figuring stuff out based on a cover. Now, having read issue 6 you may think "He didn't come up with diddly squat! He never explained anything!" Well... trust me... we'll be coming back to that eventually, so stay tuned. Also on this page is Cory's shadow guide for the cover. Cory likes to map out where the shadows are for Bill. I think they always look cool and figured it be fun to share just this once.

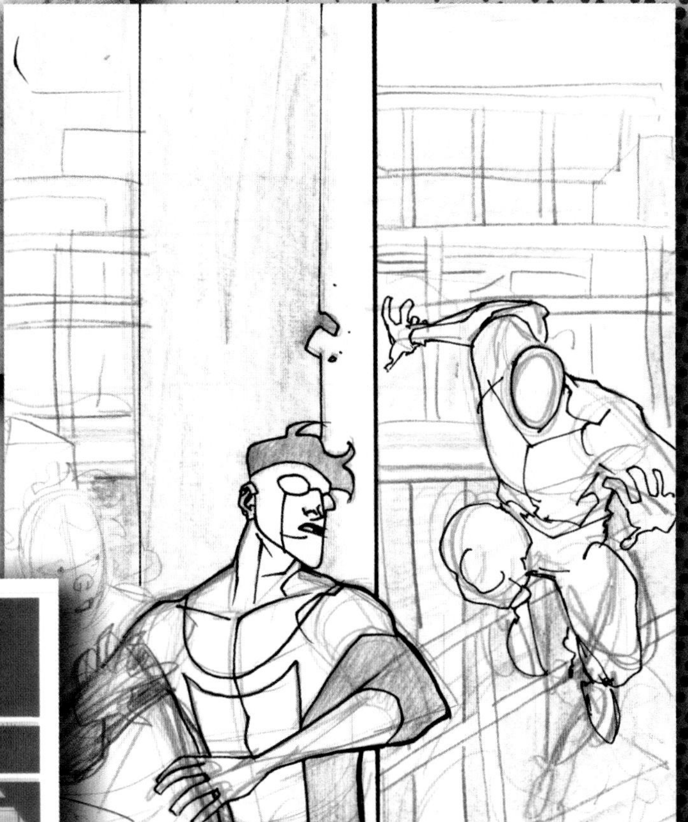

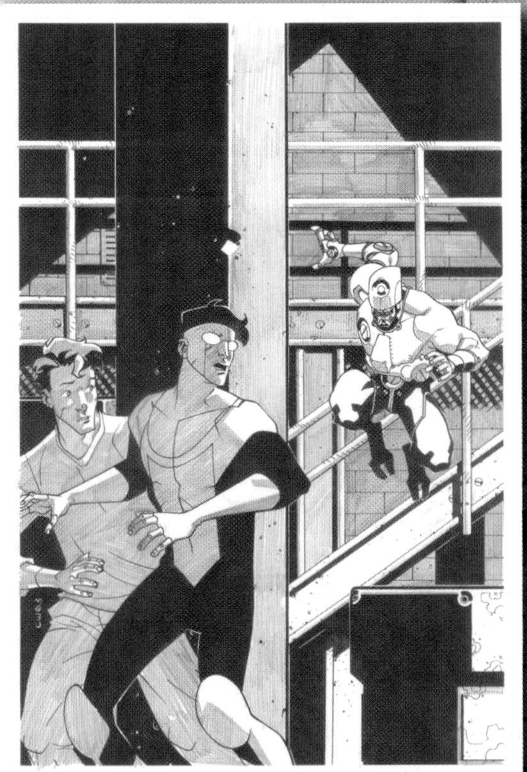

The cover to issue 8 wasn't quite as easy to nail down. Must have been all those cameos that threw him.

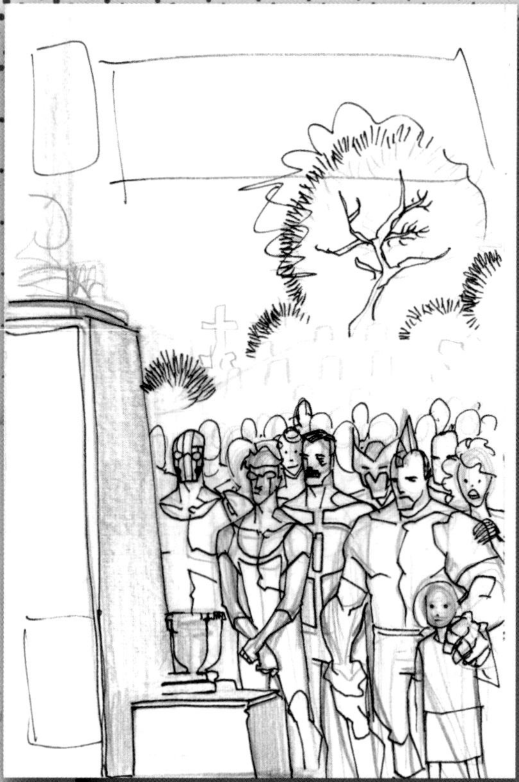

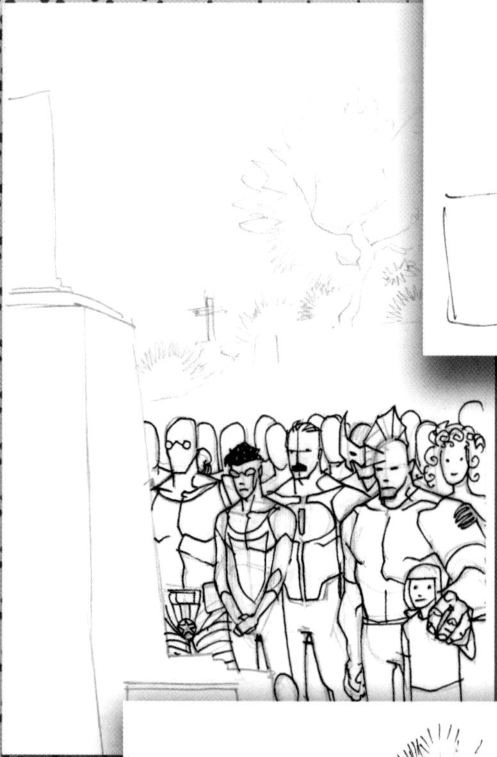

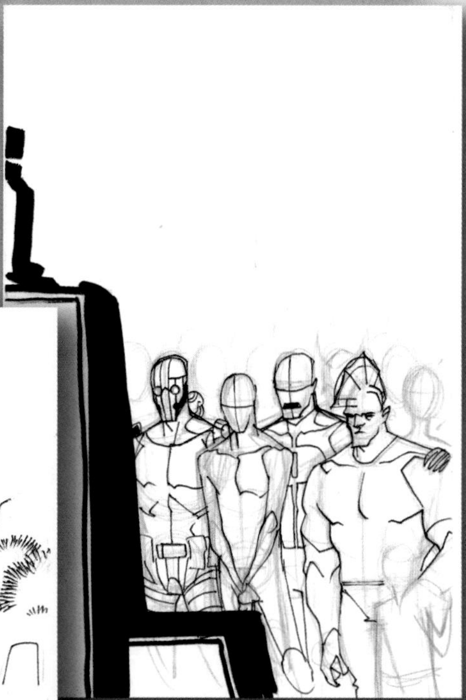

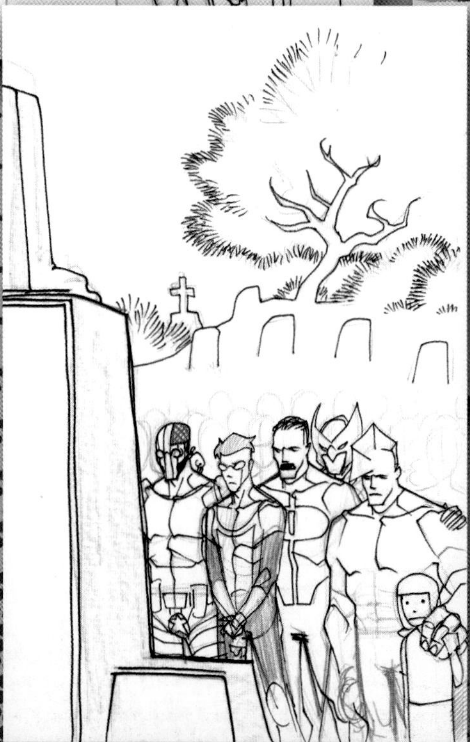

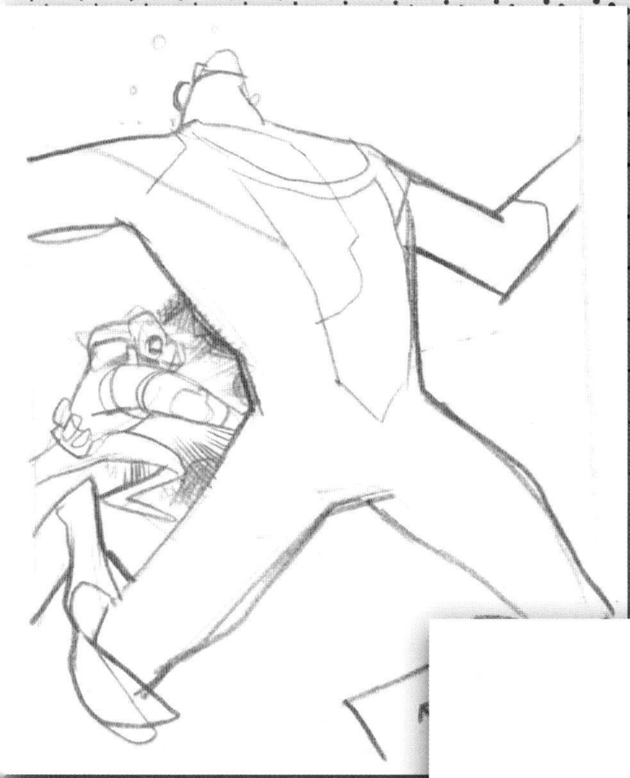

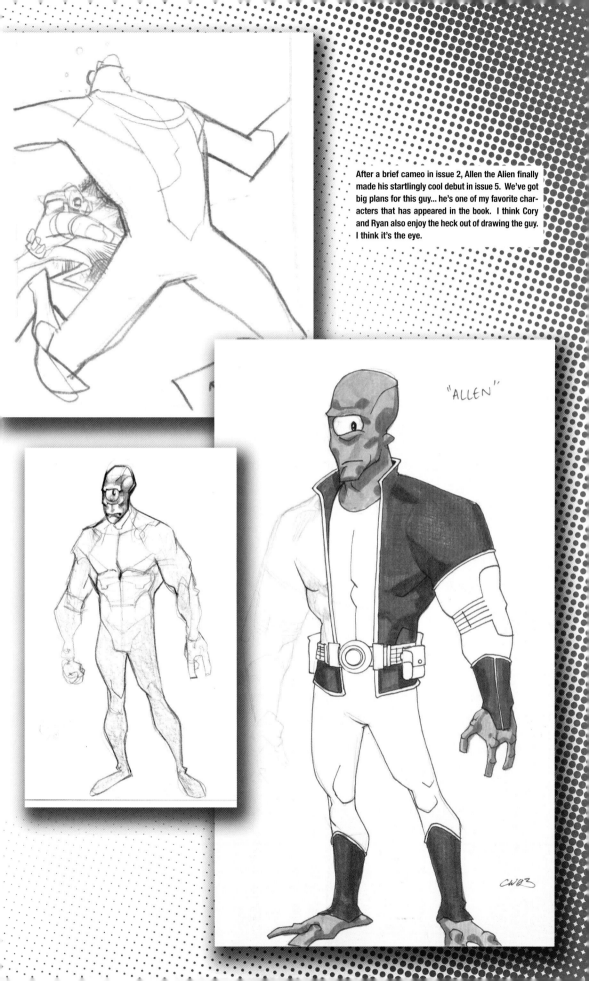

After a brief cameo in issue 2, Allen the Alien finally made his startlingly cool debut in issue 5. We've got big plans for this guy... he's one of my favorite characters that has appeared in the book. I think Cory and Ryan also enjoy the heck out of drawing the guy. I think it's the eye.

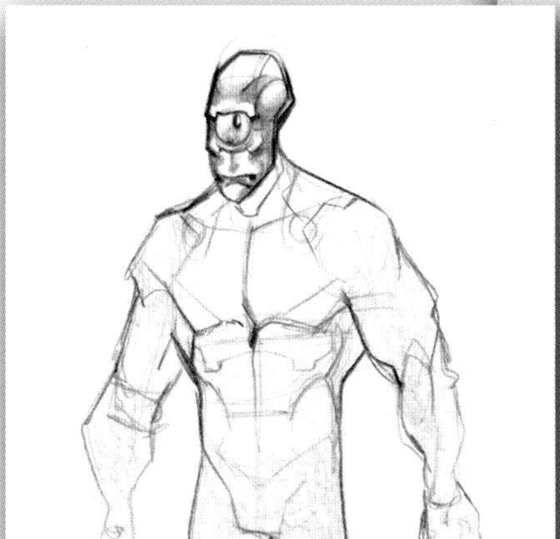

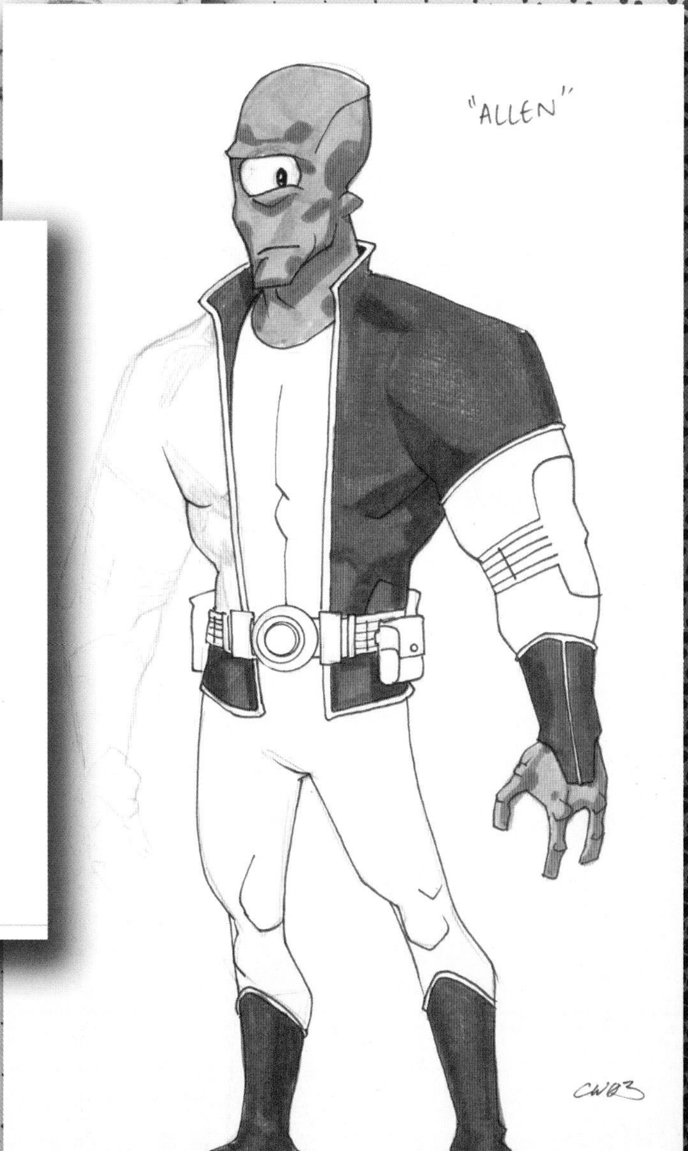
"ALLEN"

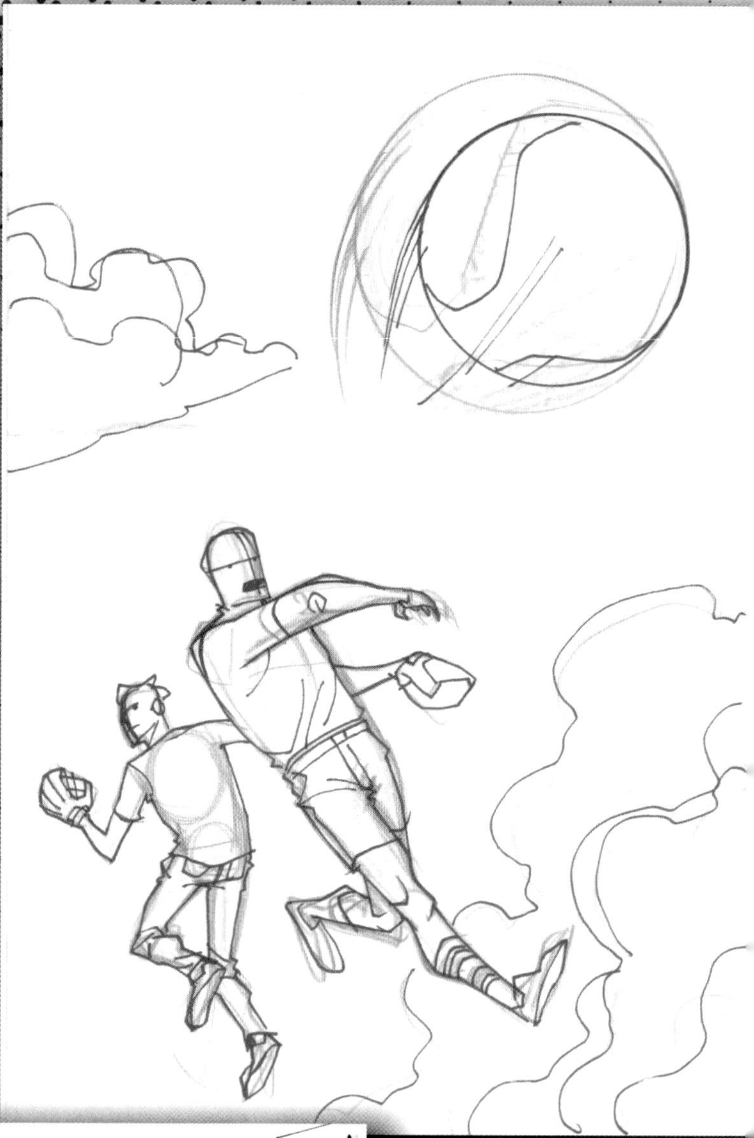

Here are some rough layouts for pages from issue 6. You'll notice that Cory eventually decided the college panel would look better without a background... the slacker.

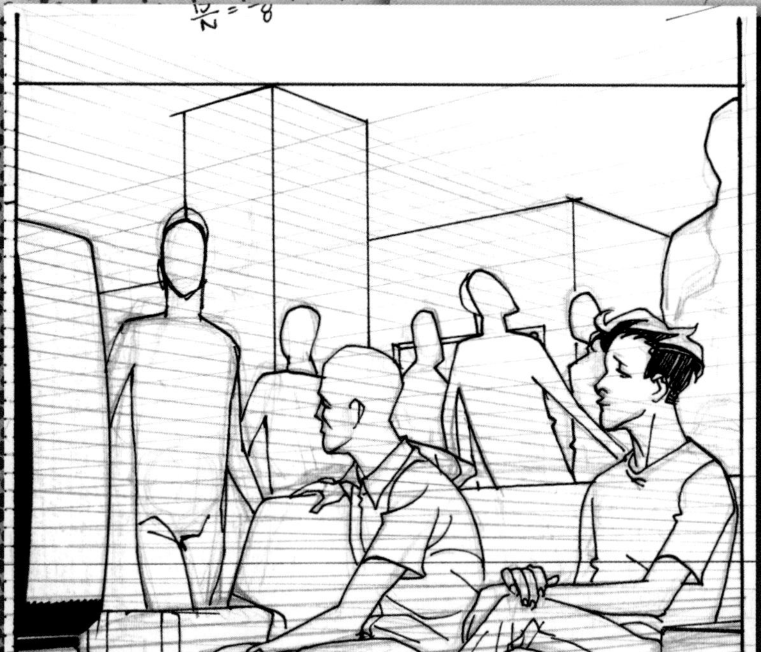

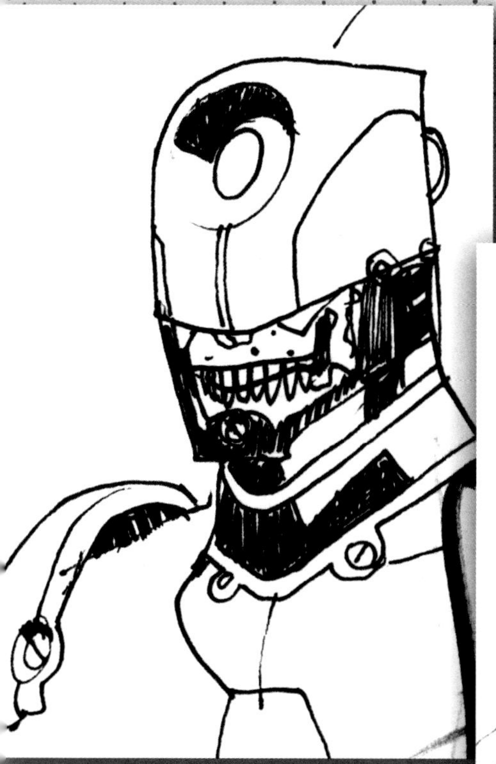

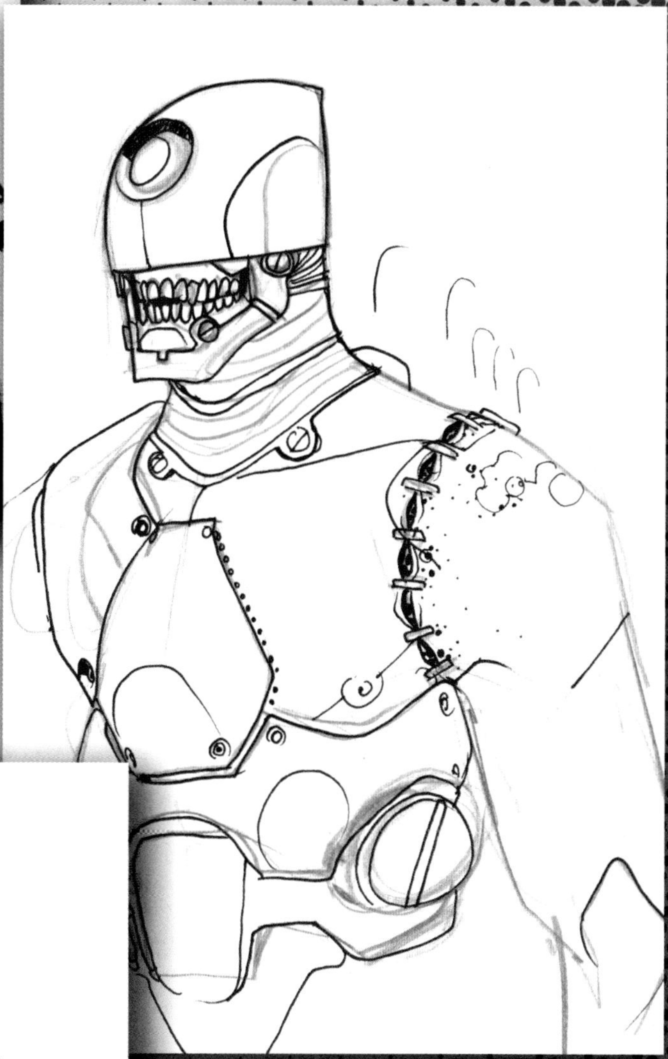

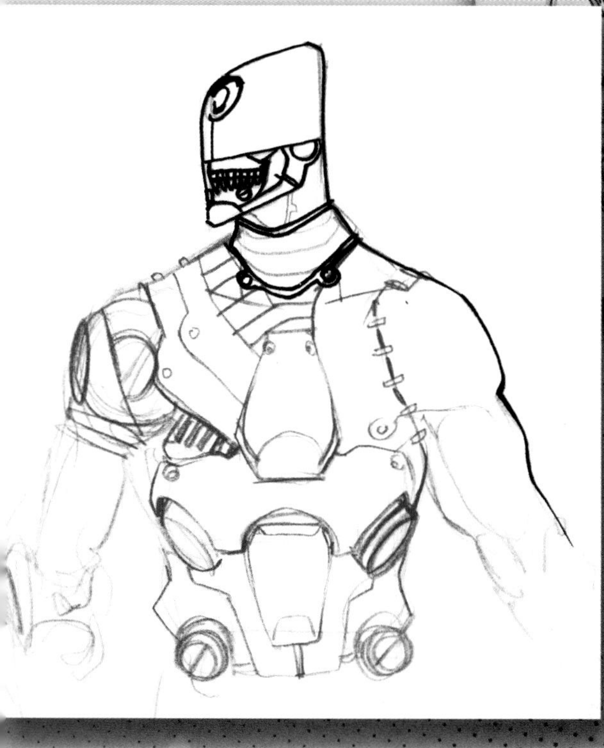

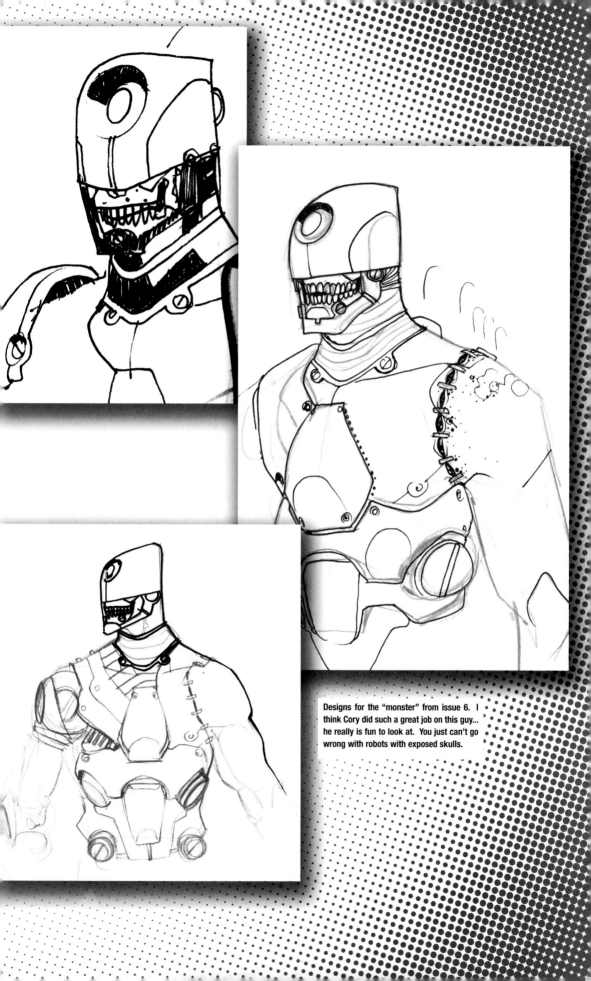

Designs for the “monster” from issue 6. I think Cory did such a great job on this guy... he really is fun to look at. You just can’t go wrong with robots with exposed skulls.

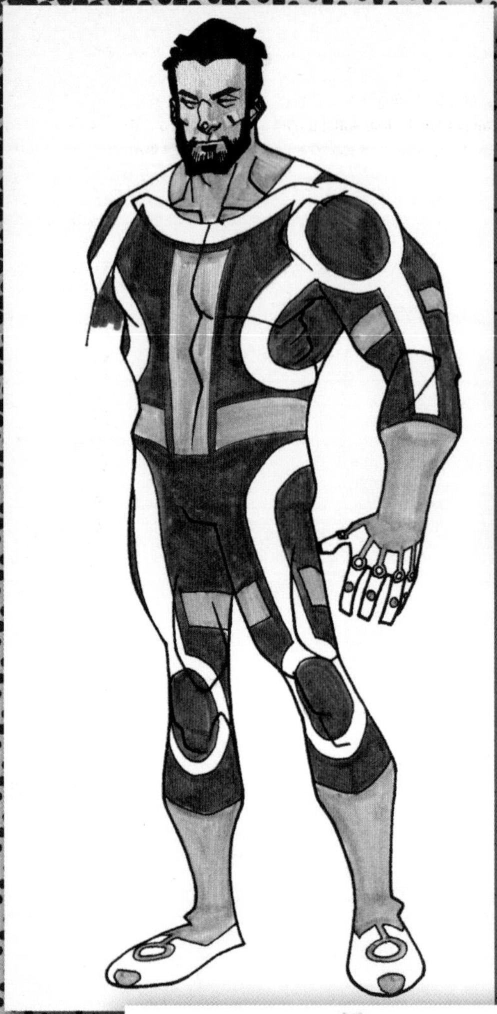

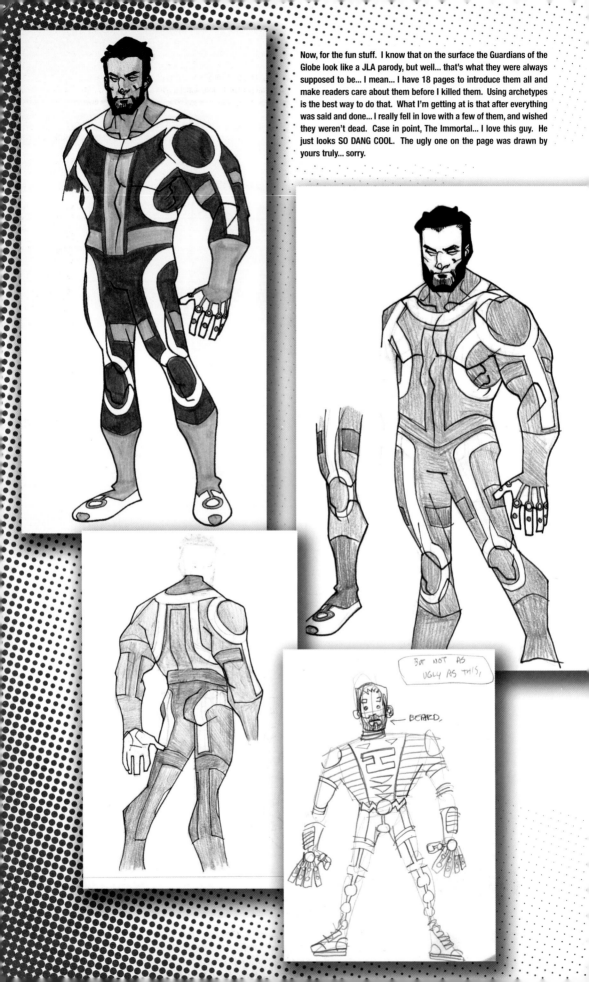

Now, for the fun stuff. I know that on the surface the Guardians of the Globe look like a JLA parody, but well... that's what they were always supposed to be... I mean... I have 18 pages to introduce them all and make readers care about them before I killed them. Using archetypes is the best way to do that. What I'm getting at is that after everything was said and done... I really fell in love with a few of them, and wished they weren't dead. Case in point, The Immortal... I love this guy. He just looks SO DANG COOL. The ugly one on the page was drawn by yours truly... sorry.

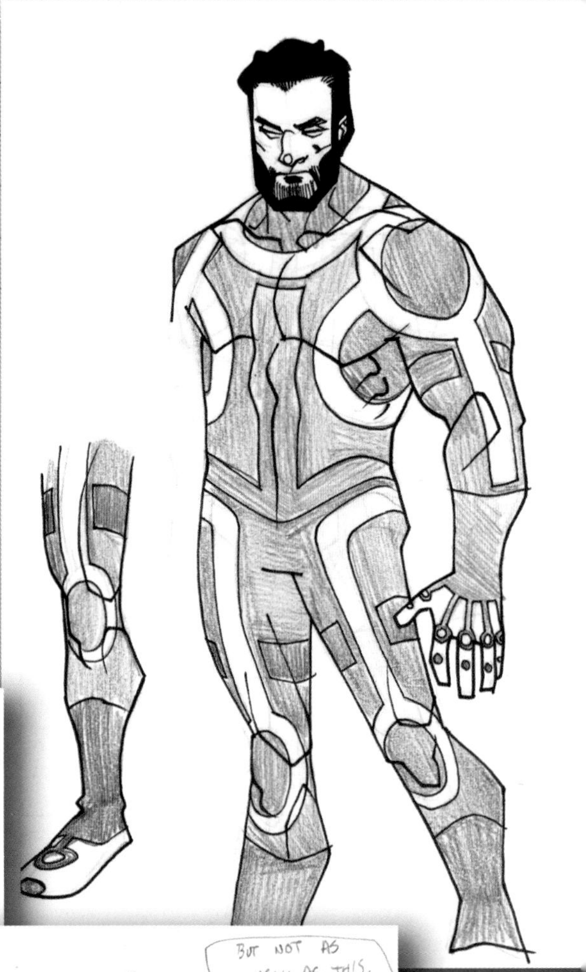

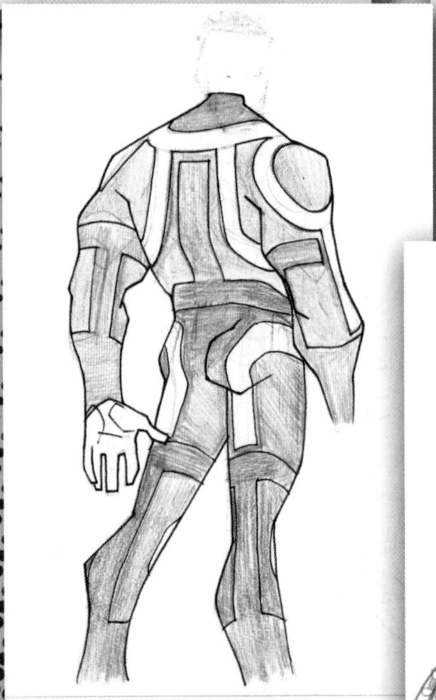

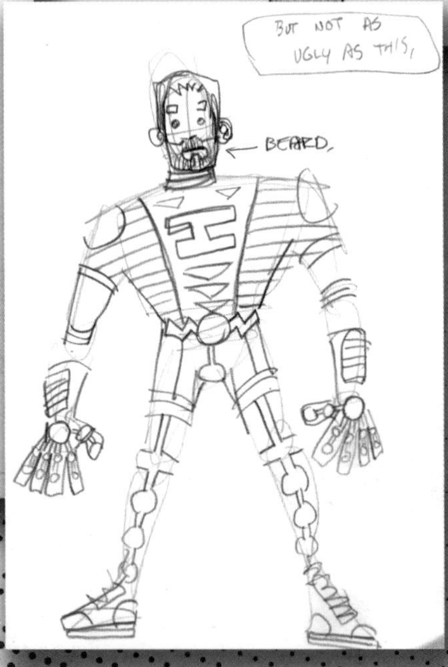
BUT NOT AS
UGLY AS THIS,
BEARD,

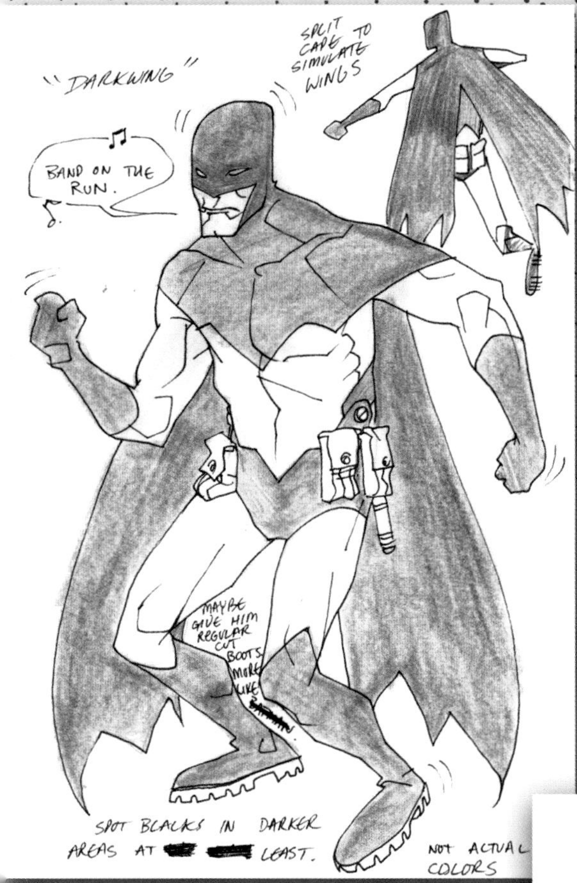
"DARKWING"
SPLIT CAPE TO SIMULATE WINGS
BAND ON THE RUN.
MAYBE GIVE HIM REGULAR CUT BOOTS MORE LIKE [redacted]
SPOT BLACKS IN DARKER AREAS AT [redacted] LEAST.
NOT ACTUAL COLORS

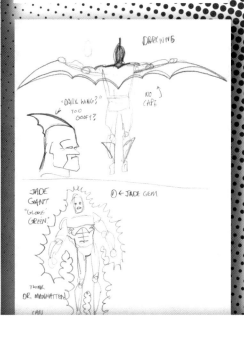

I kinda like Darkwing too. I'm so glad Cory didn't put the wing on his head... talk about stupid design. There's a little bit of Green Ghost action on the page too, but it's little.

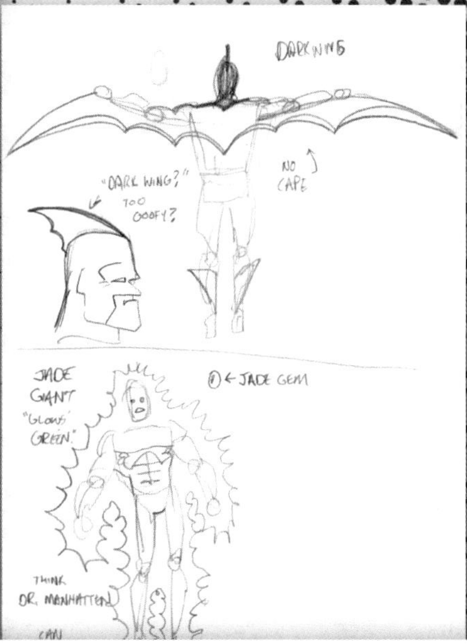
DARKWING
"DARK WING?" TOO GOOFY?
NO CAPE
JADE GIANT
← JADE GEM
"GLOWS" GREEN.
THINK DR. MANHATTEN
CAN

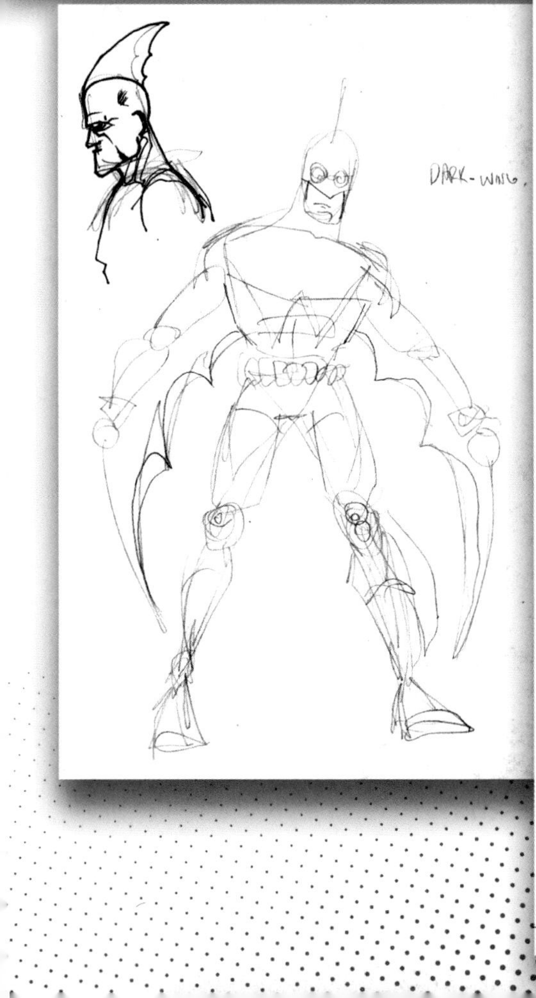
DARK-WING.

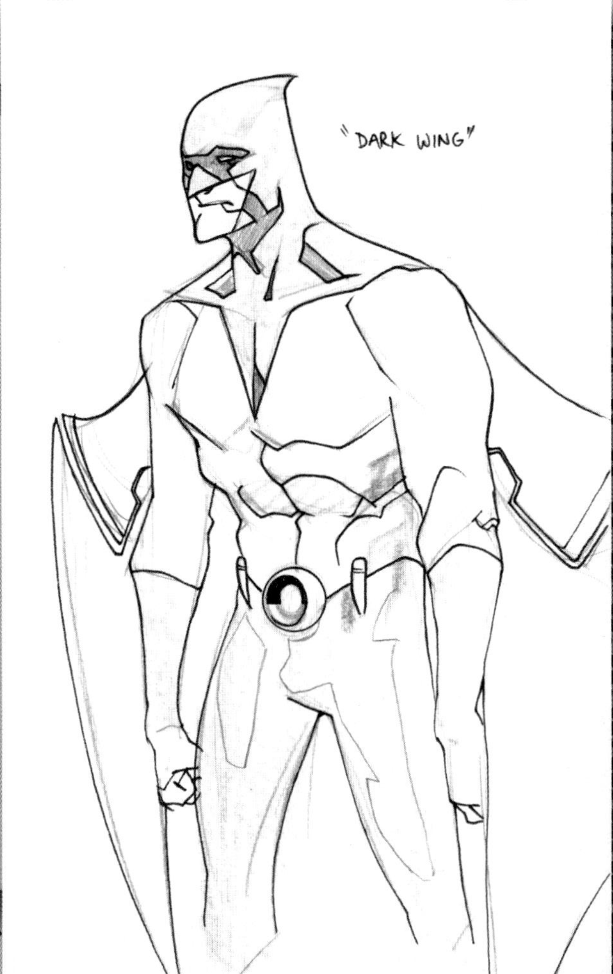
"DARK WING"

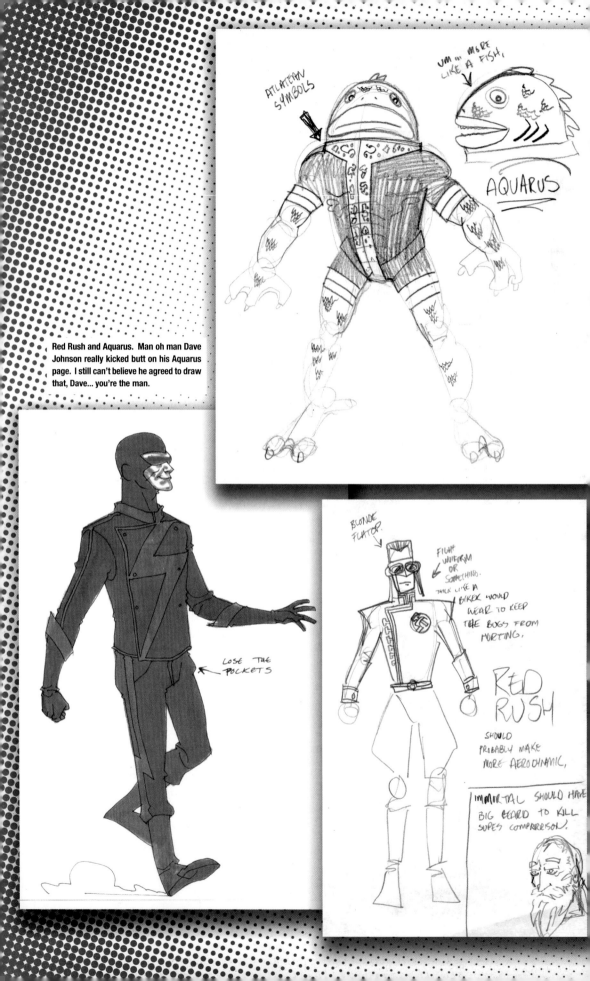

Red Rush and Aquarus. Man oh man Dave Johnson really kicked butt on his Aquarus page. I still can't believe he agreed to draw that, Dave... you're the man.

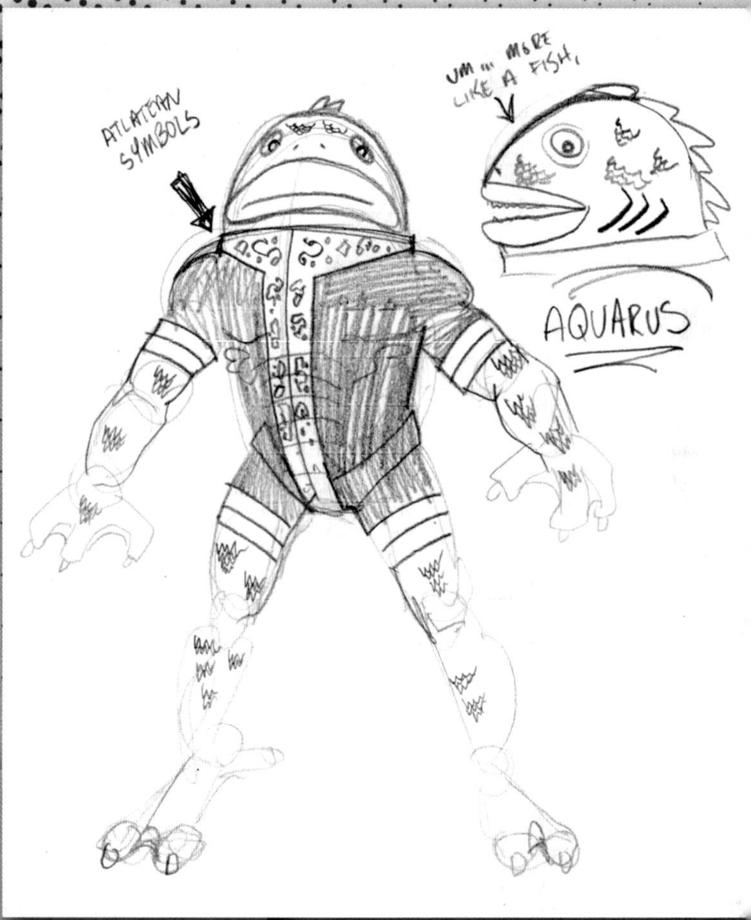

ATLANTIAN SYMBOLS
UM... MORE LIKE A FISH,
AQUARUS

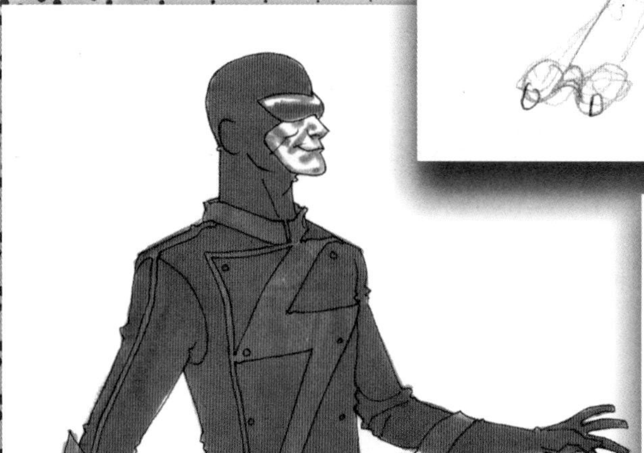

LOSE THE POCKETS

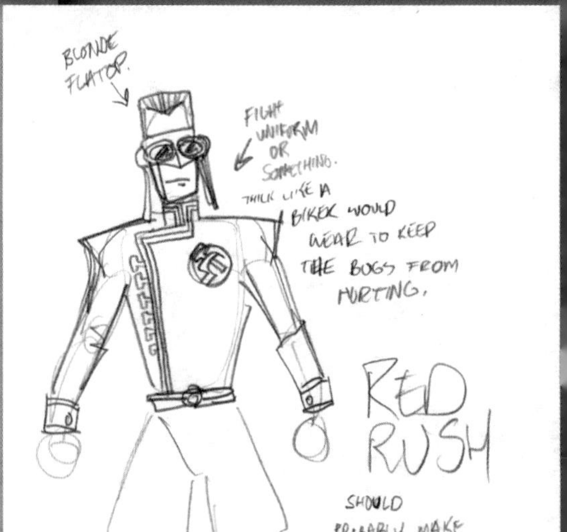

BLONDE FLATOP.
FLIGHT UNIFORM OR SOMETHING.
THINK LIKE A BIKER WOULD WEAR TO KEEP THE BUGS FROM HURTING,
RED RUSH
SHOULD PROBABLY MAKE MORE AERODYNAMIC,
IMMORTAL SHOULD HAVE BIG BEARD TO KILL SUPES COMPARRISON.

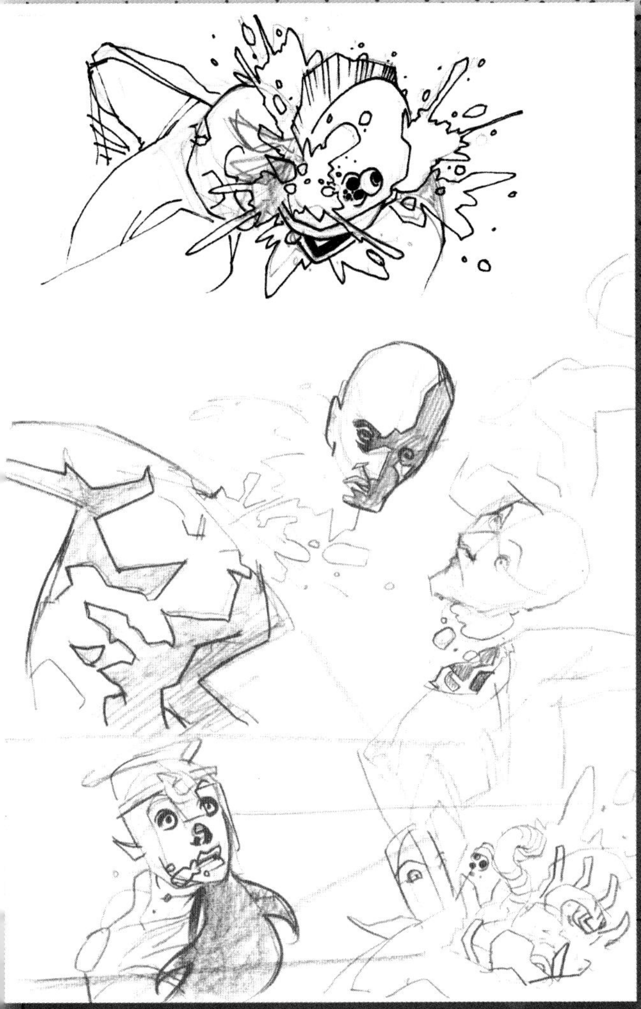

Some sketches from issue 7. I was really worried that the kill scenes in issue 7 would piss people off. Up to that point the book had been pretty much all ages. I wanted the scenes to be graphic so that they would stand out, and then when the page came in from Cory... well... it was graphic. Good stuff all around, Cory draws organs pretty well.

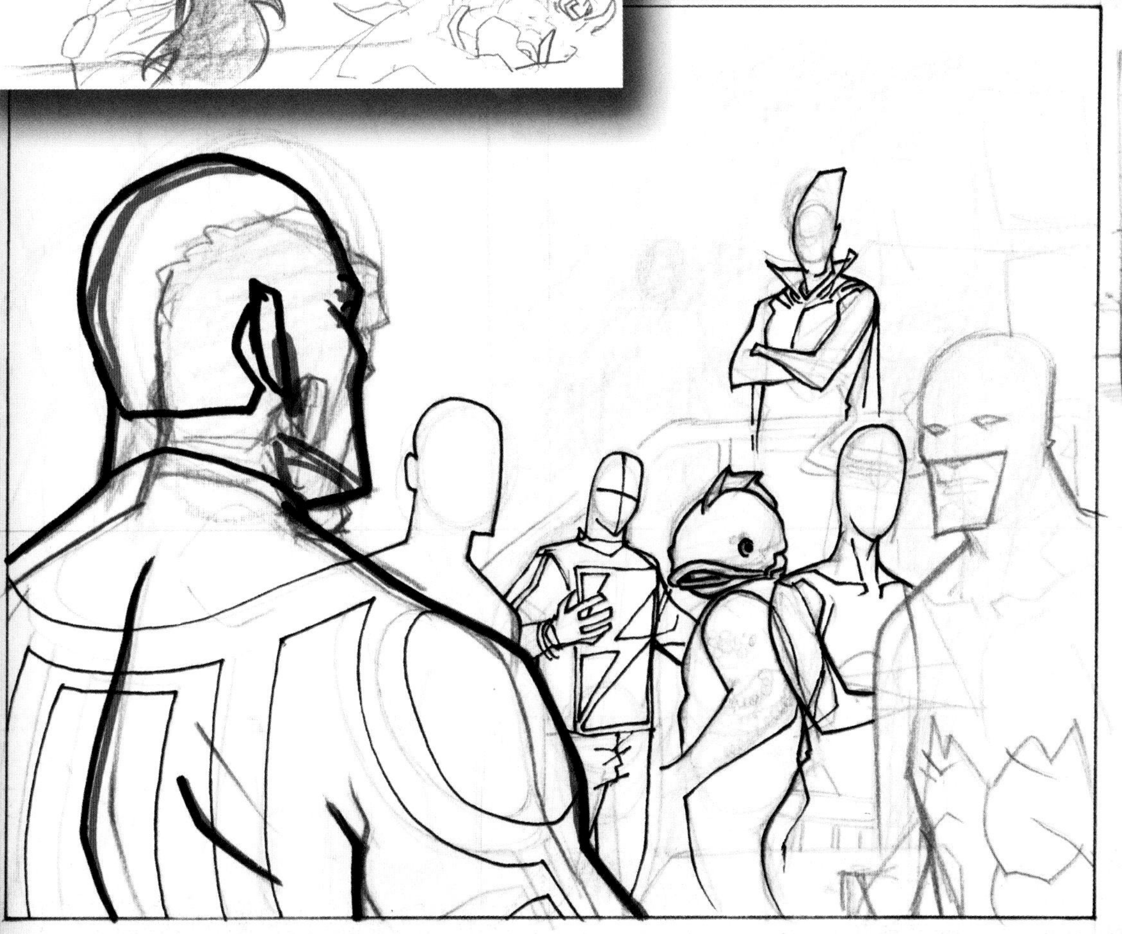

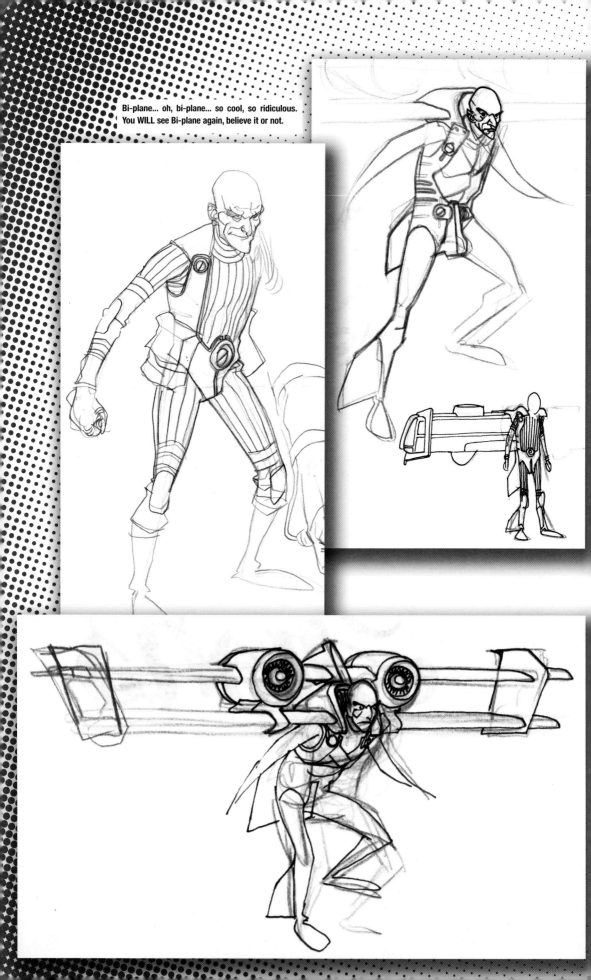

Bi-plane... oh, bi-plane... so cool, so ridiculous. You WILL see Bi-plane again, believe it or not.

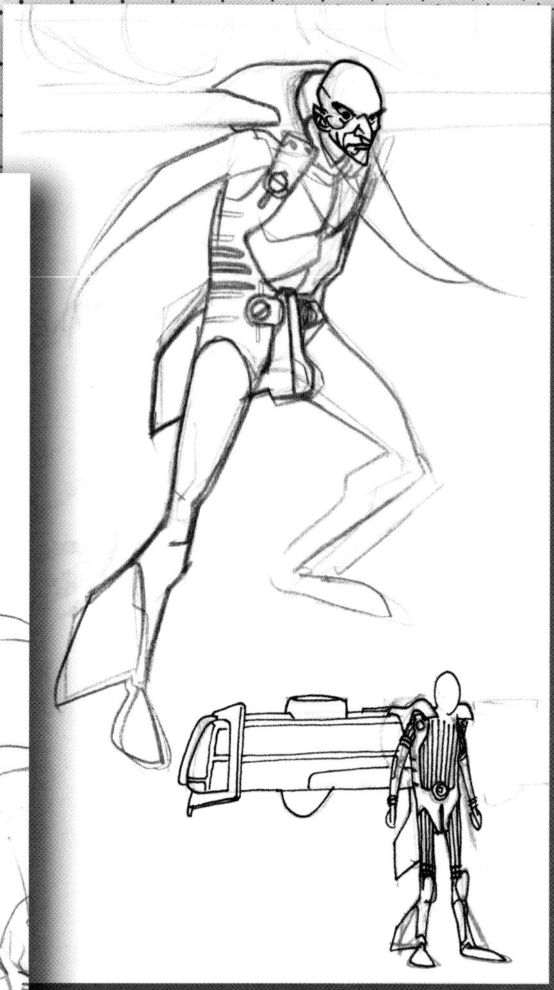

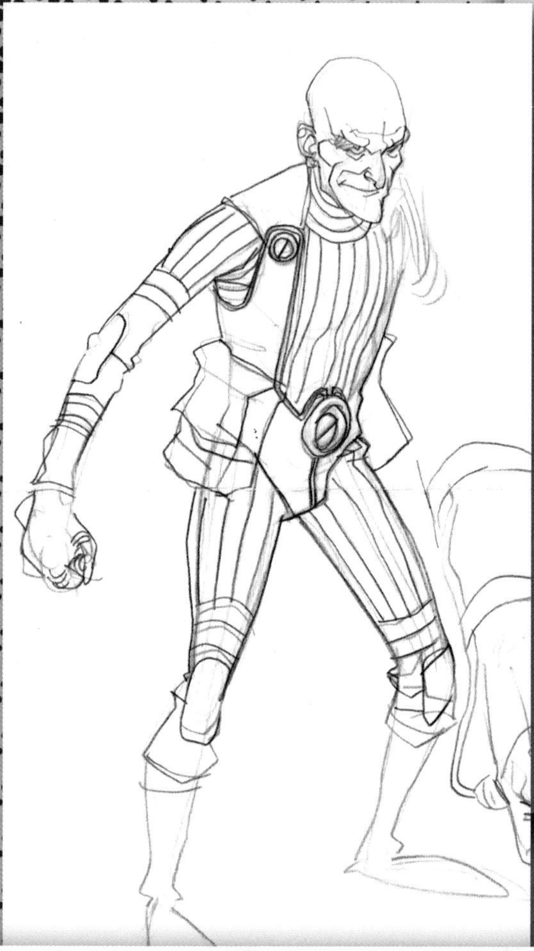

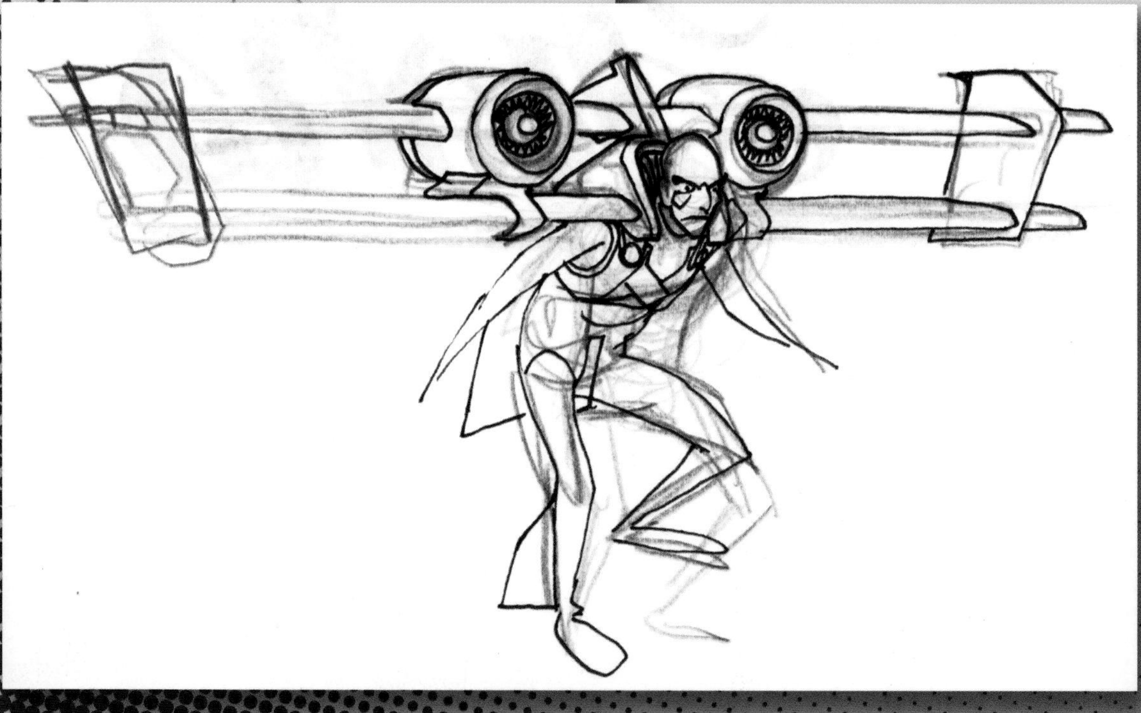

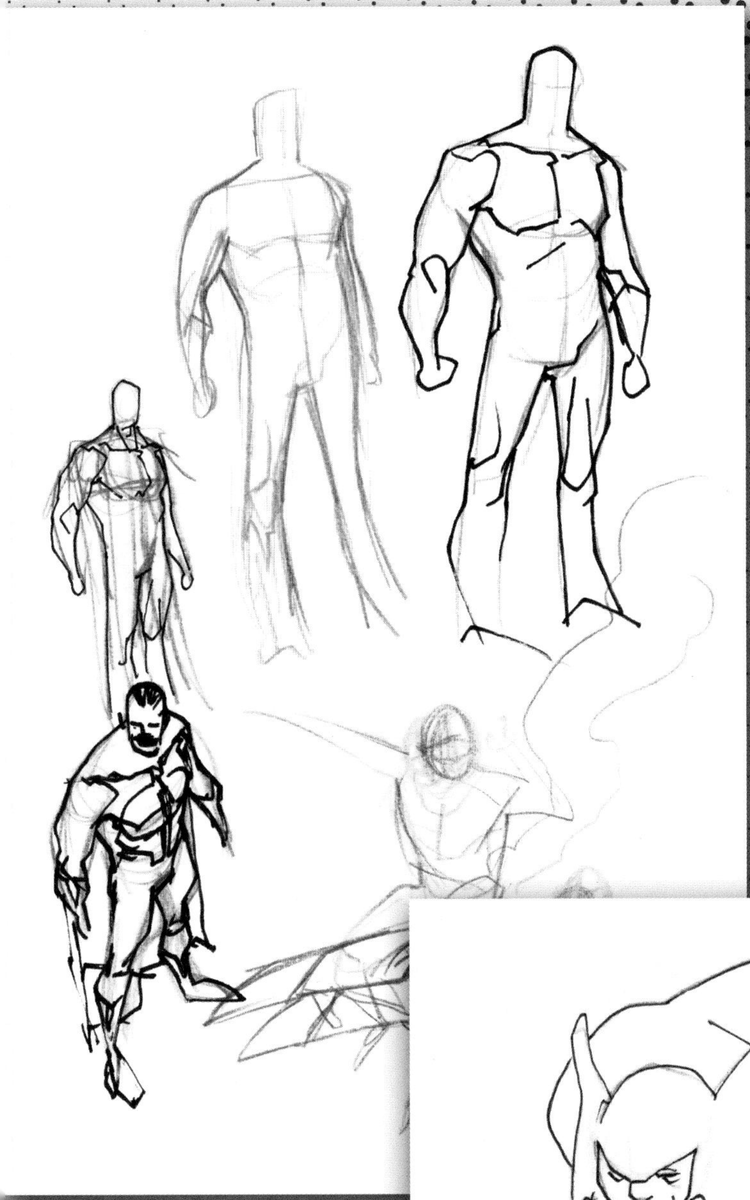

The Elephant is all Cory's fault. Blame him.
I had NOTHING to do with that guy.

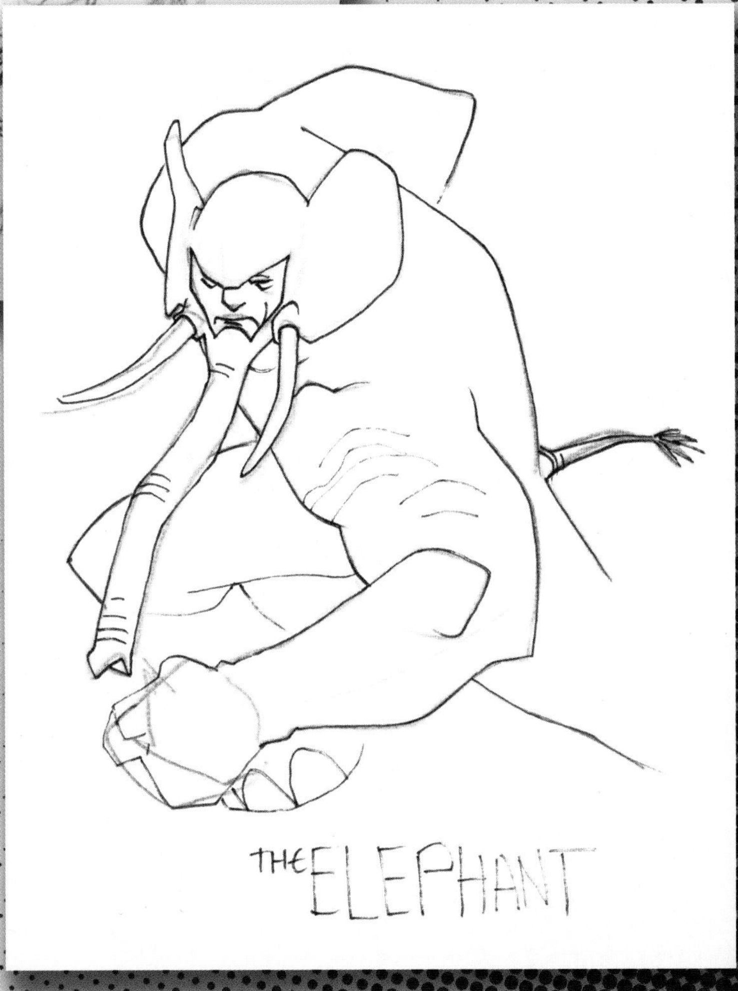
THE ELEPHANT

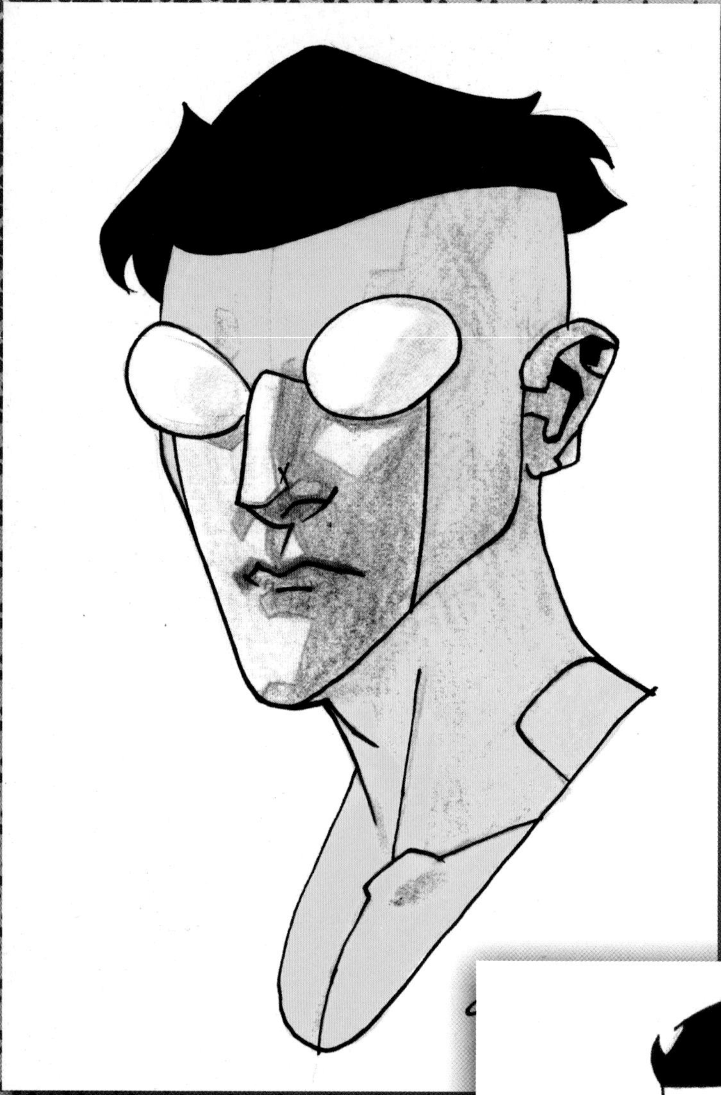

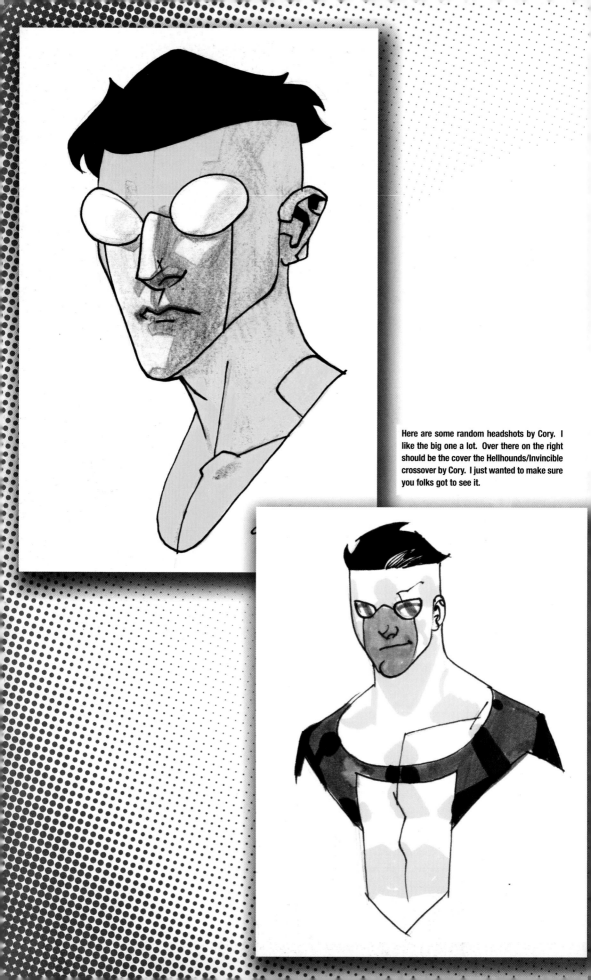

Here are some random headshots by Cory. I like the big one a lot. Over there on the right should be the cover the Hellhounds/Invincible crossover by Cory. I just wanted to make sure you folks got to see it.

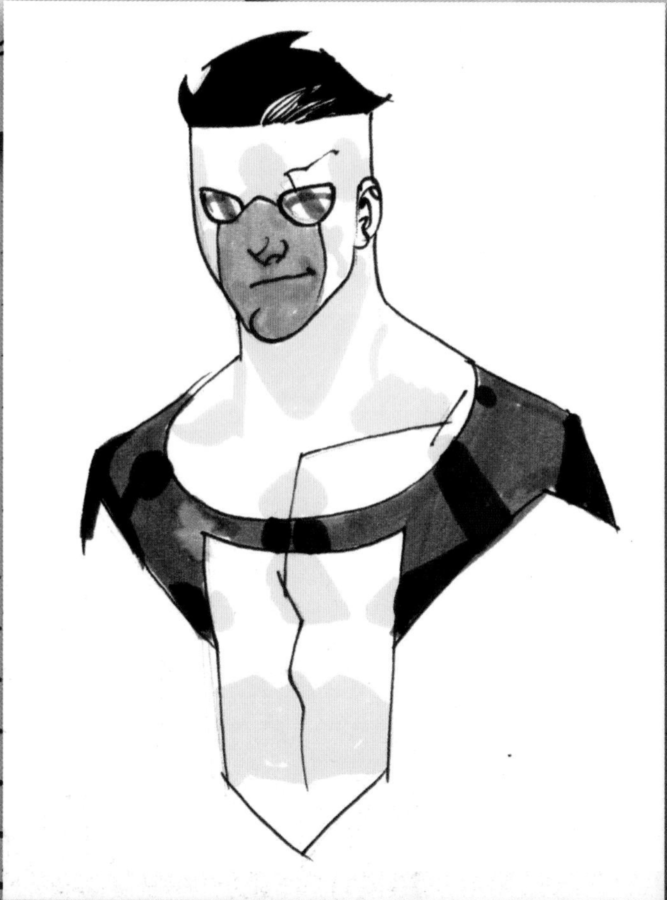

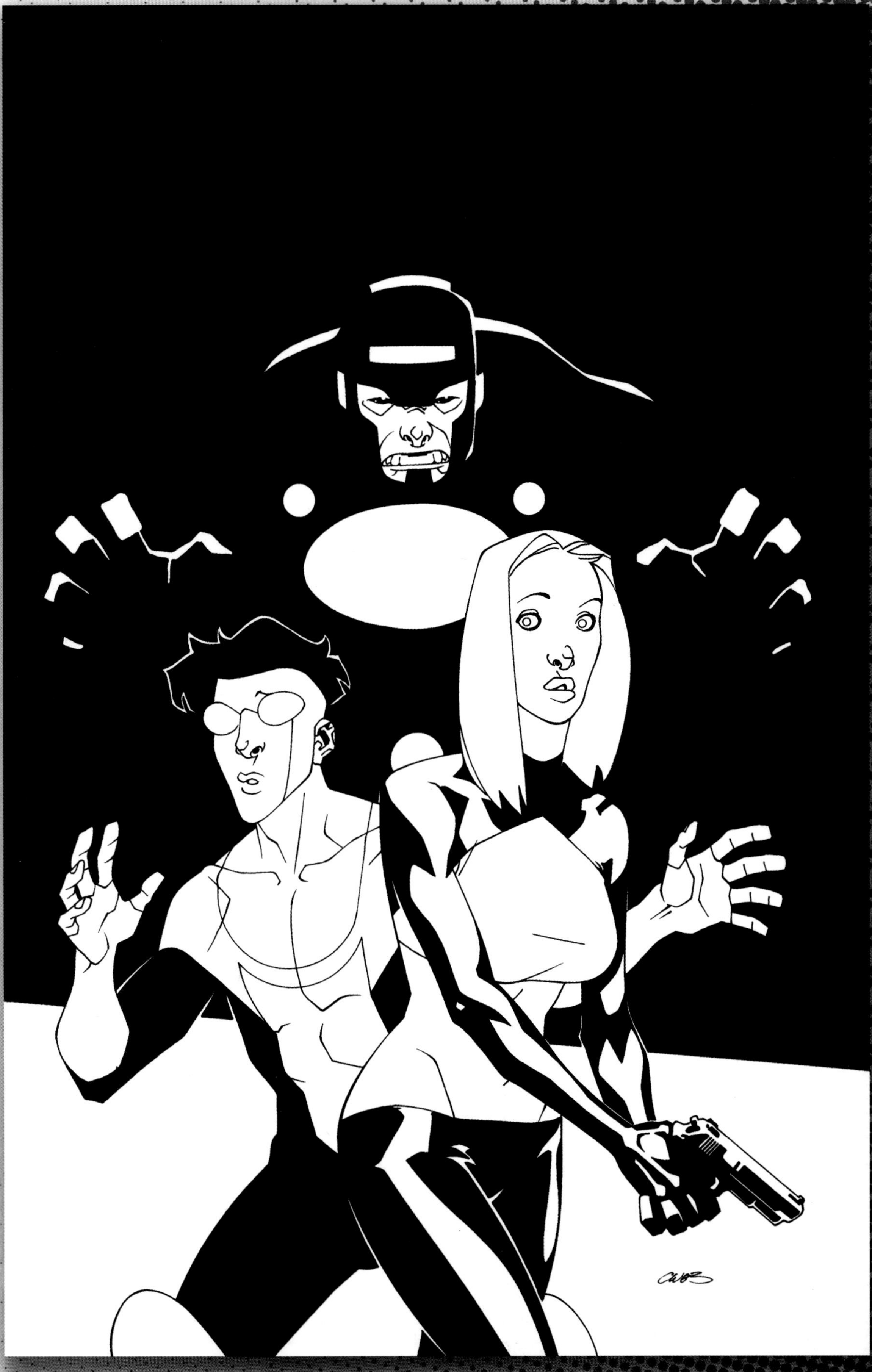

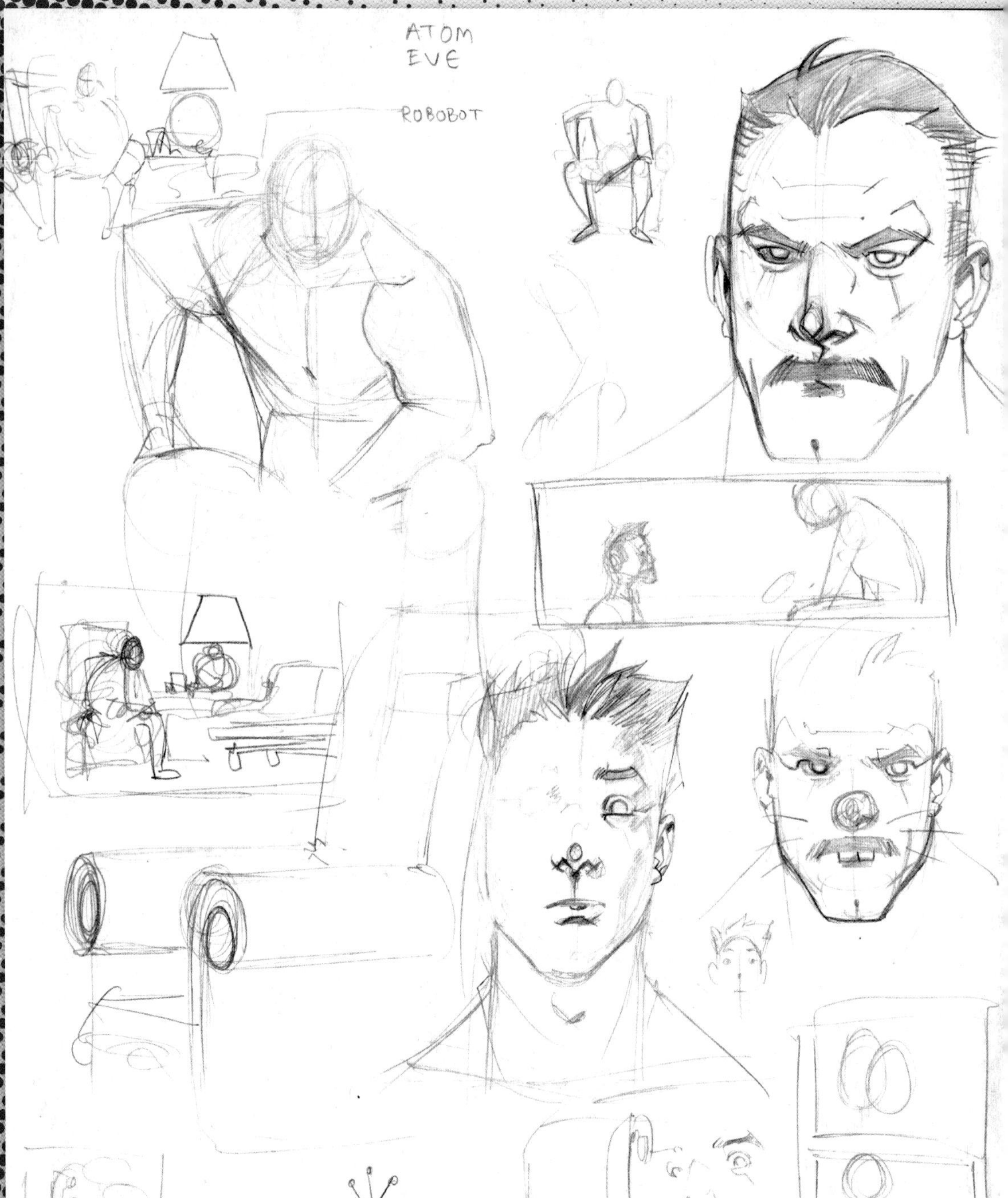
ATOM
EVE
ROBOBOT

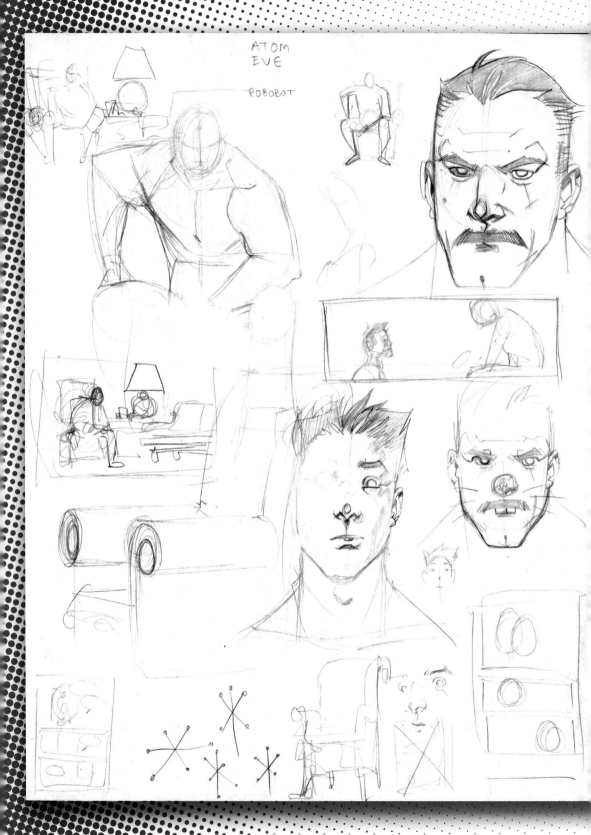

On this page are some early sketches I probably should have run in the first TPB. Sue me. On the opposite page here you should see some cool designs for robots and stuff. I like it when Cory goes crazy with the marker... neat stuff, I'm sure you'll agree. If not. Sue me.

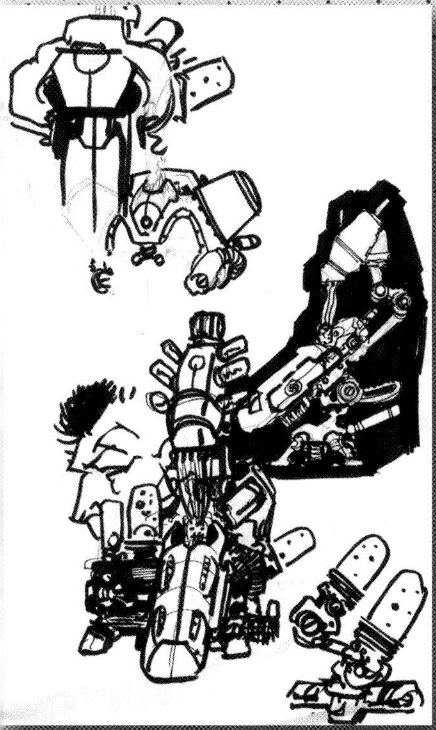
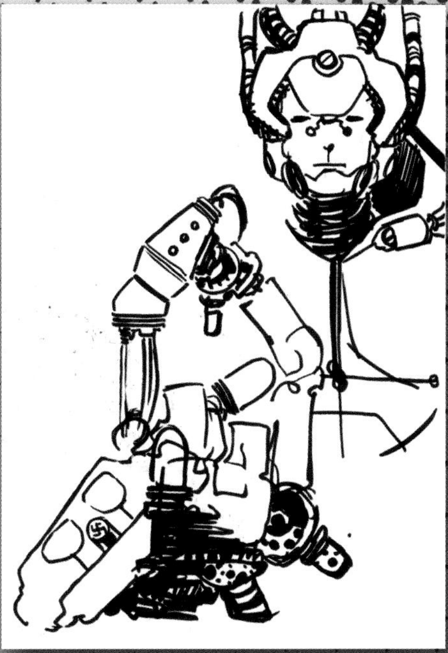
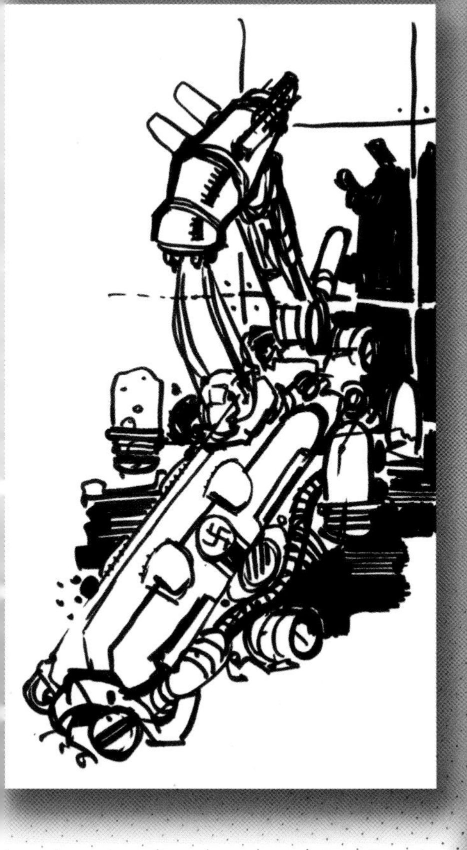
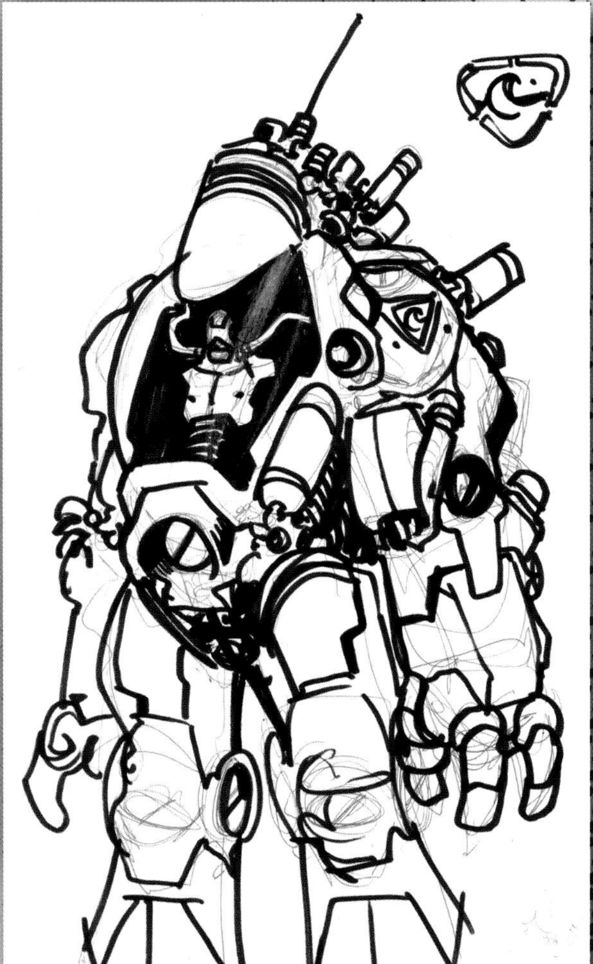

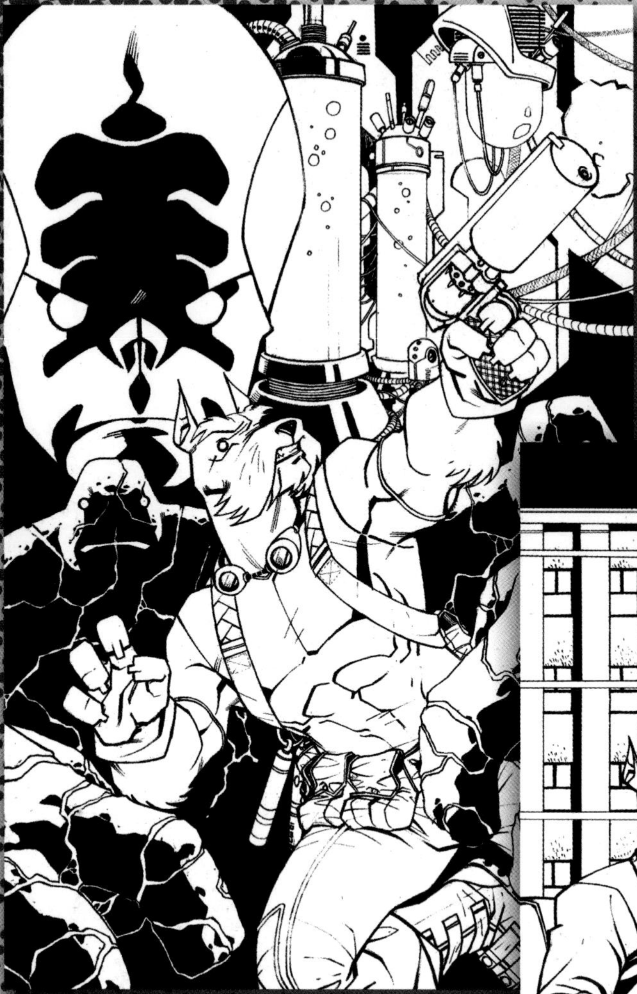

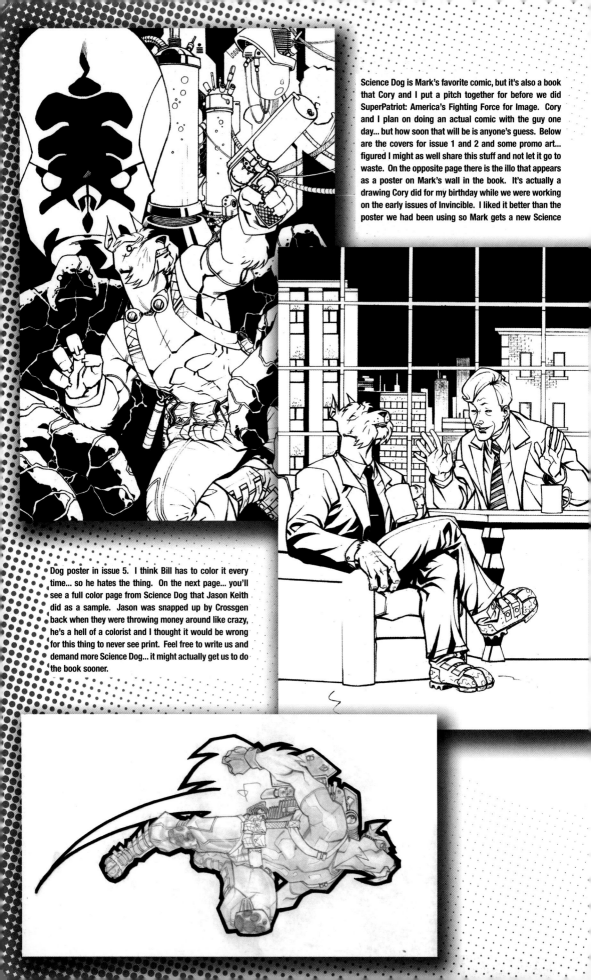

Science Dog is Mark's favorite comic, but it's also a book that Cory and I put a pitch together for before we did SuperPatriot: America's Fighting Force for Image. Cory and I plan on doing an actual comic with the guy one day... but how soon that will be is anyone's guess. Below are the covers for issue 1 and 2 and some promo art... figured I might as well share this stuff and not let it go to waste. On the opposite page there is the illo that appears as a poster on Mark's wall in the book. It's actually a drawing Cory did for my birthday while we were working on the early issues of Invincible. I liked it better than the poster we had been using so Mark gets a new Science

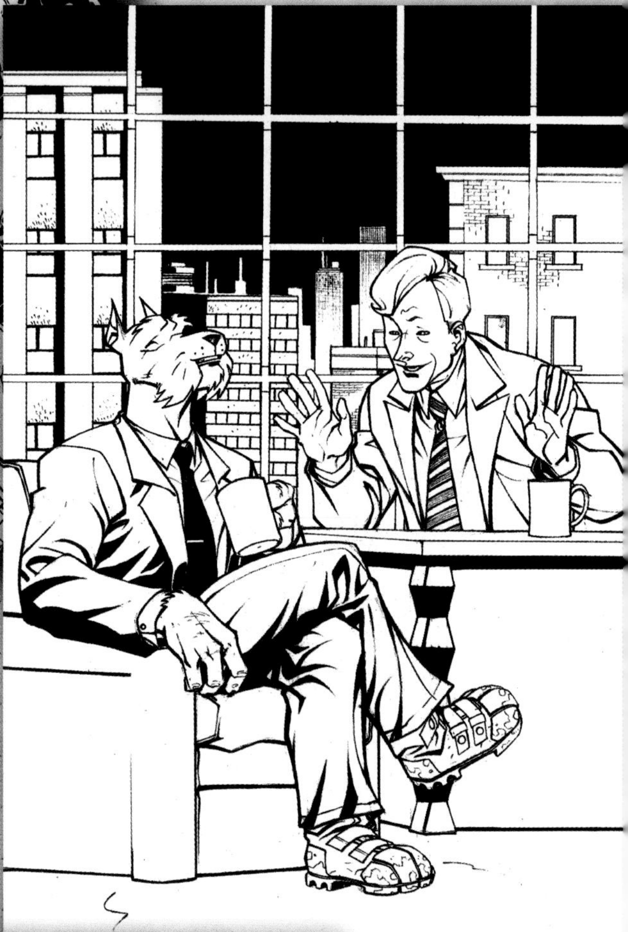

Dog poster in issue 5. I think Bill has to color it every time... so he hates the thing. On the next page... you'll see a full color page from Science Dog that Jason Keith did as a sample. Jason was snapped up by Crossgen back when they were throwing money around like crazy, he's a hell of a colorist and I thought it would be wrong for this thing to never see print. Feel free to write us and demand more Science Dog... it might actually get us to do the book sooner.

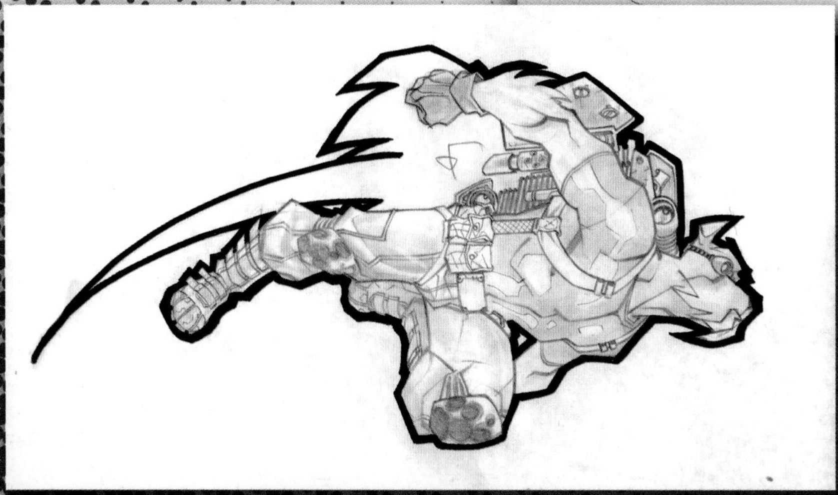

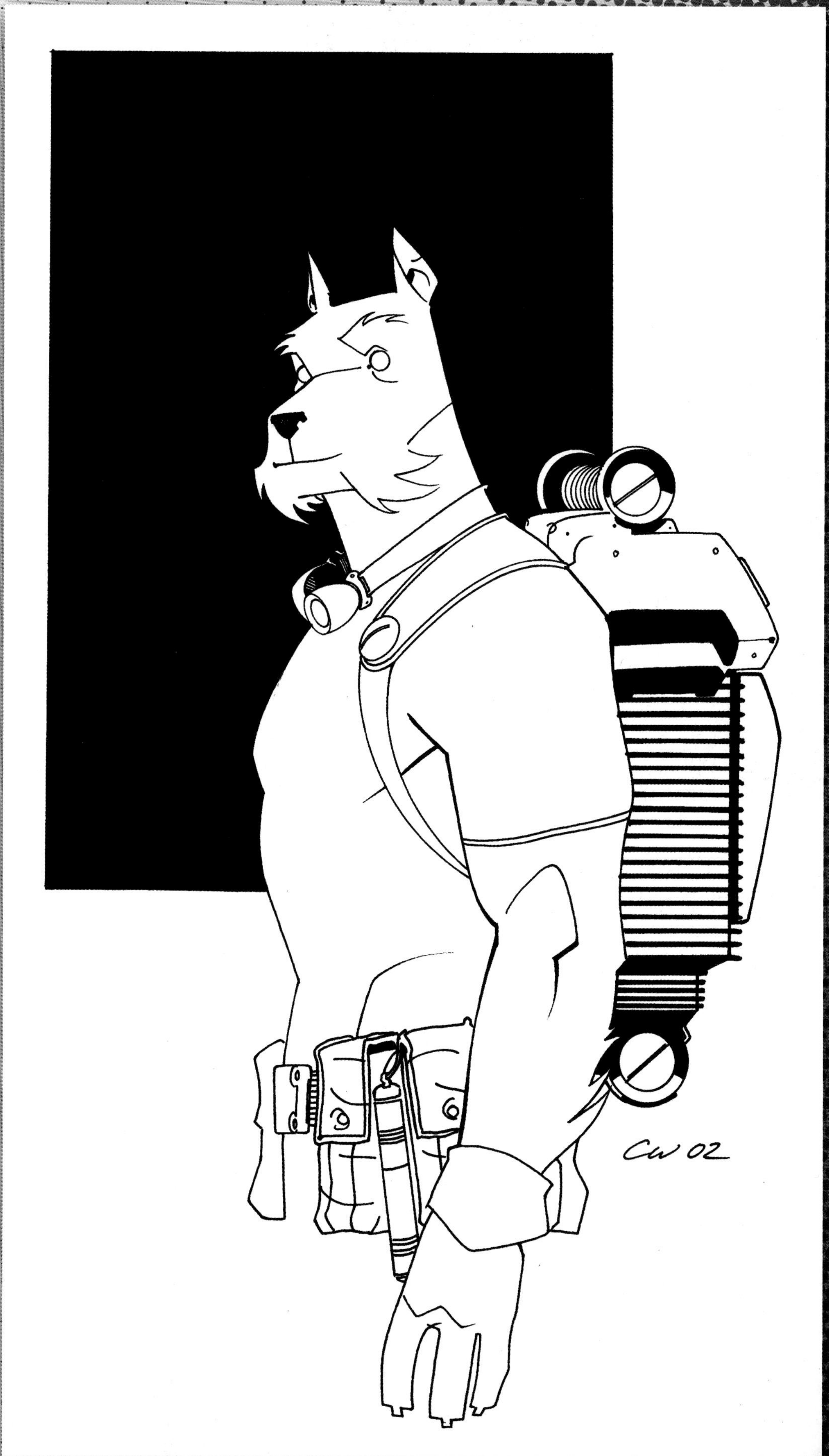
CW 02

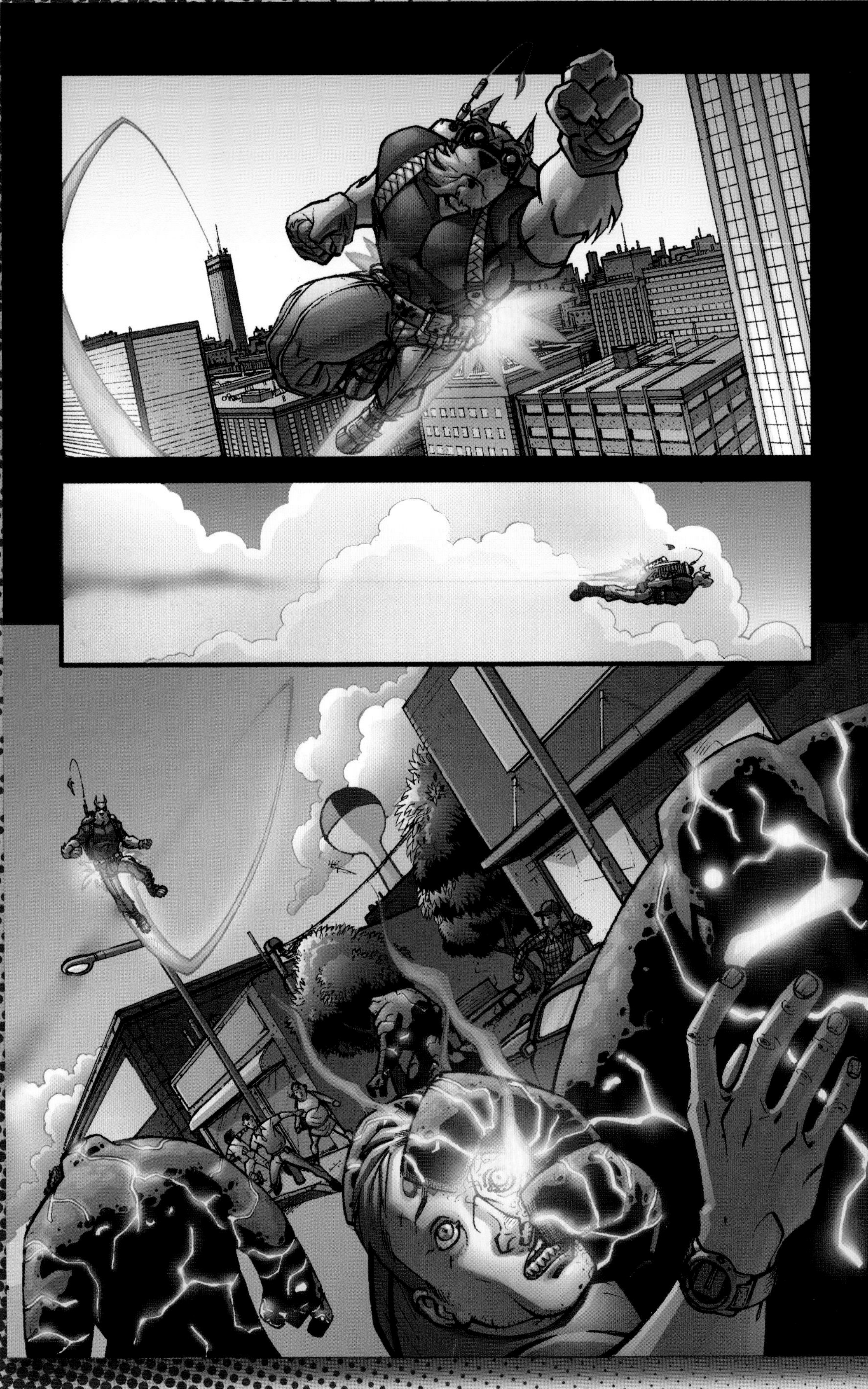

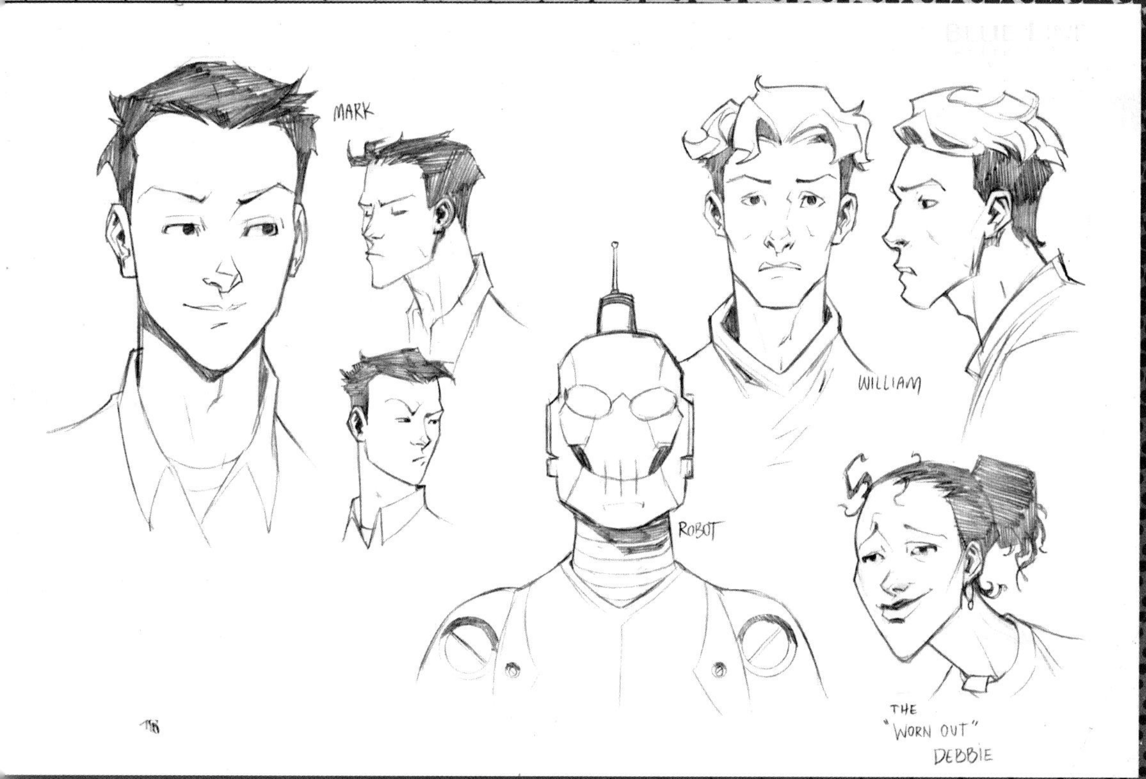
MARK
ROBOT
WILLIAM
THE "WORN OUT" DEBBIE

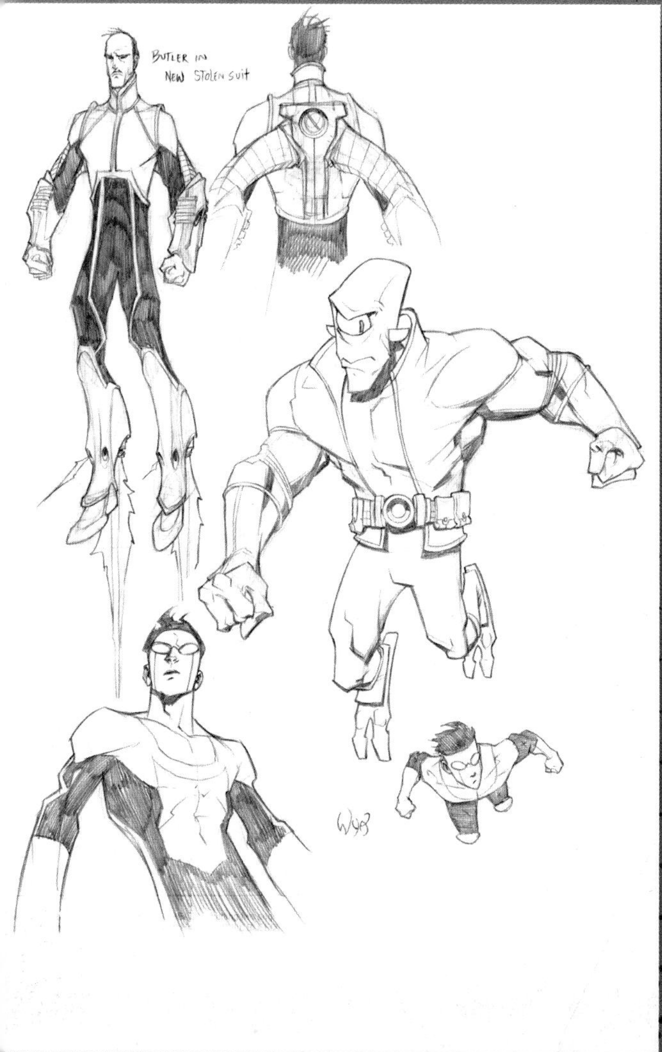
BUTLER IN NEW STOLEN SUIT

Some sketches from Ryan Ottley, the new series artist. Ryan just dove into the pages of issue 8 so there's really not that much sketch stuff to show. Needless to say he nailed all the characters and I couldn't be happier with what he's done with the book. When Cory started having trouble getting the book out on time, he decided to step aside and let Ryan take over. Now Ryan is blazing though issues at lightning speed, and Cory is working on a project with a much looser deadline that will blow you away when it sees print. All is right in the world.

-Robert Kirkman

PICK UP THESE GREAT BOOKS FROM
ROBERT KIRKMAN AND IMAGE COMICS!

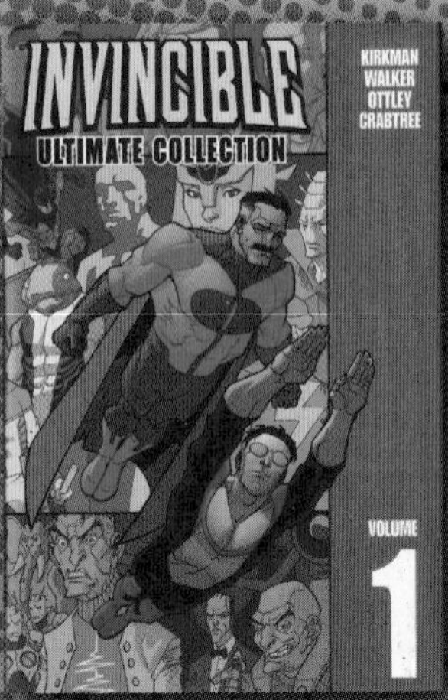
INVINCIBLE
ULTIMATE COLLECTION
KIRKMAN
WALKER
OTTLEY
CRABTREE
VOLUME
1

INVINCIBLE
ULTIMATE COLLECTION, VOL. 1 HC
$34.95
ISBN# 158240500X

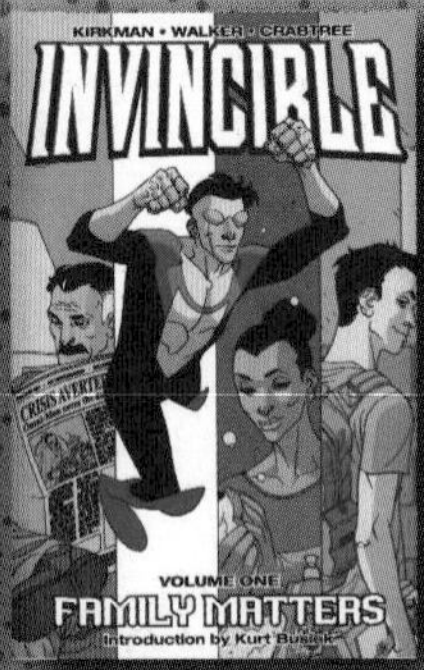
KIRKMAN • WALKER • CRABTREE
INVINCIBLE
VOLUME ONE
FAMILY MATTERS
Introduction by Kurt Busiek

INVINCIBLE
VOL. 1: FAMILY MATTERS
$12.95
ISBN# 1582403201

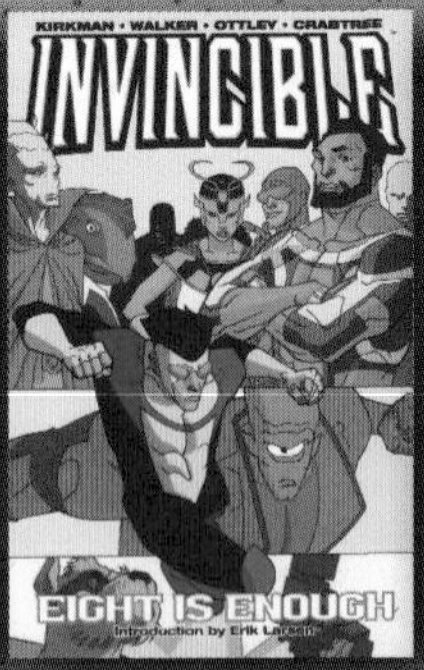
KIRKMAN • WALKER • OTTLEY • CRABTREE
INVINCIBLE
EIGHT IS ENOUGH
Introduction by Erik Larsen

INVINCIBLE
VOL. 2: EIGHT IS ENOUGH
$12.95
ISBN# 1582403473

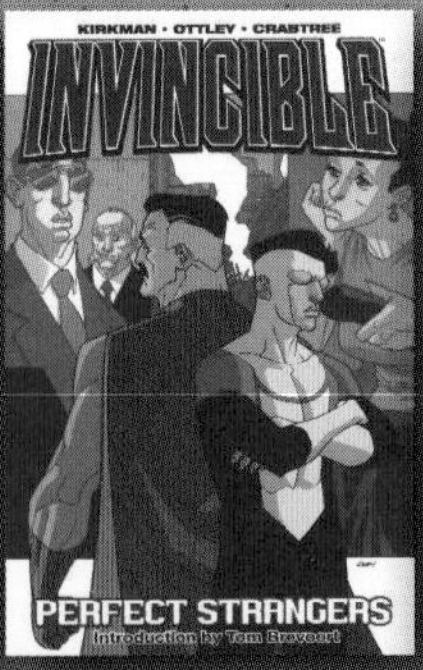
KIRKMAN • OTTLEY • CRABTREE
INVINCIBLE
PERFECT STRANGERS
Introduction by Tom Brevoort

INVINCIBLE
VOL. 3: PERFECT STRANGERS
$12.95
ISBN# 1582403910

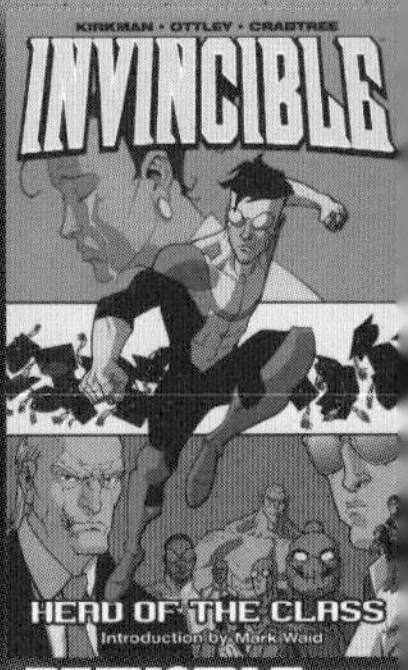
KIRKMAN • OTTLEY • CRABTREE
INVINCIBLE
HEAD OF THE CLASS
Introduction by Mark Waid

INVINCIBLE
VOL. 4: HEAD OF THE CLAS
$14.95
ISBN# 1582404402

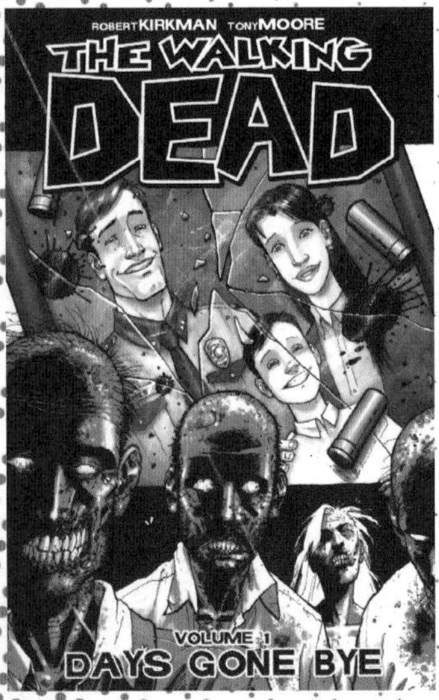
ROBERT KIRKMAN TONY MOORE
THE WALKING DEAD
VOLUME 1
DAYS GONE BYE

THE WALKING DEAD
VOL. 1: DAYS GONE BYE
$9.95
ISBN# 1582403589

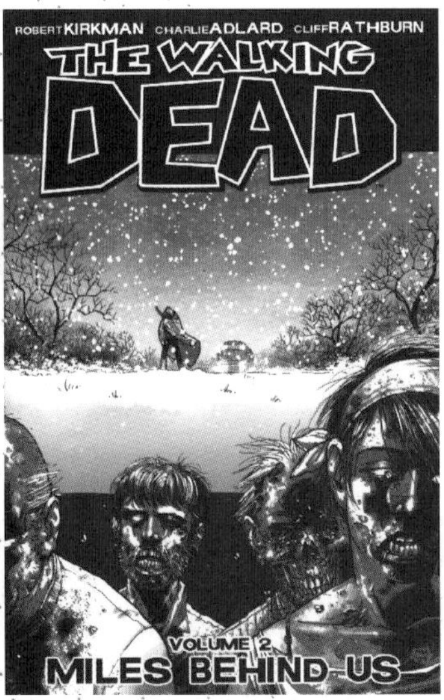
ROBERT KIRKMAN CHARLIE ADLARD CLIFF RATHBURN
THE WALKING DEAD
VOLUME 2
MILES BEHIND US

THE WALKING DEAD
VOL. 2: MILES BEHIND US
$12.95
ISBN# 1582404135

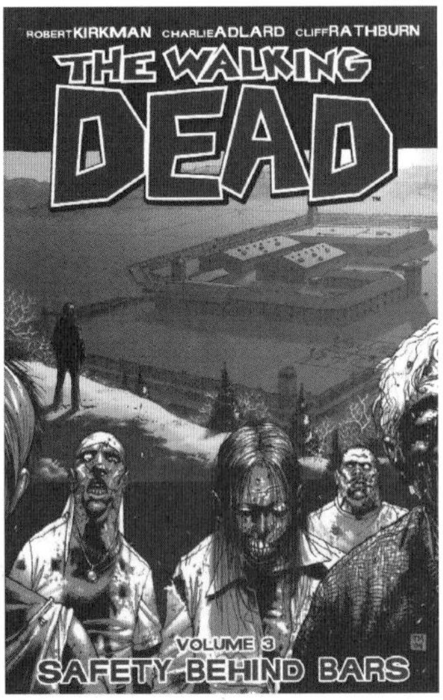
ROBERT KIRKMAN CHARLIE ADLARD CLIFF RATHBURN
THE WALKING DEAD
VOLUME 3
SAFETY BEHIND BARS

THE WALKING DEAD
VOL. 3: SAFETY BEHIND BARS
$12.95
ISBN# 1582404879

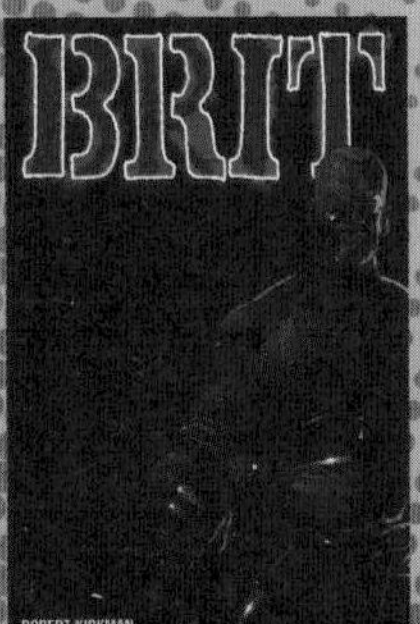
BRIT
ROBERT KIRKMAN
TONY MOORE

BRIT • $4.95
ISBN# 1582403856

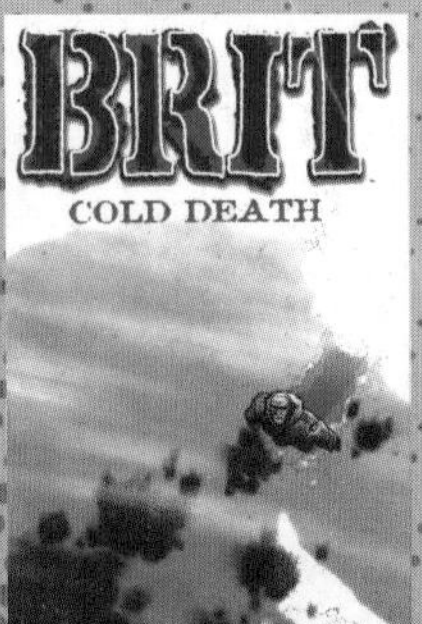
BRIT
COLD DEATH
ROBERT KIRKMAN & TONY MOORE

BRIT: COLD DEATH
$4.95
ISBN# 1582403864

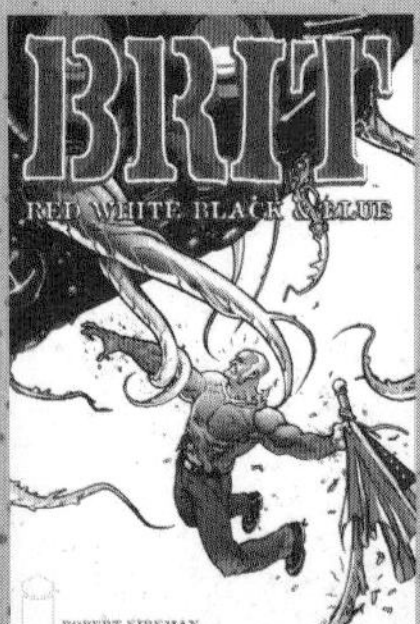
BRIT
RED WHITE BLACK & BLUE
ROBERT KIRKMAN
CLIFF RATHBURN

BRIT: RED, WHITE, BLACK & BLUE
$4.95

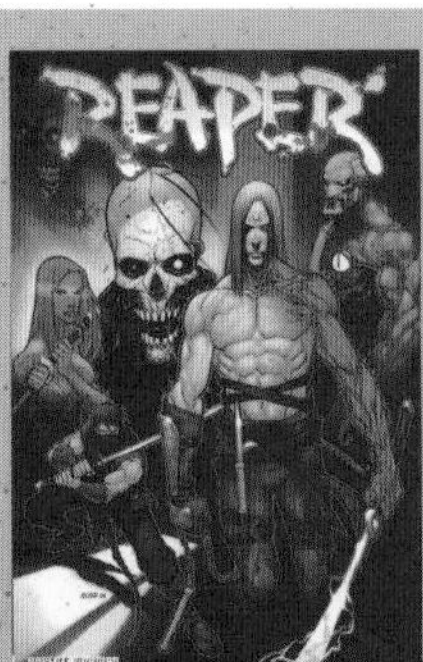
REAPER

REAPER GN
$6.95
ISBN# 1582403546

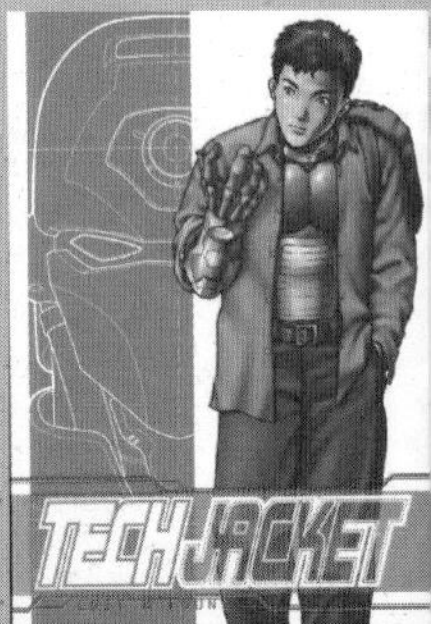
TECH JACKET

TECH JACKET,
VOL. 1: LOST AND FOUND TP
$12.95
ISBN# 1582403864